ZAREGOTO

BOOK ONE

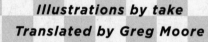

Illustrations by take
Translated by Greg Moore

BALLANTINE BOOKS
NEW YORK

ZAREGOTO

BOOK ONE
THE KUBIKIRI CYCLE

NISIOISIN

A Del Rey Manga/Kodansha Trade Paperback Original

Zaregoto Series: Kubikiri Saikuru © 2002 NISIOISIN
English translation © 2008 NISIOISIN
Illustrations © take

Published in the United States by Del Rey Books,
an imprint of The Random House Publishing Group,
a division of Random House, Inc., New York.

DEL REY is a registered trademark and the Del Rey colophon is a
trademark of Random House, Inc.

First published in Japan in 2002 by Kodansha Ltd., Tokyo as
Zaregoto Series: Kubikiri Saikuru.
Publication rights for this English edition arranged through Kodansha Ltd.

ISBN 978-0-345-50427-2

Printed in the United States of America

www.delreymanga.com

2 4 6 8 9 7 5 3 1

Translator: Greg Moore
Cover illustration: take

CONTENTS

CAST OF CHARACTERS

Akagami Iria: *the mistress of Wet Crow's Feather Island*

Chiga Akari: *oldest of the three maid sisters*

Chiga Hikari: *second of the three maid sisters*

Chiga Teruko: *youngest of the three maid sisters*

Handa Rei: *head maid at the mansion*

Ibuki Kanami: *genius painter*

Himena Maki: *genius fortune-teller*

Kunagisa Tomo: *genius engineer*

Sashirono Yayoi: *genius chef*

Sonoyama Akane: *genius and one of the Seven Fools*

Aikawa Jun: *most powerful private contractor in the world*

Me (narrator): *Kunagisa Tomo's escort*

Sakaki Shinya: *Ibuki Kanami's attendant*

Having one too many talents is even more dangerous than having one too few.

—Nietzsche

PROLOGUE

"Isn't there something really scary about people who knowingly, consciously, use others as stepping-stones?"

Hmm. I wonder.

Actually, it's the people who *unknowingly*—with all the best of intentions and delusions of just cause—use other people who are way more disturbing.

"Haha! But you're a good guy, right?" he chuckled.

Thankfully, whether or not I'm a good guy has nothing to do with anything. Instead, it's like this: it's not about two different ways of thinking, it's about different ways of *living* life. About the absolute and enormous difference between people who can get through life without even needing to walk over others—and those who aren't even worth walking over.

Yeah, I guess that's what this is really all about.

Like a painter without a style.

Like a scholar whose studies are complete.

Like a chef who has already tasted success.

Like a fortune-teller who has transcended too far.

The women on that island were far too different. Both the host and the guests were of a hopelessly different breed, of an unstoppably different breed, of a different breed you would never want to stop. Their existence was so out of reach, so distant that you could never even hope to muster a desire to approach it.

And then . . .

"In other words, this is a question of 'What is genius, and what isn't?' Now, being incompetent—that's what's best, really. To be completely obtuse. To be so oblivious as to *never think for a second* about one's purpose in life, to never think about the meaning of life, to never think about the *value* of life. Then this world would be a paradise. Calm, peaceful, and serene. Trivial things would be major and major things trivial, and life could be lived to its fullest."

Surely that was indeed the case.

The world is harsh to the brilliant. The world is harsh to the competent.

The world is harsh to the beautiful. The world is harsh to the attentive.

The world is kind to the unkempt. The world is kind to the incompetent.

The world is kind to the corrupt. The world is kind to the oblivious.

But if you figure *that* out, if you realize *that*, it's already over right then. It's a problem with no solutions and no interpretation. It's over before it's begun, and by the time it's over, it's complete. I guess it's that kind of story.

For example:

"Essentially, people live in one of two ways. Either they live in awareness of their own worthlessness, or they live in awareness of the worthlessness of the world. Two ways. Either you allow your value to be absorbed by the world, or you chisel away at the world's value and make it your own."

Which should take precedence, the value of the world or your own value?

To accept the world as boring or accept oneself as boring?

Which is really more agreeable?

There's bound to be some amount of ambiguity and uncertainty.

Is there really any defined criteria there?

Is it really just a choice between A and B?

Do you really have to choose?

"Where is the line between genius and not genius?"

Where is the line between what is true and who is a lie?

Where is the line between who is true and where is a lie?

You must not ask.

He snorted cynically. "So how about you then?"

Well . . .

"How does the world look to you?"

To me, after having experienced that island. To me, there next to the blue. To me, now with this person before my eyes, it was all just mindless babble. It wasn't even worth the trouble of even thinking of an answer.

And so I said nothing. Instead, I looked away and thought of something else.

So, how does the world look through *this* person's eyes? Just how did *I* look in this person's eyes?

THE THIRD DAY

Kunagisa Tomo,
Genius Engineer

1

SAVANT BLUE

Don't be so edgy.
Relax, okay?

1

The third morning of our life on Wet Crow's Feather Island was just greeting us. I awoke in a daze, trying to distinguish between the dreams I had just had and the reality yet to come.

The high, rectangular window admitted just a bit of light, so the room still remained dim. Since the room had no lights, I would just have to wait for it get brighter: the sun had only just risen, and it was maybe around six a.m., judging by my internal clock. I suspect this way of determining the time has no more than a fifteen-minute margin of error. But even supposing I was an hour off, it's not like it would be a problem.

"Getting up," I mumbled, and slowly rose from bed.

The room was mostly empty, its only furnishings a chair and a futon. Aside from that, it was completely bare. Its high ceilings gave it an even more spacious feel—and that hollow, dead atmosphere that evokes so vividly images of solitary confinement or something. I couldn't help but feel a little bit like an inmate on Death Row.

It was the second time in my life I'd woken up with that feeling.

But while this was in fact *not* solitary confinement, neither was it originally a bedroom. It was formerly a storage space. When I asked Akari to show me the smallest room in the mansion, this was where she brought me. The smallest room. Even so, it was infinitely bigger than my room at the lodging house. Boy, was that ever depressing.

"Nah . . . it's way beyond depressing," I said to myself.

Now then. I switched my cognitive channel from Death Row Inmate Mode to Routine Mode.

Wondering what time it really was, I glanced at my wristwatch, but the LCD screen displayed nothing. Maybe the batteries had died while I was sleeping. But wait, I'd changed them just a little while ago. There had to be some other problem. Well, I could always ask Kunagisa to fix it.

Clearing my sleep-fogged mind, I did a couple of simple stretches and then left the room. I walked around for a while. The carpet was thick, bright red, and looked like (and most probably was) super-high quality. It eventually led to the spiral case, which is where I bumped into Rei-san and Akari-san.

"Oh, good morning. You two are up early." It was only common courtesy to greet them, but they simply passed by with no more acknowledgment than a silent head-bow.

"Guess they're the quiet type," I muttered to myself.

But to be fair, they were probably working, and I wasn't exactly a "guest," per se, so I just had to live with their lukewarm response. If I expected anything more out of them, I'd have to throw my arms out wide and cry out, *"How you feelin', my freaky people?!"* And, frankly, I just didn't have the energy.

Handa Rei-san and Chiga Akari-san were maids employed at the mansion. Rei-san was the "head maid," Akari her subordinate. And there were two other maids at the mansion, of the same rank as Akari-san. A total of four maids.

Considering who owned the mansion, and the size of the mansion, it seemed as if a staff of four maids would be too small. But these women carried out their duties with the swiftness and skill of true specialists.

The mistress of the mansion, and the person these maids served, was Akagami Iria. She was the proprietress of the island, as well as the mansion. And furthermore, she was the one who had invited me and Kunagisa here.

"But wait, was I actually *invited*?" I asked myself.

Now just how old was Akari-san? You could tell just by looking at Rei-san that she was probably in her late twenties. It's not easy for kids like me to tell exactly how old a woman that age is, but that's definitely the impression I got from her. Akari-san was the real challenge. I didn't think she was younger than me, but still, she looked ridiculously young. She was one of those women you see downtown who can get away with paying half-price for everything when they're actually adults. As I went up the spiral staircase and headed down the second-floor hall, my mind filled with nonsense. *Maybe she has a thing for young guys.* Yeah, just babbling.

I was headed for Kunagisa's room. Two days ago, when we arrived at the island, a room had of course been prepared for Kunagisa, but not for me. This was to be expected: even I had had no idea I would be visiting this weird little island until that very morning, when Kunagisa called me.

Akari-san prepared a room for me at the last minute. But I'd politely refused it. Why? The reason hit me as soon as I opened the door.

I knocked once, then went ahead and opened it.

The interior was vast. Pure white carpet and pure white wallpaper complemented pure white furniture. Even I knew that white reflects light. Kunagisa was crazy about the color white, so somebody had decorated this room this way deliberately. In the center of the room was a luxurious sofa and a wooden table. A chandelier hung from the strangely high ceiling. The bed was like something straight out of a movie set in medieval times; it even had a canopy.

"Yeah, I'd never get any sleep here."

And so I had Akari-san show me to the storage room on the first floor. Meanwhile Kunagisa, lacking my more delicate sensibilities, lay there drowsily on her pure white sheets.

Looking at the enormous, antique, mechanical clock on her wall (also ever-so-thoughtfully selected in white), I saw that it was, in fact, six o'clock, just as I'd guessed. Pondering what to do now, I sat on the side of her bed, enjoying the feeling of the thick, fluffy carpet beneath my feet.

Kunagisa rolled over. Her eyes opened, just slightly. "Hmm? Oh, Ii-chan?"

Somehow she had sensed it was me, but at any rate she seemed to be awake. She pushed her mussed, Hawaiian-blue hair away from her face and regarded me with sleepy eyes. "Oh, ahhh, Ii-chan . . . ummm . . . You came to wake me up, didn't you? Thank you."

"Actually I came here to tuck you in, but what's this? Tomo sleeping at nighttime? That's pretty rare. Or did you just get to bed?" If that was the case I'd have to apologize.

"Uh-uh." She shook her head.

"I think I slept for three hours. Cuz y'know, yesterday, well, some stuff happened, Ii-chan. Give me five more seconds . . .

"Good morning! Ah, it's a bright, brisk morning, isn't it?!" She sat up, her petite little body popping up. Flashing me an ear-to-ear grin, she struck a dynamic pose. "Huh? Hey, it's not bright out at all. I don't like this. I like for the sun to be way high up in the sky when I wake up in the morning."

"You're talking about the afternoon."

"Eh, either way. That was some good sleep." Ignoring me, she kept on talking. "I'm pretty sure I got to bed at three a.m.

Some really bad stuff happened yesterday and I just huffed off to bed. Y'know, cuz sleep is the best thing when you're feeling really terrible. It's like sleep is the one and only gift of salvation God gave mankind. Now, Ii-chan?"

"Yeah, Tomo?"

"Stay still for a sec."

Without even giving me time to be confused, she hugged me. Or to put it more accurately, she draped herself on me, burdening me with the entirety of her bodyweight. She rested her tiny head on my right shoulder, with our bodies stuck together, her slender arms wrapped around my neck.

Squeeze.

Not that she was heavy.

"Uh, Kunagisa?"

"Recharging."

Evidently she was recharging. Thus, no moving allowed. I gave up on the idea of resistance and supported her weight.

But hey, what was I, an electrical outlet or something?

Looking at Kunagisa, I noticed she had slept with her coat on. As far as I knew, she wore it all the time, indoors and out-doors, summer and winter. A jet-black men's coat. On a girl of Kunagisa's tiny stature, the large-sized coat easily touched the floor. But she seemed to be madly in love with it anyway. I had told her millions of times to at least take it off when she's sleeping, but to no avail.

One thing was for sure: Kunagisa Tomo did things her own way. In that sense, she was kind of like me.

"Okay, thanks!" she said, and finally let go of me. "Battery full! Now, let's go face another day."

With a grunt she rose from bed, blue hair bouncing. She walked over to the computers by the window opposite her bed. They were the three computers she had brought from her home in Shirosaki. All three were tower models. The two on the left and right were of typical size, the one in the middle was exceptionally large. They were all white, of course. I just didn't get why she was so into a color that was so easy to get dirty.

The three computers were on a U-shaped rack, with a cushiony rolling chair in the center. Kunagisa plopped down in the chair and leaned back. That way she could simultaneously control all three computers. But no matter how you counted it up, she still had only two hands. Why she would ever think to use three keyboards at the same time was beyond me.

I looked over her shoulder. The three keyboards were neither ASCII nor JIS nor Oasis, but instead some weird, mysterious key alignment. But to question the unnaturalness of it would be futile. For an engineering whiz like Kunagisa Tomo, designing a keyboard from scratch was probably like a walk in the park.

Incidentally, Kunagisa didn't use a mouse. Because "they're a total waste of time," she would say. But to a novice like me, the sight of a mouseless computer was unnerving, just totally impossible to get used to. Not that that's the worst feeling in the world.

"Ii-chan."

"Yeah?"

"Tie my hair up."

Got it. I went up to her chair. I slipped some hair bands off her arm and tied her hair into two braids.

"Man, wash your hair already. My fingers are getting oily here."

"I hate taking baths. Cuz y'know, your hair gets all wet and stuff."

"Well, of course. Look at this, the blue is getting dark."

"I can't see my own head. Hehehe, if I leave it like it is, it'll turn ultramarine. Thank you, Ii-chan," she said, biting her lower lip with a giggle. I just looked back at her with an innocent, confused smile.

"Uh, no problem, really."

Even as we talked, her fingers never stopped moving. They moved with the accuracy of a machine at a constant rhythm with every keystroke. Her movements flowed so smoothly it was as if she were unconsciously carrying out some preplanned assignment in some preprogrammed way. Incomprehensible English characters and numbers streamed along on all three monitor displays at an unbelievable pace.

"Tomo, what are you up to, anyway? You just got up."

"Mmm, well, I don't think you'd get it even if I told you."

"Hmm. You really need all three PCs to do it?" I said.

She gave me a perplexed look. "Ii-chan, this one in the middle isn't a PC, it's a workstation," she said.

"What's a workstation? It's not a PC?"

"Nope, it's different. Well, I guess PCs and workstations are similar in that they're both intended for individual use, but, it's like, workstations are way more top-of-the-line."

"Ah, so a workstation is like a super-good PC?" I said, openly displaying my ignorance.

She groaned. "Ii-chan, a PC is a PC and a workstation is a workstation. They're both GPCs, but think of them as two completely different things."

"What's a GPC?"

She looked at me as if I were some kind of a caveman. "Ii-chan, you don't know anything, do you?" she said with a touch of disbelief. "What exactly were you doing in Houston those five years?"

"Other things."

She sighed. "Okay, okay," she said, tilting her head. Then she resumed her work as if a switch had been toggled in her brain. Letters and numbers that looked like hocus-pocus to me continued to stream by on the displays.

I wanted her to tell me a little more about the different classifications or what have you, but I'm not really that intellectually curious. Besides, it would be rude to interrupt whatever she was working on. That, and, for an "outsider" like me to try to follow this nerdy cupcake's explanations seemed as if it would just lead to a headache, so with that I ended the discussion. I massaged her shoulders for a bit, then decided to borrow her sink, where I washed my face and changed my clothes.

"Hey, Tomo, I'm gonna go for a walk."

Without looking up from her work, she gave me a half-hearted wave. The other hand kept on tapping keys. I shrugged and left the room.

2

I'd be lying if I said I knew all that much about the Akagami Foundation. They're not exactly the most well-publicized organization in the world. Plus, since they mostly operated out of the Kanto region, someone like me who was born in Kobe, grew up in Houston, Texas, and lived in Kyoto wouldn't know that much about them.

Putting it simply, the Akagami mansion was the home to a storied legacy of business barons. That business might have been some kind of trade, or a system in which money just poured in on its own. I'm not sure what exactly it is that they did, but whatever it was, one thing was for sure: the Akagami Foundation was loaded.

Holding property not just in Japan but all over the world, the Akagami Foundation was the owner of Wet Crow's Feather Island as well. And the owner of the Western-style mansion found in the center of the island was none other than Akagami Iria.

As you might guess from her name, Iria was related to the head of the Akagami Foundation—his granddaughter, in fact. She was a born-and-bred pedigreed princess, for whom no obsequious praise was too obsequious. Over time, she had inherited vast amounts of enormous wealth and unbelievable power and ruled over a great many underlings. But then, the head of the Foundation himself had completely cut her off. So maybe this is all really better expressed in the *past* tense.

Cut off.

I don't know what she did to deserve it, but it must have been something big.

Supposedly she was permanently removed from the family five years ago, at the age of sixteen. At that time, the head of the family left her with a small severance package (which was probably still an unimaginable sum to a regular joe like me) and this island, floating around in the Sea of Japan.

In other words, she had been exiled.

Maybe these days that seems old-fashioned. But far be it for me to butt into other people's ways of doing things. Especially if those people belong to a powerful institution that's practically its own world in and of itself.

Anyway, Iria had spent the last five years here with her four maids, not once setting foot off the island. Five years on this godforsaken island in the middle of nowhere, with no amusements, no nothing. In a sense, it was life in Hell, though I would speculate that, in a different sense, it was also a little like life in Heaven.

But was Iria-san lonely or bored? Indeed, you could say Kunagisa had been invited to the island to stave off Iria's boredom. But it wasn't just Kunagisa. In the same way, it would be no exaggeration to say that Akane-san, Maki-san, Yayoi-san, and Kanami-san had all been brought here for the same purpose.

Well, okay, maybe it's a little bit of an exaggeration.

So, anyway, forbidden to leave the island, Iria-san said, "Well, if that's how it is," and proceeded to invite, as her guests, the world's most prominent figures.

Now, if "prominent figures" sounds a little weird, let me

try putting it another way. Iria had decided to invite so-called geniuses to her mansion. It was a simple plan: "If I can't go to them, they can come to me."

Famous and unknown alike, all those who possessed genuine talent and amazing skill were summoned by Iria-san, one after another after another. And, of course, all expenses, including accommodations, were covered by Iria-san. In fact, visitors to the island were often *given* money, so it was pretty much always a win-win situation for them.

To me, it seemed like Iria-san was going for that whole ancient Greek salon image, collecting and cavorting with all these artists and geniuses—and thereby living a fruitful life. To be sure, it wasn't the most typical idea around, but yes, there was something amazing about it. Aside from the mansion and the forest, the island was essentially empty—almost a desert island—and for those world-weary men and women of talent who needed to rest both the body and the mind, it was the perfect place. And thus had Iria-san's plan been a tremendous success.

Now then.

Walking around aimlessly on this empty island, basking in the forest, it was by an extremely distant cherry blossom tree that I suddenly ran into Shinya-san.

"Oh, er, that is, I mean," Shinya-san said, waving a hand to greet me. "You're quite the early bird there, eh? Mister . . . er, what was your name again? Sorry, my memory's a little weak, y'see."

He had a good four inches on me, and his designer clothes were much better than mine. His expression was mild-mannered, his way of speaking was mild-mannered, and so was, somehow, his clothing and stature, but whether or not Shinya-san really was mild-mannered, I couldn't say. I don't have the skill to judge someone just based on their appearance, and I'm the last person to jump to conclusions after knowing someone for just a couple of days.

"I don't believe I ever told you," I answered with a shrug. "I'm just Kunagisa Tomo's sidekick. No need for a sidekick to have a name, am I right?"

"That's awfully modest of you. Not that it's any wonder, being on this island. But speaking of sidekicks, I suppose I'm in the same boat as you," Shinya-san said and smirked.

Yes, Shinya-san and I were no more than tagalongs. It probably goes without saying at this point, but I wasn't here walking around on this island because I was any kind of genius. Kunagisa Tomo was the "genius" here, and I was nothing more than her attendant. If she hadn't said to me, "Ii-chan, it turns out I'll be going to some island, so come with me, 'kay?" right about now I would've been in my Kyoto four-tatami-sized room getting ready for school.

No question about it: the main character here is Kunagisa Tomo. Let's just make that clear.

Now then, as for who Shinya-san was accompanying, well, she was right under the cherry blossom tree. With those thoughtful, thoughtless eyes, she gazed at the fluttering cherry blossom petals.

She had blue eyes and hair of gold. Her dress, pale in color, was out of some French movie, and was accented with dazzling jewelry. Just one of her necklaces or bracelets was likely worth more than my liver. Even if I sold off every part of my body I still couldn't pay for it.

Ibuki Kanami. One of the geniuses.

Having, supposedly, suffered problems with her legs from birth, she was confined to a wheelchair. And thus Shinya-san, as her caretaker, had tagged along on the trip. As I'd heard it, until a few years ago, she had also been totally blind. Her blue eyes were not a sign of foreign blood.

Kanami-san was a painter.

Even I, without the slightest knowledge of that field whatsoever, had heard of her. She had earned a reputation as a painter who possessed no single style. I had never actually seen any of Kanami-san's paintings, but I thought that maybe she was gazing at the cherry blossoms in that way so as to later portray them on canvas.

"What's she doing?"

"As you can see, she's watching the cherry blossoms. It won't be long before the petals start falling. She has a fondness for that 'moment just before death,' if you will, the ephemeral things in life."

Most of the trees on the island were just your standard fare, but for some reason, there was one cherry blossom tree. It looked quite old, and the fact that there was only one on the whole island was nothing short of bizarre. Most likely, Iria-san had transplanted it here.

"So they say dead bodies are buried under cherry blossom trees, eh?"

"How dreadful."

Ouch.

I was just trying to make conversation, but instead ended it in one fell swoop. Of course, it *was* pretty dreadful.

"Just joking," Shinya-san laughed.

"Personally, I think it would make more sense if that legend was about a plum tree. But then I guess it wouldn't be a legend, but a myth? Hahaha!"

"By the way, boy, have you gotten accustomed to the island yet? This is your third day here, right? Um, how long were you planning to stay again?"

"A week. So we have another few days."

"Mmm, that's too bad," he said, with a tinge of mystery.

"What's too bad?"

"Oh, it's just that I hear Iria-san's favorite will be coming here in a week. But if you're leaving in four days, you'll just miss each other, won't you? That's just too bad."

"Oh, I see." I nodded and thought about it for a moment. Iria-san's "favorite."

In other words, the genius of geniuses.

"A chef, a fortune-teller, a scholar, an artist, and an engineer. What could be next?"

"Well, I haven't heard any specifics myself, but apparently this person is capable of just about anything. Not a 'specialist,' but a 'generalist.' Hikari-san tells me this person is as sharp as a tack and full of knowledge, and has lightning reflexes."

Hmm. Yet another totally amazing person. Let's assume it was just some ridiculously over-the-top rumor. The fact that such a rumor even existed suggested that this particular genius wasn't just anyone. I'd be lying if I said I wasn't intrigued.

"Couldn't hurt to meet this person, I guess. What do you say to asking for an extension on your visit? I'm sure Iria-san would more than welcome you."

"Sounds nice and all, but . . ." I probably looked less than excited. "To be honest, this island is a little stifling. For a regular kid like me, I mean," I said.

Shinya-san guffawed boisterously. "Now, now. Now, now, now, now, now there, lad. Is *that* how it is? Kanami-san and Akane-san and all of them haven't given you a *complex*, have they?"

A complex. Even supposing it wasn't something you could put so bluntly, what I felt was certainly something similar. Shinya-san gave me a firm pat on the shoulder.

"There's no reason to feel inferior to that lot, right? Let's keep it together, brother! Whether it be Kanami-san . . ." Kanami-san glanced up from under the cherry blossom tree. "Whether it be Akane-san, Yayoi-san, or even Kunagisa-chan, if they were to play the two of us in rock-paper-scissors, they would only win one out of three times. I suppose Maki-san would be an exception there, but nevertheless."

"That's a pretty blunt way to put it."

Not to mention Shinya-san had just referred to his own

employer as part of "that lot." I'm not saying they were at each other's throats or anything, but maybe Shinya-san and Kanami-san weren't quite the best of friends.

"Talent isn't such a big deal. In fact, I, for one, am glad I don't have any. Talent isn't worth spit."

"Why's that?"

"If you've got a talent, you've got to exert effort. Being ordinary is a breeze. Having nothing to master is an advantage, if you ask me," Shinya-san said with a cynical shrug. "I think we got a little off-topic. Anyway, I don't think it would be a terrible thing if you were able to extend your stay, if you ask me. And hey, just maybe this 'generalist' will beat us in rock-paper-scissors all three times."

"Well, I'll talk it over with Kunagisa . . . It would hardly be right for the tagalong to decide something like this on his own."

"I thought so," he said. "You're a lot like me," he said, looking me in the eye.

His gaze was deeply disconcerting. It gave me that uncomfortable feeling you get when you're being watched.

"Me and you? Alike? How do you mean? In what way?"

"Don't sound so happy about it. In particular, you're practically identical in holding the idea that you yourself are a part of the world."

Seemingly with no intention of explaining himself any further, he broke his gaze and looked back at Kanami-san. Predictably, Kanami-san was still staring at the cherry blossoms with complete concentration. She was surrounded by a sort of transcendence, as if just that one spot was isolated from the rest of the world. She had the air of being unapproachable, even sacred.

"So Kanami-san's been painting even since coming here?"

"Well, it's more like she came to this island to paint. That's really all she does, after all. I suppose you could say she lives to paint. Can you believe it?" He spoke with a tinge of frustration, but if you took his words at face value, it sounded like an incredibly enviable existence; a life where what you want to do and what you have to do are directly connected. It was a way of life I could never even hope for. I, who had discovered neither what I wanted nor what I had to do.

I noticed that Shinya-san was watching me with a wicked smile, like he had just remembered a bad prank. I recoiled a little. I was getting a bad feeling, like a premonition. And then Shinya-san, with a look on his face as if to say, "I've just had a revelation from God," clapped his hands deliberately.

"That's right! It's such a prime opportunity, so why don't you try modeling?" He set me aside as I stood at a loss for words and unable to comprehend his, and faced Kanami-san. "Hey!" he called. "Kanami! This fella here says he wants to be your model!"

"Wait, Shinya-san!" Finally grasping the situation, I spun in front of him. "I can't just, I mean, give me a break!"

"Now, now, why are you so embarrassed? That hardly suits your character."

I don't think so. Asking Kanami-san to paint me? That was an incredibly intimidating idea. But Shinya-san blew off my protest with a simple "Now, now, don't be shy," and waited for an answer from Kanami-san.

Kanami-san adjusted the direction of her wheelchair and took a look at me. She scanned me up and down, from the tip of my head to the tips of my feet, observing me, assessing me, and said, "So you want me to paint you?" She sounded truly irritated.

This was a difficult question to answer. With someone as talented as Kanami-san, the simple act of hesitating would have been rude. I was weak in these situations. A real pushover. A nineteen-year-old boy who's spent his life going with the flow has not the power to alter the flow of a tale.

"Yes, absolutely, if you don't mind," I said.

Kanami-san simply looked disinterested. "Fine then. Come by the atelier this afternoon," she said, and swiveled her wheelchair back toward the cherry blossoms. She spoke with heartfelt apathy, but at least she had taken pity on me.

"Well, that's settled then. Are you free this afternoon?" Shinya-san said, strangely joyful.

I told him I was free and decided to get going before I got into any more trouble.

I returned to the mansion and visited Kunagisa's room once again. Kunagisa was just as I had left her, sitting in her revolving chair, her three PCs (I mean, two PCs and one workstation) in front of her. Right now she was focused on the workstation, and the two PCs had their power switched off.

"What were you up to, Tomo?"

No reply.

I went up to her from behind and tugged both her braids.

"Oww," she uttered in a strange voice, seeming to at last notice my presence. Without changing her position, she gaped at me in bewilderment. Surely I appeared upside down in her eyes.

"Yooo, Ii-chan. You're back from your walk."

"Yeah, well . . . Say, is that a Mac?"

The monitor on the workstation opposite Kunagisa was displaying some kind of Mac OS screen. As far as I had heard, Mac OS only worked on Macs.

"Yeah, it's Mac OS. Y'see, there are some applications that only run on Mac OS, so I'm running it on a virtual machine."

"Virtual machine?"

"Basically I'm making the workstation think there's a Mac inside it. In other words, I'm tricking the software. Of course Windows is in here, too. Most OS's are installed on this workstation, so it can do anything."

"Ah . . ."

I didn't really get it.

"This is a dumb question, but how are Mac and Windows different, anyway?"

She gave my truly amateurish question a moment's thought. "They're different because different people use them," she answered, with an air of precision.

"Well, yeah, that's true, but . . . Well, forget about that. So an OS is like the core software, right? I think that's right. So then it's like this computer has multiple personalities?"

"It's a strange metaphor, but you could say that."

"So then that PC, er, workstation, what's its *core* core OS? Like with multiple personalities you have a 'main' personality, right?"

"Geocide."

"Never heard of that. Is it like Unix?"

"That's *Unix*, with a 'yoo' sound. Come on, you studied abroad; you should know not to pronounce the alphabet like Romanized Japanese, Ii-chan. It makes you sound so stupid. Uh, well, it is compatible with Unix. But it's an original OS developed by a friend of yours truly."

"A friend . . ."

Kunagisa's friend. The only friend of Kunagisa's who could've developed an original operating system was someone from that "team." From that notorious "team."

Several years back, in the last century, during the time when the Japanese network was still underdeveloped, that group appeared. Or, no, "appeared" isn't the correct expression.

They never for an instant let their visage, nor their shadow, nor even their smell grace the public eye. They never announced their name; whatever name they had ever been known by had been applied by others. Whether you called them a virtual club, cyberterrorists, a crack unit, or a gang that made mountains out of molehills, it didn't matter to them, and they probably wouldn't respond.

They were completely peerless, species unknown. How

many people were there, and just what types of people comprised this "team"? These things were all shrouded in mystery.

And what did they do?

Everything.

They did everything, that was all you could say about it. They did so much of everything, there was nothing they didn't do. They wreaked havoc, havoc, and more havoc. I wasn't in Japan at the time, so I didn't get to see it firsthand, but they say it was such full-on, ludicrous havoc that it was practically refreshing, lending no hint as to their motives or aims. Beginning with pure hacking and cracking, they also had their hands in corporate advising and fixer fraud. It's also quietly speculated that, back then, they controlled a number of large corporations.

But you couldn't say they existed solely as a nuisance. For better or worse, it was thanks to them that the overall level of network technology improved drastically. You could even say they forced it. If you looked at it through a fine-toothed comb, sure there were losses, but in the big picture, the gains outweighed them tenfold.

But, of course, the fat cats upstairs saw them as little more than pesky, law-breaking criminals, a hacking, cracking eyesore. Thus the "team" went on, despised and pursued. But they were never caught, and exactly what they were doing was never brought to light. Then, sometime last year, suddenly and without anything in particular having happened, they were never heard from again. It was as though they had just burned out and vanished.

"Yo, what's wrong, Ii-chan? You're quiet all of a sudden."

"Nah . . . nothing."

She flipped her hair with a giggle.

"Yeah, I guess it's nothing. . . ."

It was in that way that the "team" met what was, in a sense, an anticlimactic end. Who would believe the leader of that now-defunct team was this happy-go-lucky girl still in her teens? Exactly who in their right mind would believe something so nonsensical that it couldn't even be mistaken for a sick joke?

But if that wasn't the case, Kunagisa wouldn't have been invited to this genius-ridden island. Not as a communication and systems engineering specialist.

"How could I *not* have a complex, Shinya-san?"

"Huh? Did you say something?" Kunagisa glanced up at me for a moment.

"Just babbling," I said. "So 'Geocide,' doesn't that mean 'Earth murder'?"

"Yup. Of all the existing OS's, it's probably the most awesome. Geocide is number one. Even the RASIS is perfect."

"Sometimes I think you use those big words just to tick me off. What's a RASIS?"

"It's an acronym for reliability, availability, serviceability, integrity, security. But of course, that's in English," she said a bit irritably.

"Basically it means stability. Of course it requires a high-performance system, but it won't cause errors or anything like that. Man, that Atchan really is a genius. Hehehe."

"Atchan, huh? Sounds like you two are pretty close."

"Hmm? Jealous? Hmm? Hmm?" she said with a strangely pleased tone and naughty smirk. "It's okay. I like you best of all."

"Ah, right. 'Preciate that." I shrugged and tried to change the subject. "But if it's such an amazing OS, why not market it? If it sold like Windows, you'd make a fortune."

"No can do. You know about increasing returns, right? With an OS this different, we'd never catch up. Business goes beyond skill or talent."

Increasing returns. The law of economics that states "the more you have, the more you get," which does nothing for what you don't have. It had been awhile since I'd studied it, so I didn't remember it very clearly, but to put it simply, "once a significantly problematic difference has appeared, it is impossible to bury that difference." Whether it be in regards to skill or money, it seemed to make no difference.

"Besides, Atchan was satisfied just by creating Geocide. Atchan's a very self-satisfied person."

"Hey, yeah, must be very happy."

"Even if that wasn't the case, I don't think it would be possible to market it. Even though it's just core software, it requires some pretty outrageous specs. Seriously astronomical figures. Even my machine just barely cuts it."

"Hmm. How many gigs is your hard disk? About a hundred?"

"One hundred terra."

Different unit.

"Terra . . . that's the opposite of pico, so . . . a thousand times a gig?"

"Nope, 1,024 times."

Nitpicky chick.

"Man, I've never seen a hard disk like that."

"To be specific, it's not a hard disk; it's holographic memory. Unlike hard disks, which record data with magnets, this records data onto a surface. It's capable of one terra per second rapid transfer. What you'd find on the market is, well, quite a bit slower. This is the kind of media they're using in the development of space technology."

She had those kinds of connections, too?

She belonged to an altogether dubious community.

"Of course, this goes for the machine's capacity as well, but if the motherboard specs aren't customized home brew as well, you're probably out of luck. Atchan just makes things without considering any of the surrounding circumstances, y'see. So they just end up like this. He doesn't try to suit things to other people."

"Motherboard home brew? There are people who do that?"

"Like yours truly, for one." She indicated herself with her thumb.

That's right. She was an engineer, after all. She must've been the culprit providing her "teammates" with the hardware and software that were to be their main "weapons." If you thought about it, it was fairly disturbing. It was one thing to develop a seemingly unmarketable OS like that, but to take it and build your own motherboard for it was just plain freakish.

"Mr. Earth Murder aside, haven't you ever considered selling this stuff? Like that motherboard you're so proud of?"

"I'm the self-satisfied type, too. How 'bout you, Ii-chan?"

"Hmm, I wonder."

Regardless of talent or lack thereof, in the end all people are classified into two groups: those who pursue and those who create. My own case notwithstanding, Kunagisa was overwhelmingly the latter.

"Besides, as far as money is concerned, I've got plenty and then some. I'm not thinking about making any more right now."

"Ah, no wonder."

That was true. Kunagisa wasn't in a position that demanded she immediately go into business. It wouldn't be much of an exaggeration to say she spent money like it was water. A nineteen-year-old occupying a high-class, two-floor condo in Shirosaki and spending money as fast as she could. I didn't know how many people out there had more money than Kunagisa, but surely no one individual spent as much.

Between the Akagami Foundation and the Kunagisa household, who held the greater power was beyond my realm of knowledge, but either way, they both possessed enough of a fortune to enjoy the best things in life and still get change back, that much was certain.

Speaking of which, Kunagisa resembled the master of this island, Iria, in that she, too, was semi-exiled from her family. Perhaps they were similar people. In the three days I had spent on the island, signs indeed pointed to the contrary, but, well, they were both eccentric, that was for sure. So much so that it would have been impossible for them to blend into any group or be members of any organization.

Surely that's how it was.

In which case, this island . . .

The meaning of this so-called island of wet crow's feathers . . .

Kunagisa returned to her typing.

"I'm gonna go have breakfast. What about you?"

"No, thanks. Not hungry. It's mating season. Ii-chan, go ahead on your own. Eat for me, too."

Gotcha, I said, and headed for the dining room.

3

Akane-san was in the dining room.

I tensed up.

She sat alone at the round dining table with her legs crossed in an elegant, somehow un-Japanese pose, having her breakfast. Or no, she had already finished breakfast and was enjoying an after-meal coffee.

"Oh! Good morning!" It was the bright and lively voice of Akari-san in the midst of cleaning the dining room. No, wait, it wasn't her. Akari-san never greeted me bright and lively. That wasn't the Akari-san I knew. Which meant . . .

"Hi, Hikari-san," I said, determining that it was Hikari-san. Evidently I was correct, as she then grinned at me and bowed.

Chiga Akari-san and Chiga Hikari-san.

They were sisters. Twins. To be sure, there was a third sister as well, their silent younger sister Teruko. Teruko apparently had poor eyesight and was recognizable by her glasses with their black lenses. Akari-san and Hikari-san, however, were perfectly identical, from the length of their hair to their clothes, to the point that they weren't just "similar," they were the same.

But unlike Akari-san, Hikari-san was an incredibly kind person. Even though I wasn't a true "guest," she treated me the same as everyone else.

"Breakfast? Wait one moment, please," she said, then spun around and hustled off to the kitchen. She must be so good at spinning because she's small, I thought.

With Hikari-san gone, I was suddenly left alone with Akane-san.

After a split-second's hesitation, I went ahead and took a seat near her. I thought to greet her, but she seemed completely immersed in thought, mumbling to herself in a semi-audible voice, not even looking in my direction. It was as though she hadn't noticed me. What in the world was she thinking about? I pricked my ears to listen in.

"Sente 9-6, pawn . . . Kote 8-4, pawn . . . Sente, same pawn . . . Kote 8-7, pawn . . . Sente 8-4, rook . . . Kote 2-6, pawn . . . Sente 3-2, silver general . . . Kote 9-5, pawn . . . Sente 4-4, bishop . . . Kote 5-9, gold general, take . . . Sente 2-7, knight . . ."

Meaning unknown.

That's what you get from one of the Seven Fools; even the things they mutter to themselves are different, I thought, thoroughly impressed. But listening closely, it sounded like she was reciting a shogi game record. Wow, blind shogi.

And by herself, no less.

Is this what she always did in the morning?

"Kote 2-3, pawn, checkmate, Sente forfeits," she said, and

glanced over at me. "Ah, I was wondering who that was, and here it turned out to be you. Good morning."

"Good morning."

"Heh heh. Isn't shogi tough? The pieces move around a lot more than in chess. I was playing Kote just now. It was a close victory."

"Huh."

There's a Sente and Kote in single-player shogi? Maybe Akane-san was able to divide her mind like a dolphin. Yeah, it seemed likely for someone like her.

"Are you good at shogi, or chess, whichever?"

"I wouldn't say so, no."

"Hmm, is that so?"

"Reading other people's minds isn't my forte."

"Oh no? Hmm, I suppose not. You've got that kind of face," she nodded. "I saw you from the window a little earlier. Out for a morning walk, were you?"

"Yeah, a walk in the woods."

"Ah, a walk in the woods, how nice. Very nice. The phytoncide released by the trees creates a bactericidal effect and such."

What the hell?

In Houston, Texas, in America, there's a research facility called the ER3 System. There, brilliant minds from around America, nay, around the world, gather, and it is referred to as the ultimate bastion of learning, from economics to history, political science to cultural science, physics and advanced mathematics to biology, electronic and systems engineering, metapsychology, indeed, anything that could be called a field of study or research.

It's also known as the Comprehensive Research Center. It was a gathering place for those who loved learning and research above all else. A nest for those inhuman humans whose desire for knowledge exceeded even their natural, biological desires. An entirely nonprofit organization, they dared not sell their knowledge or research findings, and they were in a sense a closed and introverted sort of secretive organization.

There were only four basic rules:

Have no pride.

Have no principles.

Have no attachments.

No whining.

They were to unbegrudgingly cooperate with one another to the fullest of their ability, to never be unproductive, even if the world should perish, and to never quit halfway, come Hell or high water.

The ultimate destination for those who wanted to do research, who wanted to *know*, who *had* to know, with means and end in complete harmony, it was the ER3 System. The people gathered there ranged from highly esteemed college professors to "frontline" researchers and amateur academics, a truly pride-free assembly of all manner of individuals. Their reputation was seemingly so bizarre that the media ridiculed them as a "cultish pack of overeducated loonies."

But their research had yielded great rewards: the demystification of Dalevio nonlinear optics, the overwhelming advancement of volume hologram technology, and the establishment of the near-magical DOP as a sensory technology were all thanks to the ER3. Not the work of individuals, but rather team efforts, and nonprofit work at that, they declined all awards and other various honors, and thus had not come to draw much attention, but their reputation within the academic world was certainly high. It was a research center with a relatively brief history—not even a century old—but it was already globally networked.

And within this research center existed the transcendental group known as the Seven Fools. Seven individuals selected in turn by the selected "seven on the verge of the answers to the universe." They were the true "geniuses among geniuses."

One of these seven individuals was Sonoyama Akane-san.

She had beautiful black hair, cut ruler-precise to lend her an air of intellectualism. She was tall for a woman, with a stylishly slender build. There was no part of her that wasn't overflowing with elegant femininity. She was a Japanese woman scholar of the highest order.

The ER3 System is relatively unknown in Japan. The fact that the ER3 itself is so exclusive is no doubt part of the reason for this, but the main reason is likely that the uncategorizable nature of the center doesn't fit with the Japanese way of doing things. But nevertheless, Akane-san had, as a pure and innocent Japanese woman (and in her twenties, no less) risen to the ranks of the ER3s Seven Fools. It would come as no surprise if one day she was a household name in Japan.

Now, this may all beg the question: if I'm just a "pure and innocent" Japanese person, too, how come I know so much? But there's no special reason, really. It's not that I'm particularly well informed, it's just that the ER3 and I have crossed paths a bit.

You see, in preparation for the long-term, ER3 System implements a study-abroad program to educate the youth of the next generation. For five years, beginning with my second year of junior high school, I participated in that program, so naturally I knew of Sonoyama Akane's reputation as one of the Seven Fools, as well as her "above the clouds" existence. And that's why I was so surprised to discover Akane-san here on this island. I'm not at all the type who surrenders unconditionally at the first sniff of authority or talent, but I can't help but be nervous. What exactly do you say to one of the Seven Fools?

I was sitting there, all clammed up, when Akane spoke to me. "By the way, that blue-haired girl—Kunagisa-chan, I mean."

"Ah. Yes?"

"She's just lovely. Last night I had her do some maintenance on my PC. She's incredibly skilled, isn't she? We have techies at ER3 as well, but I've never seen one with such . . . *mechanical* precision. She made it look like routine work. This may sound rude, but for a moment I wondered if she was really human. I was sure Iria-san would absolutely adore her."

"Ah, really? I hope she wasn't a bother or anything."

She let out a chuckle. "You sound like a baby stroller."

A baby stroller. Once again I had suffered an unfounded assessment. "You mean a baby*sitter*?"

"Well, they both mean the same thing, yes?"

"A stroller is a kind of carriage."

"Ah, right," she nodded.

For all her evident ability in math and science, it seemed Japanese was not Akane-san's forte.

"Well, either way. She was no bother at all."

Well, duh.

"Then again, she seemed a bit of the socially awkward type. I don't think she listens when people are talking. And as a result, my PC evolved about two generations."

"But that's actually the *improved* Kunagisa. She used to be terrible to talk to. Just starting and stopping whenever she felt like it. It was pretty rough for me."

"Hmm. If you want my opinion, I think there's a certain charm to her unapologeticness."

"Eh, I'm not sure I agree on that."

"Have it your way." Akane-san shrugged. "By the way, I also heard from her that you were in the ER program."

"Huh." That blabbermouth had let the cat out of the bag! I thought I told her to keep that quiet. Not that I wasn't fully aware there's no point trying to keep that girl quiet.

"You should've told me. We could've had quite a chat. I feel as if we've wasted two days. I don't suppose you were holding back by any chance? Please don't get me wrong, I'm not such a big deal."

"No, it's not that. . . . I guess it was just hard to bring up. And also, even though I was in the program, I quit midway through."

The program is a ten-year study. I dropped out after my fifth year. From there I returned to Japan and reunited with Kunagisa. Luckily I was already qualified as a high school graduate from my second year in the program, so I was able to transfer directly to Kyoto Rokumeikan University.

"It's still a big deal. Regardless of what a sprain it became for you . . ."

"That's a 'strain.' "

"Regardless of what a strain it became for you, the ER program's entrance exam is a great obstacle to have overcome. You should have a little more pride about your accomplishments."

The ER program's entrance exam *was* unusually difficult. Even in the application guidebook it said, "There are no perks. This does not guarantee your future. No one will come to rescue you. We offer only an environment in which you may sate your intellectual curiosity," yet still elite candidates from around the world gathered to take the test. So it was true, merely passing the test was something to boast about.

But.

I hadn't completed the program.

"There's no point if you drop out halfway. End results are everything in this world."

"Actually, I happen to think everything in this world *is* a result. . . . Or are you one of those 'a genius is a genius is a genius' people?" She had the slightest bit of sarcasm in her tone. "A genius is not a rose. In Japan, you often see people who take pride simply in the effort they give, don't you? 'I've endured great hardships, regardless of the end results,' they say. They say there's merit in effort alone. I think that's a valid outlook. Saying 'I worked hard' is a fine conclusion in and of itself. What I have a problem with is lowlifes who spout absurdities like 'I could have done that if I wanted' or 'I couldn't do it because I just wasn't trying' or 'I said I can do it, but that doesn't mean I will.' That's all ridiculous. There really are all sorts of people in this world, huh?"

"I didn't try because I couldn't do it."

"Hmm, hehehe, you know, you've sort of got this world-weary quality about you."

"It's probably just modesty."

"Bingo."

The right part of her lip curled up in a half-smile and she produced a pack of cigarettes from her pocket. In graceful, fluid motions, she put one in her mouth and lit it.

"Wow, you smoke? I'm surprised."

"Are you the type who doesn't like women who smoke?"

"Well, no, not women particularly. Smoking is bad for your health, you know."

"Health is bad for your smoking, you know," she retorted, slowly exhaling smoke. There's that Seven Fools wit, I thought, but she smirked with embarrassment. "It's a stupid argument, huh? Don't mind me. It'd be awful if you ended up thinking I was that kind of person," she said. "Shall we change the subject? You know, I was actually in Japan all the way through high school."

"Really?" I was a little surprised. But if you thought about it, it was really no mystery. "Which high school?"

"Just your average prefectural school. It wasn't particularly well-known. I was in the girls' karate club back then. I didn't like it at all at the time, but in retrospect it was really fun. Gee, that takes me back. It's already been more than ten years. . . . The skirts back then were this long. I didn't have the best grades, but I was good in math and English. That's why I ended up at an overseas university. My family was very against it, but I defied them. After all, don't they say 'if you love someone, set them ablaze'?"

"No."

"Anyway, it was like that, so in the end I cut myself off from my family and crossed over to America on my own. It was a hell of a big move for someone like me back then."

And thus she ended up in the Seven Fools. Maybe Cinderella was in this story, too.

"So you do like math. I had a feeling."

"Well, you know, I don't dislike it. In high school I liked how there was always one concrete answer, no vague components, so math was all I did. I liked clear-cut things. But in college, at the ER3 System, I came to realize that wasn't necessarily the case. It's just like shogi or chess. You just have to get a checkmate, but there are an infinite number of ways to get there. I felt as if I had been swindled or something."

"Like when a lover shows an unfamiliar side of themselves to you?"

She laughed as if to say, "A romantic idea, but not exactly."

"But I was also a little touched, you know. In my high school days, I always figured math wouldn't be of any use once I got into the real world, but in fact there really are cases where you have to use calculus and cubic equations and such. You use factorials in everyday life. I was definitely touched by that fact."

"I understand." I nodded.

I really did.

She smiled in a satisfied way. "Are you a math person, too? On average, men are much more likely to be mathematically inclined than women. Because of the way their brains work."

"Is that so?"

"Well, based on statistical data."

"Sounds like sexist data to me."

Besides, statistical evidence is pretty unreliable. If you roll a die one hundred times and it lands on six every single time, that doesn't necessarily mean it'll be a six the next time, too. I told her this, but she protested.

"If it lands on six one hundred times in a row, it's a die that only lands on six. It's too significant a difference to be written off as a coincidence or leaning odds. Male-female statistics are kind of like that, too, though. Hehehe, so you're a feminist. Or are you just being polite around me? Well, unfortunately I'm not a feminist. Listening to talk about expanding women's rights and women's liberation makes me sick to my stomach. I mean, right? They're obviously spouting nonsense. Sure, it's a man's world, but it's not gender equality we need, it's equal opportunity to apply our abilities. Men and women are so different that you can practically call them genetically separate creatures. So I believe they have separate roles. Of course, that rests on the major assumption that your role and what you want to do are separate, and the minor assumption that if you have to choose between the two, what you want to do should come first. Ah, and maybe the medium-sized assumption that you can do what you want to do first. But saying you can't do anything sounds like a convenient excuse to me."

"There's also the factor of environment."

"Environment, huh? But was there ever an age when women were forbidden from writing, or from sculpting? Regarding recent trends, I've become more inclined to sympathize with men. I feel as if they're closer to my own point of view, but also, until the modern day, the workplace was always exclusively man's domain, right? So it's no wonder they got angry when women wanted to butt in."

"They were just righting a wrong. That's just tough luck for the men." I wondered why I had to take the feminist stance.

"Hmm," she nodded. "Maybe you're right. I don't really know. But I can understand why women get angry at men, too. Even though they're just carrying out their roles and we're just carrying out ours, they still act all big about it and put on airs. It's no wonder women get angry. Just so long as they don't try to mix me up into anything. I guess what I truly want is for feminists to just do it away from me. Whatever the case may be, women are inherently a boring breed. Just like you men. Hmm, come to think of it, there were more men than women at ER3, too. Within the Seven Fools, five were men."

"Increasing returns, huh?"

"Eh?" She seemed taken aback. "I'm afraid I don't know that word. What is it, some kind of dieting thing or something?"

"It means Beta lost to VHS."

"Ah, you mean the bias that occurs in economics. That's right, to return a once male-biased world to equilibrium, you'd have to go through quite a bit of hardship. Really, there wouldn't be any problems if men and women weren't always acting jealous of each other. But nobody gets it, do they? And yet they claim there's no difference between separation and discrimination."

"You know, Akane-san, coming from you this all sounds convincing. I guess you must be going through 'quite a bit of hardship' yourself."

"Never," she said flatly. "I just make a little effort."

It was a loaded statement.

Suddenly I recalled something I had wanted to ask someone ever since I first learned of the Seven Fools' existence at ER3.

"Say, who's the number one smartest person in the entire ER3 system?"

In other words, who was the smartest person in the world? Akane-san answered with little deliberation.

"Number two is Froilein Love."

"And number one?"

"Come on, kid, you expect me to list *everyone*?"

Huh.

"Kidding, kidding. Hmm, to answer your question seriously, the person I respect the most, or in other words the person I place above myself *and* all others, is probably Assistant Professor Hewlett. He is number one for sure."

Almost unspeakably accomplished, he was the single greatest mind of the last century, and probably this one as well. The first and probably last man to *master* every subject when he was still in his single digits. Granted special criminal immunity by the president, he used his superior intellect to serve the good of the nation.

If Akane-san was like a god to me, Assistant Professor Hewlett was the very fabric of the universe.

"If he had been a woman, he probably would've changed history," she said, looking off into the distance. It was a curious look of admiration.

"Sorry for the wait!" With expert timing, Hikari-san appeared, pushing a cart. On top of it sat my breakfast. With experienced hands, she placed it in front of me, followed by a knife and fork on either side. "Please take your time," she said with a bow and radiant smile, and then went off somewhere once more. It seemed she still had lots of work to do.

Nine pieces of deep-fried risotto balls on lettuce. Fish soup, salad, and a sandwich made with Italian bread. Plus coffee.

"That Sashirono-san is hot stuff, huh?" Akane-san muttered, eyeing my meal.

Sashirono Yayoi.

She ran the mansion's kitchen, but she wasn't an employee. Indeed, she was one of the geniuses who had been invited to the island. Having already been here for over a year, at this point she was the longest-running guest. There was no doubt that many of the elite visitors to the island had come in hopes of trying her cuisine.

Officially, her specialty was Western cuisine, but she could just as skillfully do any other type, whether it be Chinese, Japanese, or what have you. She was a cooking master with whom no one in the culinary world wasn't familiar—or so went the tales about her. Personally, I was just as ignorant about cooking as I was about art and academics, so I had sadly not even heard of Yayoi-san until visiting the island, but having the privilege to try her dishes three times a day *plus* between-meal snacks, even I came to know of her extraordinary culinary prowess.

The typical image that accompanied a first name like "Yayoi" is either that of a stuck-up know-it-all or a short, spunky girl, but this Yayoi-san fit neither description, instead turning out to be a boisterous and lively woman with short hair. With a polite manner about her, she was the unarrogant type, despite being called a genius. She was also probably the only down-to-earth person on the whole island besides me. Likewise, she was the second-most pleasant person to talk to. Incidentally, Hikari-san was first. Nah, I'm just babbling.

Word had it that Yayoi-san possessed some power that allowed her to make any food better than any other cook, but just what was it? I was curious to know, but had yet to inquire. She spent most of the day in the kitchen (I think that's what you call a shut-in) so opportunities to speak with her were rare.

I noticed that Akane-san was hungrily eyeing my risotto balls. After a moment of my refusing to speak up, she transferred her gaze to me. Something about her eyes was slightly different from before. Like those of a carnivore hunting wild game.

"Have you ever heard that people originally didn't acknowledge any numbers past seven?"

"Well, I . . ."

Apparently, all numbers past seven were simply thought

of as "a lot." I had also heard in my program training that this was the fundamental reason why the "Fools" were limited to seven people.

"Yeah, so just looking at things objectively, if your nine risotto balls turned into eight, I don't think it would be such a great loss."

"And?"

"You're a sharp guy, huh? A good match for a girl like Kunagisa."

"It's not like that between us."

"Don't change the subject. Are you trying to get *me* to kowtow to *you*? Fine. Sashirono-san's risotto balls are delicious, so gimme one. You happy?"

I slid my plate to her without saying anything.

Akane-san began to gleefully pop down the risotto balls, one after another. Before you knew it, they were all gone. Apparently by "one" she meant "one plate."

Well, I was never one to eat a whole lot in the morning anyway. I was supposed to eat for Kunagisa, too, but it was awfully cruel of her to leave that to me.

Switching channels, I made my way to the sandwich and salad. Not to be too generic, it was really good. If you said this was the only kind of food that was served at the island (and all of it free, no less), no genius would decline. Surprisingly, even Akane-san was evidently in that boat.

"Now then, to get back to the subject you're so slyly avoiding," she said, wiping her mouth with a napkin, "if it's 'not like that' between you two, just what is your relationship? If you were just friends, you wouldn't have come to this island together. You have school to worry about."

Indeed, by coming to the island I had missed every day of class since the school entrance ceremony. Incidentally, I also missed the entrance ceremony. In other words, well, yeah.

"I met her before I was in the program. So there's a blank of five years."

"Mmm, and when you got back she turned out to be a cyberterrorist, huh? That's a sordid little tale."

Indeed.

I saw it coming even when we were thirteen years old. Nevertheless, reuniting with her after my five years of study abroad, I was honestly surprised at how little had changed from the old days. Anyone would be surprised to suddenly return to their early teens. Of course, that was just how things seemed. In reality, she had become much more human in terms of personality.

Our relationship.

Asked flat out, it was a tough question to answer.

Kunagisa needed me—that much I knew. However, it didn't really have to be me. It would be extremely difficult to explain the circumstances that surrounded us. To do so, I'd have to explain a lot about Kunagisa herself, and I didn't especially want to do that.

"Hmm," Akane-san nodded.

"I haven't talked with Kunagisa-chan all that much, but it seems to me she has too many shortcomings to go through everyday life. . . . Hmm, I guess I shouldn't say shortcomings. It's not like she's defective. But her focus is just so skewed. It reminds me of my friend whose kid is a savant."

Savant—in French, it means a person with wisdom. I was aware that Kunagisa, too, used to be called a savant. I probably knew too much about her.

"So she probably really does need someone like you looking after her. There's no doubt about that. But I mean, how does that make you feel?"

I didn't have an answer.

"It seems like you two have something of a codependent existence," Akane-san continued.

"Codependent existence?"

She tilted her head as if to say, "Haven't you heard the word?"

"It's a symptom of addiction that affects human relationships. Like, for example, let's say there's a recovering alcoholic who has a caretaker by his side. He needs that caretaker, and the caretaker devotedly looks after him. But when that devotion goes to extremes, it's a sign of codependency. They get drunk on serving. You even see mild cases of it in romantic couples. Needless to say, it's not a good thing. You end up putting each other to waste. I'm not going to say you two are like that, but you might want to take care."

"Sure."

"Few things are as meaningless as prolonging a failed relationship. But still, I'm full of nothing but awe for Kunagisa-chan's talents. Even at ER3 they're using software that she created. Er, 'they' created, rather. But certainly I never imagined I would meet her in a place like this."

"Why are you on this island anyway?"

It wasn't like the Seven Fools had the emptiest schedules in the world.

"No real reason," she said after a few moments' silence. It was a strangely blunt response, and it bothered me a little. "But more important, even if you're not the best player, you at least know the rules to shogi and chess, right? Why don't we have a game while we reminisce a little more about ER3?"

"Sure."

A shogi challenge with one of the Seven Fools.

Sounded interesting.

"But not without looking. My memory is famously bad." Not the greatest reputation to have, if I do say so myself. "If we can change locations, I'm in."

"I've got a board in my room. It was the first thing I bought when I got back to Japan. Hmm, I've actually got some work to do this morning. How's this afternoon?"

"Sounds good. . . . Ah wait, I can't. I've already got something."

"Oh? Meeting up with Kunagisa-chan or something, huh? Well, if that's the case, what can you do."

"No, with Kanami-san."

Boom.

Akane-san's expression grew unusually stern.

Damn it, I'd forgotten. When I had first arrived on the island, Hikari-san had been kind enough to let me know that Akane-san and Kanami-san were on catastrophically bad terms, but because of my famously bad memory I had forgotten.

"Hmph. We're pals, so I'll give you a bit of advice. You shouldn't hang around with someone with such a vulgar occupation. Lowering oneself like that is stupid, you know?"

"Akane-san, you really hate Kanami-san, don't you?"

"No. There's no reason for me to embrace any feelings of like or dislike toward that woman. But artists truly are a despicable race. Hmph, *seriously*!" She banged her hand on the table. "There's nothing I hate more than painters. They're the most inferior race in existence. Compared to them, thieves and rapists look like Jesus. All they do is dab a little bit of paint on something with a little brush and they think they're so damn great. A little red, a little blue, and *poof,* it's a 'masterpiece'! Hah! Anybody can do it!"

It was as if she had turned into another person. It was such an abrupt transformation, it almost made you wonder if a painter had once stolen her research materials or something.

"Ah, sorry," she said, returning to her normal self upon noticing my stunned expression. "I guess I got carried away. Not that I'm going to take any of that back, but I know it's no fun listening to someone gripe about someone else. I think I'm going to go cool off," she said, her words racing, then helped herself to the rest of my coffee and made for the door. It seemed she was regretting losing her head like that. Even if she wasn't going to take it back.

Once I was alone, I let out a sigh.

Man, I had been nervous. I'm not that used to holding conversations with people in the first place, much less Sonoyama Akane of the ER3 Seven Fools. No sweat, right?

Well, aside from that blunder at the very end, we were actually able to hold a much more natural conversation than I would've imagined, so I guess I should've been happy. And maybe, sometime in the next four days, I would get to have that game of shogi with her.

I let out another sigh, but there was no time to snooze. Having finished breakfast, I decided to pay yet another visit to Kunagisa's room, but not a second later, Maki-san appeared in mid-yawn. Fully dressed in outdoor gear, which she complemented with a high ponytail, she looked very much like she had come to this island on vacation.

"Ba baya baya baya baya bahhh," she hummed cheerfully as she strolled over and took a seat by me.

"Good morning."

"Hello."

"No no no, you gotta say 'good morning' when you greet someone in the morning. Ah, wait, is it not still morning? You've been up since six, so it probably feels pretty late to you, wow. As for me, I have extraordinarily low blood pressure, so I can't be like you," she said with another big yawn. I gave the usual nod and "yup" combo. There was no point in asking how she knew when I woke up.

I was once again nervous, this time in an entirely different way than when I was with Akane-san.

Himena Maki-san.

Of course she wasn't just here for the surfing. There was a solid reason for her being on this island.

Maki-san's occupation was fortune-telling. Just as Kanami-san was a painting genius and Akane-san was an academic genius, Maki-san was known as a genius in the world of fortune-telling.

Now that's a real talent, huh? I thought to myself.

That aside, I wasn't a big fan of Maki-san.

We had had a bad first impression of each other.

"You're a fortune-teller? I've never met one of those before. So how does *my* fortune look?"

It's not like I actually cared all that much about my fortune. I just figured that since she was a fortune-teller, it was the socially appropriate thing to say. Normally any person would be thrilled to have the conversation turn to their field of expertise. As Churchill once said, "I want to talk about what I know, but people only ask me about what I don't." I just didn't want to be one of those "people."

That's just an excuse though.

But after hearing my question, Maki-san sneered, and said, "Well, give me your year, month, and date of birth; your blood type; and the name of your favorite movie actor." I answered, but all the while wondering what possible connection my favorite actor could have to my fortune, birthday and blood type aside. In any case, I had forgotten my blood type, and I didn't really know a lot of movie actors, for that matter, so I just made some answers up.

"Okay, I see. Then, take this," Maki-san said, producing a slip of paper from her pocket and handing it to me. And with that, she left.

I opened the paper fortune and took a look. My date of birth along with the blood type and actor I had just given were inscribed on it in Mincho font.

"You were tricking me, weren't you?"

After that, I went to check with Kunagisa about it. "I figure it's some worn-out magic trick where the pocket has hidden slips of paper with random numbers written on them or something," I said.

"Mmm-mmm." Kunagisa shook her head. "No way. That might work for playing cards, but for something like this there would have to be too many. Plus, she would've had to look you up beforehand. It's not like she could've guessed you would lie about your blood type and favorite actor."

And then Kunagisa gave me the Himena Maki lecture. It seemed that although uneducated folks like myself hadn't heard of her, Maki-san had actually made quite a name for herself in the fortune-telling world. She didn't do those supposedly therapeutic horoscope-style "cold readings" like you see in magazines, but rather used her skills to advise bigwig politicians and corporate clients, never making much of a spectacle of herself.

Himena Maki, master fortune-teller.

"Also known as a good self-promoter," I commented.

Kunagisa seemed to think of her that way, too.

Her catchphrase for her: "The telepath who knows the past, the future, human beings, the world, and all inside it."

"What's a telepath?"

"She's super-powered," she said aloofly. "She's got extrasensory perception."

"Huh?"

"ESP. Super abilities are divided into the two categories of ESP and PK. What Maki-chan's got is ESP. Retrocognition, precognition, and telepathy. In translation, retrocognition means she can see the past. Precognition means she knows the future. Telepathy means she can read your psyche."

"Wait a sec, I don't follow. Slow down. Tomo, Maki-san *is* a fortune-teller, right?"

"Occupationally, yes. Using her special abilities. That's all. Being able to run fast isn't an occupation, right? But being an athlete is. Being good with your hands isn't an occupation, right? But being a craftsman is. Special abilities are just abilities, but fortune-telling is an occupation."

"Ah . . ." I nodded. "So Maki-san . . ."

"Yep. She read your thoughts in advance, even before she asked you those questions." She flashed a bright smile.

"Superpowers, huh?" I muttered softly so as not to be heard by Maki-san, now sitting next to me in the dining room. I recalled my conversation with Kunagisa. Her previous explanation had sounded somewhat convincing, to be sure, but . . .

Now, sitting next to this sleepy-eyed, spacey woman, it was really hard to imagine she was a fortune-teller. She just seemed like some drowsy chick with low blood pressure.

"I told you I'm a fortune-teller, but you seem to be dissatisfied," she said, suddenly shifting her glance toward me. For some reason, she seemed to be picking on me a little ever since our first encounter. "Perhaps you'd like me to go walking around with a black hood and crystal ball. Should I speak to you in vague, cryptic terms about your impending doom? You just take everything at face value, don't you?"

"I don't think that's the case."

"Yeah, I'll bet. I know all about it," she replied, shaking her head. "Well, whatever. You don't matter anyway."

"I don't matter?"

"Yup. You're the Japanese representative of things that don't matter."

In other words, the most unimportant guy in Japan. It was a terrible thing to hear.

"But I'll give you one piece of advice out of the kindness of my heart. Your impression of me is quite out of line. And that's not all. The ideas you hold about the residents of this island are all out of line. And that includes Kunagisa-chan. More important, it looks like you intentionally adjust all your beliefs when you're talking to other people. That's surely a very comfortable way to live, but I wouldn't call it a wise one," she rattled off at me as she let out another catlike yawn. For the last two days, I had gotten the same earful of gripes every time we met. And I couldn't say she was all that far off the mark, either. Her remarks were so accurate, I wondered if she really was using telepathy.

I'll be honest: I found her really creepy.

"Oh, I'm sorry for being creepy."

With that said, she stormed off in the direction of the kitchen, presumably to get her breakfast.

4

So as not to let this opportunity slip through my fingers, I immediately made my way out of the dining room and back to Kunagisa's room. As I expected, she was still face-to-face with her workstation. It didn't seem right to be such a shut-in while also being a guest in another person's home, but I guess we just had different values.

Kunagisa looked back at me.

"Oooh, Ii-chan. Welcome back. How was it? Did you run into anyone?"

"Almost everyone. Today I've seen everyone except Teruko-san and Iria-san. Oh yeah, Yayoi-san, too."

But having eaten her food, I felt as if I had met her.

"Hmm, well, that's almost perfect."

"What is?"

"Your score in the Meeting Everyone on Wet Crow's Feather Island by Mid-Morning Contest."

What a crappy-sounding contest.

But anyway.

There were currently twelve people on the island. Artist Ibuki Kanami-san, chef Sashirono Yayoi-san, Sonoyama Akane of the Seven Fools, fortune-teller Himena Maki-san, and engineer Kunagisa Tomo. Then there was Sakaki Shinya and myself, the tagalongs. Then there were the original residents of the island, starting with Akagami Iria, who owned the island and the mansion, plus head maid Handa Rei-san and the three all-purpose maids, Chiga Akari-san, Chiga Hikari-san, and Chiga Teruko-san. A total of twelve people.

In an ordinary-sized house, things would've already gotten quite cramped, but in this oversized palace, there was still an excess of space.

That's when I remembered.

"Hey, Kunagisa. How long were you planning to be here again?"

"Another four days. So for a week, yeah?"

"Shinya-san was asking me about something." I explained to her what Shinya-san had talked to me about. The rumor about Iria-san's favorite jack-of-all-trades coming to town. Kunagisa, however, seemed uninterested, tuning out the majority of my story.

"Is that really important? It's all really vague information, so it's hard to say, but I don't think we really need to meet this person. I didn't really come here to meet any geniuses, and I'm not really interested."

"Well, yeah, but, hey, speaking of that, I've been meaning to ask for a while, why exactly *did* you come here? If you're not interested in that kind of thing, what were you so interested in?"

I couldn't figure why someone who hated leaving the house as much as Kunagisa did would accept an invitation like this. She tilted her head a bit, and after a moment's pause said, "Eh, just 'cuz." A nonanswer. "There's no particular reason, really. Or are you the type of guy who always needs there to be one for everything?"

I shrugged.

No way.

"As long as there's a network, it doesn't really matter where I am. Home is the best in the end, though," she said in spite of still being on vacation.

Well, whatever. She was just being her usual whimsical

self. I didn't particularly mind, and it wasn't like I was supposed to, either. I sprawled myself out on the pure white carpet and stared up at the chandelier on the ceiling. Man, what an unrealistic scene. Then again, if you asked me what would be a realistic scene, I wouldn't know what to say.

Kunagisa looked at me sprawled on the floor. "Ii-chan, I don't suppose you're bored?"

"I'm bored with life."

"Y'know, that's really unattractive."

Huh.

She laid it right out for me.

"If you're free, why not read a book? I brought a few."

"A book, huh? Whatcha got?"

"Um, a Japanese-English dictionary, the Statute Books, and a modern Japanese dictionary."

"Man, bring that stuff in digital form."

Who has fun reading that kind of stuff?

Oh, right. She does.

Half giving up and half fed up, I rolled over.

"Huh? Ii-chan, your watch is broken, isn't it?"

"Eh?"

I took a look at my watch. That's right. Come to think of it, I had meant to ask her to fix it. After running into so many people this morning, I'd forgotten all about it.

"Lemme see. I'll fix it for you."

"Here. Maybe the battery's dead."

"Hmm . . ." She held the watch up to the light. "Nope, something else is wrong. Did you bump it into something hard? Anyway, I think it'll be a quick fix. But you know, wristwatches have become sort of an anachronism these days. Most people just get by with their cell phone. Huh? Speaking of which, where's yours?"

"I left it at home."

"You should bring it. That's what makes it a *mobile* phone."

"But what if I dropped it?"

"Well, I guess, but—"

"And it would be out of service here anyway. It would take a phone like yours to get any signal here."

Kunagisa uses a phone that receives signals from relay satellites anywhere in the world. Even on a deserted island in the middle of nowhere, her phone didn't know the meaning of the phrase "out of service."

Of course, it didn't come cheap. It was a terrible waste of money for an antisocialite like Kunagisa, but she wasn't the type to give much thought to such matters.

"Hmm, maybe so. Well, it's not like being an anachronism is a bad thing."

She narrowed her big eyes and placed my watch next to the computer rack.

Just then there was a knock at the door. Kunagisa showed no response whatsoever, so I had no choice but to open it myself. The visitor was none other than Hikari-san, cleaning supplies in tow.

"Hello. Thanks so much." I invited her in.

"Yo, Hikari-chan, ciaooo!" Kunagisa welcomed her with a full-faced grin. Hikari-san responded in likewise fashion. For some reason these two girls were strangely friendly with each other. They just plain got along. It's a rare thing for someone to be able to become so friendly with Kunagisa in such a short period of time, so I couldn't help but be a little surprised.

"What are you up to, Tomo-san?"

"I'm making some game software right now. I'm creating an application that converts text to music. I figured I'd give it to Iria-san as a memento of my visit."

"What kind of game is that?" I said.

"Well, shall I explain? Okay, um, okay, so, Ii-chan, what's the longest book you've ever read?"

"I quit halfway through *The Tale of Genji* and *Don Quixote*, so . . . Tolstoy's *War and Peace*. Man, that was long."

"Okay. So let's say you converted that whole book into a text document, whether by using a scanner or by typing it all by hand. Then you do a digital-to-analog conversion, like where 'i' is 'do,' 'ro' is 're,' 'ha' is 'me,' and so on. If you do that, you end up with the '*War and Peace* Song.' For that much text, it would probably come out to around . . . an hour, maybe? Of course, in reality it's more complicated than that. The code conversions and sessions and everything have to be wholly consistent. But still, it turns books into music. Sounds fun, right?"

"Well, definitely sounds interesting, anyway. What programming language are you using? VB? C?"

"Machine language."

An extremely basic-level coding language. I didn't think anybody used that kind of language these days.

"Man, it's like you can communicate with the machine like it's just some close buddy of yours."

"Heh heh heh," she laughed, just a little boastfully.

Seemingly even more ignorant than I about computers, Hikari-san wore an inscrutable expression, not revealing whether she was following the conversation, and said nothing more than "Wow."

"Seriously," I said. "But what's actually fun about this game? I guess I don't really get it."

"Making it is fun."

It was a solid reason. I couldn't object.

Hikari-san listened with apparent interest, but then seemed to remember something. "Oh, right." She turned to me. "Would it be all right if I cleaned your room later on? I stopped by the storeroom a little earlier, but you were out."

"Sure, no problem."

I sure didn't know what cleaning there was to be done in

that room, though. Hikari-san politely thanked me and resumed cleaning Kunagisa's room.

After a single sweep of the room, she stopped and crouched to the floor with a sigh.

"I apologize. I'm just . . . a little exhausted."

"Why not take a break?"

"No, I'll be fine. Rei-san would get mad anyway. I've said it before, but she's so strict. I'll be fine. I'm peppy. That's my one positive trait. I'm fine. Please forgive me for causing you concern," she said firmly, then exited the room.

I let out a sigh. "Sure seems to have it tough. Maybe it's just my assumption, but seeing her like that, it seems as if she's bearing an awfully big load on her own."

"Do you feel a little like you're watching yourself?"

"It's not like that, but y'know, I do feel a bit of sympathy for her." She did seem to be miserable, after all. Rei-san and Akari-san seemed to have a distinct division in their heads that this was just "work," but Hikari-san didn't seem to be able to mentally process it that way. It was like the concept of work hadn't been figured into her internal "circuit." Perhaps there were circumstances surrounding that.

As for the other maid, Teruko-san, I wasn't sure *what* she was thinking, so I couldn't comment.

"Everybody's suffering through something, Ii-chan," Kunagisa said knowingly. "Everybody knows hardship, or even if they don't, they're at least exerting effort somewhere. Hikari-san, your pal Nao-kun, Akane-chan—everyone. If there's anyone who lives without suffering or exerting effort, it's probably me."

5

After having lunch, I headed for the atelier as promised. Kunagisa claimed, as usual, not to be hungry and headed to bed shortly after noon. She was a chronically sleep-deprived little techie.

"Wake me for din-din, please. I hafta see Iria-chan and stuff," she said.

I knocked on the atelier door, waited for a response, then turned the knob.

The floors were uncarpeted hardwood. In some ways it reminded me of the art room in my elementary school, except of course that this room wasn't lined with scarred-up desks and there weren't any fake-looking plaster sculptures. It wasn't as big either. The total area of the atelier was probably around half the size of the room Kunagisa was staying in.

"Welcome. Take a seat over there," Kanami-san said, after briefly staring at me in cold silence. Shinya-san must have been in his room or someplace, as Kanami-san was the only person there. I walked past a shelf containing paint and paint supplies and took a seat as told.

I faced Kanami-san. "Thanks for doing this."

I couldn't deny that she was a pretty woman. With blond hair and blue eyes, she was like one of those "well-bred young ladies" you see in old films. An intellectual, at that. And even more, she had artistic talent. It was like she had God's favor.

No, maybe I can't say that.

She had bad legs, and until a few years ago, she couldn't even see. I guess it would be pretty damn low of me in all my able-bodied good fortune to gripe. But on the other hand, Kanami-san herself didn't seem to view her condition as a handicap or disability.

"God is fair. If I had been able-bodied, it would've conversely been unfair to ordinary people." "Legs are just a decoration." "Even when I gained my eyesight, my world didn't really change. The world looked just as I'd thought. Natural selection and fate have unusually bad taste."

All of these are quotes from Kanami-san's art books.

Kanami-san sat in a round, wooden chair just like the one I was sitting in. She was in a dress, so it looked mildly uncomfortable, I noticed.

"Kanami-san, is that what you wear when you're painting?"

"Are you doubting my fashion sense?"

Her face grew subtly more stern. It seemed that this was no joke. She was actually miffed. I scrambled to weasel my way out.

"No no, I didn't mean that. I was just thinking your clothes might get dirty."

"I don't go and change my clothes every time I paint something. Up to now, I've never dirtied my clothes even *once* while painting. I'm not an idiot."

"Oh, I see."

I guess it was like being an expert calligrapher. In retrospect, getting paint on your clothes is probably a pretty amateur blunder. To Kanami-san, one of the top artists in the entire world, the mere suggestion was probably rude.

I shrugged.

"But is it really okay painting someone like me?"

"What's that supposed to mean?" she snapped with the same stern expression. She seemed to be in a pretty awful mood. Or no, maybe this was her default setting.

"Er, no, it's just that, won't it decrease your worth as an artist?"

Like, for example, it was probably safe to say that Kunagisa had technological skill like no one else in the world. However, she only ever used that technology for fun, so the number of people who actually acknowledged her as amazing and brilliant was extremely small.

"Authority comes from results. Not doing and not being able to do are the same thing."

Apparently that was Kunagisa's case.

I figured it was the same with painters. If you just choose your subjects randomly and mess around all the time, it's hard to get other people to acknowledge your worth as an artist.

But Kanami-san renounced my ideas.

"Didn't I just tell you I'm not an idiot? Do you have a brain at all? I don't go around choosing subjects. You know, if you keep your mouth shut, people won't see how stupid you are, so why don't you do just that?"

My heart sank.

"I just . . . I *hate* that kind of thinking. It makes me want to puke. 'Oh, there were no good subjects to paint.' 'My model was no good.' 'The environment was all wrong.' 'That's not the kind of subject I should be painting.' And it's not just with painters either. Even you know people who say obnoxiously egotistical things like 'Oh, this isn't what I want to do' or 'Oh, I don't know what I want to do,' right?"

"Yeah, I do."

Yeah, myself.

"For god's sakes," she sighed. "I *hate* people who bitch about what they want and don't want to do, putting their own ineptitude on a pedestal. I want to tell them to stop living like pricks. I don't mean they should all die, but they should be more humble. Just paint anything and stop whining all the time. I don't care if it's some boring jerk or a pile of bug guts. I'd turn it into gorgeous art."

Regardless of how sweet and pretty she looked, she sure was full of herself. She was so uncompromising that she didn't even forgive others who compromised.

Being compared to a pile of bug guts wasn't my favorite thing in the world, but if she could paint that, surely she could paint me. It seemed that making any further thoughtful comments would just end badly, so I decided to stay quiet.

I noticed that behind Kanami-san was a canvas. An under-angle view of the cherry blossom tree was drawn on it in pencil. The one she had been looking at this morning with Shinya-san.

It was so precisely drawn, it was like a monochrome photograph. With about ten million pixels. No, that's dumb. There was no need to cheapen such an intricate drawing with that kind of metaphor.

I pointed to the picture. "When did you draw that?"

"This morning. Got a problem?"

It was early morning when she was observing the tree. That was about five hours earlier. In other words, she had drawn this amazingly detailed picture in a mere five hours. A drawing like this should've taken *at least* a week to complete. Without thinking, I shot her a skeptical expression. She grimaced back at me audaciously.

"Only idiots spend three or four months doing something you can finish in a week. Idiots or lazy people. And since I'm neither, I did this picture in three hours. It doesn't take me any longer than that."

Huh.

Being the pure embodiment of laziness myself, this was painful to hear. It stung. I wished Kunagisa could've heard it, too.

"Right? Even you have to agree a little, too, right?" she said in a cruel tone, demanding my concurrence. I couldn't help but feel as if she were attacking me with a direct insult. And I doubt that was just a false impression.

"Uh, no, well, I mean . . . yeah. Er, but anyway, you're really good."

"Yeah, sure," she answered, completely uninterested in my generic praise. It really was an exceedingly bland comment for me to make, in retrospect. *You're really good.* It sounds like something a five-year-old would say.

"Uh, so, Kanami-san, you do detail pictures?"

"I do all kinds of pictures. Didn't you know?"

Oh yeah, I'd put my foot in my mouth again. The woman before my eyes was Ibuki Kanami-san, the woman artist who denied having any style and took no stance. Whether it be detailed or abstract, there was no picture she couldn't or wouldn't paint.

She squinted just one eye at me. "I don't get hung up on one style. It's not a rule set in stone, but getting too hung up is just plain crazy. It's nuts. If there's one thing in life I want to do as I please, it's painting."

"You may be right, huh?" Unable to argue or concur, I settled with a simple nod. Perhaps able to see through me, she returned my nod with a contemptuous sneer.

"Hey, have you ever seen my art?"

"Well, a few times in some of your art books. But owing to my ignorance, this is the first time I've seen it directly."

"Hmm, and what did you think of it? Not the art book stuff, but that cherry blossom one."

To me, Kanami-san's question was a bit of a surprise. I never figured that so-called geniuses cared much about other people's opinions of them. Starting with Sonoyama Akane-san, none of the people at ER3, including that deplorable group of study-abroad participants, had any vanity or desire for glory, and nobody cared about how they looked in other people's eyes.

"I know my worth better than anyone else does. I don't need to sit here and be evaluated by a bunch of brainless slackers." This was their unanimous way of thinking. Probably why I wasn't a big fan of theirs.

"Um," I said, groping for an answer, "well, it's a very pretty picture."

"A pretty picture, huh?" she repeated my line. "You know, there's no need to try and flatter me. I won't get mad."

"Well, it's just that I don't really have much judgment or a critical eye for this kind of thing. But yeah, I think it's a pretty picture."

"Hmm . . . pretty?"

She wore an utterly disappointed expression as she stared at her canvas. She muttered something to herself.

"Pretty . . . prettyprettypretty. That's not the kind of compliment you give to art."

"Eh?"

"Hmm, you don't get it, huh? Damn, I really don't want to do this. What a waste."

She let out a heavy sigh, hunched over a bit, and picked up the canvas.

She lifted it up over her head . . .

. . . and smashed it into the hardwood floor.

The sound of splintering wood.

Of course, it wasn't the floor that had broken.

"Hey, wh-what are you doing?"

"As you can see, I'm disposing of my screwup. Ah, why did it have to come to this?"

That decidedly should've been my line. She stared down at the shattered remains of her canvas, a sorrowful expression on her face, and let out another sigh.

"Geez, it looked like it would've been worth about twenty million one day."

"Twenty million yen?"

"Twenty million dollars."

Different unit.

"Of course, we're talking about several decades later."

"Artists can be pretty reckless sometimes, huh?"

I couldn't help but feel guilty that my crappy comments had invited this disaster.

"You shouldn't feel like you did something wrong. This is my responsibility. I'm not the kind of imbecile who pushes her own responsibilities onto other people."

"But I'm just an amateur. You didn't have to do something like that based on the opinion of an amateur."

"It's not art if you get to pick who looks at it," she insisted.

So that's how it was.

I could understand that.

Her words and her manner were filled to the brim with spitefulness, but to be sure, this woman was an artist to the bone.

"But it was so realistic, it was just like a photograph."

"That's not a compliment either, you know. Listen, if you have a habit of complimenting people by saying 'it's just like blah blah blah,' I think you'd better quit it. It's really an insult of the highest order. If you absolutely have to box everything into a style, though, I guess there's no hope." She turned back toward me. "I suppose I can understand why you say it was like a photograph, though. After all, photographs originally spawned from drawings."

"Is that right?"

"Yeah. You didn't know?" She raised an eyebrow at me.

It seemed saying, "You didn't know?" was her habit.

"The person who invented daguerreotype photography was a 'factual artist.' Apparently the study of perspective is related to the invention of the camera. You've heard of the camera obscura, right?"

Heard of it, yes. The so-called dark chamber. The phenomenon where if you make a hole in one spot on the wall of a pitch-black room, the outside scenery will project onto the opposite wall. It was quite an old technology, dating back to the days of the Roman Empire, and even having been mentioned by Aristotle. Supposedly it was the origin of the camera.

"It was just one invention used to create accurate images. The main idea behind perspective is to 'show things the way they really look.' That's how the French artist Courbet put it. He also made such realist remarks as 'I've never seen an angel, so why would I paint one?' It goes against my philosophy, though. If you get a kid to draw something, it never has any perspective or depth, right? Everything's just displayed in the foreground. The size of objects is also chosen at whim, so for example a house and a person are the same size, or the most important thing is drawn the biggest. In other words, what they're putting on the canvas isn't what the objects look like, it's how the objects feel. If you believe that drawing pictures is a form of personal expression, then I think that's the correct way to do it. If you think about it like that, a drawing that looks just like a photograph isn't a good drawing at all, is it?"

"Wow."

As soon as she had broken out the professional lingo, I lost my grip on what she was talking about. And with all her chitchat she hadn't even started setting up to paint. When was she planning to get started already?

"Though truth be told, photographs aren't such an accurate representation of reality either. If you edit a photograph well, it's not hard to fool people. Maybe they're not so different from paintings, in the sense that they're both selective."

"Uh, Kanami-san, were you going to draw me?"

"Right now I'm memorizing."

Just as I thought I was about to be called incompetent again, she spoke to me with unexpected gentleness.

"Maybe you didn't know? I'm the type who has to do her work alone. When I'm with other people my focus goes wacko."

She sounded like Leonardo da Vinci. Artists who don't look and paint at the same time weren't the kind of thing you heard about every day, but they weren't the most uncommon thing in the world either, so I wasn't particularly surprised.

"So when I do portraits, I just have to rely on my memory."

"You can do that?"

"To me, memory and perception are synonymous."

Now she sounded like Hannibal the Cannibal.

"Let's just stay and talk like this for the next two hours. Then I'll start painting after you leave. Ah, after I redo this cherry blossom picture, that is. I want to turn it into something at least you can comprehend. For your painting, I'll need to put down two layers of color, so it'll take a little while to draw. I should be able to give it to you tomorrow morning."

"You'll give it to me?"

"Sure. I don't need that kind of painting. I have no interest in paintings that are finished. I'll sign it, so if you sell it you should be able to make something decent. Of course you could always destroy it if you don't like it, but that seems like a bit of a waste. It should be worth about fifty million."

What a materialistic conversation.

Sigh.

"Hey, by the way, I hear you're on bad terms with Akane-san, is that right?"

"That's right. Or really, it's sort of a one-sided hatred on her part. As an individual, as a scholar, as a researcher, as a member of the ER3 Seven Fools, I personally have nothing but goodwill and respect for Sonoyama Akane, but . . ."

"But? What's that supposed to mean?"

She gave a little smirk. "As for 'just plain' Sonoyama Akane, I despise her."

Two hours later.

After leaving Kanami-san's atelier, I headed for Kunagisa's room. She was in bed, but evidently she had awoken at some point and fixed my watch. In a world-class prank, she had changed the digital face so that the numbers were displayed backward, but at least it seemed to be working, so I stuck it on my left arm, patted the sleeping Kunagisa on the head, said thanks, and headed to Akane-san's room.

"Play me," she challenged, and then said with a delighted smile, "I'll give myself a bigger handicap."

With that, she lined her side of the shogi board with chess pieces.

"It's a Japanese-Western compromise."

"Kinda like two different martial arts styles, huh?"

Handicap notwithstanding, I was thoroughly trounced. Seven times in a row.

Himena Maki,
Genius Fortune-teller

2

ASSEMBLY AND ARITHMETIC

*If you blind yourself to the fact that your opinion is
entirely wrong, you're essentially right.*

1

I bludgeoned the slumbering Kunagisa awake, forced her to
wash her face, and tied her hair up in pigtails for her. Then
with her still half-asleep, and me half carrying her, we
headed to the dining hall, where everyone else from the
mansion was already gathered.

Round table, two empty seats.

I helped Kunagisa to her seat and then sat down next to
her. As I settled in my chair, I took a quick look around the
table at each person.

Out of the twelve people present, the most eye-catching
person—and I'm not sure whether or not this goes without
saying—was none other than the mistress of the house, Akagami Iria-san. The concept of beauty is wholly subjective,
varying from one person to the next, so to say Iria-san was
beautiful would probably be pointless. If I say she was beautiful, that was simply something I personally felt and nothing more. Besides, Akari-san the maid was way more up my
alley, as long as we're talking about personal preferences. Uh,
but none of that matters.

Seriously.

To give something more objective, Akagami Iria was a

classy woman. She wore her pretty black hair in a roll, coupled with an expensive-looking dress. She was actually somewhat mismatched, but her excessive classiness more than made up for it. She seemed to be around the same age as me, still in her twenties, but man, upbringing and lineage really do have their effects on people. Of course, there's always other factors as well, but those things are important for sure. That's always been the case.

Akagami Iria.

The black sheep granddaughter of the Akagami Foundation.

"Well then, now that Kunagisa-san is here, shall we commence with the best part of the day?" She put her hands together like a little kid. "Chow down." It seemed she was fairly immature emotionally. It was probably safe to say she wasn't the most worldly person out there, but it was probably just as well to her.

Incidentally, this island, where people were largely free to do as they wished, had a single rule: "We all eat dinner together." It was a simple rule that shouldn't have been hard for anyone to follow, but indeed, quite a few so-called geniuses had failed to do so and ended up leaving the island. There are a lot of similarities between a genius and a person with no common sense or decency.

Iria-san sat with two maids on either side of her. On her left were Teruko-san and Rei-san. On her right, Akari-san and Hikari-san. There was no way to distinguish between Akari-san and Hikari-san, so I couldn't tell which one was which. Theoretically one would've been able to tell them apart by their facial expressions and gestures and such, but for the nonobservant type like myself, it was a challenge. Kunagisa seemed to be able to distinguish between the two (which was no mystery, since it was Kunagisa, after all), but depending on the conversation, she seemed to have trouble distinguishing who was Iria-san. Nobody seemed to mind.

"Now then, everybody raise your glasses . . . cheers!" she said almost as if singing, her glass raised high in the air. Everyone else, including myself, did likewise. But it bore mentioning that my glass and Kunagisa's glass were filled not with wine, but with juice.

After all, we were underage.

A number of dishes were set beautifully around the table. They were the proud masterpieces of chef extraordinaire Sashirono Yayoi. I'll start with the dish closest to me and go in that order:

Crowned lamb roast, cappuccino-based sweet potato soup, foie gras terrine with truffle gnocchi, steamed blue mussels, Belgian eel simmered in green sauce, pickled herring, whale meat sashimi, sauce-covered ravioli, ostrich meat carpaccio, fruit salad, potato salad with egg, and, finally, oil-sautéed mushrooms.

Yup, I was clueless.

Probably because Yayoi-san had created each dish specifically to cater to the respective tastes of each guest, even after hearing the names, I had no idea what I was eating. But that was neither here nor there. It's not like a name has that profound of an influence on the thing itself.

I think.

After all this, there was said to be dessert as well. If you thought about it, it was really a copious quantity of food. And with Yayoi being the culinary maestro she was, the food was so delicious that I all but entirely neglected to watch my weight. Granted, Yayoi-san had apparently factored that into her cooking.

"After factoring in the nutritional value, it's still this amazing. She really is a genius," I muttered to myself more than a couple of times.

Speaking of which, I had spoken to Yayoi-san a bit during lunch. When I had gone to the dining hall, she happened to be the only other person around, so I used the opportunity to inquire about the popular rumors about her.

In other words, what was this secret power that allowed her to make any dish better than any other chef?

That was the question.

Upon hearing it, Yayoi-san gave a curious smirk.

"I'm afraid reality doesn't quite live up to the legends. Unlike Himena-san, I don't have any sort of wild superpowers. Basically, it's just effort and discipline."

"Really?"

"Well, I suppose I can imagine what might have started such a rumor. My senses of taste and smell are a little, well, a *lot* stronger than the average person's."

She flicked out her tongue. "To give an anecdotal example, ah, okay, like Helen Keller. She was blind, but they say she could distinguish between people just by their smell. I'm a little bit like that. My sense of smell isn't quite that amazing, but, for example . . ."

She took my arm and, without warning, licked the palm of my hand. I never would have dreamed things would have ended up like this, and I nearly let out a yelp, though somehow I managed to suppress it.

With her tongue still out, she gave an Einsteinish grin. "You've got type AB blood, don't you?" she said. "Negative, right?"

Being so told, it occurred to me that she was right. A public health doctor once told me, "You have an extremely rare blood type." So Yayoi-san was right for sure, but . . .

"'You can really tell all that just by licking my skin?"

"Well, by licking your sweat, to be specific. My tongue can distinguish between approximately twenty thousand flavors, dividing them into twenty levels of intensity. My sense of smell is probably around half that good, I suppose." She tilted her head thoughtfully. It was a cute mannerism. "I'm not smart like Sonoyama-san; I'm terrible at art, unlike Ibuki-san; I'm not particularly skilled with machines like Kunagisa-san; I certainly don't have special powers like Himena-san; and there's not much else I'm any good at, but I've had just this one strong gift since I was a kid. I figured becoming a chef was the only way to take advantage of it."

Perfect taste, they call it.

It's like the taste version of perfect pitch, except perfect taste isn't something you can acquire with training. In other words, Sashirono Yayoi-san was, to just come out and say it, one of the lucky few chosen by God. Among the highly skilled, there are two types of people: those who are chosen, and those who choose themselves—those who were born with it, and those who work for it. Of course, Yayoi-san had "discipline and effort," but she was evidently the former type.

So the path of a chef was not really something she had chosen. She had been born with this gift, and for that reason had gone on to study gastronomy, travel to the West, and polish her inborn talents even further.

The idea of flavor ultimately stems from each individual's ability to judge taste. How well a person can utilize and take advantage of flavor as if it was their own possession—that was largely connected to one's skill as a cook, and well reflected in Yayoi-san's own cooking.

Well, that's the chopped logic of it, but it doesn't mean much practically. To put it a better way, Yayoi-san's cooking was damn good.

If you thought of the round table as a clock with Iria-san sitting at twelve o'clock, then Sashirono Yayoi-san was at three o'clock next to Teruko-san and Rei-san.

At four o'clock was Sakaki Shinya-san. As you would expect from the man who had long been employed as Kanami-san's caretaker, he looked not the least bit intimidated, and was actually rather stately-looking.

Then next to him sat Ibuki Kanami-san at the five o'clock position. Behind her was her wheelchair, which she had likely used to come to the dining room. She didn't seem to be in a particularly bad mood, but she didn't look very cheerful either.

At six o'clock was Kunagisa. This meant she was sitting directly across from the mistress of the house, Akagami Iria-san. That was more than enough to make me nervous, but really that didn't matter; to Kunagisa, the word *nervous* didn't even exist in the Japanese language.

Then in lucky seat number seven sat myself.

Next to me at eight o'clock sat Sonoyama Akane-san of the Seven Fools. She was completely immersed in the devouring of Yayoi-san's cuisine. She had much more of an appetite than you might expect. Of course, she was a human being before she was a scholar—whether or not she would admit it herself—and you can't live if you don't eat, but even if you disregarded that, she was a serious eater. Even I felt satisfied just watching her eat. It seemed to me that Yayoi-san must've been really proud to see her devouring her food so delightedly.

Next to Akane-san at nine o'clock sat the fortune-telling master, the one with ESP superpowers, Himena Maki-san. At some point she had apparently changed clothes, and was now adorned in an entirely different fashion than this morning. She wore a halter-neck striped shirt with a pale, pink cardigan and sheep-printed cropped pants. Her hair was up in twin ponytails. Possibly because she noticed me looking at her, she looked back at me with a strangely unpleasant sneer and sank her teeth into some roast lamb. It was an expression that said, "I know everything, but I'm not saying anything," and it made me wholly uncomfortable.

It never ends.

At ten and eleven o'clock sat Akari-san and Hikari-san. Teruko-san was completely silent and mostly expressionless.

She just placed food in her mouth like it was a mechanical process. For someone to be able to eat this food without any sort of reaction, it made you wonder if she had any sense of taste. In the face of the three sisters' air of youthfulness, Rei-san, in contrast, had the look of a mature, uptight career woman. I hadn't heard her talk much, but judging from her appearance, she seemed to be the strict type, and I had heard the corroborating sob stories of Hikari-san several times by now.

So there you have it.

That's all twelve people.

Lucky number?

With a face like this?

Just babbling again. What kind of meaning lay in things like that? I was very obviously standing out here. You could even call me the black sheep. Then again, there had never been a place where I didn't stand out. Not Kobe, not Houston, not Kyoto, and not even on this island.

In this wide world, there's only one me.

Eh, whatever.

I like loneliness.

No bluff.

Even if I was bluffing.

"Oh by the way, if I can change the subject . . ." Iria-san said, bringing the individual conversations that had been developing up to now to an immediate halt. The power to direct the table conversation lay in Iria-san's hands alone. It was the selfish privilege befitting an upper-class girl.

She continued, raising her voice.

"It seems there are already rumors floating around, so I'll go ahead and make the announcement. This is about the next guest. The latest genius to grace this house."

All eyes were on Iria-san. Well, all except for Kunagisa, who continued to chow down on whale meat. To deliberately try and capture that girl's attention was quite a difficult task.

"I'd like to emphasize that our new guest is the possessor of such extraordinary, glorious talent that it even bears comparison to you all. I'd like very much to welcome this person, so please cooperate, okay?"

Each person gave a personalized reaction. The part about bearing comparison to everyone seemed to really shake things up. With everyone seemingly restraining themselves, only the very ordinary Shinya-san dared speak up.

"Question. Just who is this person? I don't really know a whole lot just from the rumors I've heard, but they say it's a real jack-of-all-trades. Is that right?"

"You could say that. We've only met once before, but, yeah, once was enough. This person is my hero." She gazed up, evidently deep in thought. "A truly heroic existence, to me. Like a detective in a mystery novel or a monster in a monster movie."

A monster?

I could feel my eyebrows raise of their own accord. Iria-san had just dropped a reference to monster movies, but was that really an accurate description of this person? That wasn't the kind of vocabulary you typically used to describe a person, and even if you did, it definitely wasn't a compliment.

"That's quite the hard sell. Sounds like we can expect quite a bit from this individual," Shinya-san said with a boisterous chuckle. "I hear this person can do all sorts of things . . . such as paint wonderfully and so on?"

"I've never seen it, but I wouldn't be surprised. I imagine something as simple as painting a picture shouldn't be a challenge."

As you'd expect, this seemed to have wounded Kanami-san's pride. She looked a little bit—by which I mean ridiculously—miffed.

"Might we possibly be graced with knowing the name of

this superior specimen, Iria-san?" Kanami-san said. Her tone had a bite to it.

I had thought of this that morning as well, but Kanami-san really did have a lot of pride. That's not necessarily a bad thing, but it's not strictly a good thing either. Far be it for me to cast aspersions about the way Kanami-san chose to live, but to say the least, I knew I could never live like that.

Iria's expression suggested that she didn't understand why Kanami-san was so mad (and in reality that probably was the case), and she answered plainly, "Aikawa-san."

Pure dumbfoundedness.

At this point, Kanami-san seemed like the stupid one.

"Owing to an extremely busy schedule, Aikawa-san will only be staying here for three days, but everyone, please be friendly. Aikawa-san is a big deal to me. You could even call it love."

Iria-san's cheeks turned bright red. Seeing that childish mannerism, her audience was thrown even further into bewilderment. It felt like she could've made any demand, however bossy, and everyone would've forgiven it. She innately had that sort of air about her.

Probably her lineage to blame again.

"Even still, Aikawa . . ."

I'd never heard the name, ignorant as I was. I looked over at Kunagisa to see her reaction, but she was still eating. When that girl was focused on something, she was always like that. More incorrigible than a child and harder to handle than an animal. Well, then again, at least she knew how to sit in a chair.

"Oh, I'm so looking forward to it. To think Aikawa-san is coming again. I've asked so many times. It's like a dream. Oh, what if it really was a dream?" she said as if in a daze. Judging from her current state, Iria-san must have been pretty head-over-heels for this Aikawa guy. It was like she was talking about the man she had been in love with for years and years.

She spoke his name with great reverence.

"Ah, speaking of which, Kunagisa-san," she said, turning the conversation toward Kunagisa. "You were going to leave before then, isn't that right?"

"Hmm? Oh, yup yup," she responded. She never stopped moving the chopsticks she held in her hands. The fact that she was holding a chopstick in each hand was enough of a testament to her bad table manners. "Yup, four more days."

"That's really too bad. It's going to be such a great opportunity. I'd really like you to meet Aikawa-san. There's really no way?"

"Afraid not. I'm from a world where once you've planned something you can't change it. They even call me the Living Time Table. Ii-chan, too, of course."

Don't drag me into this, I thought. Coming to this island in the first place was never part of my "time table."

Iria nodded with a truly disappointed look on her face. "Is that so? Say, could it be that you're not having a good time here? It doesn't seem like you've left your room much."

"I'm from a world where people don't leave their rooms much. But no, I'm having fun. Lots of fun. I can have fun anywhere, anytime, all the way."

Her words made me stiffen a bit. There was no exaggeration in what she said. For someone who's so completely immersed in their own world, there's never a time that isn't fun. And what of all other emotions? How tragic must it be to always be having fun, no matter where you are?

That was something I already knew the answer to.

"Ah, is that so?" Iria shrugged. "But Kunagisa-san, surely even you would find some value in meeting Aikawa-san. Meeting a person like that, you're bound to find some inspiration."

As if she had been waiting for the perfect timing, Kanami-san broke into the conversation. "Being influenced by another person is proof of one's mediocrity. Of one's impotence. How ridiculous. I don't know what kind of person this Aikawa is, but I sincerely doubt there's any need to meet him."

"Now now, is that a fact?" Playing devil's advocate with Kanami-san was the obvious choice, Sonoyama Akane. "I spent several years surrounded by the finest minds in the world, and I know for a fact that if I hadn't had that experience, I wouldn't be where I am today. You can better yourself just by spending time with brilliant people."

"The ER3? What a joke. You must be stupid. Why would anyone ever want to bind themselves to such an organization?" Kanami sneered.

"I don't consider that I'm *binding* myself. Everyone is free to move about as they please and help hone one another's skills."

" 'Free?' Don't just throw that word around. An organization with no restrictions isn't an organization at all. In the end, even you were just a member of the hierarchy, isn't that right? What a crock. I've been here on this island with you for a while now, but I certainly don't feel as if I've become any more refined. If anything, my worth is decreasing."

They glared at each other. To act this way in front of a whole group of people, they really were childish. I was a little bit appalled.

The maids tried their best to mediate, but Iria-san had a look of pure delight on her face as she watched the dueling pair, so they refrained from stepping in. This kind of situation wasn't really my cup of tea. Meanwhile, Yayoi-san looked fairly indifferent as well, while Maki-san looked entirely unimpressed, and Shinya-san seemed to have written the whole dispute off as an everyday occurrence. It was amazing that not a single person there could stop them.

Ah, wait, there was someone.

Just one person.

"After all, Ibuki-san, humans are a colonial species. People such as yourself who act like bums and expect special treatment all ought to rethink their lifestyle, if you ask me," I said.

"I suppose that means you can't function without being surrounded by other people. People aren't migratory fish, you know. And I don't expect special treatment. I just don't put myself down. I live honestly, and assess things as they really are," Kanami snapped.

"Hmm, I wonder."

" 'Hmm, I wonder'? Ah, more vague questions. You think you look clever by taking an ambiguous stance without ever clearly stating your opinion. Yeah, real clever. 'I wonder,' " Kanami said.

"This is a little hard to listen to."

A voice.

It was Kunagisa.

She pouted her lips out like a sulky kid and looked at Kanami-san.

"This is hurting my ears, Kanami-chan, Akane-chan."

In an instant, she had drawn everyone's attention. Nobody had expected Kunagisa, of all people, to say that.

I had had quite a few experiences with Kunagisa in the past, so it wasn't beyond imaginable. Kunagisa Tomo hated watching people fight quite a bit. Considering her usual happy-go-lucky attitude, it might have been a little unexpected, but it did make some sense. She was a fun-loving girl, which meant she didn't like situations that weren't fun. The logic was as simple as that.

"I'm sorry. I went too far." Somewhat surprisingly, it was Kanami-san who apologized first. In turn, Akane-san couldn't help but acknowledge that Kanami-san, too, was a prominent women of respectable status.

"I was wrong, too," she said, awkwardly avoiding eye contact.

They both hung their heads and stared at the floor. Though the atmosphere was still distinctly awkward, at least the fiasco seemed to be over.

Until Maki-san ruined it completely.

"This is gonna get worse before it gets better," she muttered with an icy voice and audacious grin. Just what was this fortune-teller chick trying to butt in with, now that things had finally settled down? Meanwhile, Iria-san's eyes were twinkling with excitement.

"Is that a prophecy?" she asked. "What do you mean it's going to get worse before it gets better? This is so fascinating. Will you tell us?"

"I won't. I'm not saying anything. Nope." As she spoke, she cast a sideways glance in Kunagisa's direction. "I'm not quite so arrogant as to get the rest of the world involved."

"What's that supposed to mean?" I protested without thinking. As for Kunagisa, she had already turned her full attention back to nutritional intake. It was as though this really was nothing more than a simple annoyance to her. "Maki-san, what do you mean by that?"

"There's no meaning. Just like there's no meaning in your actions. You know, you're, wow, so you're the kind of guy who'll get angry for the sake of a complete stranger, huh? That's not a very good thing. It's not *bad*, per se, but it's not good."

"Oh my, and why is that?" Iria-san said, stepping into our conversation. Or rather, maybe I was the one on the sideline. "I think it's wonderful to be able to get angry on behalf of a stranger. That's not so common in the world nowadays."

"That's because people who can expose their emotions

for the sake of someone else are the same people who blame things on others when something goes wrong. I despise people like you."

It had to be the first time in quite a while that someone had spoken that harshly right to my face. Slowly, she brought her glaring gaze to meet my eyes.

"You just let yourself get carried along by other people. You're the type of person who ignores traffic lights just because everyone else is doing it. You're an abominable excuse for a human being. They often say 'harmonize without agreeing,' but in your case, young man, it's like you're agreeing without harmonizing. I won't say that's bad. I won't say anything as to that. One's identity and one's worth are not always connected. A train that runs along a track is better than a train that doesn't. So I won't say anything as to that. But I hate people like you. I *despise* them. People like you always blame things on others, never acknowledging their own responsibility."

Just carried along with the flow.

To be sure, that is how I lived.

However . . .

"I don't recall . . ."

I hated it.

Meeting Kunagisa, I had grown thoroughly repulsed by it.

"I don't recall you telling me that, Himena Maki-san."

"Oh, are you angry? Gee, your boiling point's a lot lower than I expected. Are you the type who has mood swings all the time?"

"Ii . . ."

Eat me.

Go screw yourself.

Go screw yourself go screw yourself go screw yourself . . .

Go screw yourself, *bitch* . . .

"Ii-chan."

Tug.

Kunagisa yanked on my sleeve.

"This isn't worth getting angry about."

Kunagisa Tomo.

"Okay."

I felt a chill go through my body. The power drained from my body. It was beyond weakness, closer to exhaustion. I slumped in my chair.

"Sorry. I was just joking, 'kay?" Maki-san said to Kunagisa with a terribly sweet smile.

And so dinner that day was a bit of a disaster. Of course, the two days prior hadn't exactly gone off without a hitch either, but the intelligence of this jack-of-all-trades seemed to have shattered something. This Aikawa-san's coming visit to the island was becoming something to dread. Granted, I wouldn't be there when it happened, so I didn't really have much to do with it.

Nevertheless, I had no idea why Maki-san was digging into me so much. Certainly I hadn't made a great first impression on her, but that couldn't have been the only reason at this point. It was obvious that she hated me, but that wasn't reason enough to be harping on me so aggressively like this.

The opposite of affection is not animosity, but apathy. If she just didn't like me, she wouldn't go so far out of her way to pick on me like this. Why, out of this entire group of brilliant people, would Himena Maki specifically target a boring, ordinary person like me? We didn't have anything to do with each other.

It was strange.

Brooding over the subject in my mind, I didn't think for a moment about Maki-san's prophecy of the "worsening of things." If I had given it some thought, it's not likely that anything would've gone differently anyway, but looking back, I can't help but regret that a little.

I guess there was nothing I could have done about that, though.

After all, only Maki-san could have regretted things before they happened.

2

It was already past ten o'clock when I borrowed Kunagisa's bath to freshen up. Kunagisa sat in front of her PCs in the revolving chair, but all three terminals were turned off. She just wanted to spin. Must've had a strong stomach.

"You take a bath, too."

"No."

"I don't care about tonight, but take one tomorrow."

"No."

"Tomorrow I'll strip you down, tie your hands and feet, and throw you in. If you don't want that, you'd better do it yourself."

"Awww, what a drag." She half rose out of her chair to stretch. "I envy fish. They don't ever have to take baths. Hmm, but I wonder if they get cold in the winter. Oh oh oh, by the way, have you heard this before, Ii-chan? So, like, let's say you're keeping a fish in a fish tank. And say you gradually raise the temperature of the tank. Like you raise it so gradually that the fish doesn't even notice. Eventually the water gets so hot that it's boiling, but the fish's body has gotten used to the gradual change, so it can go on swimming without even noticing how hot the water is. It sounds like a lie, but it's for real. Now, Ii-chan, what lesson can we gather from this?"

"That global warming isn't a problem."

"Ding ding ding!" She looked utterly amused. What a peppy chick, I thought, then without warning, she completely collapsed. Face-first, belly-down, without breaking her fall.

I flinched.

"Owww. That hurt."

No doubt.

"What the hell are you doing?"

"I'm hungry . . ."

"You just ate a freaking feast."

"That doesn't matter. I missed breakfast and lunch, so I probably haven't eaten enough. I slept all afternoon, so I don't have to sleep again until tomorrow, but I guess you really have to make sure you sleep and eat properly."

"Human bodies aren't made for that kind of treatment."

"I guess I'm not human then. Let's get something to eat, Ii-chan. Will you tie my hair up first?"

"I think Yayoi-san's probably already back in her room. She gets up early, so don't you think she's already sleeping?"

We couldn't just go wake her up so she would make some dinner. We had to remember that she was a guest, too.

"Hikari-chan is probably awake though. Hikari-chan's cooking is delicious, too, in a Hikari-chan kinda way. If Hikari-chan's asleep, too, Ii-chan, you can make me something."

"Why me?"

"Well, 'cuz you look so a-meow-zing from behind when you're cooking."

"Ehehehe," she laughed naughtily, still facedown.

"Okay okay okay. Fine fine. Understood, Miss Tomo. First I'll tie that hair up, so get over here."

"Oh me oh my."

I tied her hair in a loose ponytail. Then we left her room, heading for the living room.

"Ah, by the way, sorry about earlier."

"About what? Ah, about the thing with Maki-chan. Yeah, it's okay. I'll forgive you. But really, compared to the old days, you've gotten soft. I didn't think you'd let her off with just a single comment like that. I wonder if living in Houston repressed you or something."

"Yeah, well, living in a desert like that for five years, your beliefs start to change. I'm not sure if it matters that it was a desert, though."

"You should tell me about it sometime. What happened over there and stuff."

"You've changed a lot, too. Not so much on the outside, but on the inside."

"There's nothing in this world that doesn't change. It's *panta rhei*."

"Handa Rei?"

"The cycling of all things . . . Ii-chan, you're supposed to be smart, so why don't you know anything?"

"I just have a bad memory. All I want is an average one, really." Just enough of one so that I wouldn't forget the fun times.

Just enough of one so that I could realize the world is full of good things, too.

"Ah, Akari-chan spotted," Kunagisa said, and charged down the hallway. I looked to see that, indeed, Akari-san was there. Or really, at this distance there was no way I could tell whether it was Akari-san or Hikari-san. It was also possible that it was Teruko-san with her glasses removed. But if Kunagisa said it was Akari-san, it was most likely her.

By the time I reached them, Kunagisa and Akari-san had already exchanged a few words. Kunagisa returned to my side and Akari-san continued down the hall in the opposite direction. I wondered about her. She must have had work left to do, even at this hour. If that was the case, she really was going above and beyond.

"What did you talk about?"

"She says Hikari-chan's in the living room."

"Oh yeah? That's convenient."

Of course, not everything in the world goes so smoothly.

When we arrived in the living room, not only Hikari-san, but also Shinya-san and my arch-nemesis Himena Maki-san were there. The three of them sat on a horseshoe-shaped sofa, engaged in lighthearted discussion. On the table were some glasses and alcohol, plus some cheese on a big plate prepared as a snack. Hikari-san promptly noticed our presence and called out with a raised hand, "Ah, Tomo-san!" Having been spotted, there was nothing we could do. We walked over and joined them on the sofa.

Awkwardly, Kunagisa quickly snapped up the seat next to Hikari-san, forcing me to sit next to Maki-san. All the same, I couldn't bear the thought of turning tail and running now. It was dishonorable to flee in the face of the enemy. But Maki-san, seeming to see right through me, greeted me with a wicked expression. "Welcome to my club," she said boastfully.

"Sorry about before. I guess I hit a touchy subject," she apologized insincerely. "Really, I'm sorry. Anybody would get mad about such a sensitive subject."

"It wasn't a particularly sensitive subject."

"Oh, it was. It was so pitiful." She sneered at me. Might she have been drunk? No, she was like this all the time. In fact, she was probably more pleasant when drunk. She slugged down her wine in one gulp, then thrust her glass at me.

"Now you drink, too, boy. Alcohol is good, you know. You forget all the bad things."

"There's nothing so bad I want to forget."

"And there's nothing so good you want to remember," she giggled. "I don't think your poor memory is to blame for not having any happy memories. There are few happy things in your life, and few sad things. There's not much of anything at all. It's all empty. It's an emptiness scarier than darkness. Ahahaha. Isn't life fun?"

Retrocognition, telepathy.

It seemed the advertisements about her weren't just baloney. She was a damn clairvoyant.

"Give me a break, Maki-san. This is just bullying."

"Yup, I'm bullying you. Now drink up."

"I don't do alcohol. I'm underage."

"How by-the-book of you. Oh dear, you're being so cold. Oh, Ii-chan, you're so cool! Is that what you want to hear? That's weird. I should call you the Boy Who's Cold Even in the Summer."

She put her glass back in front of her with a bored expression on her face.

Apparently quite starving, Kunagisa scarfed down the cheese appetizer. She ate with two hands, displaying terrible manners. Of course, knowing that it would cause no harm in this situation, it was hard to care about stuff like that.

"It's supreme, Valencay, and Maroille cheese," Hikari-san explained sweetly. Apparently they were all good cheeses to have with wine. Trying a single piece, I found that it was indeed delicious, but probably only Kunagisa would be able to stand a whole lot of it without even so much as some water.

"How did it go with Kanami?" Shinya-san asked me after a while, cheese in hand. He seemed fairly interested. "Did the modeling go well?"

"Eh, I suppose. There were no problems, anyway."

"She's got a pretty foul personality, eh?" He spoke without euphemism, about his own boss, no less.

"Oh no, she doesn't—"

"Is that so? Well, at least I've never met a woman with a *worse* personality than that."

I had.

She was sitting right next to me, drinking up.

"No, she was fine, really. . . . Oh, but she did smash one of her pictures all of a sudden, and that was surprising."

He smirked.

"Oh, that . . . yeah, yeah. When I got back to the atelier, she was all, 'Shinya-san, dispose of this garbage.' I was like, 'Who are you, Picasso?' Sorry about that. That's just her thing. Don't pay any attention to it. That woman's seen quite a bit of success without exerting much effort, so she's very obstinate. She can't live without acting like a big shot."

"Her 'thing'?"

"Yeah, you know. If she acts like that, she looks like a world-class artist, don't you think? Didn't she say all sorts of artisty things to you? Sort of snooty things? That's how she is, you see."

"Well, but, that's her true nature, right? I mean . . . I thought it was."

"Oh, of course. It's unquestionably her true nature. But she doesn't have to *say* that kind of stuff, now, does she? If she were a real artist, she wouldn't talk like that. Kanami is a genius, to be sure, but she's miles away from being an artist. She's just giving herself an image. At least, that's what I think. I'd appreciate it if she would peel away the façade, but you know how it is." He looked a little sad. "Seriously," he continued, taking a sip of wine. As he wandered slightly off topic, the glass of wine suited him quite well. It was a little enviable.

"That's the reason I asked you to be her model, too. She doesn't do many portraits, you see."

"Oh yeah? But she was saying she doesn't choose her subjects."

"Well, she doesn't, but . . . It's a taste issue. She hates people. No matter how she draws them, they complain, you see. Plus, you know, because she used to be blind, and now her legs are bad, and above all else she has that kind of personality, she doesn't get along well with anyone."

"That's how geniuses are."

The only genius I'd ever heard of who was at all good with human relationships was Gauss.

People like Michelangelo were all supposedly widely disliked. But with Michelangelo, it was because he didn't like anybody to begin with.

"You don't have to be a genius to be socially awkward," Maki-san interjected with a phony innocent expression.

Ah, indeed.

"That woman has a lot of pride about having reached where she is on her own. So it's no wonder she doesn't get along with Sonoyama-san."

Indeed, Akane-san, who had honed her talents in a group atmosphere at the ER3 system, and Kanami-san, who was a raging individualist, were practically polar opposites. It was only natural that they never hit it off.

"It was I who taught art to Kanami-san," Shinya-san said. "Her eyes got better, and . . . you have to understand, back then she had nothing. No family, no special knowledge to speak of. So I gave her a brush. I was only trying to comfort her, but just a month later, she had surpassed me."

"So you're an artist, too?"

I hadn't heard that.

He shrugged his right shoulder, a little embarrassed.

"After Kanami-san surpassed me, I quit. When Verrocchio realized da Vinci had surpassed him, he broke his own paintbrush. I, too, grew to understand his feelings in that moment. With this person of unbelievable talent right next to me all the time, there's no need for me to paint pictures."

That morning, Shinya-san had told me we were alike. I didn't know what he meant until now.

The Sakaki Shinya relative to Ibuki Kanami. It was just like me relative to Kunagisa Tomo. Though he spoke badly of her, it was clear to me now that Shinya-san had unconditional affection for Kanami-san.

"So you're the kind of guy who does everything for other people, too, eh, Shinya-san?" Maki-san said, as if reading my mind (what an analogy). "Of course in Shinya-san's case, there's a charm to it, unlike with *some* people."

"And why's that?"

"He doesn't go around blaming others."

She was going to bring me down blow by blow.

"Um, hey hey . . ." Hikari-san interjected with a worried look. "Who wants something to drink?"

"Some kind of soda would be good."

"Certainly, right away."

She pulled a small bottle of ginger ale out of the living room fridge and quickly returned. With a bright smile, she placed it beside me.

"Please enjoy."

She really was quite the hard worker. I thought it would be rude to keep fighting like this in front of her, so I forced my wound-up nerves to relax.

Gah, there I go blaming things on others.

Damn . . .

Maki-san had me in the palm of her hand.

"Hikari-chan, gimme a drink, too," Kunagisa said.

"Certainly!" She went over to Kunagisa with the ginger ale.

"Come to think of it, you're underage as well, isn't that right, Kunagisa-chan?" Maki-san said. "But it's okay, isn't it? How about it? Just one drink."

"Please don't encourage her."

"My my, playing guardian, are we?" Maki-san sneered. "Ah, how wonderful it must be to be young."

"But you're still young as well."

"No, I'm already twenty-nine." She spoke as if it were no big deal, but I was a little surprised. She was always dressed like such a kid, I figured she had to be about the same age as Iria-san.

"Wow. So that means you're the same age as Kanami," Shinya-san said. "Then Himena-san, you *are* still young. You know, I'm already thirty-two years old. Once you pass thirty, you really start to feel your age. You get winded easily and such."

"Hikari-san, how old are you?" I took the chance to ask.

"I'm twenty-seven."

"So then, Akari-san is twenty-seven, too?"

"Yup. We're triplets, after all."

Twenty-seven . . . I repeated the number a few times in my head. Twenty-seven years old. Akari-san and Hikari-san, both twenty-seven. Maybe this is rude of me, but they really didn't look like twenty-seven. I almost wondered if there was some sort of age-stopping mystery air flowing through the island.

Nah, not likely.

This wasn't Neverland.

"Akane-chan is thirty, right? And I think Yayoi-chan is about thirty as well. Boy, when you sit down and think about it, everyone sure is young. Iria-chan must really like young, female geniuses."

"Pretty lousy hobby, if you ask me."

Kunagisa nodded in agreement as she crammed her face with cheese. Apparently having picked up a spicy piece, she immediately went for the ginger ale and chugged it, but it looked as if it went down the wrong pipe, and she released a barrage of coughs. What the hell was she doing?

Shinya-san let out a sigh. "I thought if I brought Kanami here to cohabitate with other people, she might change a little. Kind of like when you send a truant kid off to camp. But this strategy seems to have been off the mark. It was kind of like a last resort. At this point, she'll probably be living like that for the rest of her life."

Misunderstood by everyone.

Not expecting anyone to understand.

Not relying on anyone but herself.

Eating away at herself all the while.

"Well, that's one way to live."

"Look who's talking."

I don't think I even have to mention whose line that was.

"Uh, speaking of which, Maki-san, why are you here on

the island?" Shinya-san said. "I've been wondering for a while. It's not just a vacation, is it?"

"It is. This place is a sweet deal. You get to live for free, and you even get money for it. It's Xanadu. If I use the Net, I can even still do fortune-telling. It's a world of convenience. Nonstop good times."

What a crappy excuse for an adult.

And pretty *damn* crappy, at that.

"I don't recall hearing *your* story," Maki-san said, breaking my silence. "Why are *you* on this island then? And please don't tell me something like you came here just because Kunagisa-chan said she was going."

Don't act like you don't know, bitch.

Seriously, why was she picking on me like that? Maybe she was really just making fun of me with no objective or reason whatsoever.

It wasn't unthinkable.

"Wrong," she said, then looked over at Kunagisa.

"Fine, assuming guys like you don't matter anyway, why is Kunagisa-chan here?"

"Just a whim, just a whim. I don't go making reasons for every little thing I do."

"I wonder." Maki-san gave a suspicious grin. I didn't know what the deal with her personality was, but she seemed to be getting along with everyone besides me rather well, including Kunagisa.

"She's clever, unlike you."

"Ah, getting sick of this? Getting tense? Hehehe, but I won't stop. I'm gonna keep playing with you until I'm bored of it."

She wore an absolutely sadistic smile.

I felt like captured game.

"Telepathy, eh? Amazing as usual, Himena-san, but lay off him," Shinya-san cut in. "You've chased a whole lot of brilliant people off this island doing that. He'll be leaving soon enough as it is, so there's no need to send him home any faster, right?"

"Everyone I try to have fun with hates me. It's discrimination against people with superpowers, I tell you."

Superpowers . . .

They talked about it like it was an everyday thing, but did such a thing really exist? Indeed, at the ER3 system, as a "comprehensive" research center, they had even conducted advanced psychological research relating to super abilities. Psychokinesis, ESP, DOP, levitation, and teleportation. I had seen any number of papers on the inexplicable, unobservable subject in my time in the ER3 program, and even met a person who claimed it was for real (though he was a phony).

But all I had concluded was that no matter how you thought about it, that stuff was a bunch of bull. None of those papers really explained anything, despite how hard they tried to arbitrarily cram facts into conclusions.

It was what they called "dry love." The dry love–filled thesis papers of these phony scientists were, to be fair, amusing in their own right, but that's all they were. They certainly didn't have what it took to convince someone of anything.

"That's just because you have a narrow mind."

"Have you ever heard of the word *privacy*?"

"It's not my fault. I see what I see and I hear what I hear. And by the way, trying to run away is futile. No matter where you go, I'll know exactly where you are."

"So, you have remote viewing and supersensitive hearing powers, too!" Kunagisa said. "I know a lot of people with special powers, but this is the first time I've ever met someone with so many. Multimulti. Amazing."

Despite knowing that our pasts, futures, and minds were all possibly being read right now, Kunagisa was without a care in the world. Or maybe she didn't have any secrets to keep.

"I really wanted psychokinesis, actually, but I ended up gravitating toward ESP for some reason. Too bad . . . I mean, doesn't teleportation seem so convenient?"

Psychokinesis—referred to as PK—and ESP were academically defined as two completely different abilities. In mainstream metapsychology, it's often said that the existence of ESP can now be proven, though the same cannot be said about PK. This is because the idea of PK is something completely inhuman, while ESP is simply an extension of actual human senses.

"Fortune-telling is about all I can do with just ESP. It's not such a useful ability," Maki-san said with a sigh.

Certainly there wasn't much she could have done apart from fortune-telling, but I still felt skeptical about the whole idea.

"Maki-san, can you prove that you have these special powers?"

"I don't think I need to. How would you, for example, prove that you are you? Would you show us your driver's license? Would you be convinced if I had a Superpowers License? It doesn't matter anyway. Whether you think it's true or think it's a lie or think it's something else, that doesn't affect anything anyway. Just like my knowing everything doesn't change anything."

"Mmm, I wonder."

"You sure have a lot of doubt. Ah, okay, how about I give you your fortune again?" she said out of the blue, grinning at me.

Damn, I hadn't seen this coming.

"You deceived me the first time, after all. Yeah, let's do it. It's a good opportunity for you. I almost never do fortune-tellings for free."

"I'll pass."

"Quick answer. You really hate me, huh? Hehehe, my

mentor always taught me to 'push people's hatred onward,' so that's what I do."

"I can't help but wonder if your mentor meant something else."

"You're quite a liar, aren't you?" She began her fortune-telling, regardless of what I had said.

"You don't like showing your emotions, but you don't like controlling them either, so you have many regrets. Even though you let yourself get pushed around by other people's opinions, you're quite independent. When faced with a challenge, you run away without deliberating, but you're not dumb. *And*, you don't like competition. Sound about right?"

"Is that what you people call a 'cold reading'?" I shot back. "You could've just said anything. Those are all things that hold true for any person, to some extent."

"Is that so? Hmm, maybe. Then let's talk about your relationship with Kunagisa-chan. What we call a compatibility reading. Hmm, both you and Kunagisa-chan are the type who don't need friends. Yet for some reason you stick together. And the reason for that is? Oh my, this part is fairly skewed. You stay by her side because you're jealous of her. And while you're jealous of her ability to express herself freely, she somehow looks unhappy, regardless of whether or not she really is. You see this girl who has everything you want and can do all the things you can't do, yet she is still, for some reason, unhappy, and that makes you feel better. That makes you feel like it doesn't matter if you can't get what you want."

"Really?" Kunagisa gave me a confused look. Whether it was true or not, it wasn't okay to say such a thing right in front of Kunagisa.

I shook my head. "No, Maki-san, I think you've got me all wrong. I'm not such a complicated guy. I'm simple as could be."

"Yeah, well, maybe, maybe not."

"Say, Maki-chan," Kunagisa said, moving closer to her. "If that's really the case, then why do I spend time with Ii-chan?"

"Sorry, but I can't seem to read your mind or past." Maki-san gave a shrug. "Occasionally I meet someone like that. I guess it's a compatibility issue or something, but the aura surrounding them is very ambiguous and hard to decipher. It's like they're in the dark, and it's a little unsettling. It puts me in a bad mood."

So maybe she was just venting on me.

How awful.

"Himena-san, in light of the occasion, I'll go ahead and ask a question, too. How does it feel to be able to see the future and read people's minds and such?" Shinya-san said. "I'm just curious."

"Hmm. That's like asking how things look to spiders with their eight eyes. To attempt a simple explanation, it's like watching TV. It's like the entire room is covered with TVs, and I don't have a remote. I can't turn them off, and I can't change the channels, so all I can do is watch. It's like having a few more brains than regular people, if you can imagine that."

I couldn't.

"Now, what's his face over there got us a little off-topic, Kunagisa-chan, but I still haven't heard why you came to this island."

"It was just on a whim, I tell you."

"No. I may not be able to read you, but I know that's not why."

Kunagisa wheezed out a strange sigh. She seemed a little troubled. I wasn't a big fan of Maki-san's way of posing the question, but to be honest, I had been wondering about it myself. For what reason had Kunagisa, the ultimate shut-in with no equal, been compelled to travel all the way out here to Wet Crow's Feather Island?

"Okay, I'll tell you," she finally said with a piece of cheese on her tongue. "I'm interested in an incident that took place here a long time ago."

3

But I didn't get the chance to learn any more. Just as I was about to ask, "What do you mean, 'incident'?" I bit down on my tongue, hard. Thus, I was unable to get the words out. But even if I miraculously had somehow, it never would've reached Kunagisa's ears, nor anyone else's ears, including my own.

It would have been drowned out by the other noise.

The shaking.

I soon realized it was an earthquake.

"Gah!" Shinya-san uttered.

"Everyone, please, stay calm!" urged Hikari-san, whose profession demanded that she remain cool no matter what happened.

Maki-san, who looked as if she had been expecting the earthquake all along, reclined on the couch without a glint of worry.

I tried to recall what I had learned about earthquakes back in my first year of junior high school, when I was still in Japan. Supposedly they would start with small tremors, and then get bigger and bigger. I couldn't quite recall which were S waves and which were P waves, or figure out which were horizontal and which were vertical tremors, but that didn't matter.

At any rate, the strength of the shaking had jumped a few levels. In a panic, I shoved Kunagisa—whose expression said "I have no idea what's going on"—onto the sofa and threw myself on top of her. There was a chandelier right above her. If that were to fall, she wouldn't stand a chance of survival with that tiny stature of hers. That was my thinking at the time, anyway.

But my efforts seemed to have been in vain, because not a moment later, the shaking died down. Of course, when I say "not a moment later," I mean in terms of real time. To me, it felt only slightly less dragging and terrible than five minutes with your hand on a stove.

In reality, the shaking had probably lasted for less than ten seconds.

"Is it over?" I asked, still on top of Kunagisa.

"Yeah," Maki-san answered. It was the word of a prophet, and probably trustworthy. Meanwhile, Kunagisa groaned with her face buried in the sofa, so I got off her for the time being.

"An earthquake . . . It was pretty big, too. I wonder what it rated on the scale," Shinya-san said, looking around the room. The glasses and bottles on the table had fallen, and Hikari-san had already reflexively begun to clean.

"Pardon me, Hikari-san. I'm going to borrow the phone. I'm worried about Kanami." He pointed to the house phone. Hikari-san nodded. He headed to the white phone by the cabinet.

"Hikari-san, do you have a radio or something?" I said. "I want to check the earthquake's level. Oh, Tomo, could you look it up on the Internet?"

"Well, there's probably already been a breaking news bulletin. We're technically in Kyoto right now, right? Oh, wait, is that wrong?"

"It was a level 3 or 4. I can't quite pinpoint the epicenter, but it's probably around Maizuru, where the level would be at 5," Maki-san said quite matter-of-factly. "And it seems like there weren't many injuries, even in urban areas."

"How do you know?" Perhaps it was inelegant of me to pose such a question, but it just felt like the natural thing to say.

She let out a big sigh before answering. "It's like I've been telling you, I just know. You may be smart, but you sure are slow. Don't have much of a memory either, it would seem. Hey wait, doesn't that make you stupid? Anyway, to use an expression, I can see these things clear as day. Ibuki-san and the others are all fine."

"Ah, remote viewing and superhearing, was it?"

Distance wasn't a factor for her. She could technically watch TV somewhere on the other side of the ocean, and even predict what would appear next. Complex ESP.

But even if she had just been making all of this up, there was no way to check. But it was probably true that the mansion hadn't suffered much damage.

Shinya-san returned from the phone. "Kanami's fine," he said. "She says she's in the atelier. Some paint cans fell off the shelf. It sounds like a big hassle, but at least she's not hurt."

"Should you go over there?"

He was her caretaker after all, and even if he hadn't been, he must've been worried about her, seeing as she couldn't walk.

"Nah, no need," he said with a shrug. "She would probably get ticked off if I did."

"Why do you say that?"

"Because she told me not to come," he said with a pained expression of humility. "She says she's working right now. In fact, she's working on your portrait. Sounds like she's going to turn it into a real masterpiece, so I'd better not bother her."

"Even with Ibuki-san's talent, there's no hope if she used such a terrible model," Maki-san said.

"You really hate me, don't you?"

"Uh-huh," she nodded.

Geez.

Well, whatever. That's how life had always gone for me anyway.

I looked over at Hikari-san.

"Does this happen here a lot? Earthquakes, I mean."

"Not a lot, really. Shinya-san, you've been through a few, right?"

"Yes, but this one was unusually big."

"I wonder if any furniture fell over. I'm a little worried."

"If you're going to fix things up, I'll help."

"No, it wouldn't be right. Tomorrow we'll deal with it depending on Rei-san's orders."

She flashed a sweet smile. If she were a mother, her kids would grow up proper for sure. If we hadn't met in this kind of place under these kinds of circumstances, I definitely would've fallen for her. Or at least, I thought I would. It was never going to happen, but I thought so.

"Teehee. That was my first earthquake in a while," Kunagisa mumbled, tossing her blue hair around as she finally got up from the sofa. "I wonder if my computers are all right. They should be. If the epicenter was in Maizuru, the mansion should be okay, too. Boy, this takes me back to the Great Hanshin quake. Say, Ii-chan, you were already in Houston in those days, right?"

"Yup. For sure."

I vaguely remembered seeing something about it on the news back in my tiny room in America.

"That was a really tough time for me. I was still in Kobe back then. Most of my computers crashed permanently. I was so startled."

Was "startled" really the most appropriate word to describe living through that disaster?

"So shouldn't you be worried about your computers? You must be fully crammed with cheese by now. Let's go back to your room already."

It seemed like the time was right, so I decided to leave the living room. I didn't trust that I had the self-control to stay cool if I had to talk to Maki-san anymore. It seemed like a good time to split.

As if able to read my every thought, Maki-san's gaze burned a hole through my back, and it took every ounce of willpower in my body to ignore her. I pulled Kunagisa by the arm and took her back to her room.

The three PCs (I mean two PCs and one workstation) in her room remained securely situated in the computer rack, and the room had suffered no other damage.

Kunagisa let out a big yawn and stretched.

"Let's turn in already. Having a full stomach really makes you sleepy, huh? Ii-chan, undo my hair."

"Do it yourself, will you?"

"Come on, it's hard to undo a ponytail by myself. I'm not flexible. It's not that I can't do it, but I'll start aching. I've broken bones that way, y'know."

"I get it, I get it. You're really adorable, you know that?"

I removed the band from her hair and ran a comb through it. She let out a naughty little giggle. Once I was finished, she dove into bed. She sunk herself into the mattress and rolled around joyously.

"Take off that coat. How many times do I have to tell you? And aren't you hot?"

"This coat has special memories attached, so no dice."

What memories? Even our dear fortune-teller, Himena Maki, couldn't read Kunagisa's past. Maybe it had something to do with what that "team."

"Anyway, Ii-chan, Kanami-chan and Akane-chan are pretty terrible, but you and Maki-chan don't seem to be on the best of terms either."

"Well, it's more like she harasses me for no reason," I said, thinking about how similar this was to what Kanami-san had said. "I don't have any problems with her in particular."

"Yeah, I'll bet. You're not aggressive enough to hate or resent people. At the very worst, you get miffed, isn't that right?"

"You think? That's interesting."

"Just joking," she snickered. "But Ii-chan, you've really never fallen in love with someone before, have you?"

"Nope."

"I love that about you."

Snicker snicker.

Strange. She was being weirdly feisty. I wondered if maybe that ginger ale had really been wine. I'd never seen her drunk before, so I couldn't imagine what she would be like.

"By the way, Tomo."

"Vat eez eet?"

"Do *you* have any special powers?"

"Hmm . . . if I did, I wouldn't mind at all," she said with a big grin. "I don't really want any, but one can always dream. It's better for Santa Claus to exist than for him not to, right? It's just like that."

"That's an odd point of view."

Even if she had special powers, she wouldn't mind.

Hmm, indeed. That was surprisingly insightful. Whether you had such abilities or not, it wouldn't have much of an effect on your daily life. Of course, now was a bit of an exception.

Because we were on this island?

Because we were on this island.

"I'm gonna go back to my room and turn in, too. See ya tomorrow. If you're planning to sleep now, I'll come wake you tomorrow, so let's have breakfast together."

"Hey, Ii-chan," she called to me, still lying face-up on her bed. "Let's fool around." She beckoned to me.

I paused, just for a second. "No," I said.

"Weirdo. Good for nothing. Coward! Chicken pot pie!"

Yeah, yeah. I shut the door, went downstairs, and headed to my room. It would have been truly awful to run into Maki-san in the hallway or something, but luckily no such incident occurred. Perhaps she was still busy chatting it up with Shinya-san.

I found a key sticking out of the door to my room. Maybe it shouldn't have been a surprise, seeing as it was supposed to be a storage room, but I couldn't help wondering about being trapped inside if someone were to turn the key while I was asleep. There was no way I could reach the window even if I stood on the chair, so it really would be like solitary confinement. Then again, there was nothing anyone could gain by locking me up, so it was probably just excessive worry.

I entered the room, curled up on my futon, and stared at the ceiling in thought.

I was of course thinking about what Maki-san had said earlier.

Oh my, this part is fairly skewed. You stay by her side because you're jealous of her. And while you're jealous of her ability to express herself freely, she somehow looks unhappy, regardless of whether or not she really is. You see this girl who has everything you want and can do all the things you can't do, yet she is still, for some reason, unhappy, and that makes you feel better. That makes you feel like it doesn't matter if you can't get what you want.

"Ha!"

Dammit.

"She's exactly right."

Akane-san of the Seven Fools had described Kunagisa and I as a codependent pair, but really, Maki-san's opinion was closer to the truth.

To me, Kunagisa Tomo represented the thing I most wanted to be.

No, that wasn't it. That wasn't it. To me, she was . . .

She was . . .

"She was what?"

The reason I chose a university in Kyoto rather than Kobe was because she had moved to Kyoto. I also couldn't deny that she was one of the reasons I left Houston.

Why had I done all that?

As Maki-san had said, I wasn't aggressive enough to have feelings like love or hate. Even if someone were to bother me, it was a feeling no different from being annoyed when it rains. No matter how much disdain Maki-san had for me, no matter how many malicious comments Kanami-san spit at me, no emotion would ever build up inside me.

I couldn't help but wonder.

Was I really human?

I didn't understand other people's feelings at all.

If they really existed.

If superpowers like the ones Maki-san claimed to use really existed, perhaps I wanted some myself.

"Nah, I don't need that," I reconsidered.

If I could understand people's feelings, it would just make life all the more annoying. I wasn't looking for a life with an open Pandora's box. I didn't have the nerve for it.

"I'm just babbling nonsense here, dammit."

I hate vacation. I just end up thinking too much. Well, I don't know if it's really too much, but they're the kind of thoughts that can only lead to one's downfall.

Four more days.

I could be patient.

I didn't hate being patient.

Or at least, I was used to it.

Suffering and pain.

I was used to these things.

"Still, they don't feel too good."

Damn, I wanted to return to my peaceful life on the other side of the sea, I thought as I fell into the night.

But the following day I would realize that these past three days had been plenty peaceful.

THE FOURTH DAY

*Ibuki Kanami, Genius Painter,
and her attendant,
Sakaki Shinya*

1

THE FIRST DECAPITATION

There's an up higher than up,
but at the very top, down is all there is.

1

was a dreadful sight.

If I were to compare it to something, let's see, yeah, okay. Gruber Norbert's painting *The River*. The same sort of creepy, marble-colored river ran through the middle of Kanami's atelier, dividing it in half.

Seemingly due to the previous night's earthquake, cans of paint lay scattered around the room, and the simple, iron-pole shelf had fallen over as well. The earthquake had caused the shelf to tip, spilling cans everywhere, their contents dumped on the floor, and this "river" was the result. It was a feasible theory, and that's no doubt how it had happened.

But while this "river" was a bizarre enough spectacle on its own, the real issue lay on the opposite "riverbank." It was beyond imagination or speculation, and couldn't be written off as the earthquake's doing. An earthquake capable of this wouldn't be found on *this* Earth.

The facedown body of a person lay on the floor, with a noticeable vacancy from the neck up.

A headless corpse.

A *beheaded* corpse.

It didn't matter much what words you chose to describe it; it was what it was.

This body with the missing head was wearing the same dress Kanami-san had been wearing the previous day. That exquisite-looking dress that Kanami-san had boasted would never get dirty while she was painting was now stained redblack with blood. It didn't look wearable anymore.

What's more, there was no longer anyone to wear it.

Or let's be more specific.

The wearer was no longer alive.

"This is . . . grotesque," I uttered reflexively. It went without saying, but the words just came out.

The room smelled like paint thinner.

Next to Kanami-san's fallen body sat an overturned wheelchair and a single canvas. It was far away so I wasn't sure, but the painting appeared to have been my portrait.

It was beautiful, a masterwork. Even from this distance, separated by the river, I could tell. I felt the shock with my body, not with my mind. In some ways it was more disturbing than the sight of the headless body.

I recalled what Kanami-san had said the previous day. *It's not art if you get to pick who looks at it.*

Point taken. With this picture, I had no complaints.

Without a doubt, Ibuki Kanami was a genius.

To the point that it made me tremble.

And this made her death all the more devastating. It had been a long time since I had felt devastated by anything, but I was truly devastated by this.

By the death of Kanami-san.

The death of Ibuki Kanami.

"Why?"

Yes, Ibuki Kanami was dead.

I mean, who could stay alive after their head's been chopped off? Even Rasputin couldn't have survived a decapitation. And Kanami-san was just a physically normal human being.

"Well, we shouldn't just leave her like this," I said, breaking everyone's silence. I looked over at Kunagisa. Her lower lip stuck out dubiously, as if she had noticed something strange about Kanami-san's body. She appeared skeptical about something. But now probably wasn't the time to be thinking about such things. If I had to give a reason for each and every one of Kunagisa's actions, I would surely die.

As I tried to take a step forward, she tugged at my arm.

"Ii-chan, wait a sec."

"Huh? Why?"

"The paint isn't dry yet."

"Hmm? Oh, yeah."

Crouching down and checking with the tip of my finger, I found that she was right. My middle finger turned marble-colored.

"But now isn't really the time to worry about things like that."

There was a cut-up dead body right in front of us. To worry about dirtying your shoes at a time like this was beyond trivial.

"Hey, I said wait!" she said. Then, before I knew what she was getting at, she took off that black coat of hers and tossed it right in the middle of the river of paint. It was like a stepping-stone in the river.

"Wasn't that your precious coat?"

"Its time had come."

I tried to say something about her just tossing her memories off like they were nothing, but as she had said, there was a bigger issue at hand right now. Besides, what's done is done. With little recourse, I jumped to the coat, then to the other side of the river.

I groaned.

It had been quite awhile since I'd last seen a headless body. I removed my sweatshirt and placed it over Kanami-san's upper body.

I looked back toward the door, where everyone was standing, and slowly shook my head.

There was no point using words.

"Everyone," Iria finally said, "could I have us all gather in the dining room? I think we need to discuss what we'll do from here on out."

With that, she made her way for the hall. The four maids—Rei-san, Akari-san, Hikari-san, and Teruko-san—quickly followed close behind. Finally, the other guests began filing out of the atelier, two by two and three by three.

The last ones to remain in the room were Kunagisa, me, and Shinya-san.

He was staring at Kanami-san's body, his face pale and blank.

"Shinya-san . . ." Stepping back on the coat, I returned to the other side. "Let's go, there's nothing we can do here." It killed me to say it.

"Oh . . . yeah. Right."

His mind was off in a very different place. Despite his response, he made no attempt to move. He stood completely rigid, his mind unable to comprehend, *refusing* to comprehend the sight before his eyes.

I understood how he felt.

If the same thing had happened to Kunagisa, I probably would have been the same way. No, that's not right. I probably would have broken down and gone on a screaming rampage. I know that's hard to imagine for a guy like me, who, as Maki-san would say, was "dead to all emotions," but that's probably what would have happened.

In that respect, Shinya-san was truly admirable.

He didn't look too good, but at least he hadn't broken down. And he could even speak. His mental faculties remained intact, albeit just barely.

This is what separated him from me. I was just a kid.

Shinya-san was an adult.

I didn't know what kind of relationship Shinya-san and Kanami-san had, whether he was just her caretaker or something more, or perhaps something less.

However . . .

Remembering the sad look in his eyes the previous night . . .

And seeing him now, I somehow understood.

"Ii-chan, let's go ahead," Kunagisa said, pulling on my arm.

"Yeah."

And thus ended our tranquil lives on this island.

And thus began the next chapter.

2

The morning of the fourth day on the island had started extremely normal. Really, *extremely* normal.

I awoke the same as always. By the time I got to Kunagisa's room, she was already awake and sitting at her computers. She said she was checking her e-mail. "Do my hair," she said, without so much as a "good morning." I put the hair on the top of her head in two tails, what we called a "twin tail." I figured it would be easy enough for her to undo it herself this time.

"I feel like breakfast today," she said, so we headed for the dining room. Peeking into the living room on the way, I found that Maki-san and Shinya-san were still there drinking wine. They must have been up all night drinking. "They sure aren't paying their age any mind," I thought, but of course I stayed quiet.

Out of courtesy, I invited them to breakfast and they accepted. The four of us entered the dining room. Sitting at the table were Akane-san and, making a rare appearance, Iria-san.

"Oh, what an unusual occurrence," Iria-san also said. "To

have everyone gathered like this even in the morning. . . . Well, I suppose it was inevitable. Shall I call in the others? It would be nice to all do breakfast together."

She summoned the nearby Akari-san and asked her to go fetch Yayoi-san, who was no doubt in the kitchen, and the other maids.

"Well, I'll go fetch Kanami-san," Shinya-san said. "She's probably all done painting by now anyway. Hmm, I wonder if she's still sleeping. Ehh, she doesn't get cranky in the morning. Despite her lousy personality."

He chuckled a bit at his own joke and looked at me. "Hope you're looking forward to seeing that picture," he said, and left the dining room.

It would have been the first time Kunagisa and I had done breakfast with the entire group, but it never actually happened.

When Shinya-san returned to the dining hall, what he brought was the news of Kanami-san's death.

"Kanami's been . . . murdered."

That's how he phrased it, anyway, but it was quite a bit of an understatement, if you ask me. There was no way she died of sickness or an accident, or even suicide—she had been beheaded.

Whatever the case.

This was a murder.

And not just a murder, but . . .

"Me? I was . . . right. After dinner, I was with Kunagisa the whole time. I took a bath in her room, then she said she was hungry, so we went to the living room. On the way we ran into Akari-san. Isn't that right? Right. In the living room we met Hikari-san, Maki-san, and Shinya-san, and then . . . the earthquake. There was an earthquake, right? We were in the living room until that earthquake occurred. After that, I took Kunagisa back to her room, and then . . . right, I went to sleep. I woke up today at six, and I've been with Kunagisa ever since." I tried my best to sound calm, even under everyone's gaze.

An alibi check.

Why we had to start with me, I don't know, but Iria-san had requested it, so there was no choice. It seemed she viewed me as the prime suspect.

The dining room.

Eating my slightly cold breakfast.

No one else seemed to be able to continue with breakfast after seeing the headless corpse, and indeed I was feeling pretty squeamish myself, but Yayoi-san's cooking was so good, I couldn't just let it all go to waste.

The round table.

Iria-san, Teruko-san, Rei-san, Yayoi-san, Shinya-san, Kunagisa Tomo, myself. Akane-san, Maki-san, Hikari-san, and Akari-san. Everyone was sitting in their assigned seats, with only Kanami-san's seat, at the five o'clock position, empty. It would never be filled.

Iria-san tilted her head at me a bit in response to my testimony. Then she glanced over at Hikari-san in the ten o'clock seat. "Hikari, is that true?"

"Yes," she nodded. "Up until the earthquake occurred . . . um . . . one o'clock, was it? Yes, one o'clock. The five of us including me were talking the whole time. I can vouch for that."

"Did anyone get up and leave for a while?"

"No," Hikari said with a bit of uncertainty. "I don't think so . . . although I couldn't say for certain."

"No one left," Kunagisa said, coming to her rescue. "And I've got a perfect memory. Nobody left the living room."

"Is that so?" Iria closed her eyes. "In that case, you and Kunagisa-san, Sakaki-san, Himena-san, and Hikari can all account for one another up until the earthquake, is that right? How about after the earthquake?"

"I slept alone, so I suppose I don't have an alibi."

"Thank you. Well then, I suppose I should go ahead and give my alibi next. Last night I was with Rei and Sashirono-san in my room talking. Yesterday's dinner was even more delicious than usual, so I was asking her about the recipe. Isn't that right, Sashirono-san?"

Possibly because her name had suddenly come up, Yayoi-san looked a bit startled. "Yes," she nodded quickly.

Rei-san shrugged a bit, but said nothing. If you thought about it, she must've been a really cool-headed person. Of course Teruko-san was quiet as ever, but Rei-san was more silent than you would have imagined. Whether she was just being loyal to her employer or this was just her natural personality, I wasn't sure.

"The earthquake happened, and . . . then I decided to go back to my room," she said as if struggling to remember.

"That's right," Iria-san nodded. "After that, Rei and I were up all night talking. Kunagisa-san will be leaving soon, so I thought we should discuss the idea of holding some kind of fun event . . . you know, like a farewell party. That's the tradition here. Anyway, we ended up forgoing sleep, so I just came straight here for breakfast."

In other words, Iria-san and Rei-san had perfect alibis. Yayoi-san, like Kunagisa and I, only had an alibi up until the earthquake.

"Shinya-san and I have complete alibis as well," Maki-san said. "Kunagisa-chan and the rest can confirm that up until the earthquake, and Shinya-san and I can vouch for each other after that. My, alcohol is just wonderful."

Just how trustworthy was a drunk person's testimony? Maki-san must've known I was thinking that, because she glared at me. But without a word to me, she turned to Shinya-san. "Isn't that right?" she asked.

"Oh, yeah, right," he replied vacantly.

"Hmm . . . Hikari, what did you do after the earthquake?"

"I went back to our room. Akari and Teruko were there, too. After that, I went to bed. I woke up today at five o'clock, and then got back to . . ."

"What about Akari and Teruko then? Akari, answer."

"After dinner, we didn't have any work left to do, so . . ." she paused, with a hand to her cheek as she tried to think. "Teruko and I were together in our room the whole time. Then the earthquake happened, and Hikari came back soon after that. That's when we decided to go to bed."

"The three of you share one room?" I asked. Akari-san's eyes shot in my direction as if she never would've guessed I would speak up.

"Yes, the three of us share a room. Is something wrong with that?"

"Oh no, nothing."

Just wondering. I bowed to her. I wanted to ask if they shared the same futon as well, but I decided to stay quiet.

Hmm . . .

That meant that Akari-san and Teruko-san had solid alibis up until the earthquake as well. After that, they had all gone to bed, so they couldn't really vouch for one another.

Teruko-san nodded a bit after listening to Akari's testimony, but ultimately said nothing. It was a simple gesture, but somehow hard to understand.

"This is becoming quite complicated." Iria-san looked toward the last possible suspect, Sonoyama Akane-san. "What about you?" she said. "What were you doing last night?"

Akane-san, who had been closely observing the situation up until now with arms folded and mouth shut, let out a sigh. "Judging from the fact that nobody's mentioned my name up until now, it's probably pretty obvious, but, yep, I wasn't with anyone last night." She spoke unhesitatingly. "After I finished dinner, I went back to my room and got on the computer. I was working on some modeling, and, well, I'll spare you the boring details. There should be a log, so you could check that for proof, but I suppose that kind of thing can be forged. I guess you couldn't call it an alibi."

"I don't know much about computers. What do you think, Kunagisa-san?"

"Hmm?" Kunagisa's head popped up (hell of a time to be daydreaming). "Oh. With a degree of skill, a person could easily manipulate something as simple as a log. Akane-chan, how much do you know about computers?"

Akane-san smirked. "There's probably no point in answering that."

"Oh, okay," Kunagisa nodded. "Yeah, I guess you're right. With the right tools, even an amateur could alter a log. It's not like it's very hard. You can find that kind of software all over the place."

"Isn't there a way to see if the log's been altered?" I asked.

"There is, but that can be faked, too. Just about anything's possible with a computer, you see, so it's hard to use one to confirm an alibi."

Kunagisa Tomo. Invited to this island as the leader of that "team." She was peerless in her field, so there was no way she was wrong. In which case, Akane-san had no alibi to speak of.

Akane-san let out another sigh. "But I suppose I have to make a defense for myself or else you'll have me on a cross. So I'll just go ahead and say it: I didn't do it. Certainly I hate artists, but I don't think they're worth killing. They're already dead when they're alive. It wouldn't be worth the effort. I had nothing to do."

She probably meant to say, "I had nothing to do with it," but at any rate, she didn't seem to be bluffing or playing tough, and it didn't seem like an act, either.

"Okay, everyone please hold on a minute. I need to work this out in my head."

"Um, before that, please hold on," I said to Iria-san. The conversation was growing bizarre. Hold on before we hold on? "Um, Iria-san, what exactly are you trying to do?"

"I'm sorry?"

"It's just that this all feels really strange to me, and . . . of course, this is your island and your mansion, so I know it's probably better not to say anything, plus I'm not even really a guest, but I'm asking anyway. What exactly are you trying to do?"

"Well, I'm trying to get to the bottom of this, of course," she smiled softly. "It seems pretty clear to me," she continued. "Ibuki-san was murdered by someone. And in this case, that means she was murdered by someone in this room. As you said, this is my island and my mansion. One of the guests I've invited here has been killed, and the murderer is right here. Surely you don't think we can just leave this alone?"

She glanced over the crowd with an ironic smile.

Indeed, she was right. This was a remote island. A remote, deserted island, completely isolated.

Wet Crow's Feather Island.

If there were twelve people on the island and one was killed, the murderer had to be one of the remaining eleven. Even elementary school students can do that sort of basic arithmetic.

"Gosh, another death," Iria-san said with a sigh.

Another? Did she just say "another"?

"And another decapitation, at that. Could it be that this island is cursed? Say, Himena-san, can you see into that?"

"You're the one who's cursed," Maki-san answered. "The island is just an island. If anything is cursed, it's you."

As disheartening a statement as that was, Iria-san replied with a strange smile. "Maybe so."

Ah, it all made sense. It had seemed strange to me that despite her attitude, Maki-san was able to get along so well with everyone other than me, but now I got it. Nobody else on this island cared about what other people said.

"Mmm, but this is a fairly simple case. Maybe there's no

need for all this questioning. After all, the time of the incident is fairly laid out for us."

"Is it?"

"It is. You saw it, too, right? All that paint got knocked over during the earthquake, and Ibuki-san's body was lying on the other side. How wide do you suppose that river of paint was?"

Nobody ventured an answer, so I went ahead. "At a quick glance, I would've said about ten feet."

"Right, not that big but certainly not small enough to jump over. So we can confirm that the murder must have happened before the earthquake."

The shelf had fallen over in the quake, resulting in that marble-colored river. What did that mean? The quake must have been more intense than I had realized, but that's not all.

What did that river really mean?

"Hold on a second," Akane interrupted. She looked a bit concerned. "This conversation doesn't bode well for me. You know why?"

Why?

Everyone besides Akane-san had an alibi prior to the earthquake.

I was with Kunagisa the whole time. Same with Hikari-san, Maki-san, and Shinya-san. Same deal with Akari-san and Teruko-san. And of course, Iria-san, Rei-san, and Yayoi-san. Everyone had an alibi and could vouch for one another.

Iria-san was right. There was no way someone could jump that marble river of paint the earthquake had created. Likewise, there was no way to cross the river without stepping in the paint and creating footprints.

In which case . . .

The murder had to have happened before the earthquake. The only one with no alibi at that time was Akane-san. Indeed, this didn't bode well for her at all.

"Iria-san," she clucked. "I'm just going to ask you straight. Do you think I did it?" That certainly was straight.

"Yes," Iria-san admitted just as directly. "I mean, who else could have?"

Akane-san broke eye contact with Iria-san and said nothing. She was at a loss for an effective argument despite that Seven Fools brain of hers. Feeling some sliver of a connection with her somehow, I wanted to jump in and save her, but if a member of the Seven Fools couldn't think of a rebuttal, there was no way a program dropout could.

An awkwardness hung in the air for a while, but it was Kunagisa who broke it.

"That's wrong," she said. "I don't think that logic completely makes sense, Iria-chan."

"Oh? Why is that?" Iria-san seemed strangely glad to hear it. "Ah, I see. You're talking about the possibility of an accomplice. I suppose there is that possibility. That would make everyone's alibis a little shaky."

"No, not that. Even if you don't consider an accomplice, you're missing something. Right, Ii-chan?"

"Huh?" I blurted out, completely surprised that I would be pulled into this.

"Come on, Ii-chan, tell her. About what happened last night."

"Last night . . . something happened?"

Looking fairly irritated, Kunagisa clammed up. This was a fairly rare thing for her.

"What can I say? Unlike you, I have a bad memory."

"Geez, you really don't remember? Your memory isn't bad, it's nonexistent! Do you always forget things this important? After the earthquake. Shinya-chan made a call to Kanami-chan, right?"

"Oh. Oh. Oh!"

Hikari-san and Shinya-san looked up in surprise.

That's right. Shinya-san had called Kanami-san after the

quake and confirmed that she was okay. Confirmed that nothing had happened to her.

Wow, that *was* important, just like Kunagisa said. What did that mean though? What would happen now?

"In other words, Kanami-chan must have been killed after the earthquake."

"Hold on a sec," Iria-san said in a bit of a panic. "But that river of paint . . ."

"Well, Iria-chan, that must mean this . . ." she paused for a moment. "The atelier was locked."

Everyone exchanged glances for a moment.

That river of paint was unjumpable for sure. It was ten feet wide. Maybe it was possible if you were a long-jumper, but even then, there was no space to get a running start. If you considered that, the murder must have happened before the earthquake, just like Iria-san said, but then Shinya-san's story wouldn't have made sense. Immediately after the earthquake, Kanami-san had neither been killed nor harmed.

"Sakaki-san," Iria-san said, "that was Ibuki-san's voice for sure, right?"

He went even paler, with a confused expression written on his face. At last, he nodded. "Yeah, it was definitely Kanami. No mistake. She said she was busy, and that the paint had fallen over so everything was a mess. She had to have been alive after the earthquake."

"I heard Sakaki-san talking on the phone as well," Hikari-san told her mistress. "He asked me if he could use the house phone and . . . I think Ibuki-san must have been alive still."

"Yeah, she was still . . ." he clutched his head in anguish. "If I had only gone to the atelier instead of neglecting my duties. Dammit! I'm scum! I'm nothing but scum!"

There wasn't much to say to that. Only that in the end, it wasn't earthquakes or blizzards or fire that was frightening.

It seems there is some kind of solace to be found in regret.

It serves as an escape from what's right before your eyes. You end up pinning all your bad deeds on the "former you." It's hardly what you would call self-condemnation.

When you are regretting something, you're technically being good.

I'm not saying Shinya-san was a monster. People are just wired that way. If anyone was a monster, it was me, for only being able to nitpick at people's flaws like this.

"This is starting to get strange," Akane-san said, stroking her chin. "According to Shinya-san, Hikari-san, and Kunagisa-san's testimony, the murder must have happened after the earthquake. But after the earthquake, the river of paint had already been formed, in which case there is nobody who could have killed her. In which case . . ."

"That's right, Akane-chan," Kunagisa interrupted. She had that look she gets when she's starting to find something interesting. "This is an incredibly strange situation."

"When you say the atelier was locked, you mean . . ." Iria-san nodded, seemingly convinced. "Hmm. Indeed, even now, that paint isn't dry, huh? Could there have been a way to climb over it and enter the room? Say, Akari, where's the house phone in Ibuki-san's atelier?"

"It's beside the window, on a phone stand," Akari-san answered with great certainty.

Iria-san crossed her arms and considered this. "Kunagisa-san, you've posed this question, but I don't suppose you know the answer already? Do you know who did it?"

"Nope," Kunagisa answered, strangely confident.

Of course, I didn't know, either.

Nobody knew.

"What about the window? Is it possible that the person entered through the window?" Shinya-san asked.

Hikari-san answered. "But it's the second floor. I don't think it's possible. And I'm pretty sure that window is locked from the inside, so—"

"So it can't be opened from the outside at all?"

"Probably," Hikari-san answered.

Check. So the window was impossible, and so was the door. It couldn't have happened before the earthquake *or* after the earthquake, so . . .

Okay.

We were at a complete dead end.

Everyone fell into silence once more. And then, eyes started shifting back toward Akane-san.

"Huh?" she seemed a little surprised. "Hey, I thought I had cleared myself."

"Maybe not," Iria-san said. "Clearing that paint river is impossible, right? So, ultimately, it *must* have been before the earthquake."

"What about what Shinya-san said?"

"He could've been tricked. Maybe it was an auditory hallucination or something."

Auditory hallucination? Nonsense. It was beyond nonsense. I had to say something.

"I think that's just what you want to believe," I said.

"I don't think so," Iria-san said, unfazed by my opinion. "Even supposing it wasn't auditory hallucination, it could have easily been some other sort of misunderstanding. There's no crossing that river of paint, that much is for sure. Thus, it's only logical to presume the murder happened before the earthquake, in which case it couldn't be anyone but Akane-san."

"This isn't good," Akane-san said, seeming truly worried. "I know this probably won't help my case any, but I can't help but feel like Akari-san and Teruko-san's alibi is a little sketchy. I mean, family members vouching for each other? It wouldn't hold up in a court of law."

"We're not talking about a court of law," Iria-san said flatly.

"I didn't think so," Akane-san said as if she expected such

a response. "Still, determining the criminal by process of elimination doesn't make much sense. It's silly. And simply ignoring Sakaki-san's testimony isn't exactly what I would call logical thinking. It's selective thinking."

"Selective thinking?"

Akane-san shot me a look, as if to say, "Will you please explain?"

"A confirmation bias," I blurted, suddenly remembering from my program training that one is never to reveal his own stupidity to a "senior." "In other words, it means when you only consider testimonies and evidence that suit your opinion and write off all evidence to the contrary as some kind of fluke. Actually, they say that in supernatural ability experiments, they"—my eyes wandered over to Maki-san—"they use it a lot. 'Dry Love,' wasn't it? They obsess over any evidence that suggests these abilities exist while ignoring any evidence that suggests they don't. It's their way of getting desirable results, I guess."

"I don't really follow you."

I had gone to all that effort to remember these things, and here Iria-san wasn't even listening. What a waste of breath.

Akane-san sighed deep.

"I suppose Ibuki-san and I were on pretty awful terms, but still . . ."

I recalled their nasty bickering from the previous night's dinner. It didn't exactly do wonders for her case. Certainly it wasn't only Akane-san's lack of an alibi that made Iria-san doubt her so much, but this as well.

Of course, it wasn't that I didn't understand Iria-san's feelings. But if you took Shinya-san's testimony into account, even Akane-san couldn't be a suspect.

It was an uncommittable crime. There were no suspects. There was one victim and zero suspects. The situation didn't make any sense. And thus to fix it . . .

"Sakaki-san's testimony seems a little shady after all," Iria-san said, staring right at him. "Even if it's not a lie, it's got to be some kind of misperception or dream or some such."

"But I heard him talking on the phone," Hikari-san said.

Iria-san shook her head. "It's not like you heard Ibuki-san's voice, right? Sakaki-san is the only one who heard her voice directly, which means . . ."

"Come on, that's—" Shinya-san started to protest, but as if realizing he had no basis for an argument, he went silent.

"Hmm. Well, if that's the way it is, I guess there's no choice but to suspect me. That's one way to look at things, anyway," Akane-san said, almost as if she was talking about someone else. Even now, she didn't seem to be lying or acting. Sonoyama Akane, ER3 system, Seven Fools. She seemed all too used to this kind of pandemonium. "But still, you don't have any proof. Iria-san, even if you are the mistress of this island and this mansion, you wouldn't treat me like a criminal without any proof, would you? This may not be a court of law here, as you say, but it's not some dusty old detective novel, either, right? You can't just assume I'm the criminal based on this unformulaic process of elimination and selective thinking. Nobody can do that."

"But Sonoyama-san, you also can't prove that you're *not* the criminal."

"You can't ask the innocent to prove their innocence. You can't prove the unprovable. I'm innocent until proven guilty."

"You're talking law again."

Akane-san's shoulders slumped. "Well, what's your point, Iria-san? So I'm the prime suspect. Fine. That's absolutely right. I'm the only one with no alibi before the earthquake. Nobody could have entered the atelier after the earthquake. Sure, I'm with you on that, too. Therefore, Sakaki-san's testimony becomes suspicious. Makes sense. So what now?"

So . . .

What now?

"What should we do?" Iria-san looked around the table

with a troubled expression. It seemed she hadn't thought any further than this. How anticlimactic.

"Throw me to the police or whatever you want," Akane-san said, brushing the bangs from her face.

Akane-san of the Seven Fools being sent off to the police?

"I hate the police," Iria-san said, still perplexed as she stared up at the ceiling. "Oh, what to do?"

A heaviness filled the air once again.

I whispered to Kunagisa. "Hey, Tomo."

"What's up, Ii-chan?"

"Isn't there some way to stop this witch hunt?"

"There is."

"Yeah?"

"Yeah, but"—she looked up at me—"you ought to do it, not me."

"Yeah, okay," I nodded, then raised my hand.

Iria-san called on me with a confused look. "Yes, you." Ah, good. It was so nice not to be ignored.

"I have a suggestion."

"Yes?"

"How about using the room I've been staying in? It looks like you can only lock and unlock it from the outside. What if we kept Akane-san there for a while?"

"Kept her there?" She eyed me dubiously. "You mean like imprisonment?"

"Not imprisonment, exactly. Not imprisonment, just . . . a brief period of seclusion. Iria-san, I think the biggest thing we have to fear right now is that this turns into a string of murders. Kanami-san was killed. Okay, that's already said and done. I hate to be so frank about it, but what's done is done. But more important, we can't let anyone else die. The quickest way to deal with a situation like this is to isolate the prime suspect. If Akane-san really is the murderer, naturally she won't be able to commit any more murders. If, on the other hand, someone else used some kind of trick and managed to sneak in and kill Kanami-san after the earthquake, then that person would be brought to a standstill. After all, if they tried anything again, it would prove Akane-san's innocence."

I looked around to see people's responses.

"In other words, create an antagonistic environment, so that the killer can't move around. This includes Akane-san, as well as everyone else. The atelier may have been locked, but locked doors are made to be unlocked. There might have been some trick. There might not have been. That doesn't matter. What matters is that we don't know either way. Akane-san might have done it. Someone else might have. Even I might have. I might not. So I think the best thing to do is create a situation where the killer can't do anything."

"Ah, I get it," Yayoi-san said, a bit to my surprise. "That makes a lot of sense. I'd have to say I agree. I don't think there's a very solid basis for suspecting Sonoyama-san alone. Iria-san's reasoning seems rather arbitrary."

Iria-san gave her a quizzical look. Nonetheless, Yayoi-san continued.

"I don't think it's a bad idea. But you don't intend to just lock her up forever, right? In that awful room?"

Hey, I've been sleeping in that awful room, dammit.

Lousy bourgeoisie.

"Well, just until the police arrive. This is a private island, it shouldn't take more than a day or two to get an investigator out here."

"I'm not calling the police," Iria-san said, completely surprising me.

Eh? Pardon me, madame, what was the horrible thing you uttered?

"I mean, what's the point, right? Even if we call the police, they'll just figure Sonoyama-san was the criminal and it'll end there. The police won't do anything."

It wasn't Iria-san's words that I found suspicious, but her

facial expression. The police won't do anything? Why did she say that with such a stern face?

"But we can't just not call the police. If we did that, there wouldn't be any point in confining her."

"Not necessarily. We just have to piece things together while she's in there. We'll track down the real culprit with evidence and reason. Doesn't that make sense to you?"

"Will *you* be the one investigating then, Iria-san?"

Something about Iria-san's idea of using "reason" didn't sit well with me at all. But to my surprise, she shook her head.

"No, not me, of course. Don't you remember? I told you yesterday, didn't I? In a week—no, six days—that wonderful, marvelous human being is coming to this island."

The detective of this proverbial mystery novel. Iria-san's favorite.

Iria-san's hero.

"Surely Aikawa-san will crush this problem to smithereens."

To smithereens. What an expression. And she didn't look like she was exaggerating, either.

"Six more days, huh?" Akane-san said cynically, letting her crossed arms drop down beside her. "Well, whatever. Fine fine fine. I know I'm not guilty, but if this is what it takes to convince you, what can I say? I presume we can trust this Aikawa-san?"

"Yes. Of course." Iria-san gave a confident nod. You could feel her utmost faith in this hero of hers just from looking at her.

Akane-san let out one more big sigh. "Fine. Let's do it then."

3

"I wonder if that was really the right thing to do," I said as I played with Kunagisa's hair. She said it was too heavy all tied up high like that and wanted me to redo it. Here I had thought it was adorable, but if she didn't like it, I had no choice.

Everybody had since split up, and the two of us had gone back to Kunagisa's room.

"I think it's okay. It's pretty much what I expected to happen. Akane-chan must be kinda grateful, too, eh? It's a way better idea than continuing that unproductive bickering, anyway."

"Hmm, I wonder . . ."

As the one who had suggested the idea in the first place, I couldn't imagine Akane-san was too happy about it. I felt a little guilty. It might well have been the only solution, but I couldn't help but wonder if there was some other way.

"All done."

"'Sankyuu." She crawled over to her computer rack and sat down with her back to me. Then she switched on the power and started typing away.

"I just . . . I feel like we've wronged Akane-san."

"Maybe so. But some things can't be avoided, y'know, Ii-chan?"

After breakfast, Akane-san had gone off to my room on her own two feet. It had been decided that Akari-san and the others would deliver meals to her directly, and that she would have to call them from the room phone every time she wanted to use the bathroom.

Akane-san had requested a reading lamp so she could pass the following six days reading books she had brought.

Six days . . . Objectively speaking, the room wasn't a particularly bad environment. But the door couldn't be unlocked from the inside and the window was way high up—there was virtually no means of escape. In that sense, it really was imprisonment.

Six days.

It really was too long to be locked up.

"If only Iria-san would call the police, we wouldn't have to do all this. It's like she's trying to cover up the incident altogether."

"But Iria-chan is right, y'know? If she had called the police, they would've blamed Akane-chan and closed the case right there. Or even if they didn't convict her, she would've been a suspect. I mean, wouldn't you want to avoid something like that? Seriously, one of the Seven Fools becoming a murder suspect?"

"Do you know a lot about the ER3, Tomo?"

"I've got a few acquaintances from over there. But I'm sure you know more than I do."

"Speaking of Seven Fools, Akane-san didn't have criminal immunity or anything, did she?"

"But it would be even worse of a situation for me, not to mention Yayoi-chan and Maki-chan, who are both well respected. Nobody needs a scandal like this to deal with. Of course the same goes for Iria-chan. So it's only natural that she isn't calling the police."

"Natural, huh?"

It was probably this island itself that was unnatural. But judging from Iria-san's manner, I got the feeling there was more to the story. Like she had some more fundamental reason for not wanting to call the cops.

"Do you suppose Iria-san has some specific reason for disliking the police?"

"Well, what if we asked her?"

"I doubt she'd tell us."

"Yeah, maybe. Anyway, why worry about it? Once this Aikawa character Iria-chan's so crazy about gets here, everything will be solved. It's just another six days."

"Yeah, but . . ."

Iria-san was the mistress of the island, and if she said no

police, there was no going against her. For what it was worth, there would probably be no more murders with Akane-san locked in seclusion. But still . . .

"Say, Tomo."

"What, Ii-chan?"

"I want to ask a favor."

"I accept. What is it?"

"Can you do something about that locked door?"

"I don't know, but for you, I'll try."

There was no need to spend the next six days just sitting around. I was the one who had proposed this course of action in the first place, so I had a duty to give the case some serious thought.

"If we can figure this case out quick, we won't have to keep Akane-chan locked up in there, whether she did it or not."

She swiveled her chair around to face me. She beckoned me closer. "Here, here." I walked over to the computers as told.

"For the time being, I've typed up everyone's alibis."

> Ibuki Kanami (murdered)
>
> Sonoyama Akane
> Before earthquake: X
> After earthquake: X
>
> Kunagisa Tomo
> Before earthquake: O (Ii-chan, Hikari, Maki, Shinya)
> After earthquake: X
>
> Sashirono Yayoi
> Before earthquake: O (Iria, Rei)
> After earthquake: X
>
> Chiga Akari
> Before earthquake: Δ (Teruko)
> After earthquake: X

Chiga Hikari
Before earthquake: O *(Ji-chan, Tomo, Maki, Shinya)*
After earthquake: X

Chiga Teruko
Before earthquake: Δ *(Akari)*
After earthquake: X

Sakaki Shinya
Before earthquake: O *(Ji-chan, Tomo, Maki, Hikari)*
After earthquake: O *(Maki)*

Handa Rei
Before earthquake: O *(Iria, Yayoi)*
After earthquake: Δ *(Iria)*

Himena Maki
Before earthquake: O *(Ji-chan, Tomo, Hikari, Shinya)*
After earthquake: O *(Shinya)*

Akagami Iria
Before earthquake: O *(Rei, Yayoi)*
After earthquake: Δ *(Rei)*

"Look about right?"

"I understand the O's and X's, but what are those triangles?"

"Akane-chan was right about family testimonies. Iria-chan, Rei-chan, Akari-chan, Hikari-chan, and Teruko-chan seem like a pretty upstanding bunch, so for now, they get a check. It's just that, well, their alibis seem kind of shaky."

She scrolled down the screen and checked the alibi chart one more time.

"For now, let's ignore the possibility of an accomplice," I said. "And that includes family ties. If we assume that much, we can remove Shinya-san and Maki-san from the suspect list. Oh, and also Rei-san and Iria-san."

Four people down.

Seven people left.

"If Shinya-san's testimony was accurate, then the locked room with the paint becomes a problem. But if it was a lie, that means only Akane-san could have done it."

"I can't imagine why Shinya-chan would lie, though."

"Well, it could've been a misunderstanding or something rather than a lie."

Well, how about that.

I was starting to sound like Iria-san.

"But you know, Akane-san really is the prime suspect here, objectively speaking."

"Yeah, you can't help but think that, looking at this chart. No matter how fair or sympathetic you are, it doesn't change the fact that she's the only one without any smidgen of an alibi. If that weren't the case, she probably wouldn't have accepted this whole seclusion idea."

"Yeah, for sure. So, Tomo, do you think Akane-san did it?"

"I wouldn't say that. Like she said herself, there's no evidence. You can't decide who the criminal is by process of elimination alone. We haven't even examined Kanami-chan's body yet, either."

"Ah, and I suppose there is still the fact that the room was locked."

"But if you take that into account, *nobody* could've done the crime. Ii-chan, you have any ideas about that?"

"I've got a few," I said as I pondered. "Maybe I'll figure something out after a little while. How about you, Tomo?"

"I've got tons of ideas," she said. "Just need to give it a little more thought and it should all fall into place. Oh, and Ii-chan? Whether or not Shinya-san's testimony is true, I think the murder happened after the earthquake."

"Huh? Why?"

"That picture of you. Do you really think she could've finished a picture like that before the earthquake? I don't think so."

"Well . . ."

It was tough to say. Kanami-san was pretty damn fast when it came to painting. But if what Kunagisa said was true, then it was all the more certain that the door had been locked. That wouldn't be the most helpful development in the case.

"And then there's the headless body itself."

I nodded.

Regardless of who killed her, why would they cut her head off?

"They say to beware of swapped identities when the bodies show up with no head, but I don't suppose there's any need for doubt in this particular case. There were twelve people, one had her head cut off, and now there are eleven. And we know exactly who and where those eleven people are."

"If it was one of those three maid sisters who got killed, it would've been a real problem, huh?" Kunagisa said. "But with Kanami-chan, there's probably no need to worry about it. If there were other people on this island it would be different, but y'know."

"We don't need to consider that notion, either. If we assume there are X number of other people on this island, all this narrowing down of suspects and alibi searching becomes pointless. I don't know what this 'detective' coming in six days will have to say about it, but for now let's just worry about the eleven people we know about."

"You said it," she said, gaping at the ceiling. "Now, if you consider the possibility of an accomplice or some kind of remote trickery, only you and I can be taken off the suspect list."

"Why me, too?" I said.

"'Cuz I trust you," she answered coolly. "Still, why did it have to be a beheading? Body-switching is the only feasible reason I can think of. But I wonder . . . maybe that's not even how she died."

"Yeah. It if was, there wouldn't have been so little blood. It would've been more like a river of blood. But at a glance, there didn't appear to be any stabbing wounds or anything, so maybe she was poisoned or strangled. I mean, just to speculate."

"I wonder if she went down easy."

"Probably. Her legs didn't work, and even though her eyesight had come back, it definitely wasn't perfect. Once you approached her, the act of killing her probably wouldn't be very difficult. And cutting off the head wouldn't be much of a challenge, either."

As long as you didn't hesitate, it would only take a few minutes.

"There's no clear motive, either. Why did Kanami-san have to be murdered?"

"Nobody *has* to be murdered. But yeah, I wonder why. Aside from Shinya-chan, everyone here only just met Kanami-chan, right? Hmm, but maybe that's not the case. Maybe somebody actually had some connection with her before coming here. It wouldn't be so strange."

"I guess you could presume just about anything on that subject."

In which case, there was no point in presuming anything. Kunagisa let out a groan.

"Well, let's just worry about these other details first, and figure out who knows who later on."

"How are we gonna do that?"

"Who do you think you're talking to?" She grinned at me. Of course.

This blue-haired girl had a "background," so to speak.

"Now then, shall we do a crime scene investigation?" She picked up her nearby digital camera.

4

On the way to Kanami-san's room, we passed by Yayoi-san. I meant to greet her, but there was something unapproachable about her, and I missed my chance. She continued walking in the opposite direction. We had passed right by each other, but it was like she hadn't even noticed our existence.

"I wonder what she's up to," Kunagisa said. "Something seems a little strange about her."

"She looked kind of worried about something. Or maybe just in deep thought."

"Hmph. Maybe she was looking around Kanami-chan's room, y'know? Maybe she had the same idea as us. Solve the case quick so we can all go home."

"Hmm, I wonder. She's been here the longest, right? I doubt she'd suddenly want to just pack up and leave."

"Eh, maybe. But personally I hate islands where murders take place."

"I *really* wonder about that."

Just before we all scattered from the dining room, Iria-san had laid down a rule. "Until Aikawa-san gets here in six days, nobody leaves the island. We're all suspects here, myself included."

In other words, Akane-san wasn't the only one being imprisoned. And it wasn't just curiosity motivating Kunagisa to dig deeper. She wanted to go home as planned. As lazy as she was, she was strangely anal about plans.

"Well, either way is good. I certainly wouldn't mind if Yayoi-chan solved this case for us."

"I don't think that's what she's up to. She had a sort of melancholy, somber vibe about her. I can't help but wonder if she was disposing of evidence or something."

"That would certainly suck a lot for us," Kunagisa said, eyeing me through the digital camera. "Let's hurry up and check it out."

Kanami-san's door had been left open. You could see the inside of the outward-opening door. Nobody seemed to be around. I wondered what everyone else was doing, except Akane-san, who was presumably in the storage room. But I decided to set that thought aside for the time being. People will do as they please, insofar as they're allowed. That was true on this island, and it was true anywhere else.

The room smelled like paint thinner as usual, but the paint seemed to mostly be dry by now. Kanami-san's body remained in the same place it had been this morning, and looked otherwise exactly the same.

"So let's check it out . . ."

There's something terribly . . . *comical* about a headless body. What makes dead bodies so creepy and terrifying is that emotionless expression on the face, but with no head to display that face, the creepiness and terror is replaced with hilarity. It's like looking at a screwed-up attempt at a plastic model or something.

The marble river. Kunagisa's tossed coat remained right in the middle.

"By the way, about that coat. How much was it?"

"It was part of a two-piece set for about twenty thousand, I think."

"Dollars?"

"Nah, yen."

Wow, an average price. I was a little surprised.

"Well, might as well go inside." I tried to take a step forward, but she tugged on my sleeve just like she had that morning. "What now?"

"Try jumping."

"Huh?"

"C'mon. It's an experiment. Get a little running start here

and see if you can jump that paint river. Your athletic skills aren't so bad, right?"

"They're not so good, either."

"Give it a shot."

"You got it."

I revved myself up a bit and gave my best leap, but as expected, I couldn't clear the river. I landed on both feet, only slightly past the center point.

"That's all you're gonna get."

"Hmm." Kunagisa stepped across, using her coat as a stepping-stone. "If you can't even do it, Shinya-san's the only person here who might even have a chance. He's the only other guy and all."

"Yeah, but those maids seem pretty able-bodied, to be honest. I mean, they carried all your luggage, including those PCs and the workstation. Those things ain't light."

"Yeah, but they're all petite. It's just a matter of width. Hmm, but then again, people always say ability matches necessity. I guess that detail is a little fuzzy. Now, let's see what's going on with Kanami-chan." She approached Kanami-san's body, camera in hand.

She seemed to be particularly interested in examining the body, while I was more concerned with Kanami-san's canvases. There were several lying around, including the cherry blossom picture she had smashed up, as well as the redo. I had to tremble at the sight of it. Even I, who had not so much as a passing interest in art or aesthetics, couldn't deny that I was looking at sheer, untainted beauty.

And then there was the picture I had modeled for. Kanami-san had promised to give it to me, but I couldn't accept something like this. I didn't have nerves of steel, after all.

"I'm probably just babbling here, but . . ."

I went to pick up the painting, but then stopped myself. It might have been bad to leave any fingerprints behind. Then again, it might not have mattered.

Huh?

"Hey, Tomo."

"Yeah?"

"Isn't there something weird about this painting?"

"You mean that picture of you? Hmm? What's weird? It's a normal painting."

Certainly Kunagisa's taste wasn't the most ordinary thing in the world, either, but that was beside the point. Something about the painting was off, in a maddeningly subtle way. It wasn't anything about the image itself, but just the strange feeling of absurdity it somehow conveyed.

"Well anyway, go ahead and snap a picture of it, will ya? Something about it bothers me."

"Got it. Hmm, I'm still not finding anything unusual over here."

She appeared to be inspecting Kanami-san's body.

"Really?" I said, walking over to her.

"Yep. I'm no professional though. The cause of death is still a mystery, and I can't narrow down the time of death, either. Without a coroner, it's probably impossible. If only Iria-chan had invited a medical genius here, too. Y'know, like Blackjack or something. Then again, even with a coroner, it would probably be pretty hard without the body's head."

"I guess we're not going to figure anything out here after all."

"Yep." She lifted the corpse up under her arm. Even years ago, she had no qualms about touching a dead body. "Kinda takes me back, y'know? It's just like the old days."

"Yeah, you're right, but . . . It doesn't feel like that to me. It's like I'm seeing a dead body for the first time all over again. It's been bothering me for a while."

There was this sort of an unspeakable, disconcerting feeling. Like when you find a scar on your own body you don't remember having.

"It's *jamais vu*."

"It's what?"

"The opposite of déjà vu. It means you feel like you're doing something for the first time, even though you've really done it many times before. Supposedly it happens when your senses have been numbed."

Then my senses must have been numbed some time long ago.

A lot of things had happened abroad, after all.

"Anyway," Kunagisa said. "There aren't any stab wounds. So maybe she was strangled after all. And then to hide the bruises, the killer cut her head off."

"It sounds crazy, but . . . here's what I don't get. Whatever the killer used to cut the head off—knife, ax, hatchet, whatever it was—why didn't they just use that to kill her?"

"Maybe they did. There are no stab wounds, but that's just on the body. Maybe they stabbed her in the head."

"Hey yeah, maybe," I said. "Speaking of that, where do you suppose the head went? I wonder where the killer took it. I mean, *if* the killer took it."

"Half the island is forest. Maybe they buried it somewhere out there. Or they could've tossed it out to sea. Disposal probably wasn't much of a problem."

"Which brings us back to the question, Why did the killer cut her head off?"

But that question was a dead end.

"I've got one more question, Ii-chan. Take a look at this. The head is cut off from the very base of the neck, right? Why is it cut like that? Don't you think that if you were going to decapitate someone, the normal place to make the cut would be around the center of the neck?"

The position of the cut was indeed unnaturally low, but I wouldn't have thought it was something significant.

I crossed my arms and said nothing. This crime scene investigation didn't seem like it would yield any clues after all. At best, we had confirmed that the river of paint couldn't be jumped. But that seemed more like a step backward than progress.

Kunagisa went over to the phone stand by the window and picked up the phone receiver.

"Hmm, nothing unusual here, either."

"You thought there would be?"

"I thought maybe the circuit had been rigged so that calls to this phone would connect to a different phone. But there doesn't seem to be anything wrong on this end. Doesn't look like it's been tinkered with, either."

"The phone, huh? Say, how'd it go again? What did Kanami-san say to Shinya-san?"

"The paint spilled, I'm busy working so don't bother me, stuff like that. But Shinya-san should've gone to check on her even if she told him not to. It may seem strict, but it's his duty as a caretaker."

"You're right about that. But there's no use talking about what's already done."

And anyway, Shinya-san already has to bear that burden himself. It wasn't particularly our place to lay the blame on him, and there was no need to do so. It's a crazy world, but it's also a world where we have to take responsibility for our own actions. And sometimes we also have to take responsibility for our own lack of action.

"Is it possible that they restored the phone back to normal afterward?"

"Well, I wouldn't say it's totally impossible, but it practically is. It's not like plugging and unplugging a cord or something."

"Yeah, good point. I guess we'll have to look at other possibilities. Like the locked door."

"You think I was lying?"

Suddenly I heard Shinya-san's voice from behind me, so I spun around. He stood in the doorway with some kind of orange bag in his hands.

"But I could hear Kanami's voice for sure. That's no lie."

From the sound of his voice, he seemed pretty worn out. Which probably goes without saying.

"I'm not saying you lied, Shinya-san. We don't have anything that certain. But is it *possible* that the voice you heard wasn't hers?"

"No," he answered. "I'd known Kanami for a long time. There's no way I would mistake her voice. Are you doubting me?"

"It's not like that. There's no reason you would have killed her, after all."

"I dunno, maybe we weren't on the best of terms." He gave a weak smile. Then he stepped through the dried paint and approached us. Upon closer inspection, it became clear what the orange bag was. It was a sleeping bag. He looked up at me. "We can't just leave her here, right?" he said. "I got permission from Iria-san and everything. I've decided to bury her on the mountain out back. It's not like Iria-san's going to call the police, and this is all her property anyway. Burying Kanami is all I can do now."

"We'll help you," I said. He tried to think of an appropriate response, but realizing the benefit of having two extra people helping him, he said nothing.

Together we lifted up Kanami-san's body and silently put it inside the sleeping bag. I know it goes without saying, but her flesh was completely devoid of warmth.

"Shinya-san, do you have something to dig with?"

"There should be a big shovel back by the entrance. Kunagisa-chan, shall we have you carry it for us? Hmm, say, is that a digital camera?"

"Yup." Kunagisa nodded. "We have to keep a record of the crime scene for when Mister Detective shows up. I don't think the corpse will demand publicity rights, after all, right?"

That was probably the worst way she could've phrased it,

but Shinya-san responded with a nod and a smirk. "I see. Shall we go, then?"

"Um, Shinya-san? About this painting . . ."

"Hmm? Ah. Kanami's painting. It's nice, isn't it? It's the last painting she ever did, but she was intending to give it to you, so please take it."

"Is it okay?"

"I want to honor her last wishes."

Her last wishes.

Yes, she was dead. Nothing left to fulfill.

"Get her feet, will you? I'll carry the head, and—" He cut himself off, most likely realizing there was no head to carry. Without saying anything, I picked up the legs.

He no doubt wished he could bury the head with the body, but its whereabouts remained unknown. Either the killer was hiding it somewhere, or it had already been tossed into the woods or thrown into the sea, like Kunagisa said.

Holding on to the legs, it occurred to me how heavy the body was. Heavier than you'd expect. It probably wasn't impossible for a single person to carry, but two people was definitely better.

From that point on, none of us spoke. In silence we lifted her body and left the mansion; in silence we headed for the mountain in the back; and in silence we dug a hole.

The sleeping bag that held her body was such a cheap-looking orange excuse for a coffin, I couldn't help but find it comical. In that moment, I felt like human death is nothing but a big joke.

People die. That was something I knew all too well, to the point that it was stifling, to the point that I wanted to vomit, and Kunagisa knew it, too. And Shinya-san, being a full-fledged adult, had no doubt been touched by death in the past as well.

That's probably why we were all so quiet.

Finally, Shinya-san spoke. "You two can go back now," he said. "I'm going to stay here a little longer."

I wanted to say something, but I didn't. Kunagisa pulled on my hand, and we left without a word. Maybe Shinya-san was going to cry. Maybe not. Either way, we no longer had a reason to linger.

After all, we were just bystanders.

"I wonder if it was okay to just go ahead and bury her," Kunagisa said.

"I think so. Shinya-san seems to be the only thing she had resembling a loved one, and that's what he wanted to do. And we couldn't just leave her lying in the atelier all week."

"True. True, but . . ."

"Say, Tomo. How big a crime do you suppose it is to abandon a corpse?"

"You'd probably get less than a three-year sentence. But you'd probably get off with parole, too. But you and I are both underage anyway, so no worries. No matter what happens, we can get off with a little money."

What a tasteless conversation.

Not that I was looking for a tasteful one.

"I'm just babbling here . . ."

Kunagisa gave me a funny look.

Sonoyama Akane,
member of the Seven Fools

2

THE TRAGEDY OF 0.14

What exactly were you trying to do?

1

Lunch was prepared by Hikari-san. Yayoi-san had complained of being under the weather and was now resting in her room. Indeed, she did seem pretty pale when we passed her in the hall.

"It's nothing like what Yayoi-san makes us, but please enjoy," Hikari-san said with a shy smile, and then left the dining room. That left only me and Kunagisa . . . and Maki-san, who seemed to be in the middle of lunch. I did my best to ignore her as I crammed Hikari-san's cooking down my throat. Kunagisa didn't seem to be hungry, so she was just tagging along, staring off into space.

"Hey, boy-o." As expected, Maki-san was going to harass me. "Looks like you've been having some fun, eh? Eh?"

"Isn't this what you said would happen?"

"Hmm? What do you mean?"

"That things will get worse before they get better. Isn't that what you said at dinner yesterday? What a lovely precognition that was."

"I sense a bit of sarcasm there, but I'll go ahead and take that as a compliment."

"If you knew this was going to happen, couldn't you have prevented it?"

"No. All I can do is watch and listen. I think you're misunderstanding my abilities. Psychic abilities aren't such a great convenience. I told you before, didn't I? It's like watching TV. Can *you* alter the contents of a TV show?"

She gave a mocking smile as she shoveled down her meal.

Something about her resembled Kunagisa, I thought. She was so emotionally immature, yet at the same time she seemed somehow enlightened. In the aftermath of Kanami-san's murder, she seemed completely unfazed. In fact, it didn't seem like *anything* could faze her.

"Then please inform us, what's going to happen next?"

"Sure. If you pay me."

Suddenly she looked furious, and without another word, she got up and stormed out of the dining room. Why was she so mad?

"That was cold of you, Ii-chan."

"*What* was?"

"Forget it. If you're done eating, let's go back to my room. We've got things to do."

"Yeah, okay."

Maki-san must just have been a moody person. I decided to assume that was the case and give it no further thought. I didn't know what darkness lurked in the heart of someone who knew everything.

We returned to Kunagisa's room. First we unloaded the digital photos onto her PC with a USB cord. Then she switched on the workstation and inserted a floppy disk.

"What's on the disk?" I asked.

"Tools. My original creations, of course. It's set up so that they only run on this workstation, so even if I drop the CD it's okay. Now let's get to the bottom of this."

To put it plainly, what Kunagisa was about to do was illegal.

But I guess you could also call it "research."

Including Kanami-san, there were twelve people. Excluding Kunagisa and me, there were ten. As planned, Kunagisa was going to run a background check on these ten people and find out who knew whom.

Kanami-san had been murdered. There must have been a reason for that. Of course, there are those murders that occur for no apparent reason, but the other type is overwhelmingly, absolutely, and depressingly more common. Supposedly everyone here had met for the first time on the island, but what if that wasn't the case? The possibility was there, and just thinking about it wouldn't do much good.

And thus it was time for Kunagisa Tomo, leader of the "team" that had thrown the cyberworld of the previous century into total chaos, to act.

"So what now?"

"First I'm gonna access the hi-spec machine I've got back home. This workstation doesn't have the power we need."

"Even though it's got so many terrabytes?"

"This has nothing to do with that. Ii-chan, you really don't know anything, do you?"

"Quit saying that. I might not know as much as you, but I know a little. I took an electronic engineering class back in Houston, at least."

"Really? Sounds like a lie to me. Weren't you the one who always used to have to go to the convenience store and be like 'Will you copy this disk for me? Here's ten yen'?"

"That was before I went to Houston."

Curse that memory of hers.

"Well, whatever. That's Ii-chan for ya," she said. "Anyway, then I'm gonna set up ten UG servers at platforms and contact Chii-kun."

"Chii-kun? Never heard that name before."

But I could've guessed it was a member of the "team." I asked if it was, and she nodded.

"Chii-kun was mainly in charge of 'seeking.' There's nothing in the universe he can't track down."

In the universe?

This was a freakish pack of talented people indeed.

"He's got a terrible personality, but he's a good guy."

"He's not the guy who made that operating system, is he? That was Atchan, right? So what's this Chii-kun doing nowadays?"

"He's in prison. He got a 150-year sentence. Oh, plus eight years—158 years. He kept hacking on his own even after the team disbanded, and tried to crack the G-eight database, but he was caught. He made it pretty far, but he got stuck at the eighty-eighth line of defense. Hehe, if you get too good at something, it's always the easy stuff that gets you in the end."

"You sure know a lot about it."

"Yup. I was the one who designed that line of defense."

I made no reply.

"I had heard a rumor that Chii-kun was after top-secret UN information. I couldn't just let the situation be, so I contacted a few friends and we set up a defense. Even then it was a close call, which is a testament to his skill."

"So that's how he got thrown in prison? You really think he'll help us? In fact, how *can* he help us from prison? They don't have the Internet in there, do they?"

"There's always an exception to the rule, y'know. And Chii-kun happens to be pretty exceptional. And he'll definitely help out. Chii-kun's not the type to sweat the small stuff."

She continued typing away even while she talked. I already had no idea what she was doing.

"Why do you call him Chii-kun?"

"His Net handle is Cheetah."

"Kind of a smarmy handle, huh?"

"Yeah, well, he's a fast guy. He says he's hit cars before."

"What, you mean while driving?"

"No, while running. I'm pretty sure he was the first person in Japan to be fined for hitting a car while on foot."

How's that for eccentric?

Did Tomo attract these kinds of people like a magnet?

Nah, maybe talent just attracted like talent.

"Don't ever introduce us."

He sounded like the kind of person I'd rather quietly observe from a distance.

Kunagisa nodded. "You got it. We all have rules, after all. We never introduce friends to each other no matter what. 'Cuz friends aren't information. I don't want you introducing me to any of your friends, either, Ii-chan."

"Sure . . . So I guess I'll just leave all this up to you then? If you're going to be talking to that guy, I probably shouldn't be hanging around, huh? And I've got a few places to go, too."

"Peace out," Kunagisa saluted.

With that, I left her room and made my way down the spiral staircase. There I paused for a deep breath, and began down the hallway. I was on my way to Iria-san's room. Hikari-san had given me directions earlier, so I didn't think there was any danger of getting lost.

Even in a mansion like this, where everything was of the finest quality, the door to her room was of exceptional craftsmanship. I doubted whether the sound of my knocking would even reach the other side of such a chunky door. Nonetheless, after giving it a try, the wave of sound did somehow appear to reach the inside, and my knock was answered with a "Come in!"

I opened the door and went inside. The room was probably twice the size of Kunagisa's. It wasn't straight out of a movie, it was an entire movie in and of itself. It was like the legendary Urashima Taro.

The words *receive an audience* came to mind.

Head maid Rei-san sat on the sofa with Iria-san standing beside her. They must've been in the middle of a conversation.

Iria-san tilted her head at me. "Is something the matter? Um . . ." Her expression was clueless. It seemed she had forgotten my name. Or rather, couldn't remember ever having said or heard my name.

"I wanted to talk to you about something."

"Certainly. Please take a seat there."

I was thrown off by her cooperativeness. As ordered, I sat myself on her sofa, which was even swankier than the sofa in Kunagisa's room. It was like sitting on air.

"I didn't get much sleep last night. I was about to go to bed, so please keep it short." She slowly began removing her dress as she spoke, presumably to change into her sleepwear. Rei-san immediately rose to her feet, but hesitated to raise complaint with Iria-san's actions and ultimately said nothing.

Seriously, this was about what you'd expect from a "woman of pedigree." The gaze of a mere plebeian meant nothing to her. What a crock.

"Iria-san, why won't you call the police?"

My question brought her to a halt. "I believe I've already explained that. If we call the police now, they'll treat Sonoyama-san like the criminal."

"But isn't that what we're doing already? We've already locked her up. And aren't we committing crimes here?"

"Sheltering a criminal, imprisonment, and . . . abandonment of a corpse, right?" She continued changing. "So what's wrong with that? Murder, theft—those are crimes. And Sonoyama-san isn't being imprisoned, really. She gave consent. And besides, aren't *you* the one who suggested it in the first place?"

Indeed, that was the case.

There was nothing I could say to that.

Iria-san continued.

"The people gathered here are the VIPs of the world. I refuse to allow them to become victims of the boorish government. And why call for excess meddling? Nobody wants that. Plus"—she grinned—"no matter who did it, I don't intend on subjecting anyone here to the law. Even if it means exercising the full wealth of my family's foundation, I'll be protecting them."

"Why?"

"Because geniuses are above the law."

Of that, she sounded totally sure of herself. But her words didn't sit well with me. It meant that if Shinya-san or I were the criminal, she wouldn't protect us.

God, what a feeling.

What a crappy, crappy feeling.

"How do you define the word *genius*?" Iria-san suddenly asked.

"Well, doesn't Kretchmar describe it as 'an individual capable of having a strong and extraordinary impact on the assertive values of a vast variety of people'?" I answered after a moment's thought.

"I asked for your opinion."

Seriously, what a crappy feeling.

But really, she was right. After another moment's thought, I answered once again.

"Someone who's 'far away.' "

"That's right," Iria-san said. "That answer is spot-on."

"I get the feeling there's some other reason you won't call the police, but . . ."

"What's that supposed to mean?"

"I'm just saying. It doesn't mean anything."

"Well then, are we done here? I want to go to bed."

What a waste of time. It was like we were having a pre-scripted debate.

"Sorry I bothered you," I said and rose from the sofa.

Rei-san stood up with me. "I'll see you out."

"You don't have to do that, Rei," Iria-san said.

"It's okay, it's my job, right? Please excuse me, madam."

Rei-san and I left the room together. It felt rather like I had been given the brush-off, but, well, I had expected as much for now. It would take more than a modest effort to convince someone like Iria-san, I thought.

"Please don't feel bad about what she said," Rei-san said softly on the way out. "She's not the most sensitive person."

"Sure."

Come to think of it, this was the first time I had spoken with Rei-san like this.

"I don't really mind anyway."

"She's really so fond of Aikawa-san, you see. That's why she doesn't want to call the police."

"Aikawa? Oh yeah, this person coming in six days."

"For her, this is sort of a welcoming present. You see, Aikawa-san's got a knack for these kinds of incidents, and, well, it's no coincidence that my mistress uses the term *detective*."

Interesting. So this whole murder fiasco was sort of a present for this Aikawa guy. If that was the truth, he must've been a hell of a guy.

No.

To say it plainly, maybe this whole incident was just Iria-san's way of killing time. Island-exiled heiress to the Akagami Foundation. She certainly had no lack of money or time. And she had already gathered all these geniuses here for her amusement. Could it be that this murder was just some sort of . . . special event?

I shook my head. I was thinking too much. There aren't people like that out there. People like that can't exist in this world.

"Well, please excuse me now."

Rei-san bowed to me in front of the door and I went back the way I had come. After talking, she had turned out to be an unexpectedly nice girl, so I was a bit taken aback. Hikari-san had made her out to be so strict.

Thinking about that made me feel a little funny as I returned to Kunagisa's room and opened the door. Inside the room Kunagisa was face-to-face with her computer rack, and one more person—that ultimate, unrivaled fortune-teller. Why?

Maki-san was smoking, but once I entered, she put out the cigarette with her own index finger. She rose from the sofa and approached to pass me without a word. But as if changing her mind midway, she butted her head into my chest and pushed me out the door with her. With a hand behind her back, she shut the door.

I eyed her suspiciously.

"Heh, heh, heh," she laughed childishly. But that's all she did, without even attempting to speak.

"In a better mood now?"

"It's not just my mood that's improved. Hehehe. You're so careless. Or maybe just rash?"

"What brought this on?"

"Do you have a favorite author?"

This conversation was all over the place.

"No."

"How about celebrity?"

"No."

"You're so boring. Fine. Well, you know how *some* people have someone they admire, right? But those people fall into three different categories. There are those who think 'I love this person, I admire him, I respect him, I want to be just like him.' Innocent, right? Then the second type is similar to the first, but they separate themselves completely from the object of their admiration, and even hold that person's life above their own. And finally, the third type of person is the one who thinks that by taking an interest in this wonderful person, they can absorb some of that wonderfulness and increase their own worth in turn. It's a despicable, rotten-minded breed of people who only live for others. Now which one of those three types do you belong to?"

"The second one, I suppose."

"Correct. And twisted as it may be, even I can't help but be moved by your loyalty to Kunagisa-chan," she sneered. "But with that said, aren't you being awfully careless? Leaving her all alone in her room like that? What if I was the killer?

"If you really, truly want to take care of something, you shouldn't let it leave your sight even for a second. Keep that in mind, boy."

Pat pat.

She smacked me twice on the shoulder and disappeared, singing some tune.

I was left alone in the hallway.

"Huh?"

Dammit.

I cursed to myself and then opened the door to Kunagisa's room and entered once again.

2

With the usual rules apparently still in effect, come dinnertime almost everyone was gathered around the table.

Almost.

Naturally Kanami-san wasn't around, and Akane-san was absent as well. Additionally missing were Akari-san and Teruko-san. Apparently they had crossed to the mainland. The reason for this was that they needed to contact our dear detective, "Aikawa-san."

"Couldn't you just call or e-mail him?" I asked.

"We can't," Hikari-san said. "Aikawa-san is famously diffi-cult to reach. It's a busy life, I guess, and I believe there's something going on in Aichi Prefecture right now. So Akari and Teruko won't be back until tomorrow."

"Busy life, huh? What's this person do?"

"Independent contracting."

What's that?

I wasn't entirely familiar with that kind of lingo.

This night's dinner was Chinese food. According to Sashirono Yayoi, master of flavors, Chinese was the quickest and easiest food to make. Of course, that was from her per-spective, so it probably wouldn't serve as reference for me in my own cooking anytime soon.

"By the way, Kunagisa-san," Iria-san said just as dinner was ending. "I hear you were conducting some covert ops this af-ternoon. Did you figure anything out? I thought you were a mechanical specialist, but you can conduct these types of in-vestigations as well, huh?"

"I do all sorts of stuff," Kunagisa said with sweet-and-sour pork crammed into her mouth. "No need to tie myself down with specialties and such."

That sounded familiar.

Ah . . . right. They were Kanami-san's words.

The words of a style-free painter.

Regardless of your strengths and weaknesses, likes and dislikes, there's no need to specialize. This was a fundamen-tal teaching at the ER program as well. Yet in a world that categorizes everything, that was no easy teaching to adhere to. It began and ended with the likes of Kunagisa Tomo, Ibuki Kanami, and Sonoyama Akane.

For me, it was an impossibility.

"So, did you figure anything out? About how they broke into the room or who the killer was or anything?"

It sounded more like she *didn't* want Kunagisa to figure anything out. I recalled what Rei-san had said earlier. Granted, if the case was solved before Aikawa-san got here, it would be something of a killjoy for Iria-san.

"I know it all. I know so much, I don't know."

Nobody seemed to understand what Kunagisa was talking about, instead eyeing her skeptically and saying nothing.

"Himena-san," Iria-san switched the conversation from the engineer to the fortune-teller. "Since coming here you've put all your effort into harassing the other guests, and have yet to do any fortune-telling. So how about it? Don't you think it's time to tell us what's going to happen next?"

"It'll cost you."

She was living here for free, and receiving a regular salary, and she still had the nerve to demand a fee? What a money-grubbing atrocity of a human being. I had never met a person like this before. She was like the devil.

"You're one to talk."

She was glaring at me.

I wasn't talking, dammit.

"Well, it sounds the same to me. I use my abilities to make a profit. I'm not so young that I can stay motivated by morality and humanity alone. Especially in terms of emotional age."

I understood what she was saying. But she must have already had enough ten-thousand-yen bills to fill ten Tokyo Domes, so what more did she want? It wouldn't hurt for her to tell fortunes for free every once in a while.

"Who gave you the right to think that?"

She snapped her attention back to Iria-san.

"Of course I'll pay for it." Iria-san put her hands together. "Please, I'm asking you."

"It ends soon."

Maki-san spoke without even changing her tone of voice. Everybody waited for her to continue, but she was already fully invested in her twice-cooked pork. It looked like that was all she had to say.

"Is that all?" Iria-san asked, evidently somewhat surprised. "I have to say, that was a little, um . . ."

"That was charity. Since *somebody* over there has so many complaints about me, I thought I'd be a little generous. Don't worry about it. It has nothing to do with the fortune."

Himena Maki.

Just what is it like to know everything and stay silent about it? For someone like me who knows nothing, it was impossible to even imagine. In that sense, Maki-san was, for me, the biggest mystery on this whole island. So much so that the mystery of the headless body and the locked door and river of paint were all blotted out.

After that, Maki-san said nothing more, and so the fourth night's dinner ended without any significant developments. Maki-san and Kunagisa made a few bizarre comments as usual, and that was it.

Yet there was one thing that bothered me. Shinya-san and Yayoi-san hadn't said a single word the entire time, and they didn't even appear to be listening to anyone else's conversation. They just sat there putting food in their mouths, just because it was there. It wasn't so remarkable, but there was definitely something unnatural about the two of them. It was one thing for Shinya-san, who had lost Kanami-san, to be like that, but what was Yayoi-san's issue? Granted, she had complained of feeling "under the weather" earlier, but . . .

3

Just past nine o'clock p.m.

I was alone in Kunagisa's room, viewing the digital camera data on the one PC that looked like even I could (just barely) operate it. It had no mouse, making it difficult to control, but it wasn't completely over my head.

Kanami-san's corpse. A shot from the chest up as well as

a full-body shot. A shot of the severed neck and a shot of the river of paint. In the middle of the river floated a coat. The paint having dried and hardened, we couldn't remove it. I suppose we could have forced the coat out, but it was already ruined with paint, so there was no point.

And finally . . .

The picture I had modeled for, Kanami-san's final work.

That unnatural feeling I had felt when first seeing the canvas during our crime scene investigation had returned.

Disharmony.

It was alien.

It was all just a gut feeling, but . . .

"Ah, I get it," I muttered to myself.

Of course. Now that I saw it, it was so simple. The bigger mystery was why it had taken me so long to spot it. It was such an obvious picture flaw.

"Hmm . . ."

But this just raised further questions.

How could something like this happen? There was no reason something like this should happen. How could an artist of Kanami-san's caliber make such a simple error?

As I thought about it, somebody knocked on the door.

"Aw, come on."

It had to be Maki-san, here to harass me again. I rose from my seat, more delighted than ever. But when I opened the door, it was actually Hikari-san. Thrown into confusion by how far off my guess had been, I stared at her for two or three seconds with no brain functionality.

"Ah, hey, Hikari-san." Somehow I managed to string the words together. "Uh, please, come in."

"Sorry to bother you," she said politely, and entered the room. She glanced around the room for a moment and then asked me, "Um, where might I find Kunagisa-san?"

"Oh, Kunagisa? I tied her up and tossed her in the tub just a minute ago."

"Huh?"

"She's like a cat. She hates taking baths. Her hair is actually supposed to be a much lighter blue, but she never washes it so it gets all dark like that. She's no good at escaping, and once she gets wet she just kind of gives up, so she could be in there for a while."

"Oh . . . ohhh, so she's kind of like a Russian Blue, huh?"

Though Hikari-san wore an expression of dawned enlightenment, what she said didn't make any sense. Seriously, I didn't know what she was talking about. Better to just ignore it.

"Um, so anyway, if you need to talk to her, I'm sorry but you're probably going to have to wait awhile." Then a thought occurred to me. Maybe this was a good opportunity. "Say, Hikari-san, are you free right now?"

"Hmm? Sure. I've finished all my work for the day, anyway."

"Then would you mind staying here for a while? It might be dangerous for me to leave Kunagisa alone," I said, recalling Maki-san's lecture this afternoon. "It should be fine now that we've made it hard for the killer to do anything, but, just in case. Do you mind?"

"No, it's okay, I guess," she said, though she wore a troubled expression. "Of course I don't mind, but is it really okay? I mean . . . to trust me?"

"No one would attack both of you at the same time."

"No, I mean, you don't think you're leaving her vulnerable?"

Oh, that.

"It's okay, " I nodded. "Unlike Maki-san, I trust you."

With that, I shut the door and headed down the hall, then descended the stairs to the first floor.

" 'I trust you'?" I muttered, mocking myself.

Since when was I the type to make such grandiose claims? Didn't sound like me.

Question.

What is trust?

Answer.

Not minding if you're betrayed.

Not regretting if you're betrayed.

"Either way, it doesn't mean much of anything, does it?"

I arrived at my destination, once my own room, now Sonoyama Akane's prison.

"It's me," I said, knocking lightly.

"Oh, you" came her reply after a moment. She sounded surprisingly calm. "What's up? Should you be away from Kunagisa-chan? It doesn't seem like you."

"Well, I had my own hesitations, but . . . I wanted to apologize to you."

"Why should you apologize?" came her reply from the other side of the door, slightly laced with crankiness. "Weren't you the one who stood up for me? Coming here and apologizing is like saying I'm too much of a thickheaded imbecile to even understand that. If anything, I should be thanking you.

"I should've suggested this in the first place, but that probably wouldn't have gone over so well, so I was thankful when you brought it up. I should express my gratitude right now." She paused for a moment. "Thank you."

"You're welcome."

She hadn't risen to the ranks of the Seven Fools for nothin'. That wasn't the kind of forgiving place where you could get by with just a little studying and a sharp wit.

"By the way, when Hikari-san brought my dinner, she mentioned you guys have been snooping around a bit. You and Kunagisa-chan. Mind if I ask about your findings?"

"Well, I still don't know who the killer is."

"*You* still don't know, huh? Heh, should I be reading into that? Heh heh, I like your style. Okay, sure. Let me ask a different question. Got any theories on that river of paint?"

"Hm, how about you?"

"I think it's a case of the post hoc fallacy."

"Is that English?"

"Latin. I think it's sort of like 'you reap what you sow.' "

Ah.

I sighed.

In that case, she must have already figured out the secret of the river of paint. She had already figured out the mystery, and now she was just staying here to preserve this "antagonistic atmosphere" we had created for the killer. She was really an amazing woman, I thought.

Hehehe, she laughed.

"It's probably best that I stay in here until Iria-san's lover boy 'Aikawa-san' gets here, huh? It's no real problem for me, anyway. I used to lock myself in my room and read all the time when I was a kid. And that room was way smaller than this."

"Do you know who the killer is?"

"No, I don't. That's no lie, seriously. That kind of thing isn't my specialty, and although I do read the occasional mystery novel, it's only for recreation. Say, do you ever read Mushanokoji?"

The subject had changed without so much as a segue. Was Mushanokoji even a mystery novel author? "I've read the anthology, at least," I answered with a slightly confused look on my face.

"Then you must know the story 'Sensei of Truth.' "

I did know that much.

"When I first read it, I thought the title was 'Mari-sensei' and that it was about a horribly brash woman. Not that I can talk. But do you remember in the opening of the story, when Shinri-sensei refers to the 'reason killing isn't okay'?"

"Yeah, he's like, 'Is there ever a time when you wouldn't mind being killed? If you can think of a condition under which you wouldn't mind being killed, please let me know.

If you don't like the thought of being killed under any circumstance, then you have no right to kill another,' right?"

Even with a memory as bad as mine, this much had stuck with me.

"Correct," Akane-san said. "Now let me ask you the same question. Under what condition would you feel it's okay to be killed?"

"There isn't one."

"But what if, for example, you had to choose between your life or Kunagisa-chan's?"

"I don't want to think about it."

"Right?" She laughed lightheartedly. "After all, you're the type who hates making decisions, right? You dislike the act of deciding in and of itself. Yesterday, Himena-san was saying the same thing about you, and I think she nailed it. You just go with the flow. You hate competition, and you hate making things clear-cut. You have to keep things ambiguous."

"I won't argue with that."

"You won't argue but you won't agree. You accepted my shogi challenge because you knew you would *definitely* lose, isn't that right? You wouldn't accept a challenge or compete otherwise."

I didn't hate losing, I hated competition. I was thoroughly put off by the idea of vying with others over something. I hated fighting as well and thus never made friends.

"Do you dislike other people?"

"Not particularly."

"But do you like them?"

"Not necessarily."

"That's right. The foundation of your values rests on the idea that people are meant to live solitary lives. That's your opinion, yes? Or no, rather that's your *will*. That's the absolute principle around which you're constructed. You try your best not to get involved and not to cause trouble or pain for anyone. Of course you can share happiness and good times with others, but you don't get close to the point that you might cause pain or sadness, isn't that right?"

I always thought couples who spend all their time fighting and stay together all the same were just idiotic. Why don't they get along? Couldn't they just do that much?

Why couldn't they?

"Since when were you such a psychologist, Akane-san?"

"Sorry, but I'm a scholar of any and all subjects. Such categorization is meaningless to me. Hehehe. You really, truly enjoy being alone, don't you?"

"Well, after all, I'm my oldest friend."

"True enough. That's the case for everyone. So how about Kunagisa-chan? Altogether, you've spent less than a year with her, right?"

"Do you like her?"

It was a straight question.

I had been asked the same one several years ago. That time it was her older brother who asked.

However the answer remained the same.

"Not especially, no." My voice came out so despairingly cold that I almost wondered if it was really mine.

Why?

Why was I being like this?

"Hmm, is that so?" She sounded a little surprised. "Because she likes you, you know. That much is certain."

"Yeah, I know. She's told me more than a few times."

"I don't particularly like this kind of discussion, but, have you ever wondered why even though the world is full of couples like this, somehow so many people are still getting together?"

"I mean isn't it strange? It would be too convenient for the person you like to ever like you back. Life isn't a shojo manga. But sure enough, in reality, you take a group of a hundred people, a whole lot of them are going to find love. Why do you think that is?"

"I have no idea. I've never thought about it. Isn't it just coincidence? Like the Law of Great Numbers of something?"

"I don't think so. A coincidence like that is unfeasible. This is the conclusion I've reached: it's because it feels good to be loved. Being loved by another person is enough to make you happy and make you love that person in return," she said assertively. I could see her clever little smile even through the door. This was becoming more than I could bear much longer. I felt like I was about to be crushed to death.

"So what are you getting at?"

"Oh, no, no . . . I was just wondering why you hadn't fallen for Kunagisa-chan, and you know how it is for us scholars. If we can't figure something out, it'll bother us to no end."

"She likes everyone. Seriously, everyone. It's not like she wants me in particular," I blurted out.

"So that's it," Akane-san said. "You don't want to be loved by her. You want to be *chosen* by her. As her one and only."

I . . .

Couldn't argue with that.

"Hmm, but why her? That's what I can't figure out. It seems like there must be some obvious reason, but I don't get it. If you two were a couple, there would certainly be some clashing factors, right? In fact, one would think you would be unattracted to someone so easy."

Easy?

Who?

"You mean easygoing?" I said.

"Right. Anyway, theoretically someone with a personality like yours wouldn't be able to endure a relationship with a girl like that, emotionally immature despite being in a superior position. Plus, you're a man."

"It's fun being with her. Or well . . ." I chose my words carefully. "Rather, it's fun being by her side."

My favorite place in the world was by her side. I had returned to Japan for that very reason.

"Mmm-hmm," Akane-san said. "You're a little masochistic, aren't you?"

"Yeah, to the bone. I got bullied in elementary school, see."

"You were bullied? No, I think this is different. I think you were neglected. There's a difference between abuse and neglect. It's the weak kids and the liars who get abused. The outcasts just get neglected. But I know how you feel. When I was in high school, I felt like I was surrounded by aliens. When we took tests, nobody shot for a perfect grade, they shot for the average. If we ran a marathon, they would say 'Hey, let's all run together!' They were a bunch of egalitarians, for better or worse. They would tell you pi equals three. Indeed, each of the other Seven Fools claims to have experienced similar feelings. It's the tragedy of 0.14. In a world of egalitarians, the outliers get to taste true isolation. Genius is born of it. But not all outcasts are geniuses."

"You mean it's a condition of being a genius, not a guarantor, huh? Well I'm sure no genius."

"Maybe not, but I think you at least know the difference between advice and an order, so let me give you some friendly advice: if you want Kunagisa-chan to choose you, I recommend you just take her. If you do that, you'll be the only one for her. She won't resist, that much is for sure. Regardless of how introverted, dark, disturbed, and deprived of an adolescent you may be, I'm sure you at least have the balls to do that."

"I don't."

"You're a real mallard, huh?"

A what?

"I may lack confidence, but you think I'm a *coward*?"

At least I wasn't a Chii-kun.

"Oh, I'm sorry. Hehehehe, I like you, y'know? It's too bad you aren't a woman."

Why was that?

I didn't know what she was trying to say anymore. No, that's wrong. It was simply becoming too painful to keep myself together any longer.

If this went on any longer, any longer at all . . .

"Well, it's okay. I'm sure everything will become clear soon enough. Time always gives things some clarity. Say, by the way, have you ever heard the theory that in zero-sum games like shogi and chess there's always one perfect move to make?"

"Is this like the Prisoners' Dilemma?"

"Yeah, that. The movement of the shogi pieces is mathematically limited, so there is always one perfect move to make. Thus, it's technically possible to decide the match in the very first move. Of course, this assumes that both opponents are perfect players. So how about the killer in our case? How will this Aikawa-san respond, I wonder? Isn't it a fascinating notion? Still, this mystery feels more like a labyrinth than a shogi board."

"A labyrinth? But labyrinths are simple. If you just stick your hand on one wall, you'll eventually find the way out. It just takes time."

"You're talking about a simple maze. I think this case is more like a multiconnected labyrinth. Still, there's a surefire strategy for this kind of labyrinth as well, but it's kind of hard to explain. If you have a chance, try looking it up. But don't you ever want to play a game with no surefire strategy?"

A game with no sure strategy.

No sure win . . .

Huh.

What if this case was like that?

Anxiety.

Like standing on shaky legs.

I felt sick.

"If you think about it," she continued. This sickening conversation. Even though it was sickening.

"Um, Akane-san?" I said, at last unable to contain myself. "I'd like to keep talking like this, but I've left someone waiting in my room." I forced the words together into a sentence. I fought the urge to throw up. "I think I'd better get back."

"Oh, okay. Sorry about that," she replied.

It must have been a bit of a letdown.

"Anyway, please come again. You sure help pass the time."

"Thanks. Well, see you later."

With that, I began to leave, but there was something that still bothered me. I knocked once again.

"Um, about your original question . . ."

"Hmm? What's up?"

"Do you have one? An instance where you wouldn't mind being killed?"

"An instance? Not an instance—always." It was a clear answer. "I'll die when my time is up. Regardless of where or how I die, or who kills me for what reasons, you won't hear a complaint out of me."

And with that I returned to Kunagisa's room, never thinking for a second that this would be my final interaction with Sonoyama Akane, that genius of geniuses of the highest order, of the Seven Fools, of the comprehensive research center ER3.

4

"Ii-chan, you're back." Kunagisa sat on her bed, her body wrapped in a pure white bathrobe. Hikari-san was on the sofa. Seeing that I had returned, she breathed a sigh of relief.

Trying to handle a conversation with a bath-fresh, spunky Kunagisa was no task for an amateur, so I knew how Hikari-san felt.

"Ii-chan, look, I washed my hair. Compliment me, compliment me."

"It's cute."

Her hair had turned a pretty, cobalt blue. "It's not easy bearing recessive genes," she herself would often say.

"Are you gonna take a bath, too, Ii-chan? You might come up with a good idea in there, y'know, like Archimedes. And then run around the mansion naked, also like him."

"That would be . . . a problem," Hikari-san said in all seriousness. It was like she thought I would really do it. I had no intention of making myself the mansion weirdo. "But Archimedes really was a strange guy, wasn't he? All geniuses are, huh?" Hikari-san said thoughtfully. I wondered which person in the mansion she was imagining. It looked as if it could have been anyone or no one.

"Nudity wasn't so uncommon in those days, Hikari-san. I don't think he was being particularly strange."

"You're so wise, Ii-chan."

"Yes, I am. So Hikari-san, what was it you needed?"

"Oh, right. My mistress sent me to come investigate what's going on with Kunagisa-san."

She was sure an honest girl. I told her there was no point if she went and told us that's what she was doing. She laughed embarrassedly.

"I know. Akari's really better at this kind of thing, but she'll be staying on the mainland tonight. She won't be back until tomorrow morning."

"She went to call on that detective, right?" I was a little bit interested, so I went ahead and asked. "So, what's this person like, anyway? Judging from the way you talk, it sounds like you've met before. Are you well acquainted?"

"Yes, I suppose so. Aikawa-san came to our rescue once before. There was an incident, and, well . . ." she vaguely trailed off. It didn't seem like it was supposed to be a secret, but maybe just an unpleasant conversation.

"Hmm, an incident, huh? On this island?"

"Yes. This was right after my mistress had been sent here, and before it had become this sort of 'salon.' So we called Aikawa-san here, and, well, the case was solved almost immediately," Hikari-san said with great emotion. "Aikawa-san has kind of a violent temper, you see. Cynical and emotional, like the entire world is an enemy. I think Aikawa-san's success in solving cases is fueled by rage alone."

"Huh . . ."

She seemed to be carefully choosing her words as she spoke, but not very effectively. I couldn't put together a concrete picture of this guy at all.

"So, pretty short-tempered?"

"Well, it's more like Aikawa-san is in a perpetual state of rage. Even if you catch a glimpse of a smile, there's always this sort of hostility hanging in the air, and . . . I'm sorry, it's kind of hard to describe. Anyway, it's like Aikawa-san has a grudge against the whole world."

"I see," I said, even though I didn't. "But all the detectives I've ever read about in mystery novels are all so cool and reserved. They're always saying stuff like 'Didn't you realize that?' You could replace eighty percent of their dialogue with 'What are you, *stupid*?' and it would still make sense.

"But based on what you're saying, this Aikawa-san sounds like some sort of hotheaded defender of justice with zero tolerance for criminals."

"Oh, well, it's not like that. It's not just zero tolerance for criminals, it's zero tolerance for the entire world. You know, always saying things like 'This world could be so much better! Why are you bastards all slacking?' "

He really was hotheaded. A rare type of person these days. It was such a contrast to me and my vague, passive babbling, it was almost beautiful.

"But despite all the anger and grouchiness, it just doesn't do any good to get frustrated with the laziness of others, so Aikawa-san would just give this cynical smile. Maybe you know the type. To say the least, it serves as quite a contrast from you and Kunagisa-san."

In describing this detective, Hikari-san seemed sort of gleeful. Like she was boasting about a close friend or something. Or more like a hero. It was just like when Iria-san had described him.

"Is that right? Well, that's probably the better way to be," I said, just trying to keep the conversation going. "Do you think Aikawa-san is reliable?"

"Yes, for sure."

"That's a relief. Even if we can't figure out the mystery in the next six days, we have a backup savior."

"Well, let's not count our chickens before they hatch."

"I'm cautious. Or maybe I'm a coward. Either way is good, I guess."

"Either way is good?" She gave me a confused look. "You know, this may be strange coming from me, but why is everyone able to stay so calm in a situation like this?"

"Well, that's a complicated question."

"Sorry. But you know, it's like, even though someone was killed, everyone is so . . . what can I say . . . ?"

"Maybe they're just used to it."

At least, that was *my* case.

I didn't really know the difference between "used to" and "numb to," though.

"Yeah, but Shinya-chan and Yayoi-chan seemed to react pretty naturally," Kunagisa said.

"That's right, but hey, Hikari-san, you and your sisters seem pretty calm, too. What about that?"

"Well, we've been trained to maintain composure." She sounded a little sad about it.

Her twenty-seven years of living probably hadn't been much of a cakewalk.

"Oh, right," she said, breaking the awkward silence with the snap of her fingers. "My mistress told me to make sure I ask you this. Earlier you said something about understanding so much that you don't understand, right? But really you must know something, right?"

About that space enclosed by a river of paint.

Hmm . . .

That "mistress" of hers must've been sharper than she was worldly.

"Nothing to brag about, really. Any mystery novel fan would've been able to solve it easily. But you know, when you're approached with a mystery like this in real life, it proves to be pretty perplexing. I guess the answers get a little drowned out by the smell of blood, the taste of death."

"Hahaha, weird, Ii-chan," Kunagisa laughed.

It was an innocent, vulnerable laugh.

It made my head spin a little.

Did I want to be chosen?

By her?

My sudden silence drew the quizzical gaze of Hikari-san, but a moment later she turned to Kunagisa. "Um, Tomo-san? If you do know, I hope that you'll tell me."

"Sure, why not? It took awhile to pin it down, but I finally figured it out," Kunagisa nodded. "Erm, where should I start?"

"Um, well first, if you wouldn't mind . . . could you tell me what you meant earlier? About knowing so much you don't know?"

"It's like the difference between bottom-up and top-down," I cut in, lacking faith in Kunagisa's ability to explain it. "Like, say, for example, that that table is a sandbox and you want to make a mound of sand as high as possible. What would you do?"

"Start from the sides and push all the sand together into a mountain."

"Right. So would I. But Kunagisa wouldn't do that. She would take a whole bunch of sand and just dump it on the table. The resulting mountain of sand would be just like the one you and I built. You and I would gradually build up to the final product, little by little. Kunagisa dumps everything out altogether. That's how her mind processes things. Right, Tomo?"

"I don't really get your analogy."

Big surprise there.

At any rate, Hikari-san seemed to get me, and she nodded along.

"Okay, so will you tell me the secret behind that paint room?"

"Sure, if you'll answer my question, Hikari-chan."

Hikari-san stared blankly back at her, as if she didn't understand the question. Kunagisa, paying no mind to that, turned back to her computer. She pointed to the screen on the computer I had been using.

"Okay, first let's review the scene of the crime. Ta-daaa. The atelier."

She used an image viewer program to display all of the pictures. That stream of marble like the Sanzu River. The headless body on the other side. Images that actualized our memories of the morning. Oblivious to such notions, Kunagisa began her explanation.

"The primary puzzle is this river of paint. The earthquake happened at one a.m., causing the shelf to fall over, which resulted in what you now see. That much is clear. The river is too wide to jump. If we suppose the murder happened after the earthquake, the killer's means of entry are a mystery. Or at least, the means of exit are. You with me so far?"

"Yes. So far."

"At this point, it's easy to pin the crime on the monster Ashinaga Tenaga, but the answer isn't that simple."

Hikari-san gave a strange laugh. Either she didn't know who Ashinaga Tenaga was or she was just giving a strange laugh.

"So you're forced to think that the murder happened before the earthquake. If that were the case, it would've been easy for the murderer to get in and out. No footprints, no blocked passages. In which case, it seems like Akane-san must be the killer, since she was the only one who didn't have an alibi. But that's where Shinya-san's testimony comes in. He confirmed that he heard Kanami-san's voice when he called her *after* the earthquake. This means that Kanami-san must have been alive at least for a few minutes after the earthquake. So, Hikari-san, what do you think?"

"Well, I, uh . . ." She tilted her head to the side. It was pretty adorable. "I guess the killer must've come through the window. It's the only other way. But the window is locked, so . . ."

"From the window, huh? There is that possibility. Glass is fundamentally closer to a liquid than a solid, after all, so a lock might not necessarily do much good. Or they could have dug a tunnel as well."

Yeah, right.

"Well, you must've figured it out by this point, right, Kunagisa?"

"Not even a little."

"It's the post hoc fallacy, Hikari-san," I said, coming to her rescue. I had been holding out so long because she was so cute when she was confused, but in the end I couldn't help but feel bad for her.

Kunagisa nodded.

"Yup. *Post hoc ergo propter hoc.* In Japanese, that's 'mistaken cause and effect.' It refers to a misinterpretation of the Law of Syllogism. You know, like false assumptions. The world isn't so neatly organized."

"I don't understand Latin."

"Hey, but you knew it was Latin."

"That's because you said *ergo*."

Cogito ergo sum, huh?

Hikari-san was sharper than she looked.

"For example, imagine I've got a hundred-yen coin and I say 'It's going to come up heads.' I said it, okay? And then I toss the coin. Okay, it's heads! What do you think? You think it was a coincidence, right? That's normal. But some people don't get it. They figure I said I would throw a heads and it was heads, therefore I must have some kind of special power to control the coin."

For the record, it was a trick coin.

"I drank some alcohol and my cold went away, therefore alcohol cures colds. I turned on my computer and a visitor showed up, therefore computers summon visitors. A man looked at a woman, and she happened to be looking in his direction, therefore she must have been interested in him. A catfish was dancing, and then an earthquake happened, so the earthquake must have been the catfish's fault. None of that makes much sense, right, Hikari-chan? In other words, just because B happens after A doesn't mean A and B have a cause-effect relationship. The sequence and timing of two events is no reflection of cause and effect. So let's think about this case now. *There was an earthquake then a river of paint was formed, therefore the earthquake created the river of paint.* Is that right?"

"Oh."

Oh. That.

It finally dawned on her.

"So that river wasn't caused by the earthquake?"

"Well, the shelf itself probably really did fall over because of it. And it probably did cause a little bit of paint to spill out. Kanami-chan even said so on the phone. But I doubt it would've caused such an incredible amount of paint to spill everywhere. The paint cans probably rolled around and let a few drops out. If you think about it, those paint can lids are relatively strong, so it's not likely that just falling over would've caused them to spill all over the place like that. But even if it was just a little bit, Kanami-chan was confined to a wheelchair, so for her it was impossible to leave the atelier."

"Oh, I see where this is going," Hikari-san said. "That makes sense. So then the killer snuck into the room and murdered her. Then, on the way out, purposely spilled paint around the room, little by little. If you did it slowly, little by little, you could make a river like that without leaving any footprints." She appeared to be imagining the killer walking around with a can of paint as she talked.

Yup. We had all assumed that the earthquake had caused the river of paint. But in reality, it didn't take a major disaster or even a major artist to make something like that. It could've been the work of any amateur.

No artistic talent required.

It wasn't a very demanding task, to say the least.

"But why would the killer do that?"

"Probably to makes us think it happened because of the quake," I said. "They must not have known Kanami-san talked to Shinya-san on the phone. So they figured by making the river, people would naturally assume it was caused by the quake."

"So this means . . ."

"Yup. It means," I said, clapping my hands together once and then spreading them out wide, "the suspect list just got way longer."

There were only four people with postearthquake alibis: Iria-san and Rei-san, and then Maki-san and Shinya-san. The remaining people were no longer cleared of suspicion.

"So then there's no point in keeping Sonoyama-san locked up, right?" Hikari-san said cheerfully. "I mean, right? She's not the only one under suspicion anymore."

She must have been feeling pretty guilty about how we had treated Akane-san. It seemed she wasn't much of a mathematical thinker. It was quite a contrast from the rational Sonoyama Akane herself. I decided to tell her.

"Akane-san already knew about the paint trick, too. She's just pretending she doesn't know."

"Why?" Hikari-san said, looking honestly baffled. "Isn't that strange? Why would she do something like that?"

"Probably to preserve this safety situation we've got here. That brain of hers sure keeps busy."

To create the best possible circumstances for everyone else, she didn't even have any reservation about putting herself in the worst possible circumstances. It was almost an inhuman way of thinking, but extremely admirable nonetheless.

"So we should keep this a secret then, huh?"

"Yeah. The killer is still at large, so I don't think it would be good to upset the situation any. I suppose Iria-san has a right to know, though. As far as that goes, do whatever you like."

I wasn't going to be that much of a roadblock.

Hikari-san let out a moan. "But it's so . . . I mean, that thing about the river not really being caused by the earthquake . . . it's so *simple*. Like I should've seen it a long time ago."

"Yeah, I couldn't believe it, either. But you know, any trick seems simple once you figure it out. By now I've seen tons of tricks that were even stupider."

"But who could've possibly thought up such a trick right

after the earthquake?" She was still unconvinced. "I mean, what were the odds there was even going to be an earthquake? It's all too much of a coincidence."

"Well, that brings us to the Law of Great Numbers, Hikari-chan."

"What is that?" Hikari-san gave Kunagisa a sideways glance. "The Law of Great Numbers?"

"It means that something looks like an amazing coincidence, but when you sit down and think about it, it's not really so amazing after all. Like, for example, if you saw someone win the lottery, wouldn't you think it was amazing? You're less likely to hit the jackpot than to spot a tear in the ocean. But if you think about it, that's only true if the guy only bought one lottery ticket. Practically nobody who plays the lottery only buys one ticket, one time. If you have a group of twenty-three people, there's a fifty percent chance two of them will have the same birthday. Even still, it seems incredible, right? That's the Law of Great Numbers. The earthquake just happened to come today, but it wouldn't have changed anything if it had happened tomorrow instead. Plus, it's not likely that the killer was counting on this earthquake trick alone. They probably considered a whole variety of ideas. It's the same concept."

"So you mean like multiple means to one end?"

"Yup yup, you got it. And it all relates back to that misunderstanding of cause and effect," Kunagisa said, poking Hikari-san with her index finger. "Now, Hikari-chan. It's time for my question."

"Oh, that's right. We made a deal," she righted her posture and nodded. "Go ahead, ask me anything."

"Why is Iria-chan here?"

It was a question that immediately changed the entire atmosphere.

Here.

This island.

Wet Crow's Feather Island.

Why was Akagami Iria here?

In a single instant, Hikari-san's usual cheerful demeanor went completely stiff. She was clearly trembling. It wasn't confusion, but utter fear, pure and simple.

Was it really that bad?

"Um, uh, well . . ." her voice wavered, unable to put the words together. "Well, um, that's . . ."

"You can't answer?"

"Just that one question—please don't make me, Tomo-san." She hung her head, as if she might even collapse. Her posture went limp, as if she were ready to pass out. "I'll answer anything else, just not this."

Hikari-san looked truly pitiable. It was like we were the devil trying to get her to do something wicked. *Give us your soul. Your most precious thing belongs to us now.* What an awful bunch of nonsense.

"No, it's okay, we don't mind," I said, breaking into the conversation. "Right, Tomo?"

"Yup. No use trying to force it out of ya." For all her selfishness, Kunagisa was being uncharacteristically sensitive. "Sorry, Hikari-chan."

"No, I'm sorry. You were just asking a question."

Hikari-san stood up. "Sorry I bothered you." She started to leave, but then paused and looked back. "Oh, by the way." She sounded like Detective Columbo or something, except much cuter so it wasn't creepy. She was even smiling. "This has nothing to do with my mistress. I'm asking you personally . . . do you really believe Himena-san has special powers?"

Did we believe?

Maki-san's ESP?

The ability to know all.

After thinking for a moment, I answered. "Right now, there's no particular reason not to."

"I don't really care if she has 'em or not," Kunagisa chimed in.

"Oh, yeah, you're probably right." Hikari-san gave a convinced nod, then left the room. My eyes stayed on the door for a while as I thought about her bizarre reaction to our question about Iria-san.

"Well, whatever."

It probably didn't have anything to do with this incident. It seemed highly unlikely that Iria-san's exile here had any influence on Kanami-san's death. Just then Kunagisa's workstation emitted a strange *boyoyon boyoyonnn* noise. I looked over at it to see Kunagisa had once again started doing something on it.

"What's up?"

"Mail, I got some mail. From Chii-kun. He's a fast one. People used to always say he ignores the theory of relativity like it was a traffic light."

She had just asked him to run a check this afternoon, so he sure wasn't slow—not to mention the fact that he was incarcerated.

"Wow, Himena-san's real name is Himena Shinari. Wow. That's a much better name. I wonder why she uses a fake one."

"Her real name? Hey, this guy even tracked down trivial stuff like that?"

"Yep. He was supposed to see how everyone was connected, but, man, he sure has a lousy personality. Seriously, he doesn't understand how to communicate with people at all. Oh, wait. Here it is. Hey, Ii-chan, we've got a connection."

I went over to her, but everything on the screen was in English, so I didn't understand it.

"Why don't you understand English, Ii-chan? Where were you studying all that time? The South Pole? Mars?"

"I forgot it, that's all. If you don't use something, it only stays with you for three or four months, y'know? Besides, my reading and writing were always worse than my conversation."

"Didn't the ER program entrance exam require English, Russian, and Chinese? How'd you get in? Backdoor?"

"It's like I'm tellin' you, I used to know it."

"Sounds like a lie to me. Anyway, I'll translate. It says 'Ibuki Kanami and Sonoyama Akane were spotted having lunch in a Chicago café. About half a year ago. It's an eye-witness account. Hmm . . . 'lunch together.' I wonder why. Don't those two hate each other?"

"They had lunch together?"

As suspected, they had a connection. But why were they doing something like that? Akane-san had lived in the States, and Kanami-san was a world-traveling artist, so it wasn't that implausible that they could've met over there, but they sure weren't the sort of pair to be having lunch dates together.

"Yup, and it wasn't just a lunch date, either. It was at a super secret-club."

"Secret-club?"

Speaking of sounding like a lie.

"Yup," Kunagisa nodded. "That's right. Those places really do exist. Even in Japan there are some, though not many. All sorts of politicians and celebrities and their families go there. Maybe 'high-class clubs' would be a more accurate description. The security at those places is out of this world."

Which raised the question of how this guy got the information, but I sure wasn't about to ask. Sometimes it's better not to touch the other end of the tunnel.

"Is that definite?"

"Chii-kun doesn't lie. But sometimes he doesn't tell the truth, either. I guess that makes him like you."

"Eh . . . I lie plenty."

I'll just let that say what it says.

So Sonoyama Akane and Ibuki Kanami had a connection. Whether or not it was important information, it was certainly something to be concerned about. I decided it was probably best to confirm it with Akane-san tomorrow. It never occurred to me that this would turn out to be impossible.

"There's some other stuff here about how everyone's doing recently. Natchan's doing about the same, huh? Ah, Satchan seems to be having some rough times. Hii-chan's gone missing. That is so him. The Admiral found a job . . . wow, a nice job. Atchan, too. Everyone else is doing well. Chii-kun, too. That's a relief. Have to admit, I was feeling a little guilty."

Feeling a little left out as she immersed herself in memories of the good ol' days, I rolled over on the sofa. "Let's get to sleep already," I said. Since Akane-san was in the storeroom now, I was stuck sleeping here.

"Okeydokey." She finished checking her mail, switched off the workstation, and dove off the revolving chair into bed. Then she rose to her knees. "Ii-chan, let's sleep together tonight for sure."

"Pass."

"It's so cold at night. If you sleep over there you'll catch a cold. This bed is a king-size. Lotsa room."

"Pass."

"Come on, I won't do anything! We'd just be sleeping together, that's all. I won't even touch you. You can even sleep with your back to me. Come on, that's not so bad, right?"

"Pass."

"Please? I'm lonely over here."

Damn this girl.

She was really digging in this time.

I got up from the couch and looked her right in the eye.

"You swear you won't do anything?"

"Yes."

"You swore. I'm gonna believe you."

"No sweat," she nodded. "I won't let you down."

And so that night I slept on a real bed for the first time in a long time. A very long time. Not that I was expecting anything, but she really did keep her promise, and I could hear her sleep-breathing behind me. But since I had my back to her, I didn't know if she was really sleeping.

I remembered.

The old days.

Way back then.

Years ago.

Wow, was it really so long ago?

"Ii-chan."

She always used to call my name like that, with that sense of familiarity in her voice.

Her heart was just as open to me now, like we had never been apart.

Wide open, no façades.

I really don't like meeting up with people from the past.

Whether they've changed or not, it's a lonely experience for me.

Nevertheless, Kunagisa's house was the first place I went when I came back to Japan, before even going to my own home, and I did so without hesitation.

The blue-haired femme.

She still looked exactly the same.

Like those years had never happened.

I closed my eyes.

Surely this was the first time we'd slept side by side in a long while.

Just take her, Akane-san said.

If you want to be her one-and-only.

If you want not to be loved, but chosen.

"Nonsense . . ."

What if . . .

If I told Akane-san I had already tried that before, would she have held it against me?

It hadn't been out of love, but out of desire for destruction.

But Akane-san.

It didn't mean anything.

Really.

Really, it meant nothing.

So then what?

Then what should I do?

Please tell me.

THE FIFTH DAY

Chiga Hikari,
Second of the
Three Maid Sisters

Chiga Akari,
Oldest of the
Three Maid Sisters

1

THE SECOND DECAPITATION

Death to wolves, and death to pigs, too.

1

I awoke to a loud knocking. My head still swirling with sleep, I got up and opened the door only to have Hikari-san charge into the room and grab me by the collar.

"You bastard!" she suddenly screamed.

No, this wasn't Hikari-san, I realized. The day Hikari-san says something like "You bastard!" is the day I change my name to Samantha. To say something like that and grab me by the collar was, for Hikari-san, literally impossible. She lacked that ability. This was most likely not Teruko-san either . . . so it must be . . . Akari-san?

"Because of you, this—goddammit! You shithead!"

Even for Akari-san, this was pretty uncharacteristic behavior. In a complete frenzy, she looked as if she was going to start pummeling me any second. Or actually, she had already beaten on my chest several times at this point. I was just too surprised by her behavior to notice the pain.

"I'm so tired of this happening." She was panting and trembling. "No more of this . . . It's just too awful. . . . It's too awful. Why? *Why?!*"

"Take it easy, Akari-san." I grabbed her shoulders and gave her a firm shaking.

"Did something . . . happen?"

She shot me a glare. It was a look of true resentment. Vengeful indignation from the core of her being.

She glared with all her might.

Hadn't Hikari-san said something yesterday along the lines of "We've been trained to maintain our composure"? It wasn't likely that Hikari-san had undergone training that Akari-san hadn't. Yet here she was, out of her mind. What the hell had happened?

At last, she shook her head gently. "I'm so sorry. Please excuse me, my behavior was very inappropriate." She hung her head in shame. "It's not even your fault. This terrible thing isn't your fault. . . ."

"Hey, don't worry about it. . . . But what exactly happened?" I repeated my question. "Whatever it was, please tell me."

Instead of answering directly, she spun around with her back to me. "Please come with me to the first-floor storage room," she said, and began walking.

I stood frozen. "W-what? But that's . . ."

Akari-san and Teruko-san had supposedly spent the night on the mainland; when had they gotten back? According to the watch Kunagisa had fixed for me, it was already ten o'clock in the morning (although it was hard to read, since the numbers were backward). It was unlike me to have overslept. How embarrassing.

But now was no time for such thoughts. When Akari-san had returned and how long I overslept were far too trivial matters at this point.

More important . . .

More important . . .

"Akari-san, what did you just say?"

The first-floor storage room?

I had a bad feeling about this. Who was down there?

A real bad feeling.

What was happening on this island?

A *really* bad feeling.

And the feeling was probably right. There was a pattern developing here.

"Hey, wake up, Tomo."

"Hnnh? Gmorning. . . . Put my hair up?"

Kunagisa sleepily raised her head. She wore a strangely content expression, like she had been having a nice dream.

"It seems like now's not the time for that."

She rubbed her eyes. "That means I don't have to wash my face, either."

2

An inward-opening door.

On the other side, Akane-san lay facedown, her body pointing toward us. As a result, the cross section of the cut—as well as all the flesh and bone and veins it revealed—was in plain sight. It was a grotesque reminder that in the end, human beings are nothing more than giant wads of organic matter.

Yes.

It was yet another decapitated body.

Just like Kanami-san's body, the head had been completely severed from the very base of the neck.

It was dressed in a suit. An expensive-looking, gray one. Ruined by bloodstains. But even supposing it hadn't been, just as was the case with Kanami-san's dress the day before, there was no one left to wear it.

The room was stark and barren. I had spent three days in here. Akane-san hadn't lasted one night.

It was an empty room. The only things inside it were a wooden chair by the wall, a house telephone hanging on the wall, a futon, a few books Akane-san had presumably brought with her, and the lamp stand.

"The door was locked, right?" Iria-san asked. "Right, Hikari?"

"Yes." Hikari-san's voice trembled. I looked over to see that her body was also trembling. "It was definitely locked. No mistake."

"Well, what about the window then?"

I looked up at the sound of Iria's voice. At the very top of the wall opposite the door, where we all stood, there was a rectangular window. But it was strictly for letting in sunlight and ventilation. As far as allowing someone to sneak in or get out, it was way too . . .

It was open.

It had an open/close lever that could be operated from within the room. If you thought about it, it was just big enough to let a single person pass through, if the person put in a little effort.

But still . . .

"It's too high," I said to no one in particular.

Breaking in through that window would be like taking a two-story dive, and breaking out would've been even worse. The impossibility of getting in or out through that window was the reason we chose this room as Akane-san's cell in the first place.

In other words, the window was impenetrable.

However.

The only other port of entry or exit had been locked.

This was a dead end. Another sealed room. A second decapitation. Two decapitations, two sealed rooms.

Kunagisa, who was standing next to me, let out a whine. I tried to say something, but ultimately stayed silent.

Lying on the floor before us was the headless body of the woman we had all suspected was the killer. In a situation like this, what words were suitable?

The head was nowhere to be found.

This meant that just like Kanami-san, accidental death and suicide were out of the question.

"Anyway, it looks like we've got some things to reconsider," Iria-san finally said. "Can we all gather in the dining room? Hikari, lock this room."

Once again, Iria-san was the first to leave. Rei-san silently followed close behind.

"Some things to reconsider?" I repeated painfully. Indeed, that was right. All of our thinking and every speculation we had made up to this point would have to be wiped clean. It also seemed as if we had a lot of new details to consider.

"I guess this makes it a serial killing, huh?"

It was really painful to say that.

A serial killing.

I had locked Akane-san in here to prevent that very thing. And she had become the second victim as a result.

Yeah, real safe situation we had created. What the hell did I think would happen? What did I expect from a person who kills others and *cuts their heads off*? Probably the good sense and strategic thinking of, you know, *a human being*.

I had felt so relaxed. Totally at ease. Completely proud of myself. I had stopped the killer from moving around. I was so confident. Carried away. Big-headed.

Akane-san's words from the previous night all came rushing back. The words she had left me with.

Could this be forgiven?

"It's all nonsense, really."

I turned on my heels and left the crime scene.

At that moment, I spotted Yayoi-san out of the corner of my eye. She looked terribly pale. Even more so than yesterday. I guess you'd expect as much from anyone who'd seen two headless corpses in two days. It wasn't like looking at pork or chicken.

Still, there was something—just then Yayoi-san seemed to notice my gaze and sped off to the dining room, as if to get away from me.

I wondered what that was about while Kunagisa tugged on my arm.

"Ii-chan, let's go already. Iria-chan'll get tired of waiting around. Everyone's already gone; there's no point sticking around."

I nodded.

Things to rethink, and new things to think about.

As such, the morning of the fifth day was total crap.

3

"It was around two in the morning," Hikari-san said.

Dining room.

Round table.

But we were two fewer people than just two days ago.

The artist extraordinaire Ibuki Kanami and member of the Seven Fools Sonoyama Akane.

The bickering duo was no more. They were no longer alive.

"I received a phone call in my room . . . from Sonoyama-san. She said she had forgotten a book in her room that she wanted me to bring her."

"And then?" Iria-san said. "I presume you did as you were told?"

"Yes," Hikari-san nodded. "It was a kind of old-looking paperback of *Bakaichi* by Mushanokoji."

"That's not really important. So at that time, Akane-san was still alive, yes? And she had a head?"

"Yes, at that time she was alive," Hikari-san said distinctly.

This meant that Akane-san had been killed after two a.m. I had assumed I was the last person to see Akane-san alive, so I was a little surprised. But really, I don't suppose I had "seen" her, per se, since we had only spoken through the door.

Her body had apparently been discovered around nine o'clock that morning. She usually woke up and went for breakfast at a set time every day, so Hikari-san was concerned when no call came from Akane-san's room, and thus became the one to discover the body.

At first she had suspected that Akane-san had merely overslept on account of being in a new environment. But reality had something else in store. At any rate, assuming Hikari-san's testimony was true, the time of the murder was limited to a seven-and-a-half-hour window. The body didn't appear freshly killed at the time it was discovered, so it seemed that the murder probably occurred in the middle of the night.

"Well then," Iria-san said, looking over the people at the table. "Let's start looking at alibis like we did yesterday."

She sounded like she was playing some kind of game. I won't claim to be able to judge what was inside Iria-san's heart, but at the very least, she seemed to have no sense of sadness or grief.

No matter who it had all happened to or what happened, it didn't happen to her. That's all there was to it.

"This time, I don't have an alibi." I decided to get the ball rolling since nobody was talking. "Hikari-san came to visit our room around ten or eleven last night, I think. But then Kunagisa and I went to bed and fell asleep."

"You went to bed together?" Iria-san teased.

"Yeah, right. 'Went to bed' is just a figure of speech. I slept on the sofa."

"But if you both went to sleep, there's no way of confirming that one of you didn't slip out in the middle of the night."

"Oh, oh, but you can rule me out." Kunagisa slid her hand horizontally across her neck. "The storage room is on the first floor, right? I can't go downstairs alone."

"Eh?" Not only Iria-san, but everyone gawked at Kunagisa in surprise. Well, everyone except for Maki-san, who wore an utterly indifferent expression, as if to say, "I already knew that." But you can always count on her to be the exception.

"That's why I always make Ii-chan come with me."

Yup. I hadn't come to this island just because I was bored or interested. I had a bona fide reason for being here, and Kunagisa needed me.

Kunagisa had a wide array of unique quirks and characteristics that made everyday life a serious health risk, but among those were three major ones, and within those three was one of special note: she couldn't handle extreme vertical locomotion on her own.

That was a rule.

I suppose it's more fitting to call it a rigid, compulsive, subconscious rule that lay somewhere within her mind than a "quirk." If poorly enforced, it would be revealed, and she would scream and shout and you wouldn't be able to lay a finger on her. It was the same way years ago. I wondered if she might have been cured, but it seemed it wasn't such a simple condition.

"Is that right?" The look of surprise remained on Iria-san's face. "But this is the first time I've heard about this."

"Well, it's not really something you bring up all the time. But if you've been observing me, you'll note that I haven't gone up or down any stairs alone the whole time I've been on this island."

I was always with her during meals, or else she was locked up in her room.

Kunagisa Tomo.

"Now that you mention it, you do always get that guy to come to your room and get you. But we don't have any way to prove this."

"We do have a medical certificate," I said. "It's a mental disorder, so to speak. So I think we can confirm Kunagisa's alibi for now."

Not mine, though.

Iria-san seemed to be pondering this for a moment, but then she switched her train of thought. "Well, what about Himena-san?"

"I was in my room drinking all night." She looked over at Shinya-san. "Together with that wonderful gentleman over there."

"Is that right, Sakaki-san?"

"Well, I don't know about the gentleman part, but otherwise, yes." He gave Maki-san a little wink. "I only meant to go bother her for a little bit, but I ended up staying all night drinking."

That makes two nights in a row that they were up drinking. They must have had incredible endurance. Or maybe that wasn't the case for Shinya-san. Maybe he just couldn't bear being sober after the loss of Kanami-san.

I could imagine how important she was to him. He had taught her painting, and even raised her to surpass him. She was special. Her existence had been important to him.

"Neither of us were particularly intoxicated, so I think we can vouch for each other," Shinya-san said. "Yeah, it was around one in the morning. I couldn't get to sleep . . . you know, because of what happened, so I went to the living room and there she was. Then she invited me to her room, and we ended up staying there until morning."

Yup. *That's* what he meant. But either way, he was in her room for a fact; so the two of them had solid alibis.

"I was sleeping the whole time," Yayoi-san said before even being asked, as if we were going in some sort of order. "I've got no alibi at all. But I think Hikari-san can at least vouch that I got up at six a.m. and that she helped me prepare breakfast."

For some reason, she was sort of mumbling her words, and she looked up to see Iria-san's reaction. There was something off about her, and something about her bizarre disposition was bothering me. It's hard to explain, but something caught my attention. I just didn't know what it was.

"Hmm," Iria-san said. "How about you, Hikari?"

"Well, I delivered the book to Sonoyama-san at two a.m.,

then I went to bed. So I don't have an alibi until the time I woke up this morning."

"I see . . . Oh, I suppose I have to give my story as well. I was in my room talking with Rei all night. We were discussing what to do from here on and what to tell Aikawa-san. Isn't that right, Rei?"

Rei silently nodded.

"I had already slept that afternoon, so I couldn't get to sleep at night. By the time we finished talking, it was already morning, so I figured it was too late to try and sleep, so then . . . the usual things, and then finally breakfast. I think that's a solid alibi, isn't it?"

For some reason, Iria-san looked at me when she said it. It was a challenging gaze. I shrugged. "Yup, sure is. So when did Teruko-san and Akari-san get back?"

"At about nine o'clock." It was Akari-san, who had only a short while ago jumped me in Kunagisa's room. She had completely returned to normal by this point, but she didn't try to make eye contact with me.

"Nine o'clock?"

Speaking of which, she had said something kind of strange earlier. "I'm so tired of this happening," or something to that effect. But what was she so "tired" of? No matter how you looked at it, there was something strange about her whole manner at that time.

Something told me she wasn't just referring to Kanami-san's death.

"Well, I guess that means Akari and Teruko have an alibi, yes? Which means . . ." Iria-san said. "The people with alibis are Sakaki-san and Himena-san, followed by me and Rei, and Teruko and Akari. And most likely Kunagisa as well. That's seven."

On the other side we had myself, Sashirono Yayoi, and Chiga Hikari. The three of us had no alibis. But while the question of who had an alibi was an important one, there was one thing more important in this case.

"Um, Hikari-san?"

"Yes?" She looked in my direction.

"Maybe I'm being too trivial here, but could you tell me whether or not the window was open when you delivered the book to the storage room at two o'clock?"

She looked off into space as she thought about it for a moment. "I believe it was closed," she answered.

"I see. Is it something a person could easily open?"

"Yes. It's supposed to be for ventilation, so if you just use the lever—you have to crank it like this—it opens and closes normally. But that's only from the inside. It's completely sealed off from the outside."

"I see."

This was a troublesome development. A *very* troublesome development. A window more than ten feet high. Without a ladder, it was virtually impossible for someone to climb out, and even more implausible that someone had climbed in.

In other words, we had another "locked room" mystery.

"Well, tell me then, how do you go about handling the key? Are there copies of it or anything?"

"I have the only key. There are no copies or master keys."

She seemed pretty worried. Which was only natural. The implications of this conversation were that she was the only one who could've possibly committed the murder. Just looking at it objectively, that was the most likely case.

But I wasn't about to point that out. I didn't want to cause another Akane-san-style mishap.

"What type of lock is it?"

"Just a normal one. You twist the key like this and the bolt latches. I don't know the official name . . ."

"And you definitely locked the door at two a.m.?"

"Yes, I locked it. For sure. I even checked several times," she answered with a somewhat pained expression. "For sure."

"I see . . ."

She was an honest girl.

To the point that it must have made life difficult for her.

Seeing her like this, it seemed clear to me that she wasn't the killer. If she were the killer, she wouldn't have gone to all the trouble to report that she had been called to Akane-san's room in the middle of the night. Anyone could have deduced that much.

Of course, you couldn't throw out the possibility that she had strategized all this to fool everyone. That kind of argument could go on forever.

I continued my questioning.

"And nobody else was in her room when you went there? What about the possibility that someone was hiding in the dark or something like that?"

"Well, I didn't sense anybody else in the room, but"—she tilted her head as if she didn't quite get the point of my question—"I can't be certain. I didn't actually go into the room. I gave her the book at the door."

"Weren't you scared?" Yayoi-san suddenly asked, her voice faint. She wore an upset expression as she continued. "I mean, didn't we all think Sonoyama-san might be the killer? And you met with her alone, in the middle of the night? Weren't you scared?"

"No, not at all," Hikari-san answered after a moment's hesitation. "I didn't think Sonoyama-san was the killer."

"Why not?" For some reason, Yayoi-san was being strangely pushy with Hikari-san. "What makes you so sure?"

"Uh, well . . ." Hikari-san looked over at me with a worried expression. Ah, it was because of her conversation with Kunagisa yesterday. Indeed, after hearing that conversation there was no reason to suspect Akane-san in particular.

I thought about things as I watched this conversation unfold between the two ladies. But I couldn't pin anything down. It had seemed to me that if something had happened, it probably happened around two a.m., when Hikari-san delivered the book, but then, after listening to her testimony, that didn't seem to be the case.

So what to do now?

How to continue?

"I don't suppose the room was completely sealed. The window was open, after all," Iria-san said to me. "In that sense it's not exactly what you would define as 'sealed.' "

"But it's impossible to get in or out through that window."

"There's a chair in the room, right? Couldn't you reach the window if you stood on the chair?"

"I don't think so. Even if you stretched and jumped at the same time, I don't think you'd reach it. Shinya-san is the tallest person here, and I don't think even he could reach it."

"Is that so? So Ibuki-san's room was sealed off by a river of paint, and this time it's a room sealed off by a height problem. . . ." Iria-san stretched out her arms with an irritated sigh. "And both women were decapitated."

Yeah, there was that issue as well.

The killer had cut off Kanami-san, and Akane-san's heads.

That was still a mystery. There was no reason to suspect switched bodies, but what other reason was there to cut off the heads? Could we just write it off as a bizarre fluke?

What's more, the fact that the killer took the severed head didn't make much sense. Of course, there was also the possibility that the killer severed the head specifically for the sake of taking it somewhere, but what in the world do you do with a severed human head?

And that question just led to another question: why were these women killed in the first place? I had no idea. This case was full of things I didn't understand. It was all hopeless and meaningless.

Dammit.

Since when had I become so dumb?

"Hmm . . . looking at things objectively, Hikari is the most suspicious one here," Iria-san said suddenly.

Hikari-san flinched for a moment. "Eh? Oh, um, I . . ."

"Hikari was the one with the key, and one of the three people with no alibi. If the window isn't a possible entrance or exit, the door is the only possibility, right? There are three people without alibis, but only one of those three has a key."

"Please hold on a second," I barged into Iria-san's monologue. "That's no good. That's not a fair assumption."

"Assumption? I believe the correct term is 'reasoning.' "

Hikari-san watched our interaction with a worried expression. She didn't know what to say.

"It's like Akane-san said yesterday. It's foolish to reach a conclusion based on the process of elimination and selective thinking. I won't go as far as to call it foolish, but I do think we're leaving things out."

"I wonder. Is that right? I don't think so, personally."

"It was that thinking that caused me to have Akane-san locked up as the prime suspect. And this is the result. This is the result of that, Iria-san. There's nothing I can say about what's already over and done, but I refuse to make the same mistake again. You understand, right? It's too dangerous for anyone to be left alone anymore."

"Now you tell me," she said with a smile. Under different circumstances, it might have even been pretty. "Wasn't it your idea to have Akane-san locked up—sorry, *secluded*—in the first place?"

"That's correct. I'm not here to debate that fact. It was I who suggested we lock her up in there, and so now it is my duty to counter that suggestion. If I have to take responsibility for what happened, making sure it doesn't happen again is how I'll take that responsibility. At this point, it's still too early to determine who the killer is. We're still not even thinking about the things we need to be thinking about."

Maki-san let out a big yawn. Possibly because she hadn't slept in two days, or possibly because she was bored by the conversation. Most likely it was for both of those things.

She was just a bystander.

"Well, I still think Hikari is the most suspicious."

There was absolutely no sense of compassion in her words for this maid with whom she had coexisted under the same roof for all these years.

She was completely devoid of sentimentality. She spoke with the icy-cold tone of someone simply reporting facts as facts, with no emotion inserted whatsoever.

I thought I knew.

The answer to Kunagisa's question from yesterday. The reason this woman had been exiled from the Akagami family.

Akagami Iria. This world was all the same to her, by and large. It all had the same lack of value. And so she was searching for something of value; unable to find it, she was able to rid her life of anything without any shred of hesitation.

I had been wondering what she had done.

I had assumed she had done something.

But in reality, maybe that was the wrong assumption. Maybe it wasn't that she had done anything wrong, but that she couldn't exist as part of the Akagami family. Furthermore, maybe it wasn't the family that had shunned her, but in fact the other way around. It wasn't out of the question.

And here I thought it was supposed to be her job to stick up for Hikari-san.

"Well, let's do this then," I suggested without looking up at Iria-san. "We can say for a fact that it's no longer safe for anyone to be alone. So let's divide into teams. No complaints about that, right Iria-san? I don't think I need to bother explaining the purpose of making teams, right? It's just safer than moving around alone. And that way we can all watch one another's backs. Now, since I've been sticking up for

Hikari-san, I'll be on her team. Her, Kunagisa, and I will be Team A. How's that sound?"

"Hmm, interesting." Iria-san seemed genuinely impressed. "You're smarter than you look, huh? Teams, eh? Well, naturally I'll be teamed up with Rei and Akari and Teruko. Then let's have Maki-san, Shinya-san, and Yayoi-san on Team C. Shinya-san and Maki-san have been confirmed as innocent twice in a row now, so Yayoi-san can put herself at ease. And even if Yayoi-san is the killer, it would be two against one. Does that sound okay?"

"What if we just had everyone stay in the dining room together? Until Aikawa-san gets here?" Hikari-san said, looking over at me with the same worried expression. "That way nobody has to be alone and the killer can't take any actions, either."

"We can't do that. You mean just stay put here? Don't be ridiculous."

I spoke not only to Hikari-san, but to the entire group.

"Kunagisa and I have some moving around to do."

4

For the time being, we decided to bury Akane-san's body. As was the case with Kanami-san's body the day before, simply leaving it there on the floor was out of the question. Iria-san didn't seem to have any plans to call the police anyway, so we went ahead and did as we felt.

We decided it would be best to use the digital camera to first take pictures of the scene of the crime as we had done the day before, then go bury the body in the mountain woods behind the mansion, so the three of us headed back to Kunagisa's room. But our plans would end up being slightly modified.

"Gah!"

The instant Kunagisa entered the room, she let out a scream that reverberated out into the hall.

I took a peek in and discovered the reason.

"This is . . . *wow* . . ."

"Ah, what the hell?" Kunagisa was uncharacteristically vocal. "This is bullshit!"

Destroyed.

It was destroyed.

Inside her room lay destruction. All three of her computers, the two PCs and the workstation. They had been completely smashed to bits.

"Wahhh! Why did this happen?!" She frantically scrambled over to the completely exposed, mostly unrecognizable mess of mechanical parts. "Awfulawfulawfulawfulawfulawfulawful! This is bullying! Demonic! There is a demon on this island! It's Diabolos, Ii-chan! A tragedy! Uwaaa! This is the ruptured organ compound fracture of computers! Even the monitors are busted! Why?! Ah, this keyboard was *impossible* to build! The holographic memory! Oh my God, the motherboard!!! What happened to—oh my God, it's been *smashed*! What the hell is this?!?!"

She had lost it. Like flipping a switch. For a happy-go-lucky girl like her, this was a fairly rare state of being. Or at least it was the first time I'd seen her like this since coming back to Japan.

"Why would they do something like this? Oh, it's too awful. . . . Ii-chan Ii-chan Ii-chan . . . So whaddaya think?"

"It's ghastly." Even supposing these computers were a nuisance, there was no need to go this far. They were smashed up so bad, it seemed like overkill. "I wonder if they used some kind of iron bar. It's not a very clean method of destruction. Or maybe it was a hatchet or something."

"Why did this happen? Who did this? You think it was the killer?" Hikari-san said in a whisper.

The killer? Maybe the person who murdered Kanami-san and Akane-san was trying to create some chaos. But what was the point? What did the killer have to gain by destroying Kunagisa's equipment?

"Oooh . . . poor me. I want to cry," Kunagisa said, as if really about to cry. "Hah . . . well, whatever. I already sent a backup to my house and all. But still, I went to so much trouble to build these. I didn't see this coming. I guess next time I'll have to make the motherboard out of unbreakable parts."

"Wow, backup to the rescue, huh? At least you won't lose the software you made."

But in reality, it wasn't much of a "rescue." Kunagisa's computers weren't the normal equipment used by your average professional. They were all completely homemade, so the external parts were actually worth even more than the internal parts.

"Now we can't even view what was on the digital camera. It looks like the camera and the mobile memory are busted as well. Oh, it's too horrible. Does this person think money grows on trees?"

I thought for a moment. "Hey wait, you're one to talk."

I snapped my fingers. As expected, the camera seemed to have been destroyed very deliberately. Which made the culprit's motive entirely clear.

"I see, I see. It makes perfect sense," I muttered to myself. "Yeah, this is surprisingly easy to understand. They must have been afraid of us snooping around any further."

"What do you mean?" Hikari-san asked. "You know why this happened?"

"Yeah, I think so. You saw them yesterday, too, right? Kunagisa's pictures from the atelier had all been sent to the hard disk through a USB connection. Whether or not the culprit knew all that, they must've figured those images were incriminating."

The workstation and mobile memory had probably been destroyed with extra care.

Kanami-san's room.

Those images.

"I think that's why this happened."

We hadn't told anybody about the mail or info from Chii-kun, so the killer wouldn't have known about that, but everybody knew about the pictures. Kunagisa slumped her shoulders in realization of this fact.

"Ah. I didn't even bother applying extra protection. I never imagined anyone would resort to something like this."

"This room doesn't have a lock, does it?" Hikari-san said. "I guess you were unlucky."

I patted Kunagisa on the head.

"Keep your spirits up. I guess this means we can't just sit around happily waiting for this detective guy to show up." I put my hands on her shoulders and sort of half hugged her. "No more playing around, huh?"

We didn't know who the culprit was, and we didn't know the motive, either. But we did know one thing for sure: the bastard had destroyed something precious to Kunagisa Tomo for his or her own selfish reasons.

This was unforgivable.

"Huh? Hey. Wait, wait a second," Hikari-san said as if having suddenly thought of something. "Who did this?"

"Uh, the killer, right? We don't know who that is right now."

"But we were all in the dining room, and then we came directly here, right? Who could've had the time to destroy everything like this?"

Whoa.

We had been in this room until Akari-san came. Then we went to the storage room where the murder had happened, but we were the last ones there. Everyone else was already gathered. Then everyone went directly to the dining room as a group.

If that was the case—or rather, that *was* the case. Logically, there was nobody here who could have committed this destruction.

"This is obviously the work of a human being, but nobody had the time to do it. What the hell?"

It didn't make sense. Yet another mystery to worry about. Just like Kanami-san's sealed room and Akane-san's headless body. No.

This was different. This was a different sort of mystery. It went beyond simply trying to figure out people's alibis and motives. It wasn't a matter of tricks or gimmicks. It was simply an impossibility.

Which meant . . .

"Which means maybe this is the key."

I looked at Kunagisa. I looked at Hikari-san.

And then I thought.

If this was the key . . .

Then where the hell was the door?

5

Determining that the equipment was beyond repair, we decided to continue with our planned course of action. And by that I mean Akane-san's burial.

We went to the storage room, placed her body on a big stretcher, and headed for the mountain woods behind the mansion. The stretcher was kept in the mansion in case of an emergency, but I doubt they had had an emergency like this in mind.

No . . .

Maybe they had.

This time we would bury the body alone, without a sleeping bag. Hikari-san took the front of the stretcher and I took the back. Despite her small frame, Hikari-san's length of service as a maid was apparent in her surprising upper-body strength.

Kunagisa followed behind me carrying the shovel.

Carrying the back of the stretcher placed the corpse directly in my field of vision, front and center. Even being used to this sort of thing, it wasn't the most pleasurable experience in the world.

On the way, I remembered something I had meant to ask.

"Hikari-san, was Akane-san wearing the same clothes when you brought the book last night?"

"Yes, they were the same," she replied. "Of course, she still had a head, too."

It wasn't the type of joke you laugh at. It was far too true to be funny.

The digital camera had been destroyed beyond all repair, so naturally we couldn't make a record of the storage room where Akane-san was killed. This was probably exactly what the killer had hoped.

Surely the killer was mocking us. But he or she was taking Kunagisa's memory too lightly.

"Hmm. Hmmhmmhmm. If we assume the killer broke everything because he didn't want there to be a record of the scene where Kanami-chan was killed, why exactly was that? Did the pictures show some concrete evidence? I don't remember anything like that."

Inside her head was an image of not only yesterday's crime scene, but also of the storage room we had just visited, just as accurate and precise as that digital camera. They didn't call Kunagisa Tomo a prodigy for nothing.

"Anything sticking out in your mind?"

"Uh-huh. Tons of things are sticking out. I'm trying to narrow them down. Ermm, ah, right . . ." She began mumbling to herself. Once she had gone into this kind of state, it was best not to bother her. I looked back over at Hikari-san.

"So where should we bury her, Hikari-san?"

"I suppose away from Ibuki-san would be best."

I couldn't have agreed more.

Walking through the mountain forest for a while, we eventually found a spot we thought would make a decent burial ground, and decided to begin digging. Yesterday we had had twice as many men, so today promised to be relatively exhausting. I had hoped Shinya-san would be able to help us, but alas, he was on a different team. That and, for the average guy, having to bury the corpses of two acquaintances in a period of two days was more than a little nerve-racking.

Unless you were a guy like me.

In which case it was nothing to write home about.

"This should do."

I brushed the hair out of my face. If this were summer, I would've been sweating like crazy. I hoisted myself out of the hole and lowered Akane-san's body into it. Then, a brief, silent prayer. I didn't know whether or not there was a point to such actions, but I figured it was better to do it than not.

Regardless of where or how I die, or who kills me for what reasons, you won't hear a complaint out of me.

The last words I had heard out of Akane-san. But did she really mean it? Even being killed like this, had she crossed over to the other side like a saint, without a single gripe?

For me, that was an impossible feat.

"I really wish we could bury her with the head, huh?" Hikari-san said. "Ibuki-san, too. Why do you suppose the killer cut the heads off anyway?"

"That's the question of the week, I guess. But we keep coming up with the same answer."

That is, "I don't know."

I scooped up some dirt with the shovel and began burying Akane-san's body. My joints would be hurting tomorrow for sure. If I still had the mental faculties to feel pain, that is.

There was no saying I wouldn't be the next murder victim. The chances weren't very high, but it wasn't impossible.

A serial killing.

Maybe it was already over with Kanami-san and Akane-san. According to the information from Kunagisa's old buddy Chii-kun, the pair had had some sort of relationship in the past, although I couldn't say what kind, so there was always the possibility that the whole ordeal was already over. But maybe that was just overly optimistic thinking.

At long last, Akane-san's body was completely buried.

"Hikari-san, since we're already out here, would you mind taking me somewhere where we can see that storage room window from the outside?"

"Certainly."

She began walking.

Kunagisa followed behind, blue hair waving. Speaking of which, I hadn't put her hair up at all today. I decided to do so properly once we got back to her room.

As we were walking, Hikari-san turned to me with a serious expression. "Thank you so much." Not knowing what that was in regards to, I was taken aback.

"At breakfast, you stood up for me. So I wanted to thank you."

"Oh, well, I didn't just do it because it was you. I just hate the idea of making the same mistake again. Even putting mistakes aside, I just hate repetitive actions, really."

Maybe that was why my memory was so bad.

"Nyahaha, that is so you, Ii-chan," Kunagisa giggled childishly. "But really you did it for Hikari-chan, right? 'Cuz she's right in the center of your strike zone."

"What exactly is my strike zone?"

"She's older than you, she's a girl, she's petite, she's got long hair, she's slender, she doesn't wear any rings or anything, and she's even wearing an apron dress."

"I've never said anything about apron dresses."

"Also girls who wear jeans on the bottom and nothing on top, librarian-lookin' girls who dress in white uniforms and wear glasses, gothy girls who are taller than you and have brown hair and wear jerseys . . ."

"Don't make me sound like such a freak."

Damn. She sure was chatty.

But to be sure, Hikari-san was totally up my alley. In terms of speed, I preferred the slight harshness of Akari-san's personality, but certainly I had no problem with Hikari-san's gentle "slowball." I suppose Teruko-san was some sort of disappearing magic pitch . . .

I don't know what the hell I'm talking about.

"Hah . . ." Hikari-san gave an ambiguous smile tinged with embarrassment. "Anyway, I wanted to thank you. My mistress can be quite . . . severe in these cases. Plus, unlike yesterday with Sonoyama-san, this time it seems like I *must* be the killer. Even I couldn't help but think so. At least with Sonoyama-san there was the pretense that it was a sealed room, so really *nobody* could have been the killer. But this time—"

"Don't worry about that anymore, Hikari-san." I was becoming a little irritated, so I cut her off mid-sentence. "You've already thanked me, and you've already shown your sincerity, so you don't have to keep thanking me for everything."

"But—"

"If the situation had been reversed, you wouldn't have just left me there on my own, right? I think you would have done the same for me."

"But I think if that happened, you would thank me."

Well I'll be damned. She was playing hardball.

"I think he means that you're a friend," Kunagisa said. "And we don't doubt our friends. That's why I don't think Ii-chan or you could be the killer."

"Friends?" she nodded, brimming with emotion. "I've

never had friends before. I've been by my mistress's side for as long as I can remember."

"I don't have any friends, either. Neither does Ii-chan. So we'd be happy if you'd be our friend."

Kunagisa took Hikari-san's hand.

Just looking at a sight like this was enough to bring a smile to your face. But realistically speaking, it would've been hard for Kunagisa and Hikari-san to continue a friendship, I thought. From here on out, Iria-san would likely need Hikari-san at her side more than ever before, and meanwhile Kunagisa was scheduled to head back home. And once back, Kunagisa was bound to stay holed up in her home all the time.

Kunagisa Tomo was a lonesome girl.

They often say that geniuses are completely self-sufficient. If that was the case, Kunagisa fit the bill.

And most likely, unable to analyze the situation in any other way, it was I who was the loneliest.

"Oh, it's over there. The window."

I looked around in confusion for a minute. There wasn't a window in sight.

"Oh, is it that one?" I said, pointing to the only window I could see, which stood at about the height of my chest.

"Yeah, that's it."

"But that height is—"

"It looks high up from the inside, but half this place is built on a mountain, so . . ."

While I listened to her, I looked into the room through the window. You could make out a small puddle of blood, the wooden chair, and the door. It was without a doubt the storage room where I had been sleeping and where Akane-san was killed.

Wow. So part of the mansion was buried in the mountain, including this room.

"In that case, breaking in wouldn't be so hard, huh?"

"But you can't open the window from the outside. And it doesn't lock with just a latch, either, so you couldn't get it to unlock by rattling it a little."

"Well, what about the possibility that Akane-san opened the window on her own, letting the killer in?" Kunagisa said. "Like maybe the killer knocked to get her to open it. Y'know, like 'anybody home?' "

"It's hard to believe Akane-san would do anything to let the killer inside. I mean, it's Akane-san. Plus, this really is quite a height. It feels all the more real when you're looking from the top down. I, for one, sure wouldn't want to jump down from the window."

The window was the kind that tilted open, and only partially, so it didn't look like there was much room to make a balanced jump, either. And it looked like if you didn't make a proper landing, you could easily break a bone, or even die if you happened to hit your head.

"But even supposing Akane-san had accidentally let the killer in, she could've easily called for help. The house phone was right by her."

"Maybe she was attacked in her sleep. . . . Oh wait, I'm an idiot. If she was sleeping she couldn't open the window," Kunagisa said.

"And even ignoring that fact, how would the killer get back out? Even an expert rock climber couldn't get up a flat wall like that."

"Teehee! Like a gecko." Kunagisa poked her head inside the window and looked around. "Oooh, it is a dangerous drop, huh? What if the killer used rope?"

"Rope, huh? But there are no trees in this area to tie it around."

I looked around the area. Whether it had been deforested or it had always been this way, the whole place was nothing but a big grass plain, and there was nothing appropriate for tying a rope around.

"And y'know, rappelling isn't the easiest trick in the book, either. I have some experience with it, but it's pretty damn tough. The skin from your hands peels off and stuff."

"Not if you wear gloves."

"Well, yeah, but I still think it's pretty unlikely. They might as well have brought out a ladder and stuck it through the window. That's probably more likely anyway," I said.

"But a ladder wouldn't fit through a gap this small. It would get caught halfway, and then a person couldn't fit through."

"Hmm, I wonder. Hikari-san, is there a ladder anywhere on this island?"

"Well, no . . ."

"What about the possibility that someone brought one with them?"

"I don't think so. I would've noticed if someone brought something that big."

"How about a rope ladder? Then they could easily hide it in their luggage, and it wouldn't get caught in the window."

"Ii-chan, you even forget stuff you said yourself? If it was a rope ladder, there wouldn't be anything to tie it to. It would be possible if they stuck some kind of metal hook in the wall, but that would've left a hole. The wall looks fine as far as I can see."

That was true. This was just common sense, not the kind of thing even worth bringing up. But for the sake of confirmation, we were discussing it anyway. It was just another form of "preestablished harmony."

I faced Hikari-san.

"Have any ideas?" I asked. "Or even just any observations?"

"Hmm, nothing in particular . . ." she said as she approached the window. "But assuming the killer didn't enter through the door, the window was the only other way to break in, huh?"

"Break in . . . but maybe they didn't even have to break in." I was just coming up with this on the spot. "The chair is over there, which means that must have been where Akane-san was sitting and reading. Maybe the killer made some sort of lasso out of rope, put it in through the window, caught it around Akane-san's neck, and then pulled her up. So she was strangled to death. Then she was pulled up as far as the window, where her head was cut off. How about that?"

Implausible, huh? At the very least, it didn't have any holes. The killer wouldn't have had to sneak in through the window, or even enter the room, and still could have killed her.

There were no holes at— "Oh no, wait, that's no good."

"Why not? I didn't think it was so implausible," Hikari-san said, confused. "If that was the case, anyone could have done it."

"Human bodies aren't so light."

For a woman, Akane-san wasn't small. She was taller than average, and she looked like she must have weighed at least 110 pounds. She probably wasn't as much as 130, but she definitely wasn't in the 90s, either. To lift her from this height would've required not only a really tough rope, but some incredible arm strength to boot. I definitely couldn't have done it. To pull someone up this high with just two arms was a crazy feat of strength.

"Shinya-san's probably the strongest one here, but he's got an alibi. And even if he's the strongest one here, that's very relative. I don't think even he could lift a human body by himself. Not to mention that Akane-san would've been resisting all the while."

And while she was resisting, the house phone would have been right beside her. If she even just kicked it over, somebody would have discovered what was happening. It wouldn't have been a very wise method.

"Plus, in that case the window would have had to be open. But would she have really opened the window and then turned her back to it? She wasn't stupid; in fact, quite the opposite. So she was probably being somewhat cautious."

Indeed.

Dammit. And here I thought I was getting a little warm, but I was still on the wrong track. I felt an unpleasant sensation, like I was in some twisted dimension. It was like searching for the corner of a circle. Something was decidedly off. Something was depressingly messed up. What the hell was I doing wrong?

I felt as if I was being given the run around, big-time.

"Anyway, let's go back to the room. There's nothing more to see here."

Not that there was anything to see back at the room.

Seemingly reluctant to leave, Kunagisa stayed gazing in through the window for a while, but finally turned and began to follow me.

"Did you spot something?"

"Uh-uh, nothing special. More important, I'm hungry."

"Oh yeah?"

"Then let's go have lunch," Hikari-san said.

"Yeah," I nodded.

Chiga Teruko,
Youngest of the
Three Maid Sisters

2

LIES

Don't you have anything better to do?

1

Hikari-san had been completely relieved of her duties by Iria-san. "Instead, go help Kunagisa-san and the other guy," she had been told. It was a soft way of saying, "No way in hell am I going to entrust any of the housework to the prime suspect," or at least that was partially what she meant.

And thus, the three of us remained together even after finishing lunch.

"Would you two go on ahead of me?" I said to the two girls on the way to Kunagisa's room. "I want to stop by Iria-san's room for a bit. Kunagisa, hold on to this."

I pulled a small knife out of my pocket and handed it to her.

"You've been walking around with something that dangerous?" Hikari-san said in surprise.

"A young man always carries a knife in his heart."

"And a young woman carries a pistol," Kunagisa joked as she took the knife. "Well, let's go, Hikari-chan."

"But . . ."

"It's okay, it's okay. Let's leave it to Ii-chan," Kunagisa said, half dragging Hikari-san along. As long as they were together, Kunagisa wouldn't have any trouble going upstairs. That was one of the reasons we were on a team of three.

"Well, I guess we're going then."

I did an about-face and began walking toward Iria-san's room.

Time to request another "audience." I gave myself some mental prep. Then I took in a deep breath.

I knocked on the thick door, waited for an answer, and then entered. Inside the room, I found Iria-san and Rei-san, as well as Akari-san and Teruko-san, which I guess I probably should've expected since they were a team. All of them were sitting on the sofa, elegantly sipping black tea.

Akari-san awkwardly avoided eye contact with me, as if trying to escape. She must have been regretting going bananas on me that morning in Kunagisa's room. That was only natural, but it was I who was at a loss for what to do with her speaking so openly to me.

Iria-san's mouth slowly curled into a smile.

"Is something the matter, Mr. . . . um . . . what was it? You're the one who proposed that we operate in teams, and now you're here alone? That's a bit of a problem, now, isn't it? Hikari is on your team, you know—"

"Iria-san," I interrupted. "Um, you still don't plan on contacting the police, do you?"

"Not a chance."

A snappy answer.

An utterly cold, curt response.

She was just amazing.

You're really wonderful, Akagami Iria-san.

"I don't think that's a good thing, to be honest," I said.

"Would you also care for some black tea?" It was Rei-san. She stood up without waiting for my reply and walked over to the pot. Iria-san shot her a look that seemed to have some hidden meaning, but then looked back toward me.

"If the police came now, you'd be a sticky situation yourself, don't you think? Akane-san was killed because of your suggestion, after all."

"It doesn't matter if it would put me in a 'sticky situation' anymore. I live to be given the run around. More important, what about you, Iria-san? Akagami Iria-san. You might be killed, too, you know. What do you think of that situation?"

With Rei-san's invitation, I took a seat on the empty part of the couch next to Teruko-san. Teruko-san made no attempt to even look at me. Her vacant eyes stared off into space from behind her black glasses. It was like her focus was out of alignment or something. Or no, it wasn't out of alignment. It just wasn't in tune with mine.

The black tea was good.

Iria-san took a long pause before answering me, as if trying to intimidate me.

"What do I think of it? Of this situation? It's terrible. It's a terrible event. Of course that's not all I think, but what if I ask you the same question? What do you think?"

"It's a dangerous situation. I have no interest in sticking around with a murderer in our midst."

And I had no interest in sticking Kunagisa in such a situation, either. I didn't know how she felt about things though. I had no idea. But as for me . . .

"Hmph. Do you think murder is a terrible thing?"

"Yes I do," I answered promptly. "I do think that. Without question. No matter what reasons they might have, murderers are the most despicable type of human."

"Hmm. So what would you do if you were going to be killed? I mean, if it was kill or be killed, what would you do? Just sit there and wait to die?"

"I'd probably kill. I'm not a saint. But in that moment, I would consider myself the most despicable type of human. No matter what kind . . . what kind of person he or she was."

"You look like you're speaking from experience." Iria-san gave me an unsavory smile. It was a wicked smile, perfectly befitting a woman of such absolute power, with such an overwhelming upper hand.

I thought she reminded me of someone.

Ah yes, Kanami-san. It was that same sort of "Didn't you know that?" kind of smile. But why would a nongenius like Iria-san have a similar smile to Ibuki Kanami-san?

"You think murder must be punished? But imagine you set some food in front of a mouse, and every time the mouse tries to eat it, it gets an electric shock. What do you think the mouse does?"

"Mice are capable of learning, so it would probably stop trying to eat."

"Wrong. Mice are capable of learning, so it would eat the parts of the food that aren't electrified."

"Humans aren't mice."

"And mice aren't humans." She clapped both her hands together. "Gee, as long as we're discussing this, maybe you'll answer this for me. Why is it wrong to kill people?"

It was the kind of question you might ask a junior high school student.

She didn't seem to be joking.

"Because it's against the law, because it's easier to function in society if you believe that, because I don't want to be killed myself."

"All of the above lack persuasive power."

"I agree. So this is my answer: there is no reason. You need a reason *to* kill someone. Like maybe you were pissed off, or you just wanted to kill the person or whatever, but nobody kills without some reason. But it's not something you choose, right? To kill or not to kill? That's not something you choose. That's just drivel that people with a Hamlet complex spout. The instant you embrace such doubts, you cease to be human."

Am I who suffers noble?

What a joke.

"Killing is wrong," I said. "That's an absolute. You don't need a reason."

"Hmm, is that right?" She nodded with blatant insincerity. "I suppose I can understand where you're coming from. But if we knew who the killer was, this case would be closed. Once Aikawa gets here, we'll find out who that is."

"I don't know this Aikawa-san."

"But I do. Isn't that enough? Akari, tell him when Aikawa-san's coming."

"In three days," Akari-san answered, still without making eye contact with me. "We asked Aikawa-san to come earlier than planned. So . . ."

"There you have it. If we knew who the killer was, of course you could just leave. You're here on this island because you're a suspect. That's the only reason a talentless, mediocre boy such as yourself is here. Speaking of which, you didn't have an alibi when Ibuki-san was killed *or* when Sonoyama-san was killed, did you?"

Thunk. I placed my still-more-than-half-full cup of tea back in its saucer, let out a deliberate sigh, and slowly rose to my feet.

"Please excuse me. I think we're speaking completely different languages here."

"Indeed," she sneered. "There's your exit."

"Teruko, see him back to his room," Rei-san said to Teruko-san sitting next to me. "So that he's not all alone. You shouldn't have a problem with that, right?"

With a quick nod, Teruko-san got up from the sofa. I didn't fully understand what Rei-san had meant by that nor how to react to it, but nevertheless Teruko advanced out of the room on her own. I scrambled after her, leaving Iria-san's room behind as well.

By the time I got out to the hallway, Teruko-san was already quite a ways ahead of me. What kind of an escort sped out the door ahead of the guest? As usual, I couldn't read her mind at all. And it wasn't just a matter of her doing things at her own pace. I accelerated to catch up with her.

But more important . . .

My conversation with Iria-san really hadn't gone anywhere at all. I had more or less expected that, but still I was surprised at how quickly it had died. It seemed Iria-san really trusted this Aikawa-san. But did such amazing detectives really exist in this world?

I hoped so.

I sincerely hoped so.

No, I was wishing for it.

Praying.

"Maybe that's all nonsense, too."

I let out another sigh. I would just have to try again. It didn't seem likely that I would be able to progress very far without the cooperation of the owner of this mansion. It was nothing to brag about, but I could be surprisingly determined. And I was a sore loser. The worst of the worst sore losers. There was no way I would give up that easily.

Huh?

Did somebody say something just now? I could have sworn I had heard someone's voice. I looked around the hall, but nobody was around besides Teruko-san and me. It must have been my imagination. My ears were playing tricks on me. Maybe I was losing it.

Hmm . . .

No.

It was the sound of a voice.

Which meant . . .

There was just one other, highly, *highly* unlikely possibility. I knew that it was nearly impossible, logically speaking, but could it have been? Was it possible?

"Teruko-san, did you say something?"

By any chance?

She stopped upon hearing my question.

"I said it would be better for you to just die."

I was speechless.

It was the first time she had ever spoken in front of me, and I never would have guessed it would be a line such as "it would be better for you to just die." That was just too much. Was she for real?

And then she turned to me and stared from behind those dark glasses, perfectly still.

It was an accusing gaze, and I couldn't help but wince. We stood like that for a while, her staring me down, but realizing I didn't have the perseverance to beat her, I decided to just ignore her and keep on walking. As I tried to pass, she grabbed me by the arm and tightly clenched it.

Squeeze.

It felt like an electric shock had run through my elbow.

Without releasing my arm, she pulled me into a nearby room and shut the door behind her. She forced me onto the sofa. From there she sat down so that we were face-to-face, and removed her black glasses.

"Those are just for show?"

"They're so we can be told apart."

She raised her face.

Her voice was exactly the same as Akari-san and Hikari-san's.

That clear, beautiful voice.

"Is that right?"

"No, I'm lying. I just don't want to look at your face."

"No, I'm lying. I just wanted to see you make *that* face."

"Can I help you with something?"

Unable to figure out her intentions, I knew that it would be bad to get swallowed up in this bizarre situation, so I tried my best to seize the initiative by asking questions. But she just sat there looking around the room without giving any response.

"I'll give you a word of advice," she suddenly said, continuing to ignore my question. It was as if she were talking to a ghost behind me. "You'd be best to live on your own. When you're around other people, you cause trouble for them."

The worst part was, without her glasses, she was completely indistinguishable from Akari-san and Hikari-san. Being told this kind of stuff by not only Maki-san but now her, too, was, to be honest, unpleasant.

I felt like I'd been betrayed.

"A person who does nothing but bother other people should just stop being a person altogether. If you can't do that, then you've got to go on living alone. That's what I think."

"Why are you saying this?"

"But I'm the same way."

A clear answer.

Her expression showed no change.

Not even a flicker.

"But you're here with other people and—"

"We've stopped being people."

We.

Exactly who did that include?

"This morning, Akari was rude to you. I apologize." She changed the subject without any segue. And her pale expression and her tone of voice remained unchanged.

"Why are you apologizing?"

"That was me."

"Huh?"

She continued, oblivious to my confusion.

"It wasn't really *me* per se, but it was my body. The three of us all share these three bodies. All three of us have three personalities each, and each of us has the same personalities and memories. So although the one screaming at you this morning was Akari, it was really my body."

"You're lying."

"Yes."

She kept a completely straight face. What was up with this girl? She kept throwing me crazy curveballs. I didn't know where she was going with this at all.

"Now then, enough with the chitchat."

And she thought this was just chitchat.

"Let me get to the point. I don't think it's very wise to be yakking on and on about the police around my mistress. She can be quite patient, but everyone has a breaking point."

"Why is Iria-san being so stubborn about it anyway? She says it's to keep the peace here, but I can't help but think there's more to it than that."

And hadn't the peace already been broken? She didn't seem to be interested in peace in the slightest.

"You really want to know?"

"I do."

Teruko-san stood up.

She came over beside me. She leaned up against me. She was stuck to me. Her body was all the way up on me.

"It's because . . . no criminal likes the police," she said, her voice completely devoid of tone or cadence. "That's why."

I was at a loss for words for a moment, not quite clear what she meant.

"Surely you've wondered why my mistress is on this island. Why do you think she's here?"

"Well, with that personality of hers—"

"She messed up."

She was being a little sparse on the details, so I had no idea where the conversation was headed. How could triplets raised in the exact same environment have such completely different personalities? It really was like multiple personality disorder.

"Huh? What do you mean by 'messed up'?"

"Kunagisa-san can't handle extreme vertical motion. That's why you're here, yes?"

"Yeah, that's right." I guess she wasn't much for flattery. "Is something wrong with that?"

"My mistress is the opposite of that," she said eloquently.

It was almost like she was reading it right out of a script. And a fairly dry reading at that.

"That's why she's on this completely deserted island."

She immediately continued.

"Have you ever seen my mistress's left arm? If you saw the scars all over her wrist you would understand, too."

The scars . . . on her wrist?

As dry and monotone as her voice was, it was deadly serious as well.

"They called it the abuse syndrome. I'm sure even you've heard of it?"

Abuse syndrome. She must have meant DLLR syndrome. Indeed I had heard of it. A form of autism in which the person *can't exist* without harming him- or herself as well as others. To be more specific, it was at the high end of the autism spectrum. At any rate, it was an exceptionally bad, impossibly unsavory, extraordinarily atrocious type of mental disorder.

In my time at the program I had read some literature about it, but I had never actually witnessed a case of it in real life, though I knew someone who had. As he had put it, "a person capable of killing without bearing any sense of guilt is truly a scary thing."

Truly scary indeed.

Was she saying *that* was Iria-san?

But DLLR syndrome was such a rare condition that its very existence was the subject of great suspicion. It was a fairly compulsive condition, so it was supposedly extremely rare. There hadn't been a single case of it in Japan, and even in the States there had only been a small, countable sample. But I guess that's the Law of Great Numbers at work again.

"Teruko-san, that's—"

"Just as we are triplets, my mistress also has a twin, Mistress Odette."

Iliad and Odyssey.

That explained that.

"Is that right? So what's her sister doing now?"

"She's dead."

"You mean it, right?"

"I mean it," she said. "And the one who killed Mistress Odette was none other than Mistress Iria. Do you understand? Do you understand what that means? Have you grasped the logic here? It means that you've just insulted my mistress with your filthy mouth. 'Murder is despicable, no matter what the reason,' huh?"

"I didn't really mean to—"

"Your intentions are irrelevant in this case. At any rate, I presume you understand why she won't call the police now? If you understand, please go back to your room. And please stop making waves."

Without another moment's hesitation, she got up from the couch. I could tell from her disposition that this conversation was over.

But oh, oh Teruko-san . . .

"Don't make waves"?

That was *my* line.

"Teruko-san!" I blurted spontaneously after her.

Contrary to my every expectation, she stopped in her tracks by the door.

"What?"

"Like . . ."

Like . . .

Liiiike . . .

"Like . . . say there was a kid who spent the first ten years of his life locked in the basement without communicating with a single person, including his own kin. Can you imagine what that kid would grow up to be like?"

She didn't answer.

Naturally I wasn't hoping for an actual answer.

I just thought I'd try asking.

This girl here. This quiet, sallow-faced girl, living her life in silence. To me, she was probably . . .

"You and I are totally different," she said in a fairly harsh tone.

It was like she could read my mind.

She spoke without even looking back.

"Don't you dare make me out to be related to you in some way. It's disgusting and it makes me nauseous and it's an incredible nuisance."

"Sorry to hear that."

"You have nothing to belong to in this whole world. Not just here, *the whole world*. If you'd like me to put it simply: you're a popped cork," she said.

"That's actually more than I wanted to hear, especially from you."

"It had to be me who said it, because nobody else will." She didn't look back. She continued all the same. "It seems you still think you don't understand why Himena-san picks on you so much, but the reason is obvious. It's because she can see what's in your mind. Nobody likes filthy things."

"I'm saying you're filthy."

"No need to repeat that . . . I'm fully aware of it."

"Oh, you're aware of it? And yet you manage to go on living. Well, that's the spirit. That must take a lot of willpower. That's worthy of respect. Or could it be that you think there's someone out there who will *like* you even after you've revealed yourself to them? Do you actually believe someone out there will choose you? Then you really are a popped cork."

There was nothing to say. Her words echoed. They were too heavy for me. I was going to collapse. Fall to pieces.

"How dare you barge into other people's lives when you're harboring such a monster inside yourself? You're lower than an insect. You're shameless. The world isn't that forgiving. How grossly conceited you are. And *that's* why—"

She opened the door. Then, for a moment, she looked back at me.

It was . . .

The expression of a woman staring at the object of her truest heartfelt loathing. It was an ice-cold look.

"You should just die."

Ka-thunk.

The sound of inorganic matter.

The door closed.

The power drained from my body. It was like the feeling you have when your shackles are removed, but without the sense of liberation.

"Jesus."

What a circus. I felt as if I were going to be crushed. Completely pulverized.

"This is the nonsense to end all nonsense, seriously."

Left all alone, I sat and thought.

Now what was it? I tried to recall everything she had said. Unlike Akane-san's conversation the previous night, there was no theorizing this time. There was no reasoning, no explaining, just the naked truth thrust in my face.

"Oh man, that did me some damage for real." I shook my head.

Don't think about it. There are other things to be thinking about now. I got up from the sofa and left the room. Looking around the hallway, not even Teruko-san's shadow remained. She was pretty light on her feet. Maybe that was another way in which she resembled me.

Anyway, all that mattered now was the information Teruko-san had left me with. The scars on Iria-san's wrist.

Her "background." The fact that she had killed her sister . . . and in so doing had been exiled to this island. Her abuse syndrome. Autism.

Thinking of that, surely it was clear why she wouldn't call the police.

"Wait a minute. Hold it."

A revelation. I had seen Iria-san changing clothes right before my eyes yesterday. The first time she had granted me an audience. But there was not a scratch on her wrist. Not that I was staring at just her limbs the whole time, but surely I would have noticed such an imposing scar if it had really been there.

"Wait wait wait . . ." I stopped in my tracks, scratching my head. "What the hell is this?"

Essentially, Teruko-san was a big fat liar.

Just like me.

2

On the way back to Kunagisa's room, I ran into Team Maki-san, Shinya-san, and Yayoi-san. They were apparently on their way to eat. I was a little jealous; with Yayoi-san on their team, they could eat amazing food whenever they wanted. Not that I had any complaints about Hikari-san's cooking.

"Ahaha . . . *boy*. Ahahahahahahaha. Aaaaahahahahaha . . . ha."

At the very sight of me, Maki-san burst into laughter. I was beyond finding this rude anymore. It was no less expected than the changing of the seasons.

"What is it this time, Maki-san? You're always so bustling with energy."

"Ahaha. Young man, it looks like Teruko-san did a real number on you. Oh, my stars. That's what you get."

"How do you know?"

"You're still asking me that? Thanks for an amusing show, Mr. Spineless. You must never get bored. I'm jealous."

For sure, Maki-san must have led a boring life. She knew all that had happened, all that was happening, and all that would happen. It was like watching a nonstop stream of movies where you already know the ending. There was no doubt that that sucked the fun out of living.

"That's not exactly true," she teased. Was she drunk? She seemed oddly high. The inside of her head must've looked like *mentaiko*.

Gah, she glared at me.

"Say, should you really be alone at a time like this in a place like this?" Shinya-san still looked a little blue, but he seemed to have calmed down quite a bit, and he was no longer pale. Even though it can be cruel sometimes, in the end, time really *is* kind to us all. "Kunagisa-chan and Hikari-san must be a little edgy on their own. They're just petite little things. And Hikari-san is the prime suspect right now, right? Your beloved Kunagisa-chan could be in danger."

He seemed to be half joking, but it was clear that he really was worried about me. I bowed to him in gratitude.

"Eehehehe. You'll have to excuse us now, Mr. Half-Baked. Don't think too hard," Maki-san teased, and then turned her back on me. Shinya-san shot her a look.

"If you're feeling responsible for Sonoyama-san's death, I don't think you should worry about it. You did everything that was in your power. You couldn't have done anything else. You did your best," he said to me.

"Thank you so much." I bowed and thanked him.

"Well, see you later." With that, he turned around as well.

Yayoi-san had given me a few odd looks that seemed to mean something, but with no more than a slight nod of her head, she went off with the other two and headed for the dining room.

"What was that about?"

There wasn't anything suspicious per se, but something was strange.

"Eh, I guess it's not really anything to worry about," I muttered to myself.

Upon returning to the room, I found Kunagisa nose-deep in busted-up computer parts while Hikari-san was doing some cleaning. Word had it that Hikari-san was a total neat-freak. Come to think of it, she did always seem to be cleaning. I supposed it was one form of workaholism. Was there not a single normal person on this island?

"Hey hey, Ii-chan. You're just in time."

"For what?"

"Putting my hair up."

Gotcha. I approached her from behind. I decided to give her a whole bunch of mini-braids, and began braiding together small portions of hair.

"Ahhhh," she sighed with pleasure.

"Tomo-san. Is it okay if I clean up that mess?"

"Don't call it a mess. I can still use some of these parts, so I'm retrieving them now. You gotta reuse stuff. Recycle, recycle, *for Mother Earth*! Recycling's important, y'know. Mm-hmm. But what should I do, huh? Maybe I can make a secret weapon to stop that killer."

She sure knew how to keep her chin up. Not that I wanted to be like her, but you had to admire her positive thinking. Even if it was just because she had never known negative emotions.

Sigh.

"Oh, right. Hikari-san, do you have a memo pad or something? And something to write with?"

"They're in that cabinet. Do you need them?"

"I want to write up an outline of the current situation."

We had made an alibi chart yesterday, but the data had been smashed to smithereens along with the computers.

Therefore I wanted to create a new chart that included up-dated information.

"I see," she said and headed to the cabinet.

"Oh, hey. Tomo, I forgot to tell you, remember that painting? I figured out what was strange about it."

"Hmm? Oh, yeah, you were saying something about that, weren't you? So what was it?"

"The watch."

"Watch?"

"Yes, the watch. When I was modeling for the picture in Kanami-san's atelier, I hadn't been wearing a watch. It was broken and I gave it to you to repair. So there wasn't anything on my wrist.

"Nonetheless, on the canvas, there was a watch painted onto it."

Kunagisa looked puzzled for just a moment, then reverted back to her usual expression and delivered a stock question. "Mmm. Don't you think it's just an error? I can't imagine it's very important."

"Well, yeah, maybe, but . . ."

"Which?"

"How about a subject and predicate?"

"The watch display. Was it the blank one, or the one after I fixed it that displays backwards?"

"Oh, well, actually, I'm sort of faced inward like this, so I couldn't tell."

"Mmm," she nodded. After a moment's thought, she said, "Yeah, I think it's just an error. More important, I thought of a clue, maybe. Akane-chan's murder was like . . . her headless body was all, errr . . ."

"Errr?"

"Her hand was kinda . . ."

She tilted her head to the side and folded her arms.

"Well, not her hand, but her fingers. There was something unnatural, I mean *really* unnatural about them, I think. . . .

Aw, man, my memory capacity has hit its peak. It feels like there's a big mosaic in my head. Hey, Hikari-chan, did you notice anything weird about her fingers?"

"Hmm . . ."

Hikari-san, who had returned at some point, sat down on the carpet next to Kunagisa so that she was facing me.

"Sorry for the wait. Here's some paper and a pen."

"Thanks."

I took the supplies from her and, while recalling the chart we had made yesterday, whipped up a new alibi list for the Ibuki Kanami and Sonoyama Akane murders, including everyone on the island.

> *Ibuki Kanami*
> *(Murdered)*
>
> *Sonoyama Akane*
> *Before earthquake: X*
> *After earthquake: X*
> *(Murdered)*
>
> *Kunagisa Tomo*
> *Before earthquake: O (Ji-chan, Hikari, Maki, Shinya)*
> *After earthquake: X*
>
> *O (can't go down stairs alone)*
>
> *Sashirono Yayoi*
> *Before earthquake: O (Iria, Rei)*
> *After earthquake: X*
>
> *X (sleeping)*
>
> *Chiga Akari*
> *Before earthquake: Δ (Teruko)*
> *After earthquake: X*
>
> *O (on the mainland)*

Chiga Hikari
Before earthquake: O *(Ji-chan, Tomo, Maki, Shinya)*
After earthquake: X

X

Chiga Teruko
Before earthquake: Δ *(Akari)*
After earthquake: X

O *(on the mainland)*

Sakaki Shinya
Before earthquake: O *(Ji-chan, Tomo, Maki, Hikari)*
After earthquake: O *(Maki)*

O *(Maki)*

Handa Rei
Before earthquake: O *(Iria, Yayoi)*
After earthquake: Δ *(Iria)*

Δ *(Iria)*

Himena Maki
Before earthquake: O *(Ji-chan, Tomo, Hikari, Shinya)*
After earthquake: O *(Shinya)*

O *(Shinya)*

Akagami Iria
Before earthquake: O *(Rei, Yayoi)*
After earthquake: Δ *(Rei)*

Δ *(Rei)*

Phew. Or something like that. Staring at the chart, I let out a sigh.

"Alibis, huh? But y'know, this doesn't really mean all that much, does it? We've pretty much shelved the idea of it being a cooperative crime up until now, but if you consider that possibility, this chart doesn't mean squat. Especially looking at these two- and three-person alibi testimonies."

There was also the possibility that people other than the killer had lied just so they wouldn't be suspected, and if you considered that, this charted information was even harder to swallow.

Well aware of the futility of it all, I decided nonetheless to write up a similar summary outline of the murder incidents themselves.

FIRST INCIDENT

Victim:
Ibuki Kanami

Conditions:
Sealed room
River of paint (solved)

Time of incident:
Night
Presumably after earthquake

Notes:
Decapitated body
Killer unknown

SECOND INCIDENT

Victim:
Sonoyama Akane

Conditions:
Sealed room
Open window in a high location (unsolved)

Time of incident:
Between 2:00 and 9:30 a m

Notes:
Decapitated body

"And . . . killer unknown."

I finished writing and put the pen down.

"You're forgetting about the third incident, Ii-chan," Kunagisa immediately objected. "The Poor Kunagisa-chan Incident."

"Oh, right. It pales in comparison, but that's a mystery, too, huh."

"Don't say that! To me this is a greater tragedy than having my head cut off! As long as they've gone this far, I wish they *would* cut my head off!"

"Okay, okay." I picked up the pen again.

THIRD INCIDENT

Victim:
Kunagisa Tomo('s computers)

Conditions:
Unsealed room
No lock, enterable by anyone

Time of incident:
Between 10:00 a.m. and the end of breakfast
However, everybody in the mansion was together at that time. A time-sealed room?

Notes:
Destructor's goal presumed to be the destruction of image data taken from the scene of Ibuki Kanami's death.

"A time-sealed room, huh?"

The first incident involved a room sealed by a river of paint. The second, a room sealed by an unreachable window.

A room sealed in terms of height. And the third incident was sealed in terms of time.

"The second, third, and fourth dimension, huh?"

"That sure makes it sound like a crime of enormous scope. Say, Hikari-san, this question pretty much completely undermines any pretense we've had up until now, but . . . is it possible there are other people on this island?"

"It is not," she stated confidently. "There's only one spot on the whole island where ships can dock, so I think I can say that for certain."

"I see."

But if that were really true, then it would have been absolutely impossible for this to have happened to Kunagisa's computers. With enough wit and wisdom, a person could feasibly get through a sealed plane or conquer height, but time was the one dominion impenetrable by man.

"So I wonder if there's some kind of trick to this as well. Like a remote control or something. Mmm, but this is obviously the work of a human being."

"Hikari-san, is it possible that one or two people maybe slipped away in the midst of all the confusion of discovering the body? I mean there *was* a headless dead body right before our eyes. Maybe someone took advantage of the situation and walked off while we were distracted."

"I . . . don't think so . . ."

Hikari-san was still unconvinced. Even I couldn't help but scratch my head at the idea, and I was the one who had brought it up. In reality, we probably would've noticed if someone had disappeared from the room.

"First incident. Anybody could have done it—that is, if you consider the possibility of a cooperative crime. But we've at least figured out *how* they did it, and we know it wasn't really a 'sealed room' after all. Now, second incident. This time, we have no idea how they did it."

"But I, as an exception, could have done it," Hikari-san said.

I nodded. "And then the third incident. *Nobody* could have done it. Moreover, there was no possible way it could have happened."

The incident itself was rapidly growing more complicated. This didn't bode well for the *next* incident.

"Jesus, what the hell kind of a cycle is this?"

"Well, I don't think this was all planned out intentionally. Hmm, but it doesn't feel right to write it all off as a coincidence, either."

"Anyway, let's stop thinking about all this disheartening stuff," I said. "Alibis, sealed rooms. Tricks, gimmicks, setups, fakes. Whatever. Let's just agree that someone is using some unimaginable method to fool us all."

"Maybe it's a virtual machine."

"Yeah, that."

I guess.

They often say in old mystery novels that it's harder to make a puzzle than to solve one, but I don't think that's true. Creating a puzzle or trick or what have you is far easier. In creating a puzzle, you're free to display events from whatever angle you please, completely catering to your own convenience. Solving the puzzle, on the other hand, can only be done from that one presented angle.

So for now we just had to place the issue aside.

"But don't you think we should at least consider alibis? That's pretty much all the information we have right now," Hikari-san said. "And if we start making emotionally charged arguments, everyone will become suspicious. I mean, didn't Sonoyama-san become the prime suspect after Ibuki-san was murdered because they hated each other so much? But look at what happened because of that."

"Yeaaah, but— It really would've made sense if Akane-san was the killer."

And now Akane-san was dead, too.

"What about the thought that Sonoyama-san killed Ibuki-san, and then someone killed her in revenge?"

"If that were the case, then I guess Shinya-san would be the most likely to have killed her. He was Kanami-san's caretaker and closest friend."

"But Shinya-chan had an alibi. Even if you set that aside, how would he have known Akane-chan killed her?"

"Maybe he didn't, maybe he just had a hunch. Mistaken revenge may not happen every day, but it's not unheard of. If you think about it, what's the deal with Shinya-san and Maki-san? They've got alibis two days in a row. In the middle of the night. Don't you think their having alibis is conversely kind of suspicious?"

"It is a little, huh? Maybe they're synchronizing stories in secret. But you know, Himena-san doesn't really seem the type."

Himena Maki. The indescribable fortune-teller with superhuman abilities. The absolute absolutist, able to gaze upon the inner workings of men's minds and hear any and all things. Something about her resembled Kunagisa. It was weird.

"What's up with you, Ii-chan? Have you fallen for Maki-chan or something?"

"Geez, don't say that. But you know, a spaced-out woman like her can't be expected to have the best common sense."

Man, this really was all futile. I felt like we had already considered every possibility. It was like we were stranded. What else was there left to think about?

"It kind of seems like maybe Akane-san knew she was going to be killed."

"Huh?" Hikari-san leaned forward in surprise. "What do you mean?"

"It just seemed that way. Last night, I had a conversation with her through the door, and at the time, well, it was like she was at peace. She was quoting Ryokan and stuff. It was really out of character."

"Hmm, I wonder if she knew who the killer was," Kunagisa said.

Indeed, that was a possibility. She *was* Sonoyama Akane of the ER3 system's Seven Fools. Even without conducting an investigation, if she had a hunch about who the killer was, it was pretty much sure to be right.

"By the way, Hikari-san. I was just talking with Teruko-san—"

"What?!" She was even more shocked than before, as if I'd just made some ungodly remark. No, not shocked, exactly. It was more like she was thinking, "Why would you tell me such a blatant lie?!"

"Y-you mean . . . Teruko talked?"

"Yeah. I was pretty surprised, too, but the real problem was *what* she said."

I explained to Hikari-san and Kunagisa what Teruko-san had told me. Of course I cut out the latter half. I was never one to go around boasting about my own faults.

"So what does it mean, Hikari-san? How much of it was true?"

Hikari-san wore a completely perplexed expression as she muddled out a vague response. "Um," she muttered. "Um, well, um . . ."

"Akari-san was ranting about something strange this morning as well. 'I'm so tired of this' or something like that. What was she talking about?"

She was still stumbling over a response. At last, she looked up at me, seeming to have made up her mind. But still, her eyes darted back and forth as she deliberated for another moment. Finally, she opened her mouth.

"It's all true."

Huh.

Admittedly, that was not the answer I expected.

This time it was my turn to be speechless. It was *all* true? Huh? What did she just say?

"I'll talk because it's come to this, and because I choose to trust you. And because I owe you." Hikari-san fell silent once again, and then, looking more lost than ever, finally continued. "Yes, my mistress is technically a criminal. We serve her in full awareness of that."

"And that's why you won't call the police?"

"We just work for her. We don't do anything else. Ever since coming to this island, various things have happened. That's how we eventually met Aikawa-san, who you've been hearing about."

Various things? What various things?

The incident on this island.

Come to think of it . . . Come to think of it, the other night . . .

"Hey, Tomo."

"Yeah, Ii-chan?"

"I seem to recall you saying something the other night along the lines of 'I'm interested in the incident that happened on this island,' but is this just another figment of my awesome memory?"

"Nope."

"Then you knew?"

"Yup," she nodded with a giggle. "It's pretty well-known info. Lots of people know, but nobody ever talks about it. Not a lot of people are looking to make enemies with the Akagami Foundation."

So, Kunagisa's hobbies hadn't changed since the good old days. Maybe the passing of five years wasn't enough to alter her nature.

"Actually, it was mixed in with the rest of Chii-kun's information, but I thought it might be better to keep it a secret from you, so . . ."

"Why?"

"'Cuz I knew you'd make that face."

Aha.

Come on . . .

I was drained.

Pallidly, falteringly, painfully, Hikari-san continued.

"Once we started planning this 'salon,' my mistress was able to calm down a bit, but . . . I can understand Akari's feelings of frustration. But you know, this is our job."

A job, huh? If she really meant that, it was quite a statement. I was honestly impressed. I respected any person who lived solely to fulfill their role, regardless of what that role was. It was something I could never do.

So Hikari-san, too, was truly immersed in the deepest depths of her abyss.

"Huh, so that's the deal, huh?"

But what did that mean? If the killer knew all this and knew Iria-san couldn't call the police, then . . .

Then the remarkable boldness, audaciousness, and fearlessness of his or her actions all suddenly made sense.

"Okay, Hikari-san, well . . ."

Just as I was about to ask for the details of this famous island incident, there came a knock at the door.

It was Yayoi-san.

3

"I have to go to the bathroom." That's what Yayoi-san had told Maki-san and Shinya-san in the middle of lunch before breaking off from her team and coming here. It was a pretty typical and hackneyed lie, and Maki-san could read minds anyway, and even under-the-weather Shinya-san probably could've seen through it, but one look at Yayoi-san's sickly blue expression, and they probably wouldn't have called her a liar if she said a pack of devils were on their way to the island on turtleback.

She sat down on the sofa and said nothing.

She seemed strangely wary of Hikari-san's presence. Maybe she, too, thought Hikari-san was the killer. It wasn't such an unexpected assumption, to be honest.

"Can we assume you came here because you wanted to tell us something, Yayoi-san?" It didn't look like this was going anywhere on its own, so I went ahead and asked.

"Yes," she nodded weakly.

"Um, you two are doing some investigating, right?"

"Well, that's the plan. It's become a personal matter at this point, after all," I said, looking at the computer parts in the corner of the room. "What about it?"

"Well, if you're investigating, I suppose the facts need to be accurate, right?"

"Yeah, well, naturally."

"If you proceeded from here with inaccurate information, there could be a third incident, right?"

"Fourth."

"That's right, Yayoi-san." We ignored Kunagisa's protest. "That's the situation. Um, Yayoi-san, I don't really understand what it is you're trying to say. It looks like you came here to help us, but am I wrong? Did you come here because you don't like being on a team with Shinya-san and Maki-san?"

"No, that's not it," she mumbled. "It's just . . . I-I told a lie I can't take back."

"A lie?"

"Yes. That night . . . I really was with Iria-san talking. It was only up until the earthquake, but that much is an honest fact," she said. "But Handa-san . . . *Handa-san wasn't there.*"

Hikari-san's face went stiff.

Rei-san—Handa Rei.

It was suddenly clear why Yayoi-san seemed so nervous around Hikari-san and why she had seemed so unnaturally detached since the other day, staying holed up in her room all the time.

The ice was melting.

The other morning during the alibi check, Iria-san had said herself that she, Yayoi-san, and Rei-san were together. Everyone else was questioned one by one, but when Yayoi-san's turn came, Iria-san spoke for her. I had thought this was simply because they had been together, but it seemed that wasn't why after all.

Iria-san . . .

Akagami Iria was covering for Handa Rei.

Yayoi-san slumped down with her shoulders drooped. It was like she had been relieved of a terrible burden or freed of a curse.

"Why?"

Why had she kept silent about such an important detail up until now? It was a question I was in no position to ask. This was Iria-san's island and Iria-san's mansion, and it was Iria-san who had invited Yayoi-san here, and she was, after all, *Akagami Iria*. If Iria-san said, "I was with Yayoi-san and Rei-san," who could argue? Who could just call her a liar? Like anyone could say that.

"I didn't think it was a big deal at the time," Yayoi-san finally said. "I just figured she was looking out for her own. But thanks to that, Akane-san became the only person without an alibi, and she was locked away and . . . killed."

She was speaking like a burst dam. I sat and listened in silence. Kunagisa and Hikari-san did likewise.

"And then regarding last night, Iria-san said she was with Rei-san again. All night long. But who could believe that? She said they were discussing what to do from here on, but why would that take all night?"

"Well, it's possible."

"I don't think so. Just because someone lied the first time doesn't mean they lied the second time, but the chances are pretty high, right? And Hikari-san"—Yayoi-san glared over at Hikari-san—"Hikari-san is one of Iria-san's inner circle, too, but Iria-san didn't even try to cover for her, did she? Why is that? Why would she cover for Rei-san but not for Hikari-san? Isn't it because she knew there was no need to cover for Hikari-san? Isn't it, conversely, because she knew *who the killer was*?"

"Are you saying Rei-san is the killer?"

I was surprised by this. I didn't think the conversation was heading in this direction. But Yayoi-san seemed absolutely serious.

"Certainly her alibi is rather dubious now—that is, if we can believe what you're saying."

"It's the truth. Whether you believe me or not, it's the truth," she said. Hikari-san looked like she had something to say, but as if having realized something, she remained silent. She chewed on her lip with a painful expression.

"Let's just hold on a second here."

If Rei-san didn't have an alibi that night, how did that change things? Maybe not all that much, but the fact that Iria-san had lied was unarguably huge.

Rei-san wasn't in Iria-san's room that night. That meant they weren't together after the earthquake, either.

Which meant . . .

"Mmm. Hey, Yayoi-chan."

"What is it, Kunagisa-san?"

"Why do you think Rei-chan is the killer? She's the head maid. She's the confidante. She's a hotshot. She's even closer to Iria-chan than Hikari-chan and the others are. So maybe Iria-chan just covered for her out of friendship. And we really don't know if she was lying the second time, even if she was lying the first time. And if Rei-chan really was the murderer, then that means Iria-chan knew about it, right? Why would she cover for—"

"What if Iria-san *ordered* the murder?"

Gulp, someone swallowed audibly. For all I knew, it could have been me.

"I don't think that's the case. Kanami-chan and Akane-chan were both invited here as guests. What's the point in bringing people over and then killing them?"

"What if she invited them here *to* kill them?" Yayoi-san pressed on. "Iria-san invited people here. And then those people were killed. If you look at it that way, it's not so un-thinkable."

Was Iria-san using Rei-san in a plot to kill those two, as well as possibly a third, fourth, and fifth? It seemed like a highly unrealistic notion, but there was no proof against it.

Yeah. And on that note, hadn't I just heard the proof *for* it from Teruko-san and Hikari-san?

Handa Rei.

The head maid.

As Hikari-san, Akari-san, and Teruko-san's boss, she was in the closest position to Iria-san herself. So how about it? Was that the answer? Was that what it all came down to?

Akagami Iria.

Named for that great ancient Greek classic epic, Homer's *Iliad*, the work that told of the great war with Troy over Helen. All of the characters in that epic thought they were being manipulated by the gods. Was that it? If that was the answer . . .

As I thought, Yayoi-san continued on.

"Do you know why I was called here?"

"Because you're a genius, right?"

She grimaced.

"Well, Ibuki-san was a painter—a magnificent artist. Sonoyama-san was a scholar—fine. Maki-san is a fortune-teller—whatever. Kunagisa-san's an engineer, yes? That's wonderful. But I'm a chef. Unless she's some kind of gourmet cuisine nut, why would she call such a person here? I don't think cooking is really that special."

I was silent. Hearing her say that, there was no possible response I could give.

"And do you know why Ibuki-san and Sonoyama-san had their heads cut off?"

"That's a sudden change in topic."

"No, it's not," Yayoi-san said with a stern expression and tone to match. "*You are what you eat.* It's an idea that exists in Chinese cuisine. If your liver is bad, you should eat liver. If your stomach is bad, eat stomachs. In other words, if part of you isn't working right, you should eat that same thing. I'm sure you've heard of this?"

"Hang on now, Yayoi-san. This is . . ."

This . . . This notion . . .

"Who called Ibuki-san and Sonoyama-san to this island? *Who?*" Yayoi-san screamed. Her voice reverberated throughout the room. The sound lingered in my ears. But I was so confused at this point I didn't even care.

Hold on . . . hold on a minute, here. Did she mean what I thought she meant? Just wait a second. Hold the phone. I'm begging you, just give me a little time.

"I'll say it one more time. No, I'll say it as many times as it takes. Why would the killer cut off their heads? Why would the killer take the heads with her? Where did she take them? And who was it who invited those two women here? Who brought these renowned geniuses here? What was inside those heads the killer carried off?"

If jewels are stolen from a murder scene, it probably means the killer was after the jewels. If cash is missing, he must've been after cash. Such thinking was just plain common sense.

And in this case, it was the victims' heads that were missing.

Yayoi-san continued. "Why was I invited here? Why was I, not an artist or a scholar or a fortune-teller or an engineer but a mere *chef*, invited to this island? Why have I been given special treatment and allowed to stay here indefinitely?" Her voice sounded like it was being squeezed out.

It was a voice seeking rescue.

She had probably been brooding over this. From the moment she had given her false testimony. From before Sonoyama-san was killed, and indeed the half day following her death as well, Yayoi-san had probably been thinking about it nonstop.

Yayoi-san turned toward Hikari-san and began her hopeless screaming once again.

"What . . . *Just what are they going to make me do?*"

Gulp—someone swallowed again.

This time it was definitely me.

Was it possible? Such a notion . . . Wasn't the acceptance of such a notion itself unforgivable?

If that was really what was going on, why now? It wasn't like this whole "salon" thing had just started. If that was Iria-san's little game, she would've done this in the past.

No, the five geniuses on this island right now were all world-class, top specialists in their respective fields. Had Iria-san been waiting for this exact timing?

"That's impossible!" Hikari-san shrieked. It was like she had exploded after holding it in until now. "The idea that my mistress would do such an inhuman thing, such a cruel thing now . . ."

"Now"?

I'm so tired of this.

The past.

Various things. So tired. Now. Why now? I'm so tired of this. Please don't make waves. I'm so tired. Tired, so tired. Even though I'm so tired.

But Yayoi-san didn't relent.

"I've been keeping an eye on Handa-san since yesterday morning," she said. "You know how the longer you watch someone, the more you start to notice their similarities to you, or you start to feel their humanity? Their humanness? Some kind of closeness. You know? It's like 'Oh, this person is just like me.' I felt that way with Iria-san. She's human, just like me. She lied, but she's still a human being. But Handa-san . . . That woman frightens me. How could I not be afraid of a woman like that whose whole life is an act?"

"That's—" Hikari-san interrupted with her head hung. "That's . . . that's . . . that's . . ."

But it seemed there was no end to that sentence. Even so, Hikari-san tried desperately to defend her mistress. In accordance with her duties. It was too heartbreaking—to the point that it was laughable.

"I see. Yayoi-san, I basically understand what you're trying to say. You're trying to say this, right?"

I tried my best to force my way into their conversation, but it was hopeless. Yayoi-san continued her relentless questioning.

"Akari-san and Teruko-san were on the mainland calling on a detective? Who can prove that? Who's the one who won't contact the police? Who's the one who won't let us leave this island? Maybe you were left out of the plans, Hikari-san, but where's the proof of that? They called you the prime suspect, didn't they? Where's the proof saying you aren't just a scapegoat here to shake things up? No, maybe you're in cahoots with Iria-san, here to make trouble for Kunagisa-san and—"

"Please stop this. Yayoi-san, that's enough," I said quietly. "Please stop insulting our friend. Kunagisa and I both dislike getting angry. But we're not afraid to do what we must."

My gaze was probably fairly cold, and she shivered for a moment at the sight of it. She had the same look of uneasiness that she had when she entered the room.

"I'm scared. I'm scared. I'm scared. I'm just scared."

"Yes, I understand that."

"This is a deserted island. There's nowhere to run. If this is all what I think it is, maybe I won't be killed. You weren't invited here as a genius, so you might not be killed, either.

But your dear friend Kunagisa-san is in danger. Not even God can guarantee that she won't be the next one to have her shoulders flattened, if you know what I mean. The time for leisurely investigations has already . . . I mean, I think we need to do something fast. I didn't come here to hiss at Hikari-san. I came here because Kunagisa-san is an engineer. Can you operate a boat, by any chance? If so, let's get out of here on that cruiser and—"

"Hold on." I held up my right hand. She looked up at me with a confused expression. Hikari-san eyed me curiously as well. Only Kunagisa remained staring off into space, a somewhat irritated expression on her face. I was probably making the same face.

Um, where was I? Why did I interrupt Yayoi-san?

Oh, right.

"Please say that again."

"Huh?"

"That thing you said. Say it again."

Yayoi-san tilted her head at me a bit.

"If so, let's get out of here on that cruiser—"

"Not that."

"Can you operate a boat, by any chance?"

"No, not that, either."

"Uh, I didn't come here to . . . yada yada yada?"

"No. Not that. Something grabbed me, but that wasn't it. Before that."

"I don't remember."

"Well remember. What did you say before that?"

"We need to do something fast. . . . The time for leisurely investigations has—"

"*No.* We already understand that. We need to do something fast? That's practically a catchphrase. I don't care about the stuff we already know. I think it was a little before you said that."

"That's all I got. That's as far as I can recall."

"Tomo!" I looked over at Kunagisa. "You remember, right?"

"Yup," she nodded.

She slashed her hand across the front of her neck.

"I'm gonna get my shoulders flattened."

"Bingo."

Yes. That. It had grabbed me. Was that because it suggested something I'd rather not imagine? Nope. It wasn't nearly something that trite. It was something totally, completely different.

Now this, *this* was the key. The Rosetta Stone.

"Um . . ."

"Silence please. I'm thinking. I think I'm on the right track. Definitely. It's simpler than the geography of Kyoto or Sapporo. We have a hypothesis and conclusion now, so all that's left to do is prove it."

I thought.

Kunagisa thought, too.

All the ingredients were probably there. I could sense it. Or we already had all the ingredients a while ago. They were all lined up in front of my face, to the point that it wouldn't have been strange if I had realized the truth as soon as Kunagisa's computers were smashed. The smashed computers weren't the key after all, they were another ingredient.

And now I had the key. This time, I had it.

And just as any door will open once you've obtained the key, so, too, would I soon arrive at a solution. It was like a zero-sum game. Like a simple maze with a watertight winning strategy. Kunagisa probably had it, too. The mountain of sand was almost complete.

"Now this really is nonsense."

And after a while . . .

"Is this it?" I muttered.

But this was . . .

"No way . . . this can't be right."

This couldn't be right. Like this could possibly be it. What logic was this?

But there were no contradictions, it was all consistent, it all made sense—it was complete. There was no other possibility left. It didn't look like there was any more sand to pile up, either.

Something felt uneasy. Something was strange. No matter how many mental checks I did, I couldn't feel satisfied about it, like the final question on an exam. I definitely wasn't wrong, but something felt off nonetheless. It was that kind of feeling. I couldn't shake it.

What was it . . . this vague, sickly feeling?

"What do you think, Tomo?"

"Mmm," she moaned.

"There's no 'what do you think' about it. There's only one possible train of thought. So that's why the fingers seemed strange, huh? But this means . . ."

It seemed Kunagisa had the same sense of anxiety. Yayoi-san and Hikari-san stared at the two of us like we were from Mars. Venus, maybe. I guess that's a trivial matter either way.

"I guess that's the only possibility, huh?" Kunagisa was first to fall before the reality of the situation. "I can't think of anything else. It must be the only possibility."

"Yeah. If there's only one possibility, it's got to be the right one, no matter how unbelievable it seems."

It looked as if we had to rely on selective thinking in the end. If Akane-san heard about it she surely would have gotten angry, but we no longer had to worry about that. At least insofar as this was in fact a case of serial murder committed by a person, there was only this one possibility. One possibility with one hundred percent odds.

Okay.

Time to just accept it.

I didn't like it at all, but this was reality, this was the

truth. And those were just my nonsense-ridden sentiments anyway.

"Looks like we've reached an agreement, Ii-chan," Kunagisa said. "So what now?"

"What now, indeed. Hmm, this place is a little too big." I continued my pondering. I was more cut out for something like this than Kunagisa was. I may not have been any good at actual shogi, but if this, too, was a sort of shogi problem, I had it down.

"Now then, Yayoi-san, Hikari-san, could I ask for a little bit of your cooperation?"

"Huh?" The lovely duo let out a collective question mark.

I rose to my feet. "The top of the inning is finally over. We're down by a lot of points, but it's not a called game yet. This is where we get that third out and launch our attack in the bottom of the inning."

"Yayoi-chan on first. Hikari-chan in center field. Yours truly as catcher and Ii-chan as pitcher."

Boing, Kunagisa jumped up off the bed and flashed a smile bright as the blue sky.

"Launching counterattack."

**Sashirono Yayoi,
Genius Chef**

3

A CROW'S WET FEATHERS

End it.

1

By the way.

In Russian, "the crow's wet feathers" supposedly means "the peak of despair." Given that, you could romantically describe this island as the ultimate destination for those in despair. Just as the opposite of affection isn't hatred, but indifference, the opposite of hope isn't despair. Surely the opposite of despair is apathetic acceptance of all things. That sheer apathy laced with the absolute conviction that allows you to approve of all things, saying, "Yeah, that's fine"—*that* is the opposite of hope.

Everything is here, so what more could I possibly need? This apathy I felt was way over the line of normality. The proverbial destination of all of one's emotions.

That noninterfering realm on the other side of the lake that we all view at some point or another with admiring eyes laced with envy. That domain on the other side of taboo, connected to reality by a big equals sign.

To reach said domain, you had to make many sacrifices. What's more, it was a one-way ticket with no guarantees.

However, even then, there are people who reach it— whether by some mistake, or through knowledge.

Ibuki Kanami, Sonoyama Akane, Sashirono Yayoi, Himena Maki, Akagami Iria, Chiga Akari, Chiga Hikari, Chiga Teruko, Handa Rei.

And Kunagisa Tomo . . .

This is all probably a big old heap of ridiculous mumbo-jumbo. Nothing but boring, worthless nonsense. And the continuation of this nonsense is unwholesome at best.

Really now, what kind of a clown was I?

"Have you figured something out?"

The fifth dinner assembly.

Teruko-san had her personal chores to attend to, so her seat was empty, but the other nine of us were all gathered together. Nine people. Until the day before yesterday, just two days ago, there were twelve of us surrounding this round table.

"Do I have to ask again? Kunagisa-san, you all are still doing some investigating, correct? Well, have you figured anything out?" Iria-san asked.

She seemed to be having an awful lot of fun. I'm sure she was. Of course it was fun.

Because she had probably created a whole world in her head. Because this island, this Wet Crow's Feather Island, was, in itself, her whole world.

"Shall I ask again?"

"We know absolutely, positively nothing at all," I answered. "So what about it? Is there a problem?"

"Oh, no. I was just thinking, I guess there's nothing we can do without a specialist after all," Iria-san said with apparent interest. "Well, I guess the best thing then is to continue operating in teams like this for the next three days."

"Three days?" Shinya-san said. "I must say, you seem to be expecting quite a bit from this person. Just what kind of person is this Aikawa-san, anyway? How did you meet?"

"That's a private matter," Iria-san smirked. "But I will tell you what kind of person. Hmm, what should I say? Aikawa-san is a very frightening person. Well, that's what you'd expect from the world's most powerful contractor. But also incredibly intelligent. I'm sure this case will be solved in no time. Hehehe, I really can't wait."

The detective, huh?

Solving the case before the lead detective even got here probably disqualified me as a supporting character, I thought. But my life was on the line here, too, and there were various complicated circumstances. I couldn't just sit around and wait for the main character to show up. It was his own fault for being late.

"Kekekeke," Maki-san snickered next to me.

She seemed to be having an awful lot of fun as well. I didn't know whether she was reading my thoughts or watching the whole farce. Surely it was at least one of those, but that probably wasn't the only reason she was laughing. Really, just who was this woman who was able to continue laughing even after knowing everything in the entire world?

She was probably deserving of respect. Still, I avoided eye contact.

"I'm told Aikawa-san will be here by the afternoon three days from now at the latest. After that, I'm sure everything will soon be—"

As Iria-san expounded over this detective of hers, she was interrupted by the sound of overturning flatware and pots banging together, accompanied by a screech.

"Enough!"

It was Yayoi-san.

Rising from her seat, Yayoi-san used her right arm to shove off the table all of the food she herself had made. She then proceeded to take the now dirty tablecloth and yank it, causing all the dishes to come toppling off the table and shatter. A string of ear-shattering noise echoed through the dining room.

"Enough of this!"

She banged her hands on the table.

"Sashirono-san . . ."

In an effort to settle her down, Hikari-san rose from her seat as well and approached her, but Yayoi-san gave her a violent shove.

"What is all this? Give me a break! I want out of this farce! Detectives? Sealed rooms? Decapitated corpses? This isn't some mystery novel. Don't you realize people are being killed? Why the hell are you eating during this kind of discussion? Their heads were cut off! Don't eat my food while you're talking about such a thing! You must all be crazy if you're able to stay so calm about all this! Why don't you care that people were killed? You're all disgusting! Since when was it okay to kill people in this country?"

"Sashirono-sa . . ." Hikari-san said from the floor. "Please calm down."

"*You're* the killer!" Yayoi-san screamed even louder. "It's obvious! We already know that! You were the only one with a key to that storage room, and you visited Sonoyama-san's room in the middle of the night, didn't you? That's when you killed her! And you must have killed Ibuki-san, too!"

"You don't have any proof. You shouldn't say such things without any proof, Yayoi-san." I tried my best to stay cool as I reprimanded her. "There's no proof that Hikari-san is the murderer."

"Proof? I don't give a hoot about proof!"

"But there's no reason Hikari-san would have done such a thing."

"It's not like you can expect to understand how a maniac's mind works! She's probably going to use it in some kind of ritual! To call upon God! No more, no more, no more!!! Why are you trying to come near me? You think you'll take my head next? Never!"

"Yayoi-san, please calm down."

"I'm plenty calm! I'm fine! You are all the crazy ones! You're all nuts! You're all disgusting! Get yourselves together! I can't stand you! I can't even talk to you! What language are you all speaking? Detectives? Sealed rooms? Severed heads? What the hell language is that? Am I the only one from Earth here? If that's the case then I'll just leave right now. I don't want to be on this maniac island anymore. I don't want to talk to you people!"

Bam! She slammed the table once again.

"I don't trust any of you! From now on, I'm staying in my room. I'm barricading myself in. Call me when you're ready to send me back to the mainland! Otherwise, leave me the hell alone! Don't come near me!"

With that said, Yayoi-san stormed off toward the dining room exit.

"Sashirono-san," Hikari-san called once more, but Yayoi-san didn't even look back, and eventually she was gone from sight.

A brief, awkward silence.

"Oh my," Iria-san eventually said with slumped shoulders. "And here I thought she was so polite. What a temper."

She continued. "Oh, what now?" She sighed. "Aikawa-san is going to all the trouble to come here, I can't just send one of the suspects home. Hikari, this is your responsibility; go do something to convince her."

"Yes, ma'am," Hikari-san said with her head down. "Understood, my mistress."

"Ohhh, dinner is all ruined. Akari, will you hurry and make us something? Now just where has Teruko gone at a time like this?"

Indeed, dinner was ruined just as Iria-san said, but it was a necessary sacrifice. It wasn't my money, and of course you shouldn't waste food, but I wasn't the one who had done it anyway. It was Yayoi-san, the one who had made the food in the first place.

Kunagisa stared at the fallen, smashed dishes with a look of despair. Not the food, but the dishes. Perhaps she was thinking of her destroyed computers, which were the same shade of white.

"Hey, catcher."

"Mmm?" Kunagisa looked at me. "What, Ii-chan?"

"I better get going. I'll leave this to you."

"Gotcha," she nodded.

I rose from my seat and headed for the door.

I could hear the sound of trouble brewing behind me. I turned to find Kunagisa had climbed over the table and jumped Shinya-san. It was admittedly a slightly enviable sight for me, but for now, I had to let it go.

Besides, I couldn't take Kunagisa with me.

Running down the hall with one eye closed, I climbed the stairs and eventually spotted Yayoi-san by her room. She was leaning up against the wall, a vacant look on her face.

She looked up at me. "Ah," she sighed with relief. "How was I?"

"You gave a star performance."

"Performance, huh? It was more than half true, really," she said as she continued walking with me. "But is it really true? Is that person really the killer?"

"You checked it yourself, right?"

"Yeah, the smell was right, but . . . I don't have that much faith in my sense of smell. I'm not a dog, after all."

"You're just like one though."

"That's not a compliment, you know."

Yeah, I knew. Kanami-san once told me something similar. It's not a compliment if you say, "You're like a such and such."

Well, what woman wouldn't be offended after being compared to a dog? I apologized innocently.

We had arrived at the door to Yayoi-san's room.

"So, what do we do from here?"

"Yayoi-san, please go back to the dining room. It's dangerous here."

"Then why are you doing it?" she asked, simply out of suspicion. "I feel like there must be another way. This is just my speculation, but it feels like you deliberately picked the most dangerous possible option."

"In this world there are people who die from eating too much and people who die from starvation, and the former is overwhelmingly more common. But it seems you're the latter type."

"Don't overestimate me."

"That wasn't a compliment."

With that she gave me a nod and slowly headed back the way we had come.

"Dangerous, man . . ." I whispered to myself. Of course, I was well aware of this. I had complete understanding of the dangers I faced when I decided to do this, which I suppose really did make me the starving-to-death type.

Now *that's* nonsense.

After a brief mental preparation, I slowly, gently opened the door to Yayoi-san's room.

Dark inside. Unable to see much of anything, I took a step inside.

Swoosh.

The sound of sliced air.

I did a forward roll and slid into the room. Then I rose to one knee and opened the eye that had been closed. This way I could make out the inside of the room at least a little bit.

Someone closed the door behind me. I could see the face clearly, and in that moment learned that my hypothesis had been correct. My opponent wore a slight look of surprise, but only held it for a moment before brandishing a hatchet—a hatchet!—at me.

Silent.

My attacker didn't say a word.

With a deep breath, I rose to my feet. It had been quite some time since I had done any acrobatics. Not that I had been bad at it, just that my skills had definitely dulled in the few months since coming back to Japan.

As if realizing the immediate need to settle this, my attacker moved first, shuffling toward me. With Kunagisa holding Shinya-san down, someone would eventually come and save me as long as I could buy some time. There was no need to go on the offensive. In fact, I wanted to get out of there, but my attacker was standing between me and the door, so that probably would've posed quite a challenge.

For now, I just had to focus on dodging attacks. This sort of passive thinking had me written all over it, but it was no good. In focusing my gaze entirely on my attacker's hatchet, I completely neglected to pay any attention to my feet.

My attacker faked with the hatchet, then came at me with a leg sweep. It made a glorious connection. Unable to even roll back to my feet, instead my back slammed into the carpet. My attacker proceeded to mount me and pin down my shoulders. It all happened in a single instant.

The match was essentially over. Maybe I should have spent those mornings running marathons instead of just going for walks. Or maybe I should have continued going to the dojo even when I got back to Japan.

"Ah . . . ahhh . . ."

Ah well, truth be told, it didn't really make much difference whether I was killed or not. At this point, Kunagisa had probably already explained everything to the others, and Yayoi-san had already returned to the dining room as well. Either way, there was no chance my attacker would escape. I had lost the match, but the tournament was ours.

So this was fine. Now then, the hatchet. Use the hatchet.

"Die."

My attacker's cold, familiar voice. I realized I had completely given up. What was this sensation? Why? Why was I even willing to give up my own life?

I didn't want to live?

It wasn't that I wanted to die, but I didn't want to live, either. Life was a big hassle, but I wasn't jumping at the idea of death specifically. Was there nothing important to me? Nothing I wanted? Nothing I wanted to protect? Is that why I was so ready to give up?

"No."

No.

It was because even if I died here, no one would be bothered. Kunagisa wouldn't be bothered.

Maki-san.

Did you know this was coming? If so, I suppose I'm grateful that you didn't let me know about it. I now knew the reason Maki-san, who knew all, had said nothing. You die exactly when you should, though I wasn't quite in that frame of mind yet.

Indeed. Just as Teruko-san said, I really should just die. Seriously.

Hey . . .

But the hatchet wasn't coming down. It was raised way up in the air, and then just stopped. Looking up in confusion, I saw not a taunting expression, but rather a twisted grimace as my attacker struggled and fought to bring the hatchet down.

"You don't close your eyes, do you?"

There was another person! It wasn't the voice of the person on top of me. I couldn't see from where I was, but this third person must have grabbed the hatchet while it was up in the air and refused to let go.

Who was it? Had Yayoi-san come to save me? Had Kunagisa followed me here? But neither of these seemed like feasible possibilities.

The third person wrenched the hatchet upward and in the same instant delivered a beautiful, truly glorious low kick to my attacker's now completely open side. Unable to take the blow, my attacker rolled off me and slammed into the nearby sofa. In another instant, though, the assailant was back on two feet and face-to-face with the third person.

In one fell swoop, I had become a mere spectator.

At this point, for some reason, the third person threw away the hatchet. And here there was such a golden opportunity to use it. Could this have been a gesture of sportsmanship? At a time like this?

Unlike when fighting me, this time my attacker attempted no reckless leaping. But there was a time limit here. If this didn't get settled fast, there was a chance Kunagisa would finish explaining everything and bring the others here.

But this third person didn't repeat my mistake. *Bam*, came the sound of feet hitting the floor as the third person sprang toward my attacker, covering as much as six feet in a single stride. In a Japanese *kenpo*-style motion, the third person used the momentum from the leap to deliver a straight punch. Instead of dodging back or to the side, my attacker instead contorted diagonally, both dodging the punch and closing in on the third person at the same time. My attacker then grabbed the third person by the throat, but the third person delivered another straight punch without even trying to avoid my attacker's clutch. My attacker, still in offensive mode, was unable to dodge. The punch connected straight with the heart.

"Huh . . ."

My attacker let out a groan but refused to release the third person's throat. Then, almost effortlessly, my attacker slid past the third person's side and delivered a back kick to the calf.

The third person stumbled.

It appeared my attacker intended to use this opportunity to slam the third person into the floor. Watching from the sidelines, even I thought this was the end. But it didn't end. The third person used my attacker's arm as a pivot axis and swung up while shifting in midair, causing them both to fall to the floor together with my attacker's arm in a lock. It was a judo offense-through-defense technique.

Another instant. The surprisingly dull, almost anticlimactic sound of breaking bone echoed through the dark room. The third person released the arm and stood up. My attacker followed suit and began to stand up, too, but before managing to get up all the way, took a merciless kick to the already seemingly broken arm. My attacker flew through the air and over the sofa. Then came the sound of the shattering glass table. And my attacker fell back on the sofa.

"Phewwww." The third person exhaled a deep breath with complete calm.

We had a winner.

I was utterly speechless.

At last, the third person faced me. And then, without so much as a smirk, said, "When you're about to die, I think you should close your eyes."

"Didn't you say guys like me *should* die?" I mumbled faintly.

"Oh, that." She tilted her head. "That was a lie."

Teruko-san said.

Slowly shaking my head, I held my hand out to her. I figured the chances were about fifty-fifty, but she grabbed my hand and pulled me to my feet.

"What are you doing here?"

"No reason. It was just inevitable."

"What are you talking about?"

"Don't worry about it. It's just nonsense."

Now that . . .

That was my line.

Sigh.

"Thank you."

After pulling me back to my feet, she let go of my hand and looked at me with those out-of-focus eyes.

"No need to thank me. More important . . ."

A brief pause.

"There's something that's been bothering me."

"What?"

This was a fairly heavy statement to make. What was she about to say? I couldn't even imagine.

Dark.

My eyes had completely adjusted to the darkness, but even still, I couldn't read Teruko-san's expression.

Just like my own heart.

Just like the hearts of others.

"Your question from this afternoon," she said, with that same old pale tone and cold gaze. "I know you were speaking metaphorically . . . were you talking about Kunagisa-san or yourself?"

The child locked in the basement.

Deprived of communication with anyone else for ten years.

"Ah . . ."

Once again, I reached out to touch Teruko-san's hand for no reason at all.

For an instant, our fingers touched. And then, in that moment of separation . . .

An eardrum-shattering sound. The feeling of a shock wave running through my entire body. Teruko-san's body slumped onto me. Like deadweight.

I held on to her as she rested her entire weight on me. But there was no time to stand there and savor the warm touch of her expectedly light body. My eyes were still glued to the sofa.

Or, to be more specific . . .

To the woman sitting there holding a handgun. Sitting there, totally aloof.

My eyes were glued to it. It was a black gun, a relatively popular model. I had even seen a few overseas. I sure didn't expect to see one in this country, though. She had a Glock?

Why she hadn't used the gun until now was obvious. No matter how big this mansion was, it wasn't big enough to stop the sound of a gunshot from reaching every corner of it. In other words, this was probably the final ace up her sleeve. It was an illegal move, the absolute forbidden method.

In which case . . .

In which case the day was mine. I still had my ace, though maybe I had l● the time to use it slip away.

And so the conclusion continued. The resolution to the final scene.

A voice. A faint voice. And then, the gun barrel turned toward me.

She said something I couldn't hear, my ears still ringing from the gun blast. My eardrums were probably okay, just momentarily paralyzed. But in a situation like this, that meant the same thing. It didn't look as if she were going to wait for my hearing to come back.

What did she say? It kind of bothered me. This was a checkmate.

Farewell. *How stupid. What were you trying to do? You want to die in a place like this? What were you living for anyway?*

She was probably saying something along those lines. Or no, maybe she wasn't saying anything at all.

Either way, there is no meaning in words you can't hear.

Just like there is no meaning in feelings you don't express.

Out of steam, I looked at her. Over Teruko-san's shoulder. Past the muzzle of the gun.

"Ah."

Just as I thought. Just as I thought, this was the end.

Naturally I didn't believe anyone was coming to rescue me from this crisis . . . and this was pretty much what I expected to happen. Of course, I didn't mean to get Teruko-san involved, but aside from that, everything had gone more or less according to plan.

That's because my one and only plan was to not involve Kunagisa. Nothing else mattered. Really, it didn't matter. I was apathetic and indifferent. There was no future. There was no past. I had forgotten about being born long ago. Oblivious to the fact that I was alive. Reality was nothing more than a synonym for illusion to me, and that was never an antonym for dream.

At this point.

Teruko-san's body resting on me. My throbbing ankle pain. My paralyzed train of thought. My breaking values. My melting ethics. My collapsing morals. Kanami-san's neck. Akane-san's neck. The truth behind the incident. The culprit. The killer. The murderer.

The splitting girl. None of it mattered now. I would forgive it all.

So . . .

Pull that trigger. Please end it.

K-chink.

The sound of the gun cocking.

A sound I had heard a million times abroad.

And so, finally . . .

Here.

"Ii-chan!"

The sound of the door slamming open. Light pierced the room with such ferocity that my eyes stopped functioning for a moment. But there was no need for visual confirmation of who was pointing the gun on me. Even with my stunned eardrums, her voice had managed to reach me.

But I could barely believe it.

Kunagisa Tomo was standing there alone.

Ridiculous. That wasn't possible. I had left her on the first floor so that she *couldn't* do this. I had left her on the first floor because she was unable to climb stairs alone. She wasn't supposed to be able to come here alone.

But she was indeed alone. With tears in her eyes. She wore a terribly exhausted expression. She was panting. Clutching her chest. She looked as if she were ready to collapse at any moment, but she forced herself to remain standing.

And she was alone.

"This is . . ."

Wait a minute here. This can't be. Someone must be with her. If no one was with her, it would have been impossible for her to climb that spiral staircase. Maybe one or two steps, but not this.

It was impossible.

Had she really come all the way up here alone, despite her affliction?

All this way?

To be sure, it wasn't *physically* impossible. But obsessive-compulsive disorders aren't something to be taken lightly. They aren't so minor that you can just conquer them with willpower. I know for a fact that defying one's own subconscious is no walk in the park.

However . . . however, Kunagisa had heard the gunshot.

And despite it being deathly agonizing, despite it being so painful that in a worse-case scenario she really might have died, she had forced herself up the stairs. Forgetting to even bring someone along. Suppressing the urge to vomit. Clutching her own heart. Forcing those reluctant legs to keep moving. Lashing at her own fear-ridden soul. With that heart much too fragile for living. Enduring the anguish of the depths of Hell. All just to reach me. Casting all things aside. Kunagisa. For me.

"Why?"

The pressure. It was heartbreaking to the point of brutality. I really was a clown . . . feeling like this.

This pathetic feeling—what was the name for this?

"Why are you . . . ?"

Why are you always, *always* . . . shaking me up?

You.

Really. Since the ancient past.

Nothing's changed.

Fwip.

The woman removed me from her sights and retrained them on Kunagisa.

"Hey!"

What are you doing? You were going to shoot *me*. Why do you have to aim that gun over there? No such necessity exists, dammit. Or are such things meaningless to you? Are things like necessity and reality nonexistent in that skewed world in which you live?

The light.

Gradually my eyes were adjusting. Hers were probably doing the same. Kunagisa, however, who unlike us was adapting to the dark, not the light, couldn't yet make out my attacker's features. Dark adaptation takes longer than light adaptation. Consequently, if she were to shoot now, there was no way Kunagisa could dodge it.

I jumped up.

But by the time I was on my feet, it was too late. There was no point. There was no way I could make it to Kunagisa in time. I couldn't outrun a bullet. Even if I could, there would be no point. I couldn't just die in front of Kunagisa. I was too late. I was too late, just as I was years ago. Just like all the time.

In which case . . .

There was nothing I could d—

"Oh."

It seemed Kunagisa was able to spot me. Without even casting a glance at the handgun, without letting my attacker even enter her field of vision, she stuck a finger out at me and grinned.

"Ah, thank God. You're okay, right Ii-chan?"

With that smile. With that selfless smile. With that ragged, worn-out smile. With Kunagisa Tomo, who was completely oblivious to the circumstances.

I was . . .

Truly . . .

"I'm in love with her," I said to myself.

Yup. It was something I had always known. It was so obvious to me there was never a need to put it into words. There was no need for words between us.

Of course, it was a completely self-aware matter. From the instant I had met her, I had chosen Kunagisa Tomo. To the point that I didn't care about anything else. I didn't need to be loved or even chosen.

"Please stop," I begged my attacker.

She remained motionless for a while, but then, "Hehe. Hehehe . . ." She spun the gun around and pointed it at the ground. She continued laughing for a while.

"Hehehehehehe . . . haaaahahahaha . . . ."

Like she was truly having a ball. Laughter like singing.

Dragging my feet, I made my way over to Kunagisa and grabbed her by the shoulders. Her body had become thoroughly hot. That was enough to discern just how much she had struggled to make it here. I held Kunagisa to cover her, and trained my eyes back on my attacker.

She was looking back at us. Looking at us holding on to each other.

"Well, I've still got some complaints, but"—she opened her mouth—"eh, from a guy like you, just hearing something that honest is good enough for now, I guess," she said. "That's what I was waiting to hear last night, after all," Sonoyama Akane said cynically, and tossed the handgun aside.

2

"Uwaaa, you've got a *huge* bruise here, Ii-chan."

With my pant leg rolled up, Kunagisa patted the bruise on my ankle. This blue-haired goon probably didn't realize how much that patting hurt. Hikari-san had brought me anti-swelling medication, so I stuck it on. It felt as if all the warmth had drained from my body.

This was comfort?

"Akane-chan was sooo tough. Not that she ever looked like much of a pushover," Kunagisa said. "Didn't you know, Ii-chan?"

"Why would I? Who could've known one of the Seven Fools would turn out to be so freaking tough? This isn't a video game or something."

She was a complete force to be reckoned with. I hadn't expected her to be so overwhelmingly tough, and I certainly hadn't expected her to have a handgun prepared. I had had a number of brushes with death by now, but this was by far the most dangerous.

"If Teruko-san hadn't come to my rescue, things would've gotten really bad."

"You have to be careful. That body doesn't belong to you alone, you know."

"Says you, woman."

Since the showdown, we had entered a phase of treating the wounded, dictated by common sense as the primary concern. At the time, I hadn't thought anything of it, but after a while, the damage from that initial leg sweep became much more apparent, so I was now undergoing treatment in Kunagisa's room.

"You hit your back as well, didn't you? Did it hurt?" Hikari-san said. "Please take care. Akane-san was in the karate club in high school, you know?"

"I think I've heard that before . . ."

"She even participated in the national tournament."

Man, teach *me* that stuff.

"Yeah, but apparently she only won five matches."

"You only need five matches to win the national tournament."

As for Akane-san's wounds, first there was her broken right arm. Then there was that first kick, which had apparently broken four ribs. Even in that early phase of the showdown she had suffered a major wound, yet she was still able to jump around like that. It was no small feat.

Meanwhile, Teruko-san was undergoing treatment with Akari-san. Skin around her throat had been scratched off from when Akane-san was strangling her, and there had been some bleeding, but she had suffered no other notable wounds. At the time of that gunshot, I had thought the bullet had hit her square in the back, but in fact it hadn't hit her at all. I thought she had fallen into my arms from the force of being shot, but it was actually the result of her dodging the bullet. Perhaps it was her reaction to the sound of the gun being cocked. She was like one of Charlie's Angels.

Not to mention that, afterward, she was playing dead.

"Actually, that's not quite right," Hikari-san said. "I'm sure she was just shielding you."

"Shielding me?" Indeed, depending on how you looked at it, that wasn't an impossibility. "So you're saying she was risking her life for me?"

"No, her life wasn't particularly in danger. Teruko's apron is bulletproof."

"Bulletproof?"

She wasn't an angel, she was a battle maid. What the hell had happened to reality?

"Yes. Spectra is sewn into her clothes. Unlike Kevlar, Spectra can withstand any number of shots without weakening. And it's light so you don't get sweaty. Teruko is nigh invincible at short range, but she takes caution with long-range defense. See how long the skirt is on this apron dress? That's because it works like an aikido *hakama*."

It sounded like a terrible joke, but it was hard to tell based on Hikari-san's expression. Maybe it was better to just let it go. "But why is Teruko-san so strong? Are *you* that strong, too?" I asked.

"No, Teruko is our mistress's resident bodyguard, in a sense. Our roles are fundamentally different. Up to now, you've never seen all three of us doing the same job, have you?"

Come to think of it, it did seem as if Hikari-san and Akari-san were always the ones at work. As a former participant in the ER3 program, maybe it was unforgivable that I hadn't noticed until now. Yeah, it sounded pretty bad.

"But I'm sure glad she rescued you. I'm sure you've noticed by now that she can be awfully cold. Saving you is one thing, but staking her own life to shield you . . . It almost doesn't make sense."

"Yeah, about that. Why did she do it?"

"Well, she's a whimsical girl."

Just like everyone else here.

But it wasn't completely beyond my comprehension. I still didn't know for sure how Teruko-san felt, but insofar as she was still a mystery to me, I was no doubt just as much a mystery to her.

Surely, she just wanted to ask about me.

"That's just a bunch of nonsense, though . . ."

Come to think of it, she had seemed abnormally strong when she grabbed my arm that afternoon, but I never would have imagined that that was some kind of foreshadowing.

"It seems like your back and hips are okay. You didn't hit

your head, did you? Well then, that's a wrap," Kunagisa said, and, sticking close to me, began to massage my shoulders. This was Heaven.

"Now then, shall we head back to the dining room?"

This was Hell.

Right. The noninjured guests had all been left waiting anxiously for Kunagisa and me in the dining room. Unbelievably. Terrifyingly.

"Tomo, you go on alone. These injuries are way worse than I thought. I don't think I can go."

"Whatever. But y'know, Ii-chan, this is your chance to look good in front of Akari-chan. If you're smooth, you might get something out of it."

"Oh my, do you have Akari on the mind? She loves smart people, you know."

Kunagisa and Hikari-san were happily double-teaming me with suggestions. What were they, middle school students?

"Tomo, you know how much I hate stuff like that. You don't need me to explain it, right? Just think something up yourself."

"Ii-chan, didn't you do this kind of thing abroad? Performances or presentations or what have you?"

"Well, yeah, but they were Hell every time. They would always bitch at me, you know, like 'Quit talking around the subject' or 'You're being too vague' or 'Nobody's interested in your problems.' Ah, I know, I know. I should just do it, right? Just do it."

"Don't weasel out of this," Kunagisa's smirk said.

"Come on, you'll get in trouble. You have to be more cheerful about this. I know that's probably impossible for you, but anyway, let's get going. Tie my hair up first."

"Huh? You don't like it that way?"

"It feels like my head is being pulled on. One or two tails is better after all."

"Mmm, and here I liked it."

"Tomo-san, would you like me to do it?"

"Uh-uh," Kunagisa shook her head.

"Putting my hair up is Ii-chan's job."

Yes'm. I redid her hair, and . . .

. . . and our preparations were complete.

"Well, let's go."

Slowly the gates of Hell opened. I was feeling quite heavy-footed, and it wasn't just because of my injuries.

"What a buncha nonsense," I muttered as I arrived in the dining room. Everyone besides Akane-san, whose wounds were severe, was gathered together.

That of course included Shinya-san.

As if he had already given up, as if a burden had been taken off his shoulders, he had a calm air about him as he watched us walk through the door. Maki-san sneered at me, making me think I was about to be harassed again, but she remained silent.

Lined up on the table was the remade food Yayoi-san had prepared while I was being treated. Possibly because Yayoi-san had calmed down, this time the food was remarkably fancier.

Akari-san, still feeling awkward, avoided eye contact. Teruko-san had bandages wrapped around her neck.

Rei-san watched over the scene in complete silence.

And then there was Akagami Iria-san. She was looking at me with challenging eyes.

"Well then, shall we have you begin?" Iria-san said to me as I took my seat. "What is all this?"

"Allow me to explain. Sonoyama Akane-san of the ER3's Seven Fools is the killer, and Ibuki Kanami-san's caretaker, Sakaki Shinya-san over there, is her accomplice."

Silence.

"And?"

"That's it."

"Give us thirty minutes," she insisted. "The first thing I want you to explain is what Sonoyama-san was doing in Yayoi's room."

"That's easy. Yayoi-san flew out of the dining room, right? Thus, Yayoi-san was the next person to be somewhere by herself, so Akane-san used it as an opportunity to kill her.

"The idea had been to have Akane-san's plan backfire, but instead things had backfired on me and Teruko-san had saved me. And ultimately I had had to rely on Akane-san's kindness."

That hatchet she had brandished at me, surely it would've lopped my head off.

"I'm very grateful to Teruko-san."

"No, I don't mean that. You know what I mean. Wasn't Sonoyama-san killed? In that sealed storage room?"

"As you saw, she's alive." I shrugged. "Assuming she doesn't have a twin, I think we can all agree that it was Akane-san."

"So what about that headless body in the storage room?"

"Well, Akane-san is alive, so that wasn't her body. That's just logical thinking."

"It was someone else's corpse?"

"If you see a headless body, beware of switching. It's a cardinal rule of detective novels, right? I'm sure your darling detective would say the same thing."

Iria-san tilted her head at me as if to show that this was beyond her comprehension. "Um, just wait a second. I'm thinking."

She wanted a moment to contemplate things alone. I was a bit impressed by her spirit. "Umm . . ."

"Well, in the meantime, might I ask something?" Shinya-san raised his hand. "I've got a question for you there."

"I don't mind," I nodded. I thought for sure I'd be asked when I realized the truth behind the incidents or how I figured out the killer or something like that, but Shinya-san's question was totally different from my expectations.

"Is that wound on your foot okay?"

"Yes. It's made a bruise, though."

"Really? So it's not broken. That woman . . ." he snorted. "Or maybe she *couldn't* break it, though that's not like her . . . or is it?"

I wasn't sure what all his whispering meant.

Finally, "Nah, it's no good," Iria-san said capitulatingly. "I don't get it at all. There was really a switch?"

"There was. Kunagisa's computers were destroyed, right? The third incident. *Nobody* could have done that. Literally, precisely nobody. Everybody served as everybody else's witness, so alibis and accomplices weren't even a matter of concern. We were all watching one another the whole time. Nobody could have done it. Nobody who was there, anyway. Therefore, the only person who could've done it would have been someone who wasn't there with us. That's just logical thinking."

"I gathered that much," Iria-san said. "You don't need to keep emphasizing that it's logical. You're kind of a smart aleck, aren't you? So *whose* headless body was that in the storage room? Everybody was here together. There wasn't a single person who could have been switched with Sonoyama-san's body. Isn't that strange to you?"

"Well, it is strange, but . . ." I decided to give her an easy-to-understand analogy. "Do you know this quiz? Or actually, it's more like a trick or a form of fraud, but anyway . . ."

I pulled out the alibi chart and turned it over to the back. There I drew a big rectangle, then drew nine lines through it. In other words, a ten-box chart.

"What is that?" Iria-san asked. "Something to do with this?"

"Please pretend these are telephone booths. Ten telephone booths. Now let's put eleven people in them."

"Phone booths?"

"Oh, I mean, they're just boxes. They could be rooms."

"Ten rooms."

"Yup," I nodded.

Incidentally, this was a magic trick I had picked up from a book I read while in elementary school.

"Okay, so let's say A-kun tries to enter the first box, but a second person enters it before him." I wrote an X in the first box. "Now for the third person." I wrote an X in the next box. "The fourth person." I wrote yet another X in the next box. "The fifth, sixth, seventh, and eighth people. The ninth person, and the tenth person. So now we've got ten people in boxes. But there's still one box leftover. So let's stick that first guy, A-kun, in there." I drew an X in the final box. "And so we've fit eleven people in ten boxes. Do you get it?"

"That's stupid," Iria-san said. "The first person never entered the box, so it was off by one person."

"Yes, that's correct. It's a rudimentary trick that anyone can figure out with a little thought. But if done with the right timing and skill, nobody notices."

"Yes they do."

"They don't. *We* didn't notice."

"I don't have any idea what you're talking about. And this is all off-topic. I'm asking whose body that was in the storage room. Everybody was gathered here. No matter how you look at it, that makes us one person short. Or are you saying there was a thirteenth person on this island?"

"Not possible. There were twelve people on this island. Let's assume that's a given."

"Well then, who was it?"

"As of now, there are eleven people alive on this island. Akagami Iria-san, Chiga Akari-san, Chiga Hikari-san, Chiga Teruko-san, Handa Rei-san, Himena Maki-san, Sashirono Yayoi-san, and Kunagisa Tomo. Then there's Sakaki Shinya-san and Sonoyama Akane-san. Then, finally, there's me. So the answer should be clear."

I allowed a brief pause.

"It was Ibuki Kanami-san."

3

"With the corpse wrapped up in a sleeping bag, it didn't get dirty even when we buried it. After we left the burial site, Shinya-san dug Kanami-san's body back up. Then, with body in tow, he headed for the storage room window. From the outside, I mean. He knocked on the window and Akane-san opened it from the inside. In went the body, and they made the switch. That's basically it."

Taking a look over the crowd to see their reaction, especially Shinya-san's, I continued.

"It was strange. When we went to bury Kanami-san's body, Shinya-san brought a sleeping bag along. It was a coffin. But hold the phone there a second. Why would he have a sleeping bag? Maybe if this was a camping trip, but nobody would bring a sleeping bag when they've been invited to a mansion. So maybe it was already at the mansion to begin with? See, that's what I had thought. I thought Iria-san had offered it to him for the sake of the burial. Certainly in a mansion like this, a mansion that offers beds with canopies even in the guest rooms, it's a little unnatural for there to be sleeping bags lying around, but it's not impossible. So that's what I thought. But the second time, when Akane-san's corpse—actually Kanami-san's corpse again—was discovered, Hikari-san brought us a stretcher. Is there some reason you would offer a sleeping bag for the first person but not for the second? Not likely. Even if there was a reason, Hikari-san would've told me. And so one assumption crumbles. There were no sleeping bags here after all. Shinya-san must have brought one himself even though this isn't camping. It's as if he knew from the start he would need something in which to bury a body. He knew that he couldn't let the body get dirty.

"So he . . . *recycled* the body?"

"Bingo, you've got it. Shinya-san and Akane-san murdered Kanami-san and from her created a new, 'phantom' corpse. That's basically it."

"But there was blood in the storage room," Iria-san said. "If that body was a day old, there wouldn't have been so much blood."

"There was no way for us to determine whether or not that was Akane-san's blood. Maybe the police could have. Indeed, if the police were here, this crazy incident never would have happened. But you didn't want to call the police. Understandable. Due to certain circumstances, you couldn't call them. Knowing that, Akane-san was free to assume that even if there was another incident, the police wouldn't come. The blood could have been from a blood bank or even from an animal. We'll have to ask Akane-san or Shinya-san to find out."

But Shinya-san remained silent, refusing to answer. I let it be and continued. "In the same sense, if the police had been here, they could have told us that the body was a day old already. But we're not professionals. All we know is the difference between dead and alive. Maybe after ten days we'd be able to discern the age of the corpse, and maybe a little faster in the summer, but this isn't the summer. This is the season of blooming cherry blossoms."

"So they changed the corpse's clothes?"

"Yes. Akane-san called Hikari-san to her room in the middle of the night just to show her what she was wearing. Kanami-san's body was already in the room at that time. That room has an inward-opening door, so all she had to do was hide the body in the shadows behind it. As long as she came out to greet Hikari-san, Hikari-san wouldn't enter the room. This was likely the riskiest part of the whole ploy. If there was ever a point that proved Akane-san was going out on a limb, it was this scene. But she had to go out on a limb. As I said before, she did it so that she could make us all think Kanami-san's body was hers. Also, to narrow down the time of the murder and to give her accomplice, Shinya-san, a solid alibi."

That night, Shinya-san was with Maki-san drinking the whole night. Maki-san had invited him, but supposing she hadn't, he probably would've invited her. Or it's even possible that he would have invited us instead of Maki-san. Of course, now that all was said and done, that was just a trivial detail.

"That's also why they smashed Kunagisa's PCs. The PCs and digital camera contained images. Images of Kanami-san's corpse. If we carefully compared those images with Akane-san's corpse in the storage room, there was a chance that we would realize they were in fact the same body."

"Actually, that's true," Kunagisa said. "Something had been bothering me. The hands, or the fingers or something. Yeah, that's it, huh? It's not like Kanami-chan and Akane-chan have the same fingerprints."

She let out a sigh. It seemed she was disappointed in herself for not noticing right off the bat. Everyone else probably thought she was joking, but I knew she probably wasn't.

For crying out loud.

"But why would they do such a thing?"

"There are altogether too many possibilities as far as that's concerned, but in my opinion she was trying to 'erase her existence.' Akane-san created a phantom 'thirteenth person' by using the same body twice, and in so doing succeeded in erasing her own existence. There are plenty of hiding places around here. It's a huge mansion, and many of the rooms aren't locked. And there's always the possibility she was outside the mansion."

"Why would she need to erase her own existence?"

"That's simple. Isn't it obvious? If she became a victim, if she herself was murdered, she would no longer be under surveillance. She would be free to move about, beyond the confines of thought and reason, like some kind of invisible woman. In which case, breaking Kunagisa's computers, for example, became a simple task. Even causing a fourth incident, such as another murder, would have been simple. But again, we won't know for sure what they had planned unless we ask Akane-san or Shinya-san."

"We were going to kill everyone."

This time he was gracious enough to answer. He spoke with a coldness that told of his complete surrender. He spoke with indifference.

"Everyone on this island. But to do so, she had to remove herself. It became apparent that her ability to move around would be cut off, either by the forming of teams or by having everyone stay together in one place, so she had to remove herself from everyone."

And once she was on the outside, she would just start picking people off one at a time, starting with the easiest prey. Shinya-san let out a weak chuckle. "And here she did such a good job of removing herself from the party. I never would've thought she wouldn't even be able to kill a single person. I thought she'd at least get through half of you."

"Shall we have you explain the rest then, Shinya-san?"

"No," he shook his head weakly. "I'll leave it all to you. That's your role here. It's your job."

I nodded without saying anything. "Well then, I don't think I need to explain the first sealed room at this point, do I? That was just a trick to distract us. They just needed to buy time until the second incident. It might not have been specifically planned to go down that way, but rather just a coincidental product of the Law of Great Numbers. Maybe the earthquake just happened to occur and she thought of it right then. Of course she was planning the murder all along, but maybe she only decided on a specific plan once the earthquake occurred. Supposing that was the case, it was some incredibly quick thinking. You can't help but be impressed. Anyway, there was an earthquake. Then Shinya-san called. However, it wasn't Kanami-san on the other end, but Akane-san. Then Akane-san killed Kanami-san. Shinya-san said Kanami-san had said 'the paint spilled,' but that, too, was a trick. He used vague wording so that even if the trick was exposed, he could weasel out of it. Even I was tricked by that."

"Heh heh," Shinya-san laughed.

"That's simply a coincidence."

"Well, I can't speak as to that, but anyway, Akane-san killed Kanami-san. Then she put together that 'sealed room.' By intentionally spilling the paint."

"Well, at least I wasn't wrong when I originally said she was the killer."

"That's right, Iria-san. Certainly it was a high possibility. But that's all it was. Because Akane-san had created that sealed room, we couldn't say for certain. Of course, that was the whole point of the sealed room. To put herself under the 'perfect level of suspicion,' she placed herself in a position where she was the prime suspect, but where nobody could prove that she did it. Then she was locked in the storage room.

"Granted, I was the one who had suggested it, but even if I hadn't said anything, Shinya-san surely would have. There were only so many rooms with locking doors, so it would have been easy for them to guess where she would be held, and there had already been plenty of time for them to get to know the mansion. Of course, we can only speculate here, and if you don't feel like talking to Shinya-san about it, we'll never know the true answer."

On that note, it seemed to me that Akane-san's big tiff with Kanami-san was also done to intentionally show their sour relationship. Akane-san had *wanted* to put herself in that risky position.

You know, for later on.

I didn't know whether the fact that Akane-san was the only one without an alibi (well, actually Rei-san, too) was pure luck, or whether she had figured out a whole strategy. But it was probably just a coincidence.

That's what I thought.

"So then she switched with Ibuki-san's body?" Iria-san said. "And then showed herself to Hikari-san in the middle of the night, put the clothes she had been wearing on Ibuki-san, escaped, and . . . then she hid away somewhere in the mansion, right? Then during dinner she was hiding right by the dining hall listening in on Sashirono-san's hysteria. She overheard her saying she was going to lock herself up in her room. So she turned back and hid herself in Sashirono-san's room. There's no lock, after all. Then there was the setup. Hmm, so that means Sashirono-san's breaking down and accusing Hikari was all a ruse you set up, doesn't it?"

"Yes," I nodded. "We could've just found her at that point if we had searched the whole mansion, but it's so huge. It just seemed like it would be a big hassle, so we set a trap instead. It was risky, though."

"The amazing thing about you is that you were able to just write that off as 'risky.' "

I didn't know who was speaking for a second, but it turned out to be Maki-san. It was the first time she had given me a compliment without a hint of sarcasm. I was just a little bit pleased.

"But hang on a second." Iria-san placed a hand on her own head and remained like that for a moment. "Something still seems off," she said. "Hmm, what is it? Something seems strange to me."

"Are you wondering how Akane-san got out of the storage room?"

"Yeah, that's it!" Iria-san said with a clap of her hands. "That's it. You haven't explained that yet. Did Shinya-san pull her up? Did she literally switch places with the corpse?"

"Nope. Shinya-san was only outside the mansion when we buried Kanami-san's body in the mountains. At that time, he did drop the body into the storage room, but he didn't pull Akane-san out. Hikari-san saw her the following night at two a.m., right? Plus, Shinya-san had an alibi that night as well. So he couldn't have pulled Akane-san out. That much is certain."

"Then did he drop a rope ladder down there or something?"

"That's not it, either. A rope ladder would've left a hole somewhere. I suppose it would've been possible if the rope was long enough, but Hikari-san saw that the window was closed at two a.m. Akane-san couldn't have tied the rope outside from the inside of her room. She would've needed an accomplice, but as I said, Shinya-san was busy at the time creating an alibi for himself with Maki-san."

"Then it's impossible," Iria-san pouted. "My head is spinning in circles. I feel like I've got cyanosis here."

"You must mean vertigo."

"That's the only kind of thing you ever explain, huh?" she grimaced. "Well? You must know the answer, right?"

"Yup," I nodded.

"She was locked in a room with a door that can only be unlocked from the outside, and a window that opens freely, and she wanted to get out. Iria-san, what would you have done in that situation?"

"I can't possibly imagine."

Spoken like a true princess.

"Well, what about you, Akari-san?"

I had already explained it to Hikari-san and Yayoi-san, so I asked Akari-san. I could've asked Teruko-san, Rei-san, or even Maki-san, but Akari-san was my favorite, after all, and I was hoping to break the awkwardness lingering from the morning's events.

"I . . . I guess I would stretch my arms up and jump."

"Right. But even if you jumped, you wouldn't reach the window."

"We're talking about the storage room, right? If I was locked in there, and jumping didn't work . . . next I would try standing on a chair, stretching my arms up and jumping."

"Even then you don't reach."

"Then it's simple," she said with a forced cheerful expression. "I'd give up."

"That won't move this conversation anywhere."

"Well, it's over, right?"

Wow, she was blunt. Maybe it wasn't awkwardness, maybe she just plain hated me. Well, whatever. Time to change the channel.

"Akari-san says she would have used a chair. That's basically what anybody would do, right? Like a monkey trying to reach a high-hanging banana."

"Are you calling me a monkey?" she screamed, her face bright red. "Aren't you rude! You don't know the meaning of the word *delicacy*, do you? Are you trying to infuriate me?"

My mistake. It seemed I had changed the channel in the wrong direction.

"No, that's not what I meant. And you don't have to get so angry. Monkeys are adorable."

"I've never been so insulted in my entire life." She cast her face away from me. "From now on you and I don't know each other."

Her disdain for me was unquestionably clear. I was a little bit shocked. Dammit, Kunagisa, what about impressing her with my smarts? It was the exact opposite outcome.

"Um, that's not good. Anyway, you stand on a chair. Just like anyone would. You jump, you stretch your arms out. You still don't reach. So what now? It's simple. You just get on a taller chair."

"There's only one chair in that room."

"Well, 'chair' is just a metaphor. It could be anything. So what was in that room?"

"Nothing. Books? The futon? A lamp and table?"

"There was something else, wasn't there? Something we all saw. It was practically *all* we saw."

A silence fell over the crowd. Maybe they couldn't think of it, maybe they had thought of it. Either way would've warranted such a reaction.

It was Iria-san who finally answered.

"It was Ibuki-san's corpse, wasn't it?"

"Bingo," I nodded.

What else needed to be said?

"Rigor mortis reaches its peak at around the first twenty-four-hour mark—well, depending on your sources. It was about two a.m., give or take, so almost exactly that much time had passed since Kanami-san was killed. Her body was probably stiff as a pole. I'm sure getting those clothes on her was no cakewalk, but there were merits here as well. I guess it had an upside and a downside."

"No cakewalk? It was a suit, for crying out loud. How do you get that on a stiff corpse? Maybe her joints were still moving, but still . . ."

"Then she could've brought two pairs of the same outfit. That way she could get it on the body while it was still relatively loose in the afternoon. Maybe Kanami's removed dress was hiding behind the door," I continued without pausing. "I arrived at this train of thought based on her reason for cutting off the head. That was, of course, so that Kanami's body could play the role of two people. Her face was a hindrance. But I believe there is one more reason she cut off the head. She may be the only person to have ever cut off someone's head for this reason. Yup. *To flatten her shoulders.*"

"You mean because if she hadn't done that, if the shoulders weren't flat, she couldn't have used them as a step? Because Kanami-san wasn't a sturdy stepping stool?" Akari-san asked weakly, as if stricken with fear, or else hoping for some other answer.

"Is that what you're saying?"

"Yes," I nodded. "Not just a step, but a 'staircase.' First she placed the chair, then stood Kanami-san's body up next to it, letting it lean against the wall a little. Then she used the chair as her first step, the body as her second, and made a final leap. Like a hop, step, and jump maneuver. Then she stretched out her arms and finally reached the window."

Kanami-san was always confined to a wheelchair, so I wasn't sure of her exact height, but considering Akane-san had thought to recycle the body that way, she was probably about as tall as Akane-san. And that was none too petite. Even without the head, she was at least five feet tall. If you added Akane-san's own height, it was a little over ten feet. Plus she was extending her arms. Plus she jumped. As long as her hand made it to the window, all she had to do was pull herself up. The impact from the jump probably caused Kanami-san's body to topple over, but that was all the better. It would be hard for anyone to tell the body had been used as a step.

And that's exactly why the head had been lopped off from the very base of the neck.

"It couldn't have been that easy. I mean, come on . . ."

"She didn't have to succeed right away. I mean, she could

have tried any number of times. It's not the type of thing you can do in one or two tries, but eventually she succeeded, and knocked Kanami-san's body down in the process. To be greedy, she probably wanted to close the window, too, but you can only do that from the inside, so she probably just gave up on it. When we went and examined Akane-san's— by which I mean Kanami-san's—body the next day, the peak of the rigor mortis had already passed, and the body had become somewhat loose again. Of course I'm no specialist, so I can't really say for certain."

"That's . . ." Akari-san was turning blue. It was the same broken down Akari-san I had encountered this morning. Infuriated, or deep in despair. "It's too terrible. It's too terrible. I can't forgive this. To kill a person, and on top of that cut her head off, and then dig up her buried corpse, and on top of *that* disguise it as the body of someone else . . . that alone is unspeakably foul. But to then use the body as a chair, as a *staircase*, as a *stepping stool?*"

" 'It's difficult to sit on a living person. To sit on a living person for nearly thirty minutes is nearly impossible. But I wouldn't say sitting on a dead person is very hard at all,' " Shinya-san recited. "The words of Oe Kenzaburo. Don't you know it, Akari-san?"

Still blue in the face, Akari-san shook her head with a look of disgust. She looked like a small frightened animal. Like she wanted to deny reality.

I couldn't help but sigh.

A corpse is something that's been thoroughly spent, with no sentience or personality or even a spirit remaining inside it, just as it no longer has a will or an essence. It is nothing more than a "thing." And the owner of that "thing" utters no complaint as to what might become of it, and even supposing it wanted to, he or she was in no place to do so.

There was a headless body. She recycled it as her own body.

There was a headless body. She used it as a staircase.

So what?

When you die, that's the end. The fact that you lived is irrelevant. It's nothing more than a fact. Everybody has a different idea about it, and that's their right; you can't complain about what others believe.

I let out another sigh.

"So that's it, Iria-san. The minor details are a pain to explain, so please think about them for yourself. I'm sure there's an easy answer for everything else. Unfortunately, I'm not a nice enough guy to explain it all. Please reason things out on your own."

"The minor details, huh?" Iria-san said. "What about the motive? I don't think you can write that off as a trivial or minor detail."

"You'll have to ask the murderers directly."

I repeated the same line I had already said a number of times by this point, and looked over at Shinya-san. So did everyone else. With a look of capitulation, Shinya-san prepared to give an answer, when a voice came from behind my back.

"You don't have to answer that, Shinya."

I looked back. Standing in the entrance to the dining room was Akane-san. She was supposed to be resting in the bedroom. How long had she been there? How much of my nonsense had she heard?

Her arm was in a brace, but she still wore a fearless expression as she looked down upon the crowd sitting at the round table.

"Akane-san . . ."

ER3 system, Seven Fools, Sonoyama Akane.

Akane-san, who had claimed that she would never complain, no matter who, when, why, or how she was killed. But did that just mean she would forgive *herself* no matter who, when, why, or how she killed?

"Hah," she laughed. "Motive? Motive, you say? How silly. What a meaningless thing that is in a world this big. It hurts my brain to think about why you would even care about such trivia. I don't get it at all." She gave a sardonic smile as she continued. "I was just trying to eat those brains of yours."

*Akagami Iria,
Mistress of
Wet Crow's
Feather Island*

*Handa Rei,
Head Maid at the Mansion*

ONE WEEK LATER

SPLIT

Where are you?
Who are you?

1

As luck would have it, just as Kunagisa and I had originally planned, we were able to return to the mainland on the afternoon exactly one week after we had arrived. Kunagisa having a tendency (albeit not as compulsive as her vertical motion thing) to hate changing plans once she's made them, this set me at ease a bit.

But if you looked back, Kunagisa's original purpose in coming to the island was, at least in part, to satisfy her interest in the "various things" that had occurred there in the past. I asked her about it.

"My investigation is basically over," she said.

It seemed *she* had been up to some "various things" herself. Not that I wasn't wondering what she had been up to, but if that was the case, there was no problem for now. I just wanted to get home anyway.

I sat on a sofa in a room on the same cruiser that had brought us to the island. Kunagisa lay sleeping on the sofa across from me.

Now that we were set to return to the mainland, I had half expected something to happen with Hikari-san or Akari-san, but they gave nothing more than the usual, dutiful formalities. *Thank you very much. Please visit again if you have the chance. Take care now.* I don't even have to get into Teruko-san's farewell. She left me without a single word, as if to say, "I've already spoken to you enough to last a lifetime."

But whatever.

That's how my life goes.

Sonoyama Akane-san and Sakaki Shinya-san.

The two perpetrators of this crime were of course no longer allowed to stay on the island, and were currently laying low in the next room. I didn't know what they might be talking about.

We were heading back to the mainland as planned, and they were heading back because they had been kicked out. It was technically the opposite of being island exiled, but if you thought about it, the word *mainland* was wholly subjective.

Yayoi-san and Maki-san remained on the island.

Yayoi-san's doubts regarding Iria-san and Rei-san seemed to have been swept away, but I wondered if that was enough. Of course, it was up to Yayoi-san to decide how she lived her own life, and not my place to butt in.

As for Maki-san . . . that woman was a sly fox to the very end.

"So how much did you really know?" I asked her before leaving the island.

Maki-san responded with an ambiguous smile.

"Well, you know. Maybe I don't really know anything. Like the whole thing was really just an act."

"You know, I get the impression you knew about Akane-san and Shinya-san's plans all along, and you were aiding them in creating alibis."

"What if I was?" she said nonchalantly. "What if I was?"

"Then you're an accomplice. That's all."

"But it's not like I had heard anything from Shinya-san, and he didn't try to tell me anything."

"If he had, you would've been abetting a murder. You invited him over two nights in a row, helping him create an alibi that was hard for me to trace. So what's the real story? If you were really cooperating with Shinya-san, then . . ."

"Then what?"

"Nothing. I guess nothing would happen," I shrugged. "Nothing at all."

Maki-san snickered at me.

In reality I wanted to tell her something, but there was no point. If she really possessed those powers there was no need to say anything, and even if she didn't there was no need.

It's just that I had doubts. Shinya-san and Akane-san's serial murder plot just seemed too perfect, like it relied on one too many coincidences. In presenting my findings to Iria-san, I had made great efforts to step around that. It's not that their plans had been sloppy. It was like they had been unrehearsed, yet at the same time, everything had been prepared ahead of time. Or rather, it felt like luck was very much on their side. . . . Yeah, it was like they had factored in coincidences and made friends with luck. As if the layout of the entire island and everything on it were on their side.

"Nonsense, huh?"

Of course they probably were all just coincidences, and probably just examples of the Law of Great Numbers, and those two had simply won a bet, so to speak. Anything will look fishy if you think about it selectively.

"Occam's razor?"

However.

On that island was someone who knew everything, and I do mean *everything*, even the future.

Was even this a coincidence?

Sigh.

Indeed, it probably was. I could draw no other conclusion. Even if it wasn't a coincidence, it was all over already, and there would be no way to prove it, plus Shinya-san and Akane-san sure weren't talking, so there was no point in pursuing it. Even if there was a point, it had nothing to do with me, and even if it had something to do with me, I wasn't interested.

So that was the situation. Instead, I asked a question.

"Are you the one who told Teruko-san I was in trouble?"

There was no reason anyone should've known I was about to be done in by Akane-san in Yayoi-san's room, and thus there was no reason Teruko-san should have conveniently busted in with all the grace and good timing of an action heroine like that.

Unless there was someone who could predict the future, that is.

"Do you think I would do something like that?"

"No."

"Then I probably didn't, did I?"

She gave me a wicked smile. I decided any further inquiry would be meaningless, so I didn't even thank her. There was no reason to.

"I wonder what's going to happen now. To the island, to Iria-san . . ."

"Mmm." Maki-san gave an expectedly short response.

I shrugged once. "Well, how about telling me what's going to happen to me and Kunagisa? As a continuation to that 'compatibility reading' from the other night. Are the two of us going to stay like this forever?"

"My readings are expensive."

"In that case I'll have to decline," I said.

"The two of you will stay that way for a little while longer," she said, answering me the very second I had given up. What a perverse contrarian.

"A little while?"

"Yes, a little while."

"How long?"

"Two years plus change."

I tilted my head at her.

"You mean it'll turn into something else after two years? Or it'll completely fade away?"

"Well, I don't know." She laughed a bit cynically. "I can't see more than two years into the future."

Hadn't heard that before. I probably failed to hide my surprised expression.

"It's a secret though," she continued. "So I don't know what will become of you and Kunagisa-chan two years from now."

"You mean that's the limit of your power?"

"I mean I'm going to die," she said plainly. "Time is not on my side. As far as I'm concerned, all time stops at that point. Two years from now, on March 21, at 3:23 p.m. That's the date and time that I will die."

All I could do was be silent.

"Spewing guts and brains all over the place, it'll be a fitting death for a heretic like me."

"Can't you avoid it?"

"When the time comes, be sure to get my killer. Just like you did this time. I'm asking you now as a favor."

"What's the point in asking a favor if you won't be able to see whether or not I've fulfilled it?"

"That's true," she seemed to say as she stuck out her right hand, her chest out as if to express pride that she, too, had an unforeseeable future.

"Let's shake hands."

"Sure. Might not be bad to pretend we're friends now that we're at the very end."

Even having said that, I couldn't grab her hand.

I still had no idea why she had picked on me so much. It probably didn't matter, and it was probably actually better that way.

However . . .

I still had some doubts.

"Excuse me." The cabin door opened and in walked Rei-san. "We'll be docking soon. Please get ready."

"Sure," I replied.

Time to wake up Kunagisa.

She seemed to be sleeping awfully comfortably so I didn't really want to, but I couldn't just leave her be. Although that would have been pretty funny.

"Um, thank you so much for everything," Rei-san took the time to say. "You, especially. We're grateful to Kunagisa-san as well, but you . . ."

"Did you have a blast, Akagami Iria-san?"

"Sure," Rei-san nodded without any particular sign of surprise. "You bet. I had tons of fun."

Akagami Iria-san grinned a genuinely happy grin. A smile she hadn't given once during her performance as Rei-san. This wasn't acting, it was a real, human smile.

"How did you know Rei and I switched? Since when?"

"I just thought of it now. It was just a wild guess. I figured if I was wrong you'd just get a little ticked off, it wasn't like a breach of your human rights or anything," I said to her. "If you had left this room quicker I probably wouldn't have even noticed, or at least I wouldn't have said anything."

"Is that right?" she nodded. "I always get sloppy at the end, huh? My grandfather used to say it all the time. But you must have had some reason to think that. Please, enlighten me."

"What's it to you?"

"I can use it as future reference."

She was going to keep doing this?

"Well, yeah. Yayoi-san still hasn't noticed, plus Maki-san . . . well, I don't know about her."

She snickered. Seeing her childish demeanor, she seemed to lack a certain refinement in comparison to the "real" Iria-san, the one on the island—Rei-san, that is. It was like the fake version was more real than the real one.

She just seemed to be very free.

"Well, let's see," I said. "You didn't talk very much, did you, Iria-san? It was so unnatural. I'm sure you thought that if you spoke you would give yourself away, but on the other hand, not talking at all was just as much of a blunder. So you made Teruko-san act silent as well to create a sort of universal 'lack of presence,' thereby covering yourself."

"No, that's just her nature," Iria-san said. "I can tell her apart from the other two even if she's not wearing her glasses. 'Cause she never talks."

Apparently that was her nature.

Well, if you thought about it, it didn't really seem like Teruko-san had been acting.

"Is that right? Well, either way, I figured if that Iria-san was an imposter, there was only one possible person it could have been. After all, Akari-san, Hikari-san, and Teruko-san are triplets. I guess it's a little counterintuitive that they couldn't have swapped places *because* they're triplets."

"You said it," she smiled.

It was the smile of someone addressing an equal.

At least that's what I thought.

"And then there was something about your aura. Like, Teruko-san never seemed to be doing much work. That's because she was mainly your bodyguard. But I never saw Rei-san do much work, either. I was wondering about that."

"I poured your tea, didn't I?"

"Yeah, it was great." I had forgotten to thank her earlier. "Oh yeah, and also, the first time I visited your room, you were sitting on the sofa and Iria-san was standing. It seemed like it should've been the other way around."

"My, my." She was gleeful. I supposed Rei-san had been copying such mannerisms all along, but there was nothing like the real thing. "Go on."

"Right. Where was I . . ."

If you thought about it, Akari-san and Hikari-san obviously knew about the switch, which meant that they, too, were quite the pair of little actresses. Especially Hikari-san. As spry and pitiable as she was, I never would've guessed she was lying all along.

Somebody owed her an Oscar.

"The nail in the coffin was when the fake Iria-san covered for you. That night 'Iria-san' and Yayoi-san were together talking all night. Makes sense, right? Rei-san was probably asking her for culinary advice. She's really a maid, after all, so it wouldn't be that strange if she had an interest in cooking."

"Yeah, Yayoi-san believes Rei is me, so she doesn't ever spend much time with the real me. That was my miscalculation," she sulked. "And hey, come to think of it, where does Rei get off imitating me like that? I don't change my clothes in front of random people, and my personality isn't that crappy."

Apparently her personality wasn't that crappy.

Hmm, sounded like another lie to me.

"So what were you really doing that night, anyway?"

"That's a secret."

"It's a secret?"

"A lady never discloses her evening's affairs," she said mysteriously.

I had a feeling if I pressed any further it would just tick her off, so I decided to let it go. I wasn't looking for any more trouble. I didn't like "making waves," after all.

"Anyway, even though 'Iria-san' did nothing to protect Hikari-san, even treating her like a criminal, she went as far as lying to save *your* hide. Why? Because Rei-san is closer to Iria-san than Hikari-san is? Maybe. But something about that answer doesn't float my boat. Living on a deserted island like that, I would think you'd all get pretty close and cozy. And I don't think human beings are such a cold species."

"That's true," Iria-san said. "Those girls are like my family.

My precious family, who stayed by my side even after I was exiled."

Exiled.

And the reason for that exile?

"Even so, 'Iria-san' protected 'Rei-san' but not Hikari-san. Why? Could it be because 'Rei-san' was really her superior, someone she had sworn allegiance to?" I clapped my hands together. "Something like that, right?"

"You're marvelous. I want to hug you."

"I don't mind."

"I will refrain," she giggled innocently.

"This time I have a question. Why exactly did you switch places with Rei-san and pose as a maid? Was it because, as the granddaughter of the Akagami family, you couldn't show yourself unguarded in front of the guests, even though you were exiled?"

There was no guarantee that there wasn't some unsavory individual mixed in with all those geniuses. As our prior investigation had indicated, sometimes these things happen.

Thus, she had prepared an imposter—a body double.

Was that it?

But Iria-san shook her head daintily. "Nope," she said. "I just wanted to see who would notice first. Just a little prank. No reason, really."

A prank.

It was the kind of line that made your knees wobble, and I didn't think she was lying this time. And until now, not a single one of those so-called geniuses had caught on.

In all these years, unnoticed by anyone, geniuses are nothing special.

Perhaps that was what Iria-san thought. And she would probably continue to think so.

"But you noticed."

"If you hadn't gone a little too far at the end there, I

wouldn't have. Even if I had noticed, I wouldn't have said anything. You should have just stayed at the mansion instead of coming on this boat with us."

"Well, I have to go apologize to Aikawa-san for all the unnecessary hoopla. There's still a visit scheduled. We're going to meet straight after dropping you off. Oh, Aikawa-san's going to be ticked. Not a person you want to see get angry. Even though it's inevitable. Plus, well, I wanted to talk to you like this. You showed me such a good time, after all."

"It's an honor."

"Say," she said sweetly, "won't you return to the mansion sometime? Kunagisa-san, Maki-san, Yayoi-san, and you. I think you'd make a terrific family. I hear you've taken a liking to Akari and Hikari. I don't mind letting you have your way with them."

"That's not the kind of thing you say to a family member."

"True, but I'm serious. I'm always serious. So how about it? Like my proposition?" She stuck her tongue out at me.

At this point I was becoming disgusted. You couldn't just write this off as free-spiritedness or vibrancy or lack of restraint.

"I don't like murderers."

"Ehehehe," Iria-san laughed.

I didn't know why she was laughing.

"Regardless of their reasons?"

"Regardless of their reasons."

She nodded. "I'm not sure what you heard from Hikari and Teruko, but you can't possibly be thinking they told you anything but the truth. Those girls are generally liars. I think the fact that they never told you about me and Rei's switch is proof enough of that."

"Eh . . . ?"

"The reason I didn't call the police was simply because it wouldn't have been any fun that way. Absolute authority is so unromantic," she said as she rolled up her left sleeve. This revealed a lovely, *perfectly unscarred* arm. "Please excuse me then," she said with a smile, and left the room.

"Hey, hey . . ."

Sigh . . .

Sure didn't see that coming.

What was real and what was fake?

Who was real and *who* was fake?

It's a mixed-up world, and I for one never claimed to know anything, nor do I think all people are honest and all things are as they seem.

What was it?

The truth.

"Man, what a load of tomfoolery."

It wouldn't be long now. I thought to wake up Kunagisa, but seeing her peaceful face as she mewed like a kitten made me lose the motivation. It wouldn't be too late to wake her up after we reached the coast. The rule of thumb is, the longer you can stay dreaming, the better.

Nevertheless.

Family?

"Man, I'm gonna regret turning down that proposition," I said to no one in particular, expecting no response. But I knew there was only one response one could give. For me, there was only one person I could ever call family. "What a load of nonsense," I muttered in the usual way.

Aikawa Jun,
Most Powerful Private Contractor
in the World

EPILOGUE

CRIMSON FAIRY TALE

A week had passed since returning to the mainland.

I finally began attending school, but finding myself hopelessly unable to adapt due to my late start, I just couldn't get into the mood. And thus I found myself cutting morning classes, walking down West Main Street. What you call a mental health day, or "playing hooky," if you want to be a jerk about it.

"What the hell was I doing all that time before coming back to Japan?" My self-directed mutterings were more or less heartfelt, but they were probably mostly meaningless. Whether I was in ER3, Kyoto, or Wet Crow's Feather Island, it had changed me little, just as leaving a five-year blank had hardly changed Kunagisa.

"Hmm, more nonsense?" I muttered as I continued my stroll. I turned south, thinking I'd head back to my Nakadachiuri apartment and do some reading, but on the way I remembered today was the day Kunagisa's favorite magazine went on sale, so I stopped in a local bookstore to buy a copy.

"Kunagisa Tomo?"

Since the island incidents, Kunagisa had stayed holed up in her house. She was deeply immersed in making all sorts of repairs on the workstation and PCs and what have you that Akane-san had destroyed. This time she was all fired up, saying she was going to rebuild them completely out of nigh-invulnerable steel, but it seemed to me that this wasn't logically possible. Of course, what she got fired up about was her business, so I didn't say anything as to that.

As for Sonoyama Akane-san and Sakaki Shinya-san, Kunagisa looked up what had become of them on the Internet, most likely employing the skills of her old pal Chii-kun.

Akane-san had retired from the Seven Fools and begun a somewhat reclusive existence, but retained her prominence as a scholar. Shinya-san supposedly remained by her side. Considering the fact that no one had reported them to the police, this seemed plausible enough.

I entered the bookstore and bought what I wanted with a gift certificate, then stood and flipped through it for a while before leaving the store. Outside, an extremely gaudy—that is, expensive-looking—convertible was parked in front of the store. It was an eccentric sort of car that would have stood out even if this was a street in the middle of Kyoto.

The kind of upper-class car you see in magazines and the like. You know, with names like "Anaconda" or "Viper" or "Japanese Ratsnake." This probably wasn't a Japanese Ratsnake, but I was sure it was something in the snake family. But what were they doing riding in a car like this on a Japanese road? Or more important, what type of person rode in this ridiculous beast of a machine? I glanced over just in time to see the driver step out of the car. So as not to lose to the car, the driver herself was adorned in attire just as flashy.

She wore a generously revealing dress shirt inside a wine red suit that was bound to catch any passerby's attention, wanted or not. On top of that she had a spring coat draped over her shoulders with nothing in the sleeves. Her shoulder-length hair was unnaturally shimmery, suggesting she had used any number of expensive hair products. Deep red sunglasses completely concealed her eyes. Her proportions were enough to make you wonder if she was a model, and she was tall to boot. She was a beautiful woman in the truest sense, but at the same time, she was the kind of beautiful woman you didn't want to approach. She looked like the type to have a lot of bad habits and lack universal appeal.

There was something offensive or disharmonious about her.

"Wow," I managed to eke out an utterance of wonderment.

So, good-looking cars *do* have good-looking drivers, I thought as I stared at her striding toward me. I cleared a path for her, thinking she wanted to stop in the bookstore, but I was wrong.

She came to a halt right in front of me. Then she stared at me over her sunglasses. Dominated by her overwhelming, abusive gaze, I found myself unable to move. Like a frog in a snake's gaze. And as such, I was unable to avoid it.

Without any warning, she brought her long leg upward, sinking her pump-adorned foot into my gut. I crumpled facedown to the pavement.

"Uguu . . ."

I felt like I was going to puke until there was nothing left in my stomach. But there was no time to scream. With no mercy nor reservation, she began stomping on my collapsed body with the heel part of her shoe, so it hurt quite a bit.

As is always the case when you're in trouble, there wasn't a single person in the vicinity. There was a bus stop nearby, but the bus must have just left because nobody was there. Damn, must be my lucky day. Still, I had no intention of making an ugly spectacle of myself by screaming for help. I rolled over in an attempt to somehow escape, but this ended in failure as soon as she seized me by the collar.

Just like that, she lifted me up.

"Huh . . . You really don't close those eyes," she said as if impressed. "Wow, it's pretty amazing. Haha. That's kinda cool. Okay, anyway . . . Hello."

"Hello."

"Come on, this isn't a funeral."

What the hell is she talking about? I wondered as she tightened her grip around my neck. She dragged me over to her convertible and tossed me into the passenger seat like a suitcase. She herself got into the driver's seat. She took off her shades and jammed her foot down on the accelerator. It seemed the car had been idling the whole time. She was a foe to the environment.

I thought as I rubbed my stomach and back.

Um, what was this? What was going on? Was this an abduction? Why me? Things were moving too fast for me to keep up. As much as I was a go-with-the-flow nineteen-year-old, I had scarcely been caught up in a torrential rapid like this before. Who was this woman?

"Um, who are you?"

"Hmm? My name? You just ask my name there, pal?"

She looked over at me. Her glare was even worse with the shades off. It was a terrifying gaze that seemed to pierce straight through my heart. What kind of life did one have to live to obtain a gaze like that?

"The name's Aikawa Jun."

Aikawa?

Aikawa, Aikawa . . .

The name rang a bell.

"Aikawa-san?"

"Jun is fine."

Her voice was brusque and surly. It seemed like such a waste, considering how beautiful she was, but maybe it suited her personality surprisingly well.

"Uh, Jun-san. Have we met before somewhere? I've got kind of a bad memory when it comes to acquaintances, but I don't feel like we've met before."

"First time."

"Thought so."

Even if we had only met one time, there was no forgetting a woman like this.

"What's that now? Eh? You mean Iria-san never told you?"

"Iria-san?" That name rang a bell, too. "Uh, Iria-san, Iria-san . . ."

Ah.

At last, the circuit in my brain connected.

Right. I remember.

"So then, you're the 'detective,' Aikawa-san?"

"I'm an independent contractor, to be precise," she said cynically. "Looks like you remembered."

"I didn't think you were a woman."

"Thanks. That's the best compliment there is."

She smacked me on the shoulder. It was more than a little surprising to learn that the Aikawa-san I had long been thinking was a man was, in fact, a woman—and such a beautiful one at that. But if you thought about it, except for the tagalongs like Shinya-san and me, Iria-san had mostly brought relatively young women to the island. Looking at it that way, I probably should have realized Aikawa-san was a woman.

But Iria-san kept using ambiguous words like "hero."

"I was going to go all the way to your college," she said with a faint smile. "But then I spotted you standing there reading in that bookstore. It was a hell of a coincidence, so I thought I'd give you a whistle."

"You mean you were looking for me?"

"Yep. Thought I ought to see with my own eyes what kind of jerk was sneaking around stealing my jobs. Thanks to you, you chump, I never had my turn. How're you gonna make up for that?"

Her gaze pierced through me. It was like she had a direct grip on my heart. In my mind, the events that had occurred on that island were already over, so this development was completely beyond my expectations.

"Because of you I missed out on a job. And here they told me it was going to be a safe and easy case."

"Uh, I . . ." Not really understanding the situation, I decided to just go ahead and apologize. "I'm real sorry. Please forgive me."

"Haha!" Aikawa-san laughed. "No reason to apologize. In fact, I should be thanking you for making things easy."

Well which was it? My unease was growing proportionally to my composure. What the hell situation had I gotten myself into? It was beyond comprehension. I had no idea what this Aikawa Jun character was trying to do.

"Um, where are we headed now?"

"Heaven. Or maybe Hell. I forgot."

"They're totally different."

"Yup, totally different. They're complete opposites. So we're bound to end up at one of them."

Where was she pulling this stuff from?

She went on driving without a care in the world. Maybe we really were headed for Hell. It seemed plausible enough. In a relatively unexpected turn, maybe my life was about to end. But then I guess the end is always unexpected.

"Well then, now that I've seen your face, that's one thing to mark off the to-do list. That leaves just one more."

Without a shred of reserve, Aikawa-san leaned that alluring face of hers right next to mine. I reflexively flinched at her whimsicalness. I wasn't very used to close contact with people other than Kunagisa.

"Um, one more? What is it?"

"Oh, I just thought I'd put one of your woes to rest," Aikawa-san said. "I'm an independent contractor. It's my job to solve people's pesky little problems. I lend a rescuing hand to those individuals with problems the likes of you could never handle. You chump."

"So that's what you mean by 'independent contractor'?"

That is to say, insofar as a detective is also someone who takes up contracts. "But what problem do I have?"

"On *rare* occasions I have been known to work for charity. Call me capricious. It'll be your reward for solving the last case so splendidly in my stead."

"Reward?"

"Don't be so tense. I may not look it, but I'm pretty much full of goodness."

Good people don't usually beat the hell out of others with their pumps on a first meeting.

"Now then, troubled one. You gonna take my hand?" she said, showing me the palm of her hand. "What's it gonna be? Your decision."

She was weird. Like, *crazy* weird. Her weirdness was in a league of its own. If you set that pack of eccentric crazies on our favorite deserted island as the average, Aikawa-san's weirdness was off the chart. Nevertheless, I grabbed her hand in a rare exhibition of assuredness.

This bizarre human being. How could I miss out on this?

"Okay, pal."

She gave a wicked smile.

Maybe that was hasty of me, I thought.

"Um, before we get into anything, what is this 'woe' of mine you mentioned?"

"That's the one thing you ought to know way better than me. Way better. Can't you guess? *I've* come to see you. *Me*. So obviously it's about the incident at Wet Crow's Feather Island."

"The incident?" I said.

"Yup." Aikawa-san gave a small nod. "After that, I ended up paying a visit to the island anyway. I was originally planning to make it a vacation, so I was lucky the case had already been solved. I really mean that. Anyway, I talked to Iria, Hikari, Akari, and Rei. Incidentally, Teruko didn't say a word. She was silent as always. Even I've only heard her voice one time. Oh yeah, there was also one hell of a chef and some creepy fortune-teller. Ah, I don't want to think about her. What was up with that lady?!"

Suddenly furious, she slammed down on the steering wheel, practically breaking it. Evidently something had transpired with Maki-san on the island. What had that woman done now? To be sure, you could tell just by looking that those two women were incompatible.

"Hmph," Aikawa-san grumbled before continuing her story.

"Anyway, I talked to them about the incident. No detail left out."

"So you think there's still something wrong?" I said. "I mean, what do you think personally, Aikawa-san?"

"That's Jun," she said in a suddenly low and grim voice. "Don't call me by my last name. Only my enemies do that."

"Do you still think there's something wrong, Jun-san?" I corrected myself and asked again.

"That's better," she smiled. Her moods changed like mad. I'd say they changed like the weather, but not even mountain weather changed this often.

"No no . . . I'm not the one feeling discontent, buddy. It's you, right? You solved the case. And you did it damn well. You did it so damn well nobody could even raise an objection. But you yourself still have doubts, don't you? Isn't something missing from your detective work?"

I was at a loss for words. Indifferent to this, she continued.

"Am I right? You solved the case in three days. It's only natural someone with brains like yours would still have doubts. Stop me if I'm wrong."

I couldn't say anything, and obviously it wasn't because she was out of line. It was because she was exactly right.

Exactly.

I . . . Kunagisa and I had made solving the case quickly a priority and shoved our own doubts into a dark corner. She had submitted a solution we personally didn't approve of.

Aikawa-san grinned.

"That feeling of discontent, those doubts, those things that seem less than agreeable to you, you chump—have you got them pinpointed?"

"Uh, well . . ."

"Why would Shinya kill Ibuki? Why would Shinya and Sonoyama be working in cahoots?" She flicked out her dark red tongue provokingly. "That's it, isn't it?"

"Yes," I nodded reluctantly. "But that's their problem and, ultimately, no one else's, right? It has to do with their motives, and that's something beyond my grasp, so . . ."

"You're similar," Aikawa-san said. "Didn't you think so? Didn't Shinya tell you that himself? That you and he are 'similar.' Now why would this guy so much like you kill Ibuki Kanami, the one person irreplaceable to him, his version of that 'blue-haired girl' of yours?"

"It's probably just a misunderstanding. If it wasn't . . . Yeah, it's probably actually Akane-san who's 'irreplaceable' to Shinya-san."

"Are you satisfied with that?" Aikawa-san said with sarcasm. "No way, right? There ain't no *way* you're satisfied with that. I fully understand your sentiments."

"You're beating around the bush, aren't you? You're right, Aikawa-san, I'm not totally convinced. But . . ."

"That's Jun. I told you not to call me by my last name."

I got glared at again. It was frightening.

"Jun-san. You're right, I'm not totally convinced, but there are no other possibilities, so there's nothing I can do. When you've erased all the impossible possibilities, the remaining one is the truth, no matter how impossible it seems."

"That's a myth. So you mean you've been taking that ridiculous motive about eating people's brains seriously?"

Huh. I was at a loss for words. Aikawa-san snickered, reveling in my response.

"Now now now, get yourself together. Get yourself together, man.

"Do you really think there's a single idiot in this whole world dumb enough to believe if you eat the brain of a genius, you *become* a genius? It's not a bad thing if there is someone like that. People are free to think what they want. Everyone has the right to be feeble-minded. There's nothing wrong with that. We have freedom of thought, and freedom to be stupid. But would someone willing to use a corpse as a stepping stool, someone who has absolutely no respect for humans, really be thinking something like that? What do you think, bud?"

Well, indeed, that was a good point.

"Well, so what? What are you saying? I've always been confident in my ability to talk around subjects, but even I never go this far."

"That's because you're below me. I know something you don't know. Not to say you're incompetent or nothin'."

"You're just calling yourself competent?"

"I'm a jack-of-all-trades. If I wasn't, I couldn't do this kind of work," she boasted. She was almost frighteningly narcissistic.

"Well then, what do you think about it, Jun-san? You say you know it all, right? Please enlighten me."

"If you had just asked me that in the first place we could've cut right to the chase," she laughed. "Come on, bud. You noticed something unnatural, didn't you? I heard from Hikari. You noticed it, right? That painting you modeled for. *Why was there a watch painted in?*"

The watch?

I had completely forgotten about that.

"You didn't forget about that, did you?" she said. "Please don't tell me you forgot something that important."

"Of course not. How could I forget? But I thought it was just a painting mistake. Kanami-san relied on her memory to do the painting, so I thought it was just a memory issue."

"Not likely. It's essentially impossible for someone who claims her memory and perception are synonymous to make a blunder like that. Even supposing it was possible, don't you think there's some other reason, bud?"

"Okay, Ai . . . Jun-san. What do you think?"

"I don't know what other people think, but this is what I, Aikawa Jun, the world's most powerful contractor, have concluded: that picture wasn't painted by Kanami.

"Right. That's the only viable possibility. I mean, think about it the other way around. Let's say Ibuki painted it. If she painted it, it would be weird for there to be a watch, right? You weren't wearing a watch when you were sitting in front of her. So it probably wasn't painted by her."

"Why?"

"What do you mean 'why?' You didn't actually see her painting it, right? Sure, maybe there are artists who always work alone, but I don't think Ibuki was one of them. I submit that Ibuki *could not* have done that painting."

"She 'couldn't' have? Kanami-san was an artist. She was famous. Surely she could've painted that."

"Plenty of artists have used fraudulent ghost painters," she said as if it was obvious. "Roughly fifty thousand. It wouldn't be odd if Ibuki was one of them. Not odd at all."

"So you think Kanami-san was a fraud?"

"Just think about it," Aikawa-san said. "You're not a painter?"

"Art is not my forte."

"So you were probably thinking something like 'this person is an artist all the way to the bone,' weren't you?"

Why did this woman know what people were thinking so

damn accurately? She reminded me of Maki-san, but telling her this would anger her, so I remained silent.

"Don't compare me to that sketchy character."

Hey now.

She looked at me with a smirk. "Don't clam up now. That was just a basic mind-reading trick. It's just a technique. With a little training, anyone can do it. But that aside, why did you think Ibuki was an artist?"

"Why? Well, I . . ." Cat had my tongue.

"It's not like you ever saw her paint anything, right? She only told you that, bud. You heard what she had to say, and then, based *solely* on that, you assumed she was an artist."

"I saw her paintings, too. Like the one of the cherry blossoms and stuff."

"But you didn't see her paint it, did you? Man, for someone who doesn't trust anyone, you sure are naïve. It's like you don't trust anyone but you don't doubt them, either, or like you just withhold all conclusions indefinitely. You just took Ibuki's steaming pile of doo-doo for fact."

Doo-doo?

Did she say doo-doo? Was everything Kanami-san said nothing more than doo-doo? How was I supposed to kn—

"Oh, how were you supposed to know?" Aikawa-san beat me to the punch with my own line. "I wonder. I really wonder, buddy."

"If there's something you want to say, go for it."

"That's no way to ask for a favor."

"Please tell me."

She smiled. She was probably a little more childish than I had thought.

"Like the whole dress thing. When you modeled for her, you saw her wearing her dress, and what did you say? You said, 'You're going to paint like that?' right?"

I didn't know who she had heard that from (and only Maki-san was likely to know), but she was exactly right.

"A real artist never dirties her clothes with painting materials," Aikawa-san muttered. And then suddenly, "Like anybody like that really exists!" she yelled. "That's impossible! Even if she didn't get her clothes dirty, they'd be soaked in stench! It's not a matter of can and can't—people *don't* do that! Don't you notice these things, you moron?"

This was no act, she really seemed mad. I cowered in all seriousness. I thought I was about to get pounded. Suddenly I understood what Hikari-san had meant.

A "violent-tempered" person, huh?

"Anyway, when you're working with paint on canvas, you at least put on an apron. Even if you suck at art, that much is just common sense."

"Sure. But if that's the case, then . . ."

Then what did that mean? Kanami-san lied to me? No, not only that: she didn't know anything about art?

There was no way an artistic genius like Ibuki Kanami didn't know something as simple as that. Why? Because it was a fact that anybody with a little experience would realize . . .

Which meant . . .

"Yup, didn't know anything," Aikawa-san said with a slightly mocking tone. "Ibuki Kanami, the genius painter who couldn't paint. So, how will you solve this conundrum?"

"Well, uh, are you saying Kanami-san was a fraud then?"

"No. Think. And then realize, man. Ibuki didn't paint that picture. *But* Ibuki was the painter. *Thus*, by the law of syllogism, Ibuki was a fake. And *thus, of course*, she couldn't paint."

"A fake? But, a fake would . . . Why? Um, sorry, I'm totally confused." I clutched my head and thought. "So . . . in other words . . . an imposter Kanami-san was killed, and the real one wasn't?"

"Yes. And the real Sonoyama Akane was killed."

Bam, another whack on the shoulder.

My brain ceased for a moment.

"Say what now? Akane-san?"

"Yeah, Sonoyama Akane. If you think about it, that clears up all the confusion, doesn't it? Why did Shinya kill Ibuki? Simple. He *didn't*. Why did Shinya go into cahoots with Sonoyama? Simple. He *didn't*. He was working with Ibuki. His irreplaceable Ibuki."

"So Kanami-san and Akane-san switched places? When? Hold on a second here. I spent three days on the same island with those two. I may have a bad memory, but I definitely would've known if they did a switch."

"What I'm saying is they switched *before* that, before they arrived at the island. I don't know how long those two were there, but it was before that."

"One has blond hair and blue eyes. The other is an intellectual-looking brunette. How in the hell do two people that different switch pla—"

"Hair can be dyed. You can put on color contacts. If you really want to look like someone else, it's simple. Especially when the person has such notable characteristics. Think about it."

"But— So those pictures—"

"It's like I've been tellin' ya, Sonoyama painted those. That day, I bet you were wearing a watch every time Sonoyama saw you. Thus, she's the one who painted you. Sonoyama . . . *as* Ibuki."

Sonoyama Akane *as* Ibuki Kanami. Come to think of it, where was Akane-san that morning? Was she in the atelier doing that cherry blossom picture? Did that mean Akane-san was the one painting me that night?

"Why would she—"

"To make everyone think she was Ibuki. Surely you would never have guessed the painter of that wasn't her. But you gotta admit, the whole watch mistake isn't like her."

"But . . . but, Iria-san . . . she's the one who invited them. She should've noticed right away, right?"

"How do you figure?"

"I mean, she must've at least seen pictures of them before."

"Pictures? Hey now. Hey now, man. Don't make me laugh here, buddy. You trying to make me laugh to death? Gimme a break here. Do you think people's faces look the same in real life as they do in photos? They leave different impressions, don't they? That's why wanted posters never work. Photos are still motion, reality moves. And the human eye chooses things arbitrarily. So naturally, when you compare the two, your mind favors reality."

She was right. Kanami-san herself had said the same thing. Suddenly I had the bizarre, *truly* bizarre feeling that *I* was the real criminal and detective Aikawa-san here was hot on my tail.

"Why . . . why were they doing that?"

"It was a prank. They switched places as a prank. Iria and Rei switched places, too, right? And they said it was a prank when you asked why, right? It's the same deal. I wonder who will notice. Will any of these so-called geniuses notice? Can this salon-running princess even tell the difference between us?

"That's at least what Sonoyama was thinking. Oh, the real one, I mean. So she, Shinya, and Ibuki got together and made these plans. Sonoyama was on board. She probably thought it would be funny. Scholars can be surprisingly willing to take part in such hedonistic pleasures. Especially those ER3 system goons. I'm sure you know that though. You were right smack in the middle of it."

That information from Chii-kun.

Ibuki Kanami and Sonoyama Akane had met in Chicago. They were acquaintances. It wasn't so impossible that they had planned such a thing. Kanami-san and Akane-san, who had gotten into countless arguments. But did this mean all that fighting was just something they planned so their switch wouldn't be obvious?

"So, what now?"

"It goes like this. Ibuki and Sonoyama switched places. Ibuki became Sonoyama, Sonoyama became Ibuki. Then one of them was killed. The remaining one was Sonoyama. The switched Sonoyama.

"Who would've thought the woman once thought dead and then pronounced the murderer was actually someone else?"

"You mean it was Kanami-san posing as Akane-san?"

Akane-san had retired from the Seven Fools and begun a somewhat reclusive existence, but retained her prominence as a scholar. Shinya-san supposedly remained by her side.

"Considering the fact that no one had reported them to the police, this seems plausible enough," Aikawa-san said cynically.

"Are you saying *that's* the motive? But why would they do—"

"Ha!" Aikawa-san laughed as she narrowed her eyes at me. "That's an indescribably irrelevant question, my man. Man, I mean what would *you* say if I asked you why you're alive?

"Granted, a guy like you probably never thought about it. Have you ever wanted to become something? Haven't you ever wanted to become some*one*? If not, then you'll never understand Ibuki Kanami's feelings, no matter how many times I explain it. You, with your one established *style*, will never understand Ibuki Kanami, even if you travel to the four corners of the earth."

It was another virtual machine, I realized. A fake. There to trick the software.

"Does that mean you understand?"

"Nope. Other people's feelings are beyond my comprehension. But insofar as I have a working brain, I can at least imagine it. Yeah. All that sealed room stuff was just child's play to them. A diversion to keep people from learning their real objective. Even you got so distracted by all the sealed rooms and headlessness going on that you didn't even consider the possibility that they had switched, right?"

She was right.

But . . . but it was all too sudden.

"Hey, I can't just believe all this up front."

"That's right. For sure. It's so convoluted it's unbelievable. It's so convoluted, my words lose all meaning and even your personality isn't an issue. But one thing is clear. That woman discarded her former shell known as 'Ibuki' and succeeded in being reborn as 'Sonoyama.' She completely hijacked Sonoyama Akane's background."

"But won't she be found out?"

"Hell no. She'd probably been preparing for this for a long, long time. And don't you think the whole crazy idea to replace Sonoyama, to turn into her, came from the fact that their faces were similar to begin with?"

"To turn into her . . . So you're saying that's why she killed her? I mean I guess if you wanted to 'become' someone you'd also want to get rid of the real person, but still . . ."

To be sure, killing someone was the fastest way to get rid of them. And indeed, a deserted island beyond the influence of the police was the prime place to do it.

"If that's the case, then it should've just ended once Ibuki-san was killed. There was no need to make herself a victim and play dead."

"Get a hold of yourself, man. Geez, you're useless. If she did it like that, surely the question of why Ibuki was the only one killed would come up in no time. That's why she had to make it look like a serial killing. To hide her true intentions. She had to pose as a lust murderer going after everyone. That business about eating everyone's brains was probably added on as an afterthought; no doubt after she overheard you guys talking about it. But even if she had to kill someone, she probably couldn't bear to kill an innocent, so she pretended to be the victim herself instead. It's so clear-cut. Her calculations were so disgustingly sharp."

"Would a murderer really put so much planning into it?"

"Not all murderers are bloodthirsty maniacs. Just like not all wolves act the same. In reaching your objective, it's only natural to try and avoid danger as much as possible. The more incidents you cause, the more clues you give everyone. Am I wrong?"

Shinya-san had told me they were planning to kill everyone, and I believed him. After they had already killed two people, plus trying to kill Yayoi-san and myself, I never would have dreamed they knew anything of mercy.

However . . .

"But she tried to kill Yayoi-san."

"She didn't kill her." Aikawa-san cut off my objections in one fell swoop. "You made an assumption. You assumed 'Sonoyama Akane' would kill again after she went as far as recycling a corpse to hide herself. That's why you thought up that trap, using Sashirono as bait. But you were blind.

"Think about it. Then realize, man, you were dancing in the palm of Ibuki and Shinya's hand. Why would Shinya show you the sleeping bag? Why would Ibuki smash those computers in the morning when everyone clearly had an alibi?"

"Even that?"

Everything, even *that*, had been precalculated? They had predicted—no, *dictated*—our actions *that far*? The showdown in Yayoi-san's room, Kunagisa's anguish, all of it, *all* of it was in the palm of their hand? Had we all been nothing more than chess pieces subject to a strategy so devious there was no room to anticipate the next move? Thinking all the while we were so clever, we were really just being controlled.

And me with no basis to argue. But wasn't this all just a little too outrageous?

That vague sense of disconcertion I felt had now disappeared without a trace.

Aikawa-san stretched her right hand in front of me and, using those long, slender, white fingertips, began brushing my lips. Though I can't speak from experience, I thought it felt very much like being raped.

"Surely they had fallen in love with their target's work. Those paintings of Ibuki Kanami's, completely errorless, sans wristwatch and all. 'Now *that's* an artist,' they probably said. Haha, I'll bet they were originally planning to use *me* in their scheme. It didn't matter who they used. All they needed was someone to solve the mystery of the sealed rooms. As long as somebody figured out and exposed the truth that 'Sonoyama Akane' wasn't dead and then fingered her as the killer, Ibuki would be reborn and that was all that mattered."

And she would obtain a magnificent new identity.

Enjoying worldwide recognition as a comprehensive scholar.

"But, hey, even if she switched backgrounds and managed to turn into someone else, you still have to account for ability. 'Akane-san' is still to this day continuing her life as a well-rounded and outstanding scholar, even though she's retired from the Seven Fools. If those two really did switch places . . ."

"If, huh?" Aikawa-san said. "You're still talking about it in those terms, man? You sure don't know when to give up, do you?"

"Based on your detective work, Akane-san is really Kanami-san. But as far as Kunagisa has researched, she's still an active scholar."

"What's wrong with that? She can paint and study pictures, obviously she's capable of murder, and she's even capable of changing her identity entirely. Doesn't that essentially make her . . . a genius?"

"A genius?"

Why had Ibuki-san been summoned there? Was it not because she possessed extraordinary ability? She was the outsider of all outsiders. The penultimate. Transcendent of boundaries. Yes, that was absolutely . . .

"What was your definition of a genius again, buddy? Someone who's 'far away'? I heard from Iria. But you're wrong. It's a vector, basically . . . someone who devotes all of the time in his or her entire life to a single direction, to reach a given maximum potential. Human beings can do all sorts of stuff. But if, instead, they just focus on one skill, they can hone it to a ridiculous level. So much so that they seem 'distant,' as you might say."

A prominent function.

The direction of a vector.

A restrictive bias.

If you set that arrow in a single direction, instead of dispersing every which way . . . The power of focus. The savant syndrome. An inexhaustible motivation.

Pon pon, Aikawa-san smacked me on the shoulder.

"You did well, pal. But you're still an amateur. In baseball terms, you're a Little Leaguer, Mr. Pitcher. And just when you thought your opponent was a Little Leaguer, too, she turned out to be Domo-kun, figuratively speaking. You know him? Domo-kun. Before your time?" Aikawa-san said, getting a little friendly as she reeled my shoulders around. "It was just a little premature, trying to end the story before the lead detective arrived, my man. And you were still too green."

"But . . . hang on a second here. Kanami-san was in a wheelchair."

"Any old schmo with working legs can sit in a wheelchair," she said cynically. "That's all there is to it, really. Even Ibuki

Kanami said legs are just a decoration. Sure, they helped in kicking you around, but that's about it."

"Maybe that's the case for Akane-san. All she had to do was sit in a wheelchair. But Kanami-san was born with bad legs. She couldn't just jump around all over the place like—"

"Ibuki Kanami wanted to become Sonoyama Akane. She wanted to take over the identities of others. I wouldn't be surprised if that wasn't the first time Ibuki Kanami had switched places with someone."

Just how long had Shinya-san been serving Ibuki-san?

He had said it was a long time.

Since when, exactly?

And even now he remained by Akane-san's side.

How long would this go on? It was a virtual machine. Simulating the presence of multiple machines. Possessing no one style. Shunning the very concept.

"Did . . ."

What about Maki-san?

Had the famous, transcendental Himena Maki "known" even this fact? Was she just watching over—or blowing off—the situation with a goofy grin, despite knowing *everything*?

What was real? What was fake? *Who* was real? *Who* was fake?

"You can't ask questions," Aikawa-san giggled.

And at last, she pulled the car over to the side of the road.

"Tough break, kid. That's all I can say. And you did good. You did real good. How's that for a compliment? But you gotta try a little harder than that. If you've got lingering doubts, don't just blow them off. Settle your suspicions. Make the inconceivable conceivable. Don't write your thoughts off as just a pile of caca. Okay?"

"Okay."

"That's the A answer," she said, sticking out her dark red tongue.

"Well, I'm done bugging you. It's thanks to fellas like you that life's worth living. I really think so. But pal, you just need to cut down on the slacking a little bit. Human beings can do so much more, so get out there and do it, dammit."

Then, with a little tilt of her head:

"Well, that's it for today. See ya. Hey, get outta here, kid, you bother me."

She had a hell of a nerve tossing me into the car and then kicking me out. But naturally I couldn't muster the energy to contradict her, so I opened the door and stepped out.

Looking around to see where I was, I discovered we were right in front of Kunagisa's condominium. If there was ever a street in this world that didn't belong in Kyoto, it was this swanky residential one, Shirosaki. Even Aikawa-san's blood-red car didn't seem out of place here.

"Well, there you go . . ." I nodded, looking up toward the roof of the building. "This really *is* Heaven."

"Or Hell. Haha. This is where you were headed anyway, right?"

"How'd you know?"

Aikawa-san pointed at the bag in my hands from the bookstore. Come to think of it, I *was* on my way to deliver the contents to Kunagisa. But this lady really figured that out just from this bag? She was like . . . like one of those famous books of yore. Like . . .

Like a detective.

"Ha," Aikawa-san laughed.

"Well, if our fates are linked, we shall meet again. Like there's any doubt about that."

She gave me a regular, noncynical smile and patted me once each on the head and shoulder. Then, pointing to the top floor of the condominium:

"Say hi to Kunagisa for me, too," she said.

Now that was a little suspicious. If there was anyone to commend in this case, Kunagisa deserved at least half the credit. So why had Aikawa-san only come to see me? Was she planning to see Kunagisa later?

"Aren't you going to see her?" I asked. "You came all this way. You might as well."

"Nah, that's okay. I saw her yesterday."

So I was the one on the back burner. The strength drained out from my shoulders.

"Ha," I sighed.

"Jun-san . . ."

My final question.

"Then . . . then what do you live for?"

"Like you have to ask. I'm the same as you, Mr. Ii," she said before stepping on the accelerator, and in another instant the red car had vanished from sight. I stood rigid in that spot for a while, unable to think. Unable to *want* to think.

Sigh . . .

"I feel as if I just ran into a street bandit."

It was a fairly accurate analogy. I felt an emptiness, like the luggage had been snatched off my back.

What was with that lady? Why did she start everything off by kicking the crap out of me? Was she just testing what she heard from Teruko-san? Or was it just payback?

Considering she had come all this way to meet me, that was probably it. Payback . . . for stealing her turn? Maybe that was it, or maybe she was just in "one of those moods," or maybe it was just as she had claimed, some kind of reward.

But maybe none of that mattered, either. At any rate, she didn't seem like a very nice person, and even if I was wrong about that, I wasn't so far wrong that it was uncorrectable.

Really . . .

Dammit.

What is this?

I'm surrounded by it here.

Really now.

"*Really* now, this is just a bunch of crappy nonsense."

Take Akagami Iria.

She brought together geniuses, deceived them, tricked them, did anything she wanted only for the sake of her own enjoyment, for the sake of the little world that was all her own.

Take the Chiga sisters.

All three of them seeming somewhat off, all three were the same, all the while being totally different. They were like the Sierpinski gasket, bearing complete self-similarity, the individual parts and their sum all uniform, all of them exactly the same while being completely different, an infinite abyss inside them impossible for anyone to view.

Take Himena Maki.

She who had the end of her life to look forward to in two years, she who knew the truth of all things, the truth of everything, and yet all she did was laze around yawning and purring like a kitty.

Take Aikawa Jun.

A big blur of red in the guise of a detective with a reputation as the world's best contractor, she had shown up on the island and solved the already solved case beyond any shred of doubt, no blade of grass left unchecked, all for no reason, and then vanished in a cloud of cynicism.

Take that woman whose name I didn't know, that woman who was no one. Surely, she was a genius.

"And then . . ."

And then.

And then, take Kunagisa.

Nothing really matters to me.

The world just does what it wants, and even if it didn't, that would have nothing to do with me, and even if it did have something to do with me, I wouldn't be interested. I've never wanted to become someone, and I've never felt like there was something I had to do. Sometimes I wonder if that's okay, but in the end, that doesn't really matter to me, either.

Somewhere along the way I just cooled off. No, that's not right. Probably, I dried out. Apathetic and indifferent. And that's why Kunagisa was moisture to me.

"Moisture, huh," I thought to myself.

Was Shinya-san the same way? Sakaki Shinya, stuck to that woman like a shadow. If so, he and I really were of the same breed, almost *too* much so.

"Hah . . ."

Sigh.

I didn't know who our worlds revolved around, but this world revolved around the sun. That's all there was to it, really, and it never amounted to anything more. And that goes for everyone.

The truth is always out of my reach.

And what's more, I never really care to reach for it.

Maybe that was the problem. This was probably what Aikawa-san meant by "slacking."

"Eh, that doesn't matter. I don't live to sit here and think about those kinds of things, and it's not like I'm trying to change the world or solve its mysteries. When I'm confronted with a puzzle, it's just annoying. If I can just keep on living like this tomorrow, that'll be enough."

Done talking to myself, I finally began to proceed on foot.

Any more thinking would just be a bother. I'd leave it to the people who wanted to do the thinking. No offense to Aikawa-san, but I wasn't looking to give some kind of worth to the world.

If anybody asked me why I was alive, I'd probably say just in case. That's about the only reason people have, and that goes for me, you, and everybody.

But . . .

But Kunagisa is different.

You know, if you were to put it in words.

"Whatever."

With Kunagisa's condo in plain sight, I thought about just going back home right then. I just wanted to throw off that haughty contractor's expectations, that's all. Even if we didn't meet today, we could always meet tomorrow. We could meet up anytime we wanted. Nothing more to it.

Hmm, but . . .

My legs came to a halt once again. And I thought.

Five years ago, before meeting Kunagisa Tomo, I had nothing. But even reuniting now, even now that we were able to be together forever, I still had nothing.

I was empty. It was like . . . meaningless routine work. Just functioning, just living.

"Ah, dammit."

The contractor's cynical smile crossed my mind. I recalled the "prophet's" words. The lying sisters' words, too.

And then, the advice of that woman whose identity remained a mystery.

"You should just go."

Aggravating as it is, my life amounts to little more than just going with the flow. Letting myself be manipulated however people like, however they please, however they desire. Like a doll. Like a heartless machine. As half-assed as that may seem.

And so this ambiguous and mechanical scrawling of unanswered questions, accompanied by a certainty so under-cooked it's practically unnatural, comes to its almost predictably anticlimactic end, like a vague, crimson fairy tale.

I'm ready to go stand by Kunagisa's side, I thought.

AFTERWORD

Let's imagine for a moment that what you hold in your hand is an extraordinarily enthralling work of fiction of the highest order. As you know, that's not truly the case, but let's pretend. Now let's say you finish reading it, and in that very instant, you scream: "This writer is a genius!" I don't know if you would really scream that sort of thing, but let's say the writer of this book is oft the subject of such praise. But such expressions sound not unlike excuses of the common man, as if claiming, "That person is a genius; in other words he's of a superior race totally separate from you and me, so of *course* he can do things we can't do" or something to that unseemly effect. "We're not to be looked down upon, we're simply looking up." And indeed that statement is correct, but I can't shake the feeling that something is off there. When it comes down to it, I don't think it's a very good thing to rely too much on this word *genius*. Moreover, not all geniuses are so evaluated. Or rather, *most* genius goes unnoticed. Meanwhile, those who achieve some sort of result are arbitrarily given the label and people forget that it's really a complex issue based on factors such as effort and environment, none of which should be written off as "genius" if you ask me. Now, it really is a complex issue, so I won't get into the nitty-gritty of it, but when a person sets out to do something, you've got to consider natural-born talent, skill, and effort, not to mention luck and fate as well, so it seems to me that the term *genius* is putting it all too simply.

That said, you may find yourself a bit surprised by the number of times that word comes up in this book. You've got Ibuki Kanami, Sashirono Yayoi, Sonoyama Akane, Himena Maki, Kunagisa Tomo, and Aikawa Jun.

The narrator uses every possible opportunity to utter things like "because she was a genius" or "that's just what you'd expect from a genius." But as to whether any of these women are really true geniuses, well, that's a sketchy matter. From their personal standpoint, it's probably more like "if you just do whatever you want all the time, you'll be labeled a genius." Or no, I'm sure they'd have more to say about themselves, but if you asked Ibuki Kanami about it, she'd probably just say, "What do you mean 'genius'? *You're* just extra dumb." *Kubikiri Cycle* is an installment in the Zaregoto series that depicts geniuses gathered on an island, and yet there isn't a single genius there.

In having this book published, there were so many people looking after me that this author almost doesn't know whom to thank. If this book can be called anything good, it's thanks to the efforts of these people as well as the bookstores. Incidentally, this puts me in the nerve-racked mindset that if this book turned out to be bad, it's my fault alone, but at any rate I would like to extend my utmost special thanks to the editor-in-chief Katsushi Ota for his goodwill and guidance, illustrator take-san, and Ryusui Seiryoin for decorating this book with undeserved endorsement.

—NISIOISIN

ABOUT THE CREATORS

Born in 1981, the prolific NISOISIN has already revolutionized the Japanese literary world with his fast-paced, pop culture-fuelled novels. He debuted with *The Kubikiri Cycle* in 2002, beginning his seminal *Zaregoto* series, and *Bakemonogatari* was published under Kodansha's popular Kodansha Box imprint. 2007 saw the magnificent conclusion to his twelve-month consecutive serial novel, *Katanagatari*—for which NISIOSIN wrote one novel a month for an entire year—also for *Kodansha Box*. NISIOISIN has also created novels based on popular manga franchises: *xxxHOLiC: ANOTHERHOLiC*, based on the series by superstar artist collective CLAMP, and *Death Note Another Note: The Los Angeles BB Murder Cases*, based on Tsugumi Ohba and Takeshi Obata's blockbuster series.

Born in 1983, TAKE made his debut with the gorgeous, ultra-modern illustrations for NISIOISIN's Zaregoto series. Just as that novel cemented NISIOISIN's reputation as one of the leading lights of Japanese pop culture, TAKE's illustrations for these best-selling novels made him a star in his own right. His first-class character designs have captured readers' hearts, and he is now ranked as one of the top young illustrators in Japan. TAKE loves cats and manga genius Osamu Tezuka.